Swan AND SHADOW

Kaki Olsen

PRAISE FOR *SWAN AND SHADOW*

"*Swan and Shadow* is a charming and bittersweet coming-of-age story, framed in a modern retelling of Swan Lake. Poignant, funny, and self-aware, it's the tale of two sisters trying to navigate the perils of late teenhood together, while the eponymous cursed twin learns to literally and figuratively spread her wings. With so much teen literature focused on dystopian horrors, it's nice to find such a gem of hopeful, current-day storytelling."
—Marianna Roberg, author of the Broom Closet Mysteries

"Kaki Olsen's wonderful characters and great sense of humor make this reimagining of Swan Lake unique and compelling. I found myself engaged and rooting for the main character as if she were real, which is a particularly remarkable feat considering the fact that she is a swan for roughly half the novel. The romance is one well worth rooting for."
—Caitlin Jans, editor of *AuthorsPublish* magazine

"Hold onto your seat—you're about to be swept away into a captivating world where things are not as they seem, where black and white are delineated but also blurred, and [where] the power of love is explored and challenged. This remarkable novel is cleverly created and utterly captivating, with a (spoiler alert!) surprise ending."
—Marci McPhee, editor of *Sunday Lessons and Activities for Kids* and a founding author of PrimaryinZion.wordpress.com.

KAKI OLSEN

SWEETWATER
BOOKS
an imprint of Cedar Fort, Inc.
Springville, Utah

*For Jenn, who was promised 16 years ago that I'd dedicate my first book to her.
For Kate, who believed in this Swan Lake when it was still an ugly duckling.*

ISBN 13: 978-1-4621-1814-4

Published by Sweetwater Books, an imprint of Cedar Fort, Inc.
2373 W. 700 S., Springville, UT 84663
Distributed by Cedar Fort, Inc., www.cedarfort.com

Library of Congress Cataloging-in-Publication Data on file

Cover design by Rebecca J. Greenwood
Cover design © 2016 by Cedar Fort, Inc.
Edited and typeset by Justin Greer

Printed in the United States of America

10 9 8 7 6 5 4 3 2 1

Printed on acid-free paper

ACT I

"There's no workman, whatsoever he be,
that may both work well and hastily."
Geoffrey Chaucer

PROLOGUE

Black/White

Simple fact of life: being an identical twin sucks.

White

The night was thick enough to turn the world into nothing but shadows. There was no telling how long I'd been unconscious, but I remembered seeing daylight last.

Darkness had become my friend years ago, so that barely even registered on my panic scale. I was human, bleeding and completely lost, so I was probably in the worst trouble of my life. The hot blood covering my shoulder was bad enough, especially since I've never been comfortable with blood, including my own.

I tried sitting up, but the pain nearly made me vomit and it was clear that I wasn't going anywhere for a while. That was a massive concern for various reasons. I didn't know if this kind of injury could cause me to bleed to death.

I also didn't know if my attacker was going to return. It had left me alone this long, but I could only desperately hope that I was safe. I'd put up enough of a fight to escape the wild animal, even if I'd eventually crash-landed in a glade.

Help wasn't likely to stumble across me this far from civilization, so I would have to find a hospital before dawn. They'd want my ID, my insurance information, and an explanation for my nudity.

All of those concerns paled next to the probability that I was to be grounded for eternity. It was enough to make me consider picking another fight with my attacker.

After mulling that option over for a while, I tried lifting my head again. This time, the world didn't spin as much. Whenever the pain flared up, the nausea spiked, but it wouldn't be long before I could walk. Maybe I'd be out of the woods by then.

My body disagreed when I tried to stand, of course. I got as far as resting on my elbow before I fainted.

I tried it a little more slowly upon waking a few minutes later and finally managed to sit upright without unpleasant side effects. I next braced myself on my good arm and got one foot under me. When it was clear that my body was okay with that, I planted the other foot and crouched uncomfortably until I felt steadier. When I finally stood upright, I had to plant my hand on the rough bark of a nearby tree until I remembered how to breathe and the vertigo passed.

Thanks to the density of the forest, I had no way of telling time by the moon's position. It could be an hour until dawn or just after sunset. I was fairly certain that I wasn't making it to safety before the sun came up. I had spent hours traveling without caring when or where I would turn back and I had no map to use as a handy reference, but I couldn't just stay here. After another break, I got moving.

Black

Thanks to missing my train from Park Street, I didn't make it home until *technically* ten minutes after curfew. Family rules said I should have called the house line, but it had been busy. Dad was at work and Mom's cell went to voicemail, so it wasn't my fault if they didn't know where I was. I also had a sheepish/contrite/indignant story to tell about lost tourists around Faneuil Hall if either of my parents interrogated me about my late arrival.

"I'm home," I called as casually as possible.

"Is Aislin with you?" Mom demanded from the living room.

I stopped and checked behind me in case my sister was slipping in unnoticed. "Negative," I replied. "Is she supposed to be?"

Mom just sighed loudly and I was immediately grateful to have Aislin in trouble. I found Mom hunched over on the couch, tapping her phone furiously.

"The person you have called . . ."

Mom hung up like the phone had offended her personally.

"I haven't seen her all day," I said cautiously.

When Mom didn't answer me, I checked my own phone, but I hadn't missed anything. "Guess her battery ran out."

Mom didn't seem to hear me. She pocketed her phone and walked away without even looking at me. Mom was only like this in a crisis, so I felt alarmed instead of insulted by the snub.

"Hey, it's not the first time this has happened," I pointed out. I could have cited a dozen of Aislin's minor infractions, but I chose to save those for later self-defense. "She'll be here soon."

Mom finally glanced up and looked frankly surprised to find me there. "Every time she's been this late before, she's called by now," Mom said firmly.

I didn't dare to claim that Aislin could handle herself just fine—I would get an earful about crime statistics. It was all about knowing my audience, and right now, my audience was bordering on a meltdown.

Mom called one more time and when the nice computer still sent her to voicemail, she reached for her purse. A moment later, I caught the car keys that she had lobbed at me and jingled them restlessly.

"Do you know where her stashes are?"

I had picked out half the hiding places and knew the rest. "Naturally."

"Check them all," she ordered. "I'll wait for her here."

I didn't need marching orders and had just gotten my jacket when a thought struck me. "You haven't told Dad yet, right?"

Mom smiled very unconvincingly. "Of course not," she said. "Once he's off work, he can sentence her for violating curfew. That's all he needs to know."

The up side of having an at-risk sister was that she occasionally made me look well-behaved. The down side was that I was in charge of the wild goose chase, but Aislin's methodical nature made that easier.

Aislin left clothes all over the Boston area, but nowhere that she could run into an acquaintance. Depending on the night, I could meet her near the Charles or the public gardens. Tonight, I parked the car by the YWCA and tried to look inconspicuous. I found jeans, a top, and sneakers in a bag behind a sign, along with subway fare and the burn phone she wasn't answering.

I went back to the car and plugged the phone into the charger before checking in with Mom. "She hasn't been here," I announced. "What's your next plan?"

"Wait there for a while," she instructed, sounding breathlessly relieved that we could explain the radio silence. "She might just be running later than usual."

"Define a while. She might be somewhere else."

"Use your judgment."

After hanging up, I turned my attention back to the loading dock. Foot traffic was light this time of night, so I'd notice immediately if Aislin arrived. The thought of her trying to preserve her modesty behind a recycling bin made me smile for the first time since I'd gotten home.

After twenty minutes, Aislin was still MIA, so I put her partially charged phone in the pocket of the jeans and left a note on top: CALL HOME RIGHT NOW.

By the time I got home, Aislin was still incommunicado and Dad was involved. He threatened to ground her for life, but I knew he just wanted her to come home at all.

SCENE 1

White

According to the ER nurse in charge of small talk and vital signs, the police escort wasn't optional. I was under a doctor's care, but I was still in custody.

If Maeve were here, she would admire the cuteness of the cops. Mom would say that someday I'd look back on this and laugh. Brendan would laugh at me right now. Dad would be arguing with everyone except for me.

On my own, I felt a little sorry for myself. I had burst into tears one minute into police questioning and they'd decided to save the interrogation for later.

I'd been impressed by the lack of a wait time for medical attention at this time of night. The good news was that, while I would need a decent number of stitches, I wasn't in immediate danger.

The police officers on duty outside my door weren't there as a courtesy, but I couldn't do anything about them. I'd giggled hysterically when one of them called me a flight risk, which probably should have earned me a TV-variety psychiatric consultation, but it hadn't happened yet. The officers didn't do much more than make sure I was still there and not a danger to anyone.

My doctor wasn't so easy to avoid, though, and he arrived just as I was dozing off. "I'm Dr. Gagnon," he introduced himself, picking up my chart. "And you are?"

I blew off the question. "Can I use your phone?"

Gagnon waited another minute for my name, but I didn't feel like having good manners. He ignored my question and checked the shoulder injury that had earned me a ride to the hospital. "That will need stitches," he announced. "Why did you wait to come in?"

Admitting that I had curled up under a nice bush until sunset and gone on a shoplifting spree wouldn't make me seem lucid.

"I got lost."

"Try not to do it again," he murmured.

"Yes, sir."

The doctor backed away and picked up my chart again to make a few more notes. "I'd like to have a closer look at your shoulder, which will mean x-rays."

"Okay." That was no surprise, but I still needed a phone and pain was making me argumentative. "I need to call my parents for a ride home."

He still didn't meet my gaze. He probably couldn't make promises without police input. "If you have an emergency contact, I'll call them," Gagnon offered. "What is your name?"

Thanks to TV, I knew to not say much until I had a lawyer present. I'd stick to really short answers until then.

"Aislin Byrne."

He nodded, apparently proud that he'd gotten me to answer a question at all. "You're at Montreal General Hospital for treatment," he continued. "Do you know how you got here?"

"Cop car."

My answer failed to amuse him and probably made me sound generally snotty instead of honest. "How old are you?"

"I'll be seventeen in October."

He grimaced at that and pulled out a pen. "Parental permission is definitely needed, then," he said. "Do you know where they can be reached?"

After bottling up so much stubbornness, the question felt like a punch to the chest. My eye muscles tightened and my throat ached, which meant I was about to cry again. I stared at my hands until the symptoms improved.

"Massachusetts."

Unflappable Dr. Gagnon smoothly dropped his pen at that moment and didn't even seem to notice. "Where are you staying here in Quebec?" he asked.

"So far, here," I admitted. "Nobody knows that."

That was more than I'd divulged before and I saw one officer turn to pay closer attention. Gagnon handed me another pen and his clipboard.

"If you give me their number, I'll ask them to come for you," he offered.

He apparently suspected I was a runaway. I only had a few numbers memorized, so I scribbled Maeve's down and handed the clipboard back.

"I'll be right back," he promised.

I went back to my self-pity and waited for the other shoe to drop.

Black

On Wednesday night, I was expected to man the phones at home. In a bigger crisis, we'd have called extended family by now, but Mom was touring likely hiding places from Walden to Winnipesaukee. She would probably also check every riverbank in the state too. Dad hadn't disclosed his itinerary but had checked in with me twice.

I had no reason to stay home during the day, but they had wanted me near a working phone in case someone else called with information.

Late on Wednesday, my cell phone rang with an unknown number on the ID. I picked up in case Mom was calling from a pay phone or something.

"May I speak to David or Sarah Byrne?"

The man's voice was oddly formal and slightly accented. "This is her daughter," I answered. "Can I help you?"

"This is Jean Lamont," he identified himself. "Do you know how we might reach your parents?"

I immediately headed for the kitchen where we had family contacts listed and rattled off both parents' numbers.

"Thank you for your help, miss," he said before hanging up.

I ended the call and tapped my phone on my palm, ready for the inevitable call from one of my parents. Five tense minutes later, Mom's name flashed on the caller ID.

"We're headed home," she said breathlessly. "Pack your sister enough clothes for a few days and have them ready to go in ten. Her passport and birth certificate are in her file."

"Five minute warning," Dad called eight minutes later on his way upstairs. "We have to *move*."

"Okay," I shouted back.

Mom burst through the bedroom door and immediately checked the bag before grabbing a couple of tank tops from the top drawer.

"We don't want anything that will be too uncomfortable for her to wear."

That choice was a weird one, since family dress code discouraged spaghetti straps. I stepped out of her way so she could open the closet and pick a dress.

"What's going on?"

"We'll explain later," Mom said curtly. "Her situation is currently complicated."

"Where is she?"

"Canada."

Well, that wasn't the expected answer, but I didn't care if she was on Mars. "She's okay?"

"She'll be fine," Mom insisted, not helping my nerves with the future tense. "Do you have . . ."

"Everything's in the backpack," I said.

Mom folded a conservative shirtdress into the bag. "Passport?"

"Got it." I added a matching pair of shoes and zipped the whole thing shut. "Are we good to go?"

"You're staying here," Mom corrected.

"For three days?" I shot back. "I don't think you're that crazy."

"I don't think you'll try making trouble in the middle of a crisis," Mom pointed out. "Brendan can stay with you."

"Brendan's got work," I reminded her.

"He'll understand."

Aislin could use a friend and Brendan wasn't what you'd call a responsible adult, even if he was the older brother. I did my best bouncer impression and tried a different tactic.

"You're going to pick up your daughter in a foreign country. It might be a good idea if it looked like you have one with you on the return trip."

"That shouldn't be a problem," Dad argued from the doorway. "We'll cross the border before dawn."

"You want to risk it?" I challenged.

Mom's lips thinned into a line and she dug my passport out of the file I'd brought upstairs. "It'll be one less person to worry about."

"I promise I'm not in this for the road trip," I stated.

Dad sighed and grabbed the keys from Mom's other hand. "Be ready to go in two minutes," he ordered. "After that, I make no promises to take you along."

It made me nervous that someone other than Aislin had called. I also hadn't seen Mom this discombobulated since Grandma's funeral two years ago. "She'll be fine" was turning into something like a self-help mantra.

In the interest of not invoking their wrath, I stopped asking questions. I dragged my own bag out of the closet and packed it with clothes, toiletries, and my MP3 player in case I needed to tune out. I didn't know how long the trip would be, but being able to escape would come in handy when things went south.

"Maeve!"

Dad sounded threatening, so I shoved my phone charger into my pocket and practically flew downstairs. He stepped aside to let me out and locked the door behind us.

No one talked while my police officer father was peeling through town at illegal speeds. Once we were on the highway, Dad broke the silence to ask for directions and I voiced one of my main questions.

"Wouldn't it be quicker to fly?" I checked my watch. "We don't want to cut it too close."

"We don't have time to wait for an available flight," Dad countered. "We'll just burn rubber and hope no one stops us along the way."

He glanced at me in the mirror and his expression was one of either fear or righteous anger. I interpreted it as bad news for Aislin.

"Who's Jean Lamont?" I asked after a few more moments of silence.

Dad sighed in annoyance, but I probably wasn't the focus of that emotion. "He's with the United States Consulate General in Montreal. He gets involved when American citizens have Canadian legal trouble."

"Montreal?" The part of me that wasn't busy being shocked was a little impressed. "That's a seriously long haul for one day."

"I'm going to generously assume this wasn't planned," he replied tersely. "The hospital will release her to us once she's patched up."

My stomach dropped into my knees as soon as Dad mentioned a hospital and my mind flashed through a dozen possible reasons for medical treatment. It couldn't be too serious if she had been awake enough to remember my phone number.

"How bad?" I asked once the moment of panic passed.

"She'll be fine, but the officials are making the arrangements to . . ." His gaze flicked to Mom. "Deport her."

"We spoke to her doctor and he said she'll need stitches and x-rays," Mom answered.

"She'll be fine," Dad reiterated as if we were getting off-topic. "What we need is an explanation for her being in Canada."

"Camping trip?" I suggested.

We hadn't even pitched a tent in four years, since Aislin didn't want to spend more of her days outside. We were probably one of the few families we knew who went on vacations to stay out of the fresh air.

"Do we know what she told them?" Mom asked.

"No." He tapped his fingers restlessly on the steering wheel. "If we claim she's a runaway, they'll want to know why we hadn't reported her as missing."

"If we saw her on Tuesday, has enough time passed for that?" I asked.

"That depends," Dad replied tersely.

"Why did we go home without her?" Mom added. "She had no ID or clothes and was three hundred miles from home."

"She *what?*"

"Your sister decided to shoplift before asking for medical help," Dad summarized.

This was exactly why we'd stashed her wardrobe across Greater Boston in the first place. "Well," I said fairly, "I would have done the same thing."

"I don't think she had many options," Mom agreed.

"Which is why she's only grounded for a month," Dad concluded. "We're not unfair."

When they didn't talk for another five minutes, I plugged my headphones in and closed my eyes, hoping I could get some kind of rest before we had to deal with all of this.

I woke up when we pulled into a gas station and paused the song at a look from Mom.

"Last chance for a bathroom break before Canada," Mom announced. "Be back here in five or we might have to leave without you."

I could dawdle all I wanted, but I decided to cooperate and didn't even browse for snacks on my way back.

Before I could plug my earphones in, Dad cleared his throat and I reluctantly sat at attention. "Okay," I said as casually as possible, "what's the plan?"

"I called Mark McInerny," he said. "Since this is a first offense, the sentence will be light and carried out here in the States."

Mark, Dad's old college roommate, was the unofficial family lawyer. Dad studied criminology, so we usually didn't need a legal second opinion. Dad apparently wanted to know about options. I wasn't too worried—teenagers were always getting busted for shoplifting on TV and getting nothing more than community service.

"I'm going to have to pick up trash, aren't I?"

Mom grimaced in sympathy. "We'll find something you'll like," she promised.

"And the court will probably mandate counseling," Dad added with an almost apologetic expression.

"At night," I demanded. "The perpetrator is getting her head shrunk, not me."

"He said that we will have to stay for a few days," Dad continued as if I hadn't made a peep. "They probably suspect foul play, so they'll want to make sure they get the real story."

"When does she get charged?" Mom asked.

"That will happen before we leave," he said. "We'll have orders and a new court date before we leave."

"And you'll want my best Aislin impersonation the whole time," I guessed.

He nodded to himself, hands tapping restlessly on the wheel. "Once we know what she told them, we'll know what's next," he mused.

SCENE 2

White

Once stitches were in and I had my arm in an immobilizing sling, Gagnon compassionately doped me up and said he'd check in later. The medication helped with the dislocated shoulder, so I fell asleep after that, but gave up on dozing after the third time I rolled onto my injured side.

I didn't have anything to read and I couldn't exactly chat up my escorting cops. One of them *had* told me around midnight that my parents were on their way, but he'd kept their ETA under wraps. By three o'clock, no one had turned up and I was starting to panic.

The next time my vital signs were checked, I spoke up. "What time is dawn?"

The nurse raised one eyebrow and started checking my pulse. "Why, do you have somewhere to be?" Apparently satisfied that I was alive, she made a note on my chart. "Dawn breaks around 5:45."

"Where are my parents?"

"Far enough away for you to get some sleep."

It wasn't a suggestion, but I couldn't sleep again. She still turned the light behind my bed to the lowest setting possible and left me to stare at the ceiling. The next thing I heard was Dad's voice. Being a cop himself, he was first checking his facts.

Maeve didn't wait for permission. She plopped herself on the end of the ER bed and hugged me like I'd just been pulled from a burning building. Eventually, she decided to let me get some oxygen and glared at me.

"You owe me big."

"You didn't have to come along," I groused, secretly glad to have an ally right now.

"Not that," she corrected. "I'm here on your side."

I doubted that it was the pain meds' fault that she wasn't making any sense. "Okay."

Mom entered first, looking paler than usual and wearing the look that I'd seen when Maeve had survived her first fender-bender, but not angry.

"How are you feeling?"

"Drugged," I admitted.

"I can imagine," she sighed. "Dr. Gagnon said there shouldn't be any permanent damage from the bite or the dislocation, so that's good news."

I had to wonder if there were any vets who did physical therapy. Having follow-up care instructions was something new for us.

"When can I go home?"

Mom glanced at Maeve and her mouth thinned to a line. "We'll explain that complication at the hotel."

It wasn't going to be a quick grab-and-go then, and Maeve was here to cooperate with the police when I couldn't. Before I could apologize to either one of them, Maeve smirked in fond exasperation.

"I told you."

Dad entered at that moment, accompanied by Gagnon and the two officers from Service de Police de la Ville de Montreal. He crossed the small room in two strides and kissed me quickly on the forehead.

"Thank goodness you're all right," he said as expected.

"I didn't mean to . . ." I let the sentence trail off. After two days as a missing person, I wasn't making excuses. "It won't happen again."

The obligatory introductions followed, but I didn't remember much. I was lucky to remember my own sister's name at this point.

"You're being released into your parents' custody," the taller officer stated. "We'd like all of you to come in for some questioning, but Dr. Gagnon agrees that it's best if you rest first."

"Yes, sir," I responded meekly.

Once they determined where we were staying, the other officer scribbled directions on a slip of paper and handed it to Mom. "I'll be there until six tonight," he informed her.

"We won't be late," Mom promised, tucking the paper into her pocket.

He nodded approvingly. "We'll be as brief as possible. The department's number is on that paper if you should have any questions before then."

"Thank you, Officer," I said. "I'll see you later."

I was certain that Maeve could keep that promise and tell me the details later. With the official business out of the way, Gagnon stepped forward.

"You are very lucky," he informed me. "You dislocated your shoulder, but you don't have muscle tears . . ."

I let him ramble on in medical jargon until he got to what I'd been hoping to hear: "With time and physical therapy, you will have full use of your arm again."

"That's good."

Gagnon smiled. "It's very good. If you'll wait here, I'll get your paperwork and prescriptions in order."

"Thank you," I responded.

I didn't speak again until the room was a Byrnes-only zone. "I think we're going to make it."

Mom glanced at her watch. "Unless they're very slow, we'll have time to spare," she agreed.

"But we should have a backup plan just in case," Maeve said. "One where we stash you in a janitor's closet . . ."

I didn't let her finish that thought. "That's not funny."

"It would be an adventure," my clever sister pressed on with a wicked grin. "Getting you out would be almost as hard as making sure no one came across you . . ."

"If you don't stop right now, I will report you for conspiracy to put your parents in an early grave," Dad interrupted. "Anything you say can and will be used against you."

"*Not funny,*" I reiterated.

Maeve shrugged, put kept her grin in place. "If you say so," she said. "Want some help dressing?"

"We'll give you some privacy," Mom offered.

Maeve had unpacked sweats, underwear, and a t-shirt from the bag by the time they left. "It's not much, but we have other options in the car."

"It's fine," I said dismissively. "I won't be wearing it long."

She set out flip-flops with a smirk. "My thoughts exactly."

"I'm sorry about this," I said, in case I had forgotten to make that clear earlier. "I had no idea what I was doing."

Maeve paused in shaking out the sweatpants to give me a don't-be-an-idiot look. "No one really blames you," she said.

"But I owe you big . . ."

"That's a fact of life." She waved a hand with unconcern. "You'll get the details after your nap."

"I still feel bad about it," I insisted.

"And that's your choice, not what I want for you."

If I had the use of both arms, I would have hugged her. I settled for smiling at her once I was properly dressed. She returned it and squeezed my hand after guiding my arm through the armhole.

"This isn't the disaster your sleep-deprived brain thinks it is."

A moment later, she let the others in and I tried to look less like someone facing a firing squad. "So, does this hotel allow pets?"

"That won't be a problem," Mom explained. "It's next to Lafontaine Park."

Mom was always in charge of hotels; they were always somewhere scenic. Part of me had hoped she'd let me crash indoors, though.

"Anything you need to know?"

"Sure," Maeve laughed. "Would you mind explaining your nudist shoplifting spree?"

Black

The receptionist at the hotel seemed barely awake enough to notice our arrival, but he politely got us checked in well before dawn. Aislin let me steer her towards the nearest elevator, looking as exhausted as the poor clerk. She hadn't said a word since we left the hospital, but she was probably too groggy to care.

"First things first," Mom announced. "We should leave for the park soon, so . . ."

"Park sounds good," Aislin muttered. "Sleep *now*?"

"We'll drop off the luggage and then get you settled in," Dad promised.

Before someone could elect me to the post of escort, I stepped in to volunteer. "You settle in," I offered, "and I'll find our runaway a nice hideout for the day."

"I'd prefer it if you didn't go alone," Mom pointed out.

"I'll be outside for ten minutes," I argued. "I'm not going on a crime spree."

Neither of my overly protective parents dignified that with a response.

"I'll bring my cell phone," I added, waving it for emphasis.

"And I'll be with her most of the time," Aislin interjected a little more lucidly than before. "Don't worry about it."

"Call us if there are any problems," Dad ordered.

Lafontaine Park wasn't very different from Aislin's usual stomping grounds, but she wouldn't be in any shape to enjoy the two lakes or scenery. She looked disgruntled as we hunted for a shaded place for her to avoid tourists, children, or squirrels.

"This is pretty much the epitome of a no-win situation," she commented as I ducked under another branch.

"I know," I assured her, "but four years in, I'm surprised this is your first major infraction."

"I didn't mean to," she restated her earlier defense. "I just lost track of time and international borders."

I turned abruptly so we were face-to-face instead of side-by-side. "I'm truly not mad. It's just . . ." I shook my head, remembering what Dad had outlined on the drive up 93. "I'll expect you to do my chores for a year."

Aislin probably hadn't slept since getting arrested, so I wasn't surprised when she didn't disagree. She turned left and circled a tree that was partially hidden behind another where she could probably go unnoticed for hours.

"Here?" I suggested.

"I think so," she agreed. "I don't have much choice or time."

Usually, she could undress in private, but she'd had already had a hard time dressing. I followed her into the shadows and helped her strip down before returning to the bag with her clothes. I heard a rustle of wings and a quiet honk, which meant we were all clear.

"See you tonight," I called out.

I circled back a couple of minutes later, just to be sure she was all right. Her head was tucked under her uninjured right wing and after a whole minute, she still hadn't moved except to breathe.

Satisfied, I shouldered my backpack and headed back to the hotel.

It was easy to sleep in something more comfortable than a car seat, so I woke up to find lunch on the table. Mom was unpacking and Dad was in work mode. That was never a reassuring thing.

"What time is it?"

"Two," Dad responded. "Are you ready to get our stories straight?"

"As ready as I'll ever be," I conceded.

"Good. I had words with Jean Lamont while you were sleeping. Your sister says she got lost and doesn't know where her clothes ended up. They want more details."

"So they think she's a nudist or worse . . ."

"I wouldn't be that glib when telling your side of the story," he said sharply.

Of course. I'd managed to forget for thirty seconds that not only did we have to come up with a plausible explanation for Aislin's nudist heist, but we had to avoid adding charges to the list.

"They probably think of her as at-risk," Dad explained. "If you're covering for someone else, they'll want to know about it."

"So my story can't be that I was sold into slavery."

"Or that you came here with a boy and can't remember what happened next," Mom agreed.

"And don't even joke about drugs," Dad concluded.

"If we're going with a hiking story, where are my boots and gear?" I challenged. "I could have gotten lost on a camping trip."

"That still doesn't explain how she crossed the border and made her way to Montreal."

That was the problem with making it up as we went along. The logic went in circles until we all got sick of it.

"This isn't really helping," I complained. "Can't we just wait until dark, grab Aislin and go?"

Dad withered me with a look. "That's would probably hurt your sister's chances of a light sentence."

"Okay." I glanced at Mom and tried to crack a smile. "How many times can we work 'flight risk' into this conversation?"

She responded by burying her face in her hands, but she groaned instead of crying. "She's grounded for life," she announced through her fingers.

"Come on," I chided. "If she's grounded forever, how is she ever going to get married?"

"Classified ads, online dating, and smoke signals," Mom listed. "I'm not letting her out of the house until she's thirty."

This was definitely not the time or the place to tell her to lighten up. I turned my attention back to Dad. "I played a prank. We were camping in Vermont, I stole her clothes during the night and she wandered off northward."

"For roughly fifty miles," he echoed my earlier calculation.

We had less than four hours before the nice officer left for the day and all we had was that I was a jerk and my sister had no navigational skills. She'd also vanished for most of a day before anyone noticed. No matter what, we looked bad.

"This isn't really helping," I said again, detangling my hair with my fingers. "Can I take a shower if I promise to brainstorm?"

Dad exchanged a look with Mom and apparently decided something through telepathy. "Go ahead," he ordered. "Maybe by the time you're dressed, we'll have a better idea of how to handle this."

That was a better plan than reinventing the same wheel fifty times. I saluted jauntily and grabbed fresh clothes on my way to the shower.

I emerged with a mental list of things to remember, like looking uncomfortable under my bandages and feigning a headache. I also needed to be reserved and polite, since that was her default setting.

My parents were looking more optimistic at first glance—not happy yet, but sanguine.

"We have a plan," Mom announced.

White

The sun was still up when I was shaken awake. My nightmares had ranged from being chased by French-Canadian children to being ambushed by my original attacker.

I still couldn't picture the animal clearly. It had looked like a wolf and I had only managed to escape by fighting back. Beaks aren't the most effective weapons, but having one had been handy for my escape. The problem had been that trying to fly with one good wing was like trying to paddle a canoe with one oar. I had gotten lucky.

I was luckier that the maybe-wolf had given up, but in my nightmare, it tracked me to the park. This time, when he grabbed me, I was too weak to fly away. My wings strained at the stitches and hot blood ran down my feathers. This time, it forgot about the shoulder and went for my throat.

When something grabbed me by the wing and shook me awake, I flapped defensively and snapped my beak at my assailant. Maeve jumped back, hands raised defensively.

"It's me," she hissed. "Settle down, will you?"

Heart pounding, I tucked my wings against my sides and sank to the ground. By the time I stopped shaking, Maeve had closed the gap between us and sat down.

"I brought you some food," she said as a peace offering.

I hated eating as a bird, but by the time I'd eaten the third croissant, I'd forgiven her for scaring me. I laid my head in her lap like an obedient dog and she laughed, stroking my back affectionately.

"We thought you'd like that," she said. "We'll have to come back sometime when all of us can go to dinner."

I nipped at the band of her wristwatch and she obediently displayed the time. It was just after 9:00, so the sun was about to set and she was here to make sure I got back to the hotel safely.

I withdrew my head from her lap and struggled to my feet. As soon as I was upright again, she unzipped her backpack and started unpacking while she reported on her day.

"I spent a few hours with that bandage on and that shirt was all wrong," she explained. "I know you don't like tank tops, but you'll probably be more comfortable in one. Mom got you some slip-ons so you don't have to worry about keeping your shoelaces tied."

Maeve's rambling was comfortingly familiar. She rarely erred on the side of caution so I wouldn't feel left out. Around the time that she started telling me about dinner, though, the sun disappeared from the horizon. My back arched and my arms flew out in an instinctive spasm. I could feel them lengthen and fingers replaced feathers, but overwhelming pain followed. I hadn't been careful of my injury and while no stitches popped, it felt as though I had come very close to re-dislocating my shoulder. I also brained myself on a low-hanging branch and curled in on myself out of agony and modesty.

"You okay?"

I gritted my teeth so my jaw would stop shaking, but the rest of me quivered at the pain and it was a while before I could speak.

"Didn't expect it to hurt that much," I finally admitted.

Maeve was silent for a moment of genuine concern. "Do you need to go back to . . ."

"I'm fine," I barked out. "I just . . ."

Maeve's next question was anxious: "Do you need a doctor?"

"I need painkillers," I said. "I don't suppose you brought any?"

"No," Maeve answered, rounding the tree with a pair of jeans, "but I can fix that at the hotel."

"Bring it on," I requested.

With the top on, I had to admit that a strap felt better on the injury than a shoulder seam. Once Maeve brushed my hair out, I looked less like a lunatic and more like your average brunette tourist.

"Much better," Maeve pronounced. "Let's go."

Halfway back to the hotel, I remembered her appointment with the SVPM. "So," I said warily, "what exactly did you tell them?"

"About your adventure?" She shrugged. "Camping trip gone awry. Brendan backed us up."

"You told Brendan?" My only brother felt morally obligated to tease us about everything. "Why does he have to get involved?"

"He says we always go camping on vacation," Maeve reasoned. "In return, he wants to talk to you as soon as we get back to the hotel."

"Please tell me he's not here," I begged.

"He's coming up for the 4th of July and an obligatory lecture," Maeve assured me.

"Thanks," I groused, readjusting my straps. "Any other unpleasant things I should know about?"

Since hugging me around the shoulders would be cruel, Maeve squeezed my waist. "Cheer up," she said. "We're not here that long and Dad says room service is up for grabs."

I let her drag me back to the safety of the hotel, where I could reasonably expect dessert to go with my painkillers.

Dad greeted me with a side hug. "Your mother has run out for a few supplies, but if anything on the menu tempts you, I admit you deserve some kindness."

That sounded like half of a parental decree, but I thumbed through the menu on the nightstand and placed an order for something reasonably priced.

When I turned back to face Dad, he had stopped looking happy to see me. "Have a seat," he ordered.

I chose the closest chair without argument, but Maeve stayed between us like some kind of referee.

"Obviously," Dad said tersely, "we are thrilled and relieved that you're all right."

"Me too."

"But this can't happen again."

Rather than feeling indignation at the directive, I was sure I'd heard him wrong. "What makes you think it will?"

"I didn't think it was something to expect," Dad argued, "yet here we are."

In the interest of not making things worse, I didn't dispute that. "I promise to never get arrested again," I said.

"I don't think that's what he means," Maeve interpreted for me. "I think none of us want to question whether you're safe again."

"But all of us have to deal with that doubt," I protested. "Anything could happen to Dad at work. Mom has to survive Boston drivers in rush hour. Brendan isn't what you'd call street-smart. Even if you and I stayed home all day, there's no guarantee that we'd be safe."

"Those are normal family worries," Dad rejoined. "Do you think that they excuse what you've done?"

There was only one right answer, but it was an honest one. "*No,*" I said. "This shouldn't have happened, and it's been a nightmare for me too."

I caught a glimpse of guilt in his expression, but it disappeared behind paternal sternness. "What I mean to say is we can't have you running off like this again. Asking for forgiveness isn't better than asking for help and if you pull something like this again, you're wearing an ankle monitor until grad school. I'm sure you feel very repentant about the incident, but that's not enough."

I had promised not to get arrested, but that wasn't a sure thing. I might also someday give in to the temptation to run away from home. I could only tell him what he needed to hear today and try my best to keep my promises tomorrow.

"I promise that I will never consider this to be a good idea," I said.

Dad glanced at Maeve as if to gauge whether or not he was supposed to find my response amusing. When she gave away nothing, he sighed.

"I won't ask for it in writing, but I'll expect you to honor that promise," he decided. "And you're still grounded for a month."

All things considered, it could have been worse.

INTERLUDE

Black

The summer before we turned thirteen, Aislin and I got to spend a whole month away at camp. It was one of those all-purpose places that had a name worthy of Thoreau or a retirement home.

The camp had something for everyone, from hiking to skits, but they stuck Aislin and me in different cabins and we rejoiced. Aislin was in Bunk 3 with Jill and Bekah, who taught her how to sail and talk to boys. I was in Bunk 9 with girls who wanted to try makeup and fawn over Derrick Ferrell. They traded diving lessons for eyeliner tips.

New friends aside, we couldn't stand ignoring each other, so we ate dinner together and teamed up for canoeing. We once swapped bunks and would have gotten away with it if Aislin's counselor hadn't noticed that I had been cured of my hay fever.

Just after the Fourth of July, disaster struck. Aislin's counselor pulled me aside to ask where she was. I hadn't seen her and the same went for her friends and counselors. I headed to my bunk after dinner in case my sister turned up there.

Shortly after dark, Aislin started throwing rocks at my screen. I snuck out of the bunk and found her hiding behind a birch tree.

She was crying and naked and promised to tell me everything if I could bring her some clothes and a tampon. I brought both of them without asking questions and while she got changed, I sought out Nina, her counselor.

Aislin told the higher-ups that she'd gone skinny-dipping on a dare and someone had swiped her clothes. Terrified that someone from camp would see her, she'd hidden in the woods until night. Nina was sympathetic to the awkward teenager, but skinny-dipping and going MIA were both against the rules. Aislin got kitchen duty for her infraction and got told that the next time, parents would be called.

Once we were alone, Aislin told me that she'd spent all day with wings and the conviction that she'd gone bonkers. I had no reason to doubt her, but I witnessed her transformation the next day to prove that it wasn't a hallucination. After seeing my twin sister's hands sprout feathers and watching her shrink to swan size, I'd wondered if I was bonkers too.

When Aislin went missing again, I knew exactly where to find her, but there was no way I was telling Nina. So I shrugged miserably and said I hadn't seen her that day.

The camp director decided that both of us had problems with authority. My parents didn't believe that, but they didn't argue when we were asked to leave camp early.

White

Every young girl I've known has grown up addicted to fairytales. There's an undeniable attraction to the idea that you can start out every story with "Once upon a time . . ." and end up with "happily ever after." My Halloween costumes were almost always fairytale–themed because I was happy with any variety of princess dress.

I didn't believe fairytales happened nowadays, so I didn't expect to be part of one. They required fairies and magic and I stopped believing in those at age nine.

The summer *it* happened, I already had enough reasons to be uncomfortable. Maeve liked being taller than half the guys in our class and shopping for our first bras. She placed bets on which one of us would get her period first. She convinced Mom to buy us tankinis and started swiping the hairdressers' magazines for beauty and boyfriend advice. The only trick was learning such things on the sly so Mom wouldn't get the chance to disapprove.

Maeve couldn't wait to grow up, but I felt like a pimply dork. I had to pack deodorant and razors for camp. At my last checkup of the school year, Dr. Michaels had talked about fixing my overbite with braces.

Maeve lost one of her bets—I got my first period about two weeks into camp. She asked me a million questions and gave me her leftover Oreos to celebrate. I would've been happy to lose that bet, but I hugged my sister and said I was sure she'd catch up soon. I was the baby of the family; it was a little nice to pull ahead in some way.

And then, as if I didn't feel like enough of a spaz, I woke up the next morning with wings. Like some demented version of *The Ugly Duckling*, I grew up one night and turned into a swan the next morning. I flapped out of the bunk before reveille and spent the day trying to figure out how to turn off the nightmare. Then I realized that I was too hungry for this to be a dream and simultaneously decided that I had gone nuts. I couldn't go back to camp for fear of turning human at an inconvenient time, so I hid in the bushes until I turned back into a gawky 12-year-old.

Mom was the one to drive our getaway car on the second night and she didn't say anything until we were well on our way back to Cambridge. I did catch her having a grim, whispered conversation with Maeve when I came out of my cabin with my bedroll, but they clammed up as soon as I was in earshot.

Mom should have put on an oldies station and asked us a million questions about camp, but the radio stayed off and she just stared at the road ahead of us until we had a good fifty miles behind us. Then, instead of yelling at me for getting us both kicked out of camp, she quietly apologized for not telling me before.

I was so furious that she would leave something like this out of the family history that I didn't speak to anyone, even Maeve, for the next two days. It was better than talking about my opinion of my newly discovered fate.

Every family has a story in its history that's more rumor than fact. On Dad's side, we have someone who lived in a cave for ten years. On Mom's side, we had a stowaway who had come to America by way of Japan.

A few generations before that was our personal fairytale. An unnamed maiden on Mom's Romanian side had the misfortune to attract a young sorcerer. When she fell for someone different, he spat at her and told her that the next second daughter born into her family line would be cursed until she found true love. The exact curse was so close to *Swan Lake* that I wouldn't have believed it on hearsay, but it had popped up in a few generations since then. The curse *was* breakable, but it was devilishly complicated. All of this was supposed to kick in once she became a woman and back then, it had meant when she was old enough to have children.

For six hundred years, the Albescu side of the family had been populated mostly by only children and groups of brothers. When Mom found out she was expecting twin girls, Aunt Diane reminded her of the family legend, but not even ballet fanatics believed in that sort of thing.

I now hate fairytales for obvious reasons. If I'm lucky, someday I'll have kids and all of their bedtime stories will start with a different phrase: "They should have known better."

SCENE 3

White

Montreal was a charming city with many things to see and do and a rich history, but none of us got to play tourist. By the time Maeve helped with my seatbelt for the ride home, I felt like we'd worn out our welcome and never wanted to come back.

Road trips were usually a time for car games and inside jokes, but today, Mom stuck to directions and driving. Maeve and I shared a box of crackers while enjoying an audiobook. I fell asleep around the Vermont/New Hampshire border and didn't wake again until we got onto Route 2, about twelve miles from home.

Mom was the one to help me out of the car this time and kept one hand on my good shoulder as we headed up the walk. "What do you need?" she asked. "Food, bath . . ."

"Bed," I responded immediately. "I can take all the showers I want while under house arrest."

She didn't take that as surliness or defiance, just led me through the front door after Dad. I lumbered up the stairs with every intention of passing out fully clothed. The problem was that Maeve had other things in mind.

"I've got painkillers," she announced. "I thought you might want help with pajamas."

"Sure," I mumbled. "Bottom drawer on the right."

"Where they've always been," Maeve pointed out. "Any preference on which ones?"

I shook my head. "I wasn't going to change."

"You'll feel better this way," my sister asserted. "Take your medicine."

I obeyed without argument, but took a seat on the bed first. Maeve patiently wrangled me through the costume change as she had on the trip and pulled the covers back so I could slide in. I spent a few moments rearranging my pillows into the configuration that had helped me sleep for the last few days, but getting comfortable still wasn't easy and Maeve pulled the covers to my chin as soon as I stopped squirming.

"Lights off, please," I requested.

"As soon as you answer one question."

I had already closed my eyes and it took an effort to reverse the process. "You couldn't have asked during our three days in Quebec?"

"We were with our parents for three days in Quebec," Maeve reminded me.

Which meant her question was something a bit more personal than she'd like to ask in front of authority figures. "Go on."

"Why Montreal?" I opened my mouth to protest and she amended her question immediately. "What made you want to take a long trip in the first place? Boredom? Teenage rebellion?"

I had answered that question for myself before leaving; it hadn't been an impulse fly and the reason made perfect sense to me.

"It was June 21," I stated. "I'm a swan longer on that day than any other."

"So you celebrated all that time by having an adventure."

"That was what I meant to do, yes," I confirmed. "Next June, I'm taking a red-eye to Miami and spending all day on the beach."

She laughed quietly and backed away to turn off the lights. "I'll come with you," she offered, "but keep that under wraps. If they know you're planning your next escape, you'll be locked up until Christmas."

Being grounded usually didn't mean much, since my social life wasn't really affected by it. I couldn't meet Maeve for a night out or have a friend over and always felt like I was on house arrest. I didn't mind much because I was able to get my stitches removed before we left Montreal, but it would be a while before I went flying under my own power again. Our family doctor referred me for physical therapy, but I couldn't ask her about improving flight speed. We were also hard-pressed to find a physical therapist with suitably extended hours.

There was some disagreement on how to punish me properly, but Mom and Dad weren't trying to be cruel, just stern. Since I was a night owl, spending all night in my house wasn't a punishment. It was just tragically typical.

Instead of extra chores, I got assigned a lot of homework. Mom knew my pet peeves and decided to hand me a stack of books and a set of deadlines for the associated essays. I was so bored by my imprisonment that I didn't mind it this time, but I looked unhappy for her sake and got down to contemplating Arthur Miller. They could have locked me in my room instead of letting me waddle around the house during daylight hours, but Maeve was the one who suffered most. Every penitentiary had to have a warden and I had orders to stay upstairs when she had friends over, but we spent several of her hard-earned summer days sitting on the couch and trying to find something other than *telenovelas* and talk shows to watch. She soon came home with a stack of movies borrowed from various friends and we spent a memorable day watching a few of them together. I had to hide when the UPS guy showed up, but it was nice of Maeve to keep me entertained.

On the fifth day, Mom woke me up before dawn. "You're out on compassionate furlough," she announced.

"For how long?" I asked groggily.

"Just for the day. Thanks to Maeve's impassioned plea, we decided that you could use some fresh air. I will drop you off wherever you would like and be back to pick you up at sunset."

I was at the point where I would kill for a few minutes outside of the house. "Wherever?"

"Within reason," Mom amended. "We're not going back to Canada."

I had a few places that were old favorites and I picked one of those instead of considering how far I could go. "Castle Island?"

"Sure." She turned on a low light. "I thought you'd pick Walden."

Castle Island Beach had trees, but they weren't the kind that would shut out the rest of the world and I could live with that, so I shrugged indifferently.

"I need a change of scenery."

Mom sighed with a touch of envy in her expression. "The weather's supposed to be good and you can find some toddlers to play with."

"And maybe steal a hot dog or two."

"It sounds nice."

I could have invited her, but she would have been immensely bored by my usual agenda. It was even more tedious when I was injured.

"I'll be in the car in twenty minutes," she said.

Even though I was now used to dressing one-handed, I chose sweatpants and a tank top, which didn't require me to handle zippers or buttons.

"If this goes well," Mom commented nineteen minutes later, "we might try it again sometime."

"'If this goes well?'" I echoed. "Do you really think I'll try something?"

"Fine," Mom sniffed. "I'll stop trying to cheer you up."

She had claimed that this was Maeve's doing, but she wasn't giving off a prison guard vibe.

"I'll be on my best behavior," I promised solemnly.

One furlough led to another, mostly because I didn't do anything scandalous or dangerous to jeopardize myself. Mom dropped me off at Todd Pond one day so she could find Dad's birthday present in Concord. I had been there a dozen times on my own, but it felt like parole for good behavior. While I wasn't going flying, I liked the option of paddling around for a few hours and napping under a tree when I got too tired to twitch.

On July 3, she didn't let me out of the house until late in the day when she had business to take care of in Arlington. I spent two hours swimming and Mom got me home three minutes before sundown.

No one in the family had ever denied me nightly shower rights, since they had more flexible bathing schedules. Maeve had asked once why it was my first human act every day; I had explained that it required opposable thumbs. When I smelled like shampoo instead of loam, I wrapped myself in a towel for the trip back to my bedroom.

The problem was that Brendan had arrived home while I was in the shower and all 6'1" of him was blocking the hallway.

"Hey, you," I said with my first human grin of the day. Usually, I wasn't thrilled to see him, but right now, I would have been friendly to Jack the Ripper because he provided human interaction.

"Hey, you," Brendan answered casually. "Going somewhere?"

"My closet," I said. "I like wearing clothes around the house."

He nodded thoughtfully, not budging an inch. "You're acting like a normal teenage girl. We might turn you to the dark side after all."

He was the only one who dared to make fun of me in equal parts before and after the change and that was one of the reasons I allowed it.

"I've been on the dark side for a while now," I pointed out. "You probably heard the thrilling tale."

"I heard the rumors," my brother confirmed with a smirk. "Problem is, that's Maeve's style. Why should I believe you were involved?"

"Maeve wouldn't have gotten caught."

"I've seen your social calendar, though," Brendan reconsidered. "I could see motive for a jailbreak."

I was *not* up for an argument, teasing or otherwise, when I was practically naked and starting to shiver. I tried to sidestep him again, but he was used to this game and he had me at a severe disadvantage.

"Do you mind letting me pass?"

"What, no hug?" he teased.

"I'm dripping wet and wearing nothing but a towel," I pointed out. "I hope this isn't how you think women should be treated."

Brendan planted a hand on my uninjured shoulder as soon as I tried to get around. "Hold up," he ordered. "We need to have a talk."

I gave up on going around and tried to muscle my way past. That was something best accomplished when I wasn't afraid of accidentally dropping my towel, so I held up both hands and decided to bargain.

"We can have a talk when I'm wearing pants."

Brendan ignored my argument and stared at me with an imitation of my father's "Officer Dad" expression. "Aislin," he said quietly.

"Brendan," I replied.

His grip tightened a little to underline the importance of this conversation and I braced myself for whatever 'wisdom' he had to impart next. I wasn't disappointed.

"I know you're boy-crazy, but becoming a nudist isn't the answer."

I couldn't punch him, but I kicked him daintily in the shins for that. "Shut up."

"Don't worry," he chuckled, finally moving out of my way. "I'm sure there are plenty of cute guys in juvie."

"SHUT UP!"

Maeve's admonition from downstairs was a perfect imitation of Mom. "Brendan, stop teasing your sister."

"Yes, Mother," he called back with mock deference.

Once he moved, I bolted for my room and could hear him laughing his way down the stairs.

Five minutes later, I entered the backyard to find Brendan holding out a plate with our usual Third of July dinner. Since we always went to the Boston Pops Fourth of July concert on the Common, we did all the family stuff the day before.

"Welcome home," I addressed Brendan, taking the plate. "When are you leaving again?"

"Friday," Brendan answered.

"Are you sure? I'm sure your boss can't live without you," I suggested. "And your roommate's probably burned the house down."

"I had laundry for Mom to do . . ."

"Please tell me you've found a laundromat down there," I interjected.

"Yeah." He shrugged. "Only Mom understands fabric softener, though."

"Very true."

Brendan grinned and gave me a quick hug. "It's good to see you too, runt."

With some teasing of my own out of the way, I crossed the lawn and claimed the lawn chair next to Maeve. I'd last eaten at breakfast, so I didn't talk until my plate was half-empty. With Dad on hamburger duty and Mom handling drinks, no one tried to stop me. It was unusual for my sister to go this long without talking, though, and her concentration on a pad of paper only supported my theory.

"What are you doing?" I asked when my mouth was empty again.

"Scavenger hunt, what else?" Maeve replied.

In our family, Maeve was the natural-born coper. I was decent at keeping a cool head in a crisis, but she was the one who could help with the aftermath.

Brendan had done his share of freaking out when the reasons for my homeschooling were explained. He had been sixteen and didn't take the news very gracefully. His anger made me feel a little less lonely. Dad had known since the pregnancy that this could happen, but twelve years of knowing hadn't helped. It had always been a possibility, but the reality was a crisis. I had been reprimanded for antagonizing my mother, but he never claimed that I didn't have a right to be angry about it. He just thought I was being disrespectful.

I shouldn't have been surprised when my twin sister's loyalty left them both behind in the dust. Maeve had wanted to know why she couldn't change as well. I thought she was jealous of this stupid curse in the same way that I envied her getting the chicken pox first. It sounded like age-old sibling rivalry until she pointed out that Odette in *Swan Lake* had been given a flock of fellow swan-maidens. She didn't want to have equal share in the family curse; she wanted to make sure I wasn't alone.

No such luck, of course. It wasn't as if we could track down the sorcerer and negotiate some wiggle room. Everything but the curse itself was based on conjecture. So Maeve started making scavenger hunts for me to keep me busy and sometimes entertained. At least once a week, she would leave a post-it on my nightstand and expect me to report back at the end of the day. They were usually things like "7. Find a guy wearing a Green Bay Packers shirt" or "3. Five autumn leaves that haven't fallen off the tree yet." Around holidays, they got thematic, so I peeked over her shoulder to see if this year was any different.

"No snooping," Maeve snapped, circling her arm like she was trying to keep me from cheating on a test. "You don't get any advance warning."

"You have the same two things on there every year," I pointed out. "Swipe an American flag and a hot dog."

She turned and glowered sternly at me. "Are you trying to ruin this for me? You'll see it tomorrow."

"So," I said once she had tucked the rough draft in her shorts pocket, "what did I miss?"

"Your lawyer called me and wants to meet up tomorrow morning before he heads off to enjoy the holiday weekend," Maeve informed me.

"Ah. That explains the bad mood." A morning meeting meant that instead of staking out a spot on Boston Common, Maeve would be stuck inside, discussing my problems and wondering if Brendan knew what a good view meant. I offered my watermelon for peace's sake. "Should I be worried?"

Maeve took the slice and broke it in half, passing the leftovers back. "The Canadians will support a diversion program, since this is your first offense. I'm stuck with a summer of community service, but I won't do any time. Your doctor doesn't want you doing any strenuous activity, so I don't even have to worry about manual labor."

That was good. She could do something like the community literacy program. On the other hand, Maeve's idea of community service was coaching some kind of sport and she couldn't do that with my kind of injury.

"I'm very sorry," I said meekly.

"I have ideas for you to make it up to me," Maeve announced.

"No, you don't." I gestured to my arm. "I can't do laundry or paint toenails like this."

"You can start by meeting this guy from my Chem class."

"No."

"He's heard all about you and wants to meet the less-gregarious Byrne sister."

"*No.*" The way Maeve talked, I would sound like a brilliant-but-agoraphobic supermodel. "I refuse to blind-date."

She grabbed my wrist, which meant she was about to beg. "Come on," she wheedled. "He's funny, nerdy enough for you, and coming tomorrow."

"Natalie let a nerd tag along?" Natalie Church thought of my introversion as unforgivable. "Did he let her cheat off his midterm?"

"He plays basketball with Darren, and Natalie likes Darren, so she'll be strategically nice to him." Maeve paused for breath. "He's funny. You'll see."

While I couldn't stand Natalie, Darren had always treated me as my sister's equal, so I sighed resignedly and decided to give up the fight.

"What's his name?"

"Ethan."

I groaned this time. "So far, you've suggested Esteban, Emile, Eric, Ernest . . ."

"And let's not forget the two Edwards and an Eduardo," Brendan added; he had given up on talking to Dad in favor of bothering us. "That was a fun month."

"Aren't there any other letters you could explore?"

"I'll try to find you three Mikes and a Miguel next week," Maeve deadpanned. "Tomorrow, you're meeting Ethan. And stop stressing; it's just an introduction."

"It's never just an introduction," I groused.

"I'm going to court for you," Maeve snapped. "You can put up with my friends for a few hours."

When she put it that way, I felt a little less resistant to the idea of doing her a favor. "Yes, ma'am," I said dutifully. "Other than Natalie, Ethan, and Darren . . ."

"Natalie isn't coming," Maeve interrupted. "Laurie Crenshaw has a cabin and it beats sunburns on the Common. Nick, Sosi, and Avril are coming too."

She had picked her allies well. No one in the group terrified me outright and I liked Avril and Sosi without trying.

"So, you'll come."

It wasn't a question. Maeve didn't budge when it came to this kind of thing. I decided to answer it anyway.

"I'll come," I conceded.

Black

To meet with the lawyer, I picked out a very Aislin-esque outfit. Mom couldn't talk me into a plaid skirt and saddle oxfords, but I raided my sister's closet for a pair of khakis that weren't cargo pants and paired it with a peach button-down sweater that made me look like a second-grade teacher. My parents wanted me to make a good impression and I figured that going preppy and remembering my manners would do the trick.

Mark McInerny's office was almost completely deserted, with no paralegals or partners scurrying around. He met us in the outer office, wearing the lawyer equivalent of "casual Friday." I felt ridiculous wearing a cardigan to impress a guy in a polo shirt, but didn't say so.

"Aislin," Mark said affectionately. "I didn't give you permission to grow a foot."

"I'll remember that next time," I answered. He wasn't the kind of family friend that I was expected to hug on sight, but I shook his hand warmly. "You haven't come to visit since, what, Brendan's graduation?"

"I think you're right," he chuckled. "Sarah, good to see you as always."

Mom, being a parent, was comfortable with a cheek-kiss and shoulder squeeze. "Thanks for seeing us, Mark."

"Any time."

He closed the door behind us and indicated the empty chairs in front of the desk. I sat, crossed my ankles, and tried to look innocent.

"So, you are being charged under the Trespass to Property Act and with shoplifting," Mark said without further preamble.

"Not public indecency?

He didn't return my hopeful smile. "You weren't very public, it seems, and Canada has a slightly different standard where it comes to streaking."

I didn't want everyone in the courtroom imagining my nude search for boot-cut jeans, so that was welcome news.

"Thank goodness for small favors," Mom murmured as if reading my thoughts.

He shook his head slightly and I saw a hint of an amused smile, but a moment later it was gone. This was the guy who had sung terrible karaoke at our New Year's party more than once, but right now, he was on the job and smiles weren't allowed.

"All right," he said, "I have the report from your friends in Montreal, but I'd like you to briefly tell me how we got here."

I gave a more casual version of what I had told the Canadians while he took notes and managed not to laugh at me. I would have to work on my own facial expressions for the next time a judge asked me about the fiasco.

"So," I concluded, "I had a good reason for being there and it was more trespassing than breaking and entering."

"I wouldn't say that at the hearing," Mark advised. "Were you under the influence?"

"No!" I blurted out. "Did they say I was?"

"No," he said, "but I don't have any reports on whether they tested you for drugs."

"I don't know," I said, "but I was very lucid and very desperate when this happened."

He nodded in understanding. "This I can work with," he promised.

"Whose idea was the diversion program?" I asked.

"That's what the court favored," Mark agreed. "You had no previous record and you were in extenuating circumstances. You have no intention to repeat your offenses. The authorities will want to interview your family before the next hearing. Do you think Maeve will be willing to help you with that?"

I tried to keep my expression neutral, but I nearly failed. "I think Maeve would move heaven and earth to back me up."

This time, Mark did smile back. "I thought she might."

"I'm not reading to the elderly," I announced as soon as we got in the car. "It would be like summer homework."

"I was thinking along the lines of finding an inner-city sports program that could use someone with your skills," Mom suggested.

"Except every college-bound goalie is already working there," I said. "If I'm going to do this for Aislin, I'm not going to suffer."

I could see her roll her eyes at my attitude. "That wasn't the plan."

"Good."

I kicked off the annoyingly proper shoes and flexed my toes. "I think that went well, though."

"You did just fine," Mom replied. "Where do you want me to drop you off?"

"I was going to ask you the same thing," I said with a smirk. "Don't you think I've earned some quality time with the car?"

"Not today," she said. "We'll talk about bribery later."

That was reasonable, if a little annoying.

"Take me home," I requested. "I'm not watching fireworks dressed like this."

Getting Aislin to hang out with my friends was a small achievement next to her agreeing to meet a boy. She stipulated that I have my own scavenger hunt, she wasn't obligated to stay for the concert, and she was in charge of the dress code.

The scavenger hunt she invented outshone my own. Finding a tent made of a space blanket and a security barrier was easy, but tracking down an Armenian-American who didn't know Sosi was harder. The hardest part was getting 100 signatures on a petition to save the completely fictional Pacific narwhal.

About five minutes before sundown, I wove through a giant patchwork of picnic blankets and lawn chairs on Boston Common. Aislin had arranged a rendezvous by the concession stands instead of trying to find us in the crowd.

When I finally caught up to Aislin, though, she wasn't alone. I stopped ten yards away and resorted to spying, because if Aislin knew I was witnessing this, she would have completely overreacted.

I didn't recognize the guy, not surprisingly. Aislin claimed to know every cashier working a graveyard shift in the Greater Boston area, and he could have been one of them. He could be someone who pulled all-nighters at the BU library or he could be a complete stranger.

All I could tell for sure was that he was older, maybe even college age, and she wasn't cowering in terror. That was a good sign if I'd ever seen one.

Unfortunately, she then spotted me skulking and beckoned

with her good arm. The guy walked off a moment later, after she said something about "my sister."

"Ash." I drew out the word the way I would when talking to a disobedient five-year-old. "What's the meaning of this?"

I recognized that look as guilty and nervous, even by the dim light on the Common. I'd caught her enjoying herself, which made her mystery man all the more interesting to me.

"Don't worry," Aislin sighed. "I'll still be charming for Ethan."

"That's not what I mean," I protested. "When did you meet him?"

A span of thirty seconds was apparently enough to make her forget that she had just had some kind of meaningful conversation with a member of the opposite sex.

"Him?" she echoed blankly.

"Your tall friend," I prompted.

"Oh." She gestured to the plate of elephant ears on her lap. "I met him about five minutes ago at the stand and he chivalrously carried my food for me."

She was again missing the point. "Uh-huh."

"Uh-huh," she echoed. "Never seen him before in my life."

"And you got his name and phone number?"

Aislin smirked at my curiosity. "And his blood type and two references."

I hated it when she sassed me about this sort of thing. It gave the impression that I was the only one making an effort. As the older sister, I had every right to hold her to certain standards.

"Be serious," I advised her. "I can go chase him down if you didn't do your job."

She grabbed my shoulder to stop me from doing just that. "Don't," she requested. "He was a nice guy, but that doesn't mean he's The One."

Before I could come up with a counter-argument or plan of attack, she shoved the plate of food into my hands and stalked off in the direction of our blankets.

"Wait," I called, "you don't know where you're going."

"I did a fly-by," Aislin responded. "You're three blankets left of a barrier and Avril needs her roots done. Mom and Dad are five rows to the right of you with the Sandovals."

Aislin was in a better mood by the time we reached the blankets, hugging our mutual friends and exchanging pleasantries with the others. A crowd was the only way to stop my interrogation.

"Ethan, Aislin," I said as I sat down. "Aislin, Ethan."

Ethan made room for her in the circle without prompting and Aislin settled in before shaking hands politely.

"How was work?" I asked after another round of Crazy Eights.

I'd cleverly invented a summer job at a day camp to explain my sister's long absences. The fictional employer even had Fourth of July festivities and was something of a slave-driver.

"You know," Aislin joked, "running around like a chicken with its head cut off."

Everyone laughed at that and Sosi paused in mid-shuffle to respond. "I'm surprised you had to work."

"I get holiday pay to kid-herd," Ash said with a wave of her hand. "We made patriotic lanyards, listened to one of the counselors do his George Washington impression . . ."

"Torture with benefits," Avril chuckled. "I'm jealous."

"Why?" I teased. "We had that lady who called the fly-overs alien invasions."

"Are we sure they're not?" Ethan countered. "They're probably waiting for the *1812 Overture*."

"What about the scavenger hunt?"

Aislin dug her list out of her shorts pocket and scanned it for effect. "I got everything. The guy wearing a flag as a skirt was the hardest one, but he was at the Charles/MGH stop."

"No fair," Ethan protested. "We couldn't use the T."

"You had the whole Esplanade and worked in teams," my sister pointed out. "How did the petition go?"

"Ask the boys," I suggested. "We were trying to find a World War II veteran."

"One hundred and thirty-seven signatures and an offer to post on an animal rights website," Darren announced. "I bet we could have gotten more if we hadn't stopped for lunch."

"And just what are we saving the Pacific narwhal from?" I asked.

Darren and Ethan exchanged looks and said, in unison, "Surfers."

"Did you know," Ethan said very seriously over our laughter, "that over the last twenty years, reckless surfing habits off the coast of Maui . . ."

"*Far* off the coast of Maui," Nick added.

". . . have cut the population of this beautiful mammal in half? We're campaigning for a safe haven for the narwhals, but we eventually hope to get laws passed to ban surfing in narwhal territory . . ."

"Which makes sense," Aislin interrupted, "since you shouldn't be surfing off the coast of Finland anyway."

"You'd be amazed at how many people don't know that," Darren said.

"Very convincing," Aislin said with the first grin I'd seen on her all day. "Where do I sign?"

While Darren was digging out a pen, she kicked off her sandals and nodded very slightly to me so I would recognize that she was surrendering. Apparently, getting her to stay around wasn't going to be a problem.

SCENE 4

White

The subway on the Fourth of July was definitely the worst possible place to have a private conversation. The T was always loud and crowded, but it was stifling when everyone who had taken it to the concert tried to get home simultaneously.

I was eye-level with a guy's armpit and squashed against a woman who hadn't heard of personal space, but Maeve apparently felt like it was time to resume questioning.

She started out with a little subtlety: "So. You liked him."

"Ethan?" I shrugged casually. "He was funny, like you said."

As the train reached the next station, she latched on to the pole nearest me and moved closer. "Well, that's good," she drawled, "but I meant your cute stranger."

I had completely forgotten about him, honestly. I tried to remember a single thing about his looks, in case I ran into him again, but all I had committed to memory were his height and his major.

"The Boston University guy?"

"You didn't say he went to BU," Maeve said eagerly. "Have you seen him there?"

"No."

She lowered her chin for a death glare. "Details."

I wasn't in the mood for a mid-transit interrogation, but Maeve was unlikely to let this go until she found out why I'd voluntarily talked to an older man.

"I don't know much," I said truthfully. "He asked me about my arm in line because he's studying physical therapy. He kindly offered to carry my food to my seat and that's *it*."

"But he's at *BU*," Maeve insisted. "That at least means he's smart."

"Which is nice, but I'm not ready for college boys."

"College men," she corrected, "and why not?"

"Because I don't understand high school boys and until I do, I'm not ready to embarrass myself at a frat party?"

My more gregarious sister rolled her eyes in exasperation. "You have no sense of adventure."

"I disagree," I said with a smirk. "You didn't go streaking in Montreal."

I saw several heads turn. Maybe people were afraid that I was going to strip right there on the Green Line. Maeve's smile disappeared at the mention of her missed adventure.

"Next time, you're taking me."

"I don't think so," I said firmly. "Then we'd both have gotten in trouble."

"That's untrue," Maeve reasoned. "Instead of being stranded abroad, you would have had an uber-organized . . ." I snorted and she amended her statement. "You would have had a sister who could carry spare clothes."

"You're missing the point," Mom said, squeezing past several kids. "Aislin is grounded until she's sixty and you're not allowed to flee the country either."

"I thought we agreed on a month," I called back.

"The sentence can be changed by the parole board," she said. "Don't either of you even *think* of doing that to me again."

"We weren't," Maeve interjected. "I was just pointing out the flaws in her rebellion."

"You're not helping," I muttered to her.

"But she promises to be boring from now on," Maeve added. "That reminds me . . ."

"No," I cut her brainstorm off.

Maeve put on her best kicked-puppy expression and sighed dramatically. "I was just going to ask if you wanted me to invite Ethan to our birthday party."

"I'd like to know him a little better before I let you do that," I said after a moment of consideration.

"Of course," she said. "You'll see him soon, anyway. He'll be at Kerry's party next week."

Kerry was one of Natalie's hangers-on, but not nearly as annoying. There were two major problems.

"Kerry's not going to invite me to a party."

"Kerry said I could have a plus-one," Maeve assured me. "It's a pool party and you're coming."

"I'm not going to a pool party with this thing," I argued, pointing at my sling. "I can't swim lopsided."

I was spared further argument by the train grinding to a halt in the Park Street station. I pushed past the rest of the passengers to make my escape and headed for the Red Line.

"I can't go to a party anyway," I said once Mom was in earshot. "Grounded until July 21, right?"

"This is for the good of her love life," Maeve informed her.

Those were usually magic words, since my escaping the curse relied on that completely non-existent love life.

"We'll see" was all Mom would say.

I should have known she was stalling—it was her code for "Dad's the tie-breaker." I didn't have a chance to bring it up before the next day's transformation, so I had to wait until after dinner for their answer.

"Your request for early parole has been denied," Dad began.

I hadn't hung my hopes on leniency, so this wasn't a major blow. I nodded my head deferentially and waited for the rest of the verdict.

"Maeve proposed that we allow in-house visitors," he continued. "That will be allowed once a week until your time is up."

So I couldn't mingle at Kerry's party, but no one would be

turned away if they decided to visit. It wasn't much, but it was an improvement.

"Thank you."

"Consider it a reward for good behavior," Mom said, waving her hand like a queen. "In unrelated news, we think you should earn your GED this fall."

If I'd still been eating, I would have choked, which was probably why they'd waited this long to break the news.

"I'm a junior," I said intelligently. "Is that allowed?"

"You can take the exams early with the right paperwork," Dad explained.

"Books can help you where you aren't completely prepared," Mom added.

"Fall semester is out of the question, of course, but you could start attending night courses in January."

It was like they'd each assigned parts in a play. Nothing they'd said so far had been offensive or inaccurate, but there was one glaring problem with the idea.

"What about SATs?"

"There are many colleges around here that are SAT-optional," Mom provided.

I decided right then that I didn't need to hear the rest of the brochure they'd memorized. "Why the sudden rush?"

I could have asked what they were doing to kick Maeve out of the nest, but left that unsaid. It took them a minute to decide who should answer.

"It's not a rush," Mom said. "It's, well, concern."

"It's because I got deported."

"That's a symptom," Dad replied. "You obviously felt trapped."

"Stuck," I corrected. "It's like a rut, not a cage."

"And we can understand that," Mom said quickly. "It might help if you had something more than my history final to look forward to."

I didn't much like it when they treated parenting like therapy, but she wasn't wrong.

"And Maeve and Brendan are okay with this?"

"They haven't been consulted," Mom admitted. "Maeve will say she's in full support of you meeting college guys."

"And Brendan will refuse to take his toddler sister to frat parties," Dad concluded, grinning. "It's up to you. We'll support your decision."

I was far from being ready to decide, and I wasn't deciding either way until Maeve gave her input.

"I'll let you know."

Black

My parents were kind enough to warn me about the GED proposal before I next ran into my sister. The night after that, Aislin invaded my room with a notebook and a purpose. That was unusual—we'd shared a womb, but Aislin kept a lot of her opinions to herself. I was glad she sought me out, so I didn't stop her. It could be considered payback for when I borrowed her green shirt last week. I kicked my sneakers off and sat down so Aislin had my undivided attention.

"I've got a list," she started.

"You always do," I observed. "What are the pros and cons?"

"Con: being the youngest person in every class I take."

"Not necessarily. There could be some fifteen-year-old genius out there."

"I'm not going to take classes designed for geniuses," Aislin said. "I'll start with easy classes and build up to average."

"Go on," I encouraged.

"Second con is probably being the dumbest person in every class I take."

I shouldn't have teased her about geniuses, but this was Aislin, the girl who did extra homework voluntarily. Given the chance, she'd have been in every honors class at my school.

"Don't sell yourself short," I ordered.

"I'm being realistic," Aislin argued.

"No, you're being nervous." I paused the debate to stretch, but she didn't continue. "Give me some pros."

It wasn't like I didn't want to hear her whole list. I was just trying to balance things. She scanned down the list for about five seconds.

"I could pick my classes," she pointed out, "and I'd meet a wider variety of people."

"Such as boys," I prompted. "Even if you don't date every guy on campus, you *will* meet boys. It's a given."

"Okay, number thirteen is now 'older men.'" At my pointed stare, she obediently wrote that down. "I was kidding."

"I wasn't," I countered. "What's number twelve?"

She turned a little pinker than usual. "Getting out of the house more."

"I'd make that Number 1, but okay." I reached over and grabbed the pad. "Number 1 is 'lording it over Brendan'?"

"He doesn't think we're allowed to be teenagers," Aislin explained. "Just think how much he'll object to *this*."

I was mildly impressed by her devious priorities. Tormenting siblings was usually my assignment.

"You've got four cons and thirteen pros."

"The pros are stupid," she protested.

"I think they're not as stupid as you think and they just might make you happy."

Aislin grabbed the legal pad back and spent a few moments looking it over. I knew she was close to buckling, since the pros spoke for themselves.

"I wouldn't get to be a kid anymore," she said finally.

She was a sixteen-year-old looking for true love instead of worrying about zits. Clever or not, she was a little delusional.

"I don't think you've really been a kid in four years."

Aislin's quick smile didn't reach her eyes. "Not for lack of trying."

This would have been the perfect time to ask when she was going to appeal her sentence again. I stood up and opened the door instead.

"Dad's downstairs. You should tell him yes now."

She stood as well, but made no moves towards the door. "What makes you think I'm saying yes?"

"Numbers 1 and 13," I said. "It's what I would pick and you wouldn't be here if you didn't trust my judgment."

At that, she ditched the notepad and started taking deep, calming breaths.

"Do you want me to do it?" I offered. "I'm getting good at impersonating you."

Aislin tried to crack another smile. "No," she said firmly. "It's the only way I'd have it."

"Life is pleasant. Death is peaceful.
It's the transition that's troublesome."
Isaac Asimov

SCENE 1

Black

I hoped that Aislin would be let out for Kerry's party, but Mom didn't see the point of letting her attend a pool party where she couldn't dive in. It was unsurprising that they expected me to limit my time there if Aislin couldn't attend, but that was an unspoken family rule.

I arrived fashionably late, but early enough to enjoy two hours of daylight and pool time.

"Anything I can help with?" I offered after greeting Kerry like we'd been separated for years, not days.

"Sure." She turned me around and I immediately saw Ethan, still fully dressed and looking uptight on a lounge chair. "I have nothing for him to do. Can you entertain him?"

Darren's car was parked out front, which explained how Ethan arrived, but his ride was probably talking to Natalie and this wasn't Ethan's usual crowd.

"I'm on it," I promised.

He looked desperately happy to see me as soon as he saw me, which made me irritated at Darren for abandoning him.

"Ethan," I said. "How's Natalie?"

"With Darren," he confirmed my suspicions. "I think it's getting serious."

When Natalie liked someone, she'd make it serious or die trying. There was a chance that we wouldn't see her before Christmas.

"My condolences," I said with a straight face.

"I'm sorry for your loss," he replied just as seriously. "You don't have to entertain me."

I didn't see this as a chore at all, no matter what he thought. "I don't see why not. I like hanging out with friends."

He nodded a little distractedly, glancing around us. "Is your sister coming?"

I resisted the urge to dance when he showed an interest in her whereabouts. "She's being held captive."

Ethan raised an eyebrow to encourage me to elaborate. "Why?"

"Grounded," I groused.

"For how long?"

"A month," I supplied.

He grimaced sympathetically at such a harsh sentence. "That's rough. Arson or robbery?"

"It wasn't that bad," I reassured him. "She rebelled impressively recently and a month is a light sentence."

"I'll have to get her to tell me the story sometime."

Ethan had always seemed nice, but right now, I loved that he was having a very Aislin-centric conversation after only having met her once. Most people would have begged *me* for details.

"It's hard to believe," I commented. "I'm usually the one grounded."

"So she's not as much of an adventurer as you?"

I considered how to keep him interested without spilling any secrets. "She's very outdoorsy, but she doesn't like taking risks."

"So, she'll climb Katahden, but she won't go bungee jumping?"

Actually, Aislin would probably like bungee jumping. It would rival flying, and doing a swan dive might thrill her.

"Pretty much."

"What about you?" He shrugged a shoulder in my direction. "You're more of a risk-taker?"

"I like adrenaline and pulling off the impossible."

"Which is why you're hanging out within spitting distance of the pool," he guessed.

"I had other priorities," I said with a hint of indignation. "This isn't a charity conversation."

His smile was a little self-deprecating, but he didn't look irritated or insulted. "I know."

"I can last a whole twenty minutes outside a pool," I informed him. "Longer if I have good company."

"And you've been here five minutes already. Do you really think you should push your luck?"

I waved a hand to dismiss his concern. "I've got plenty of time before I dehydrate, and then I'll cannonball."

"I might join you," he suggested.

"You should." I nudged him with my shoulder and his smile reappeared. "So, who else is coming to this thing?"

He could give me a rundown of the guest list, but he stuck to the ones he'd enjoy talking to: "Sosi's bringing Josh. Kerry invited a bunch of sophomores and John said he'd come if Nick does, but Nick can't come until after he gets off of work . . ."

Thanks to his weird social circle, Ethan wasn't always in on the excitement but paid attention to what was going on in everyone's life. Aislin had the same habit, mostly because she lived vicariously through me.

". . . and, of course, you and I."

I hadn't really been paying attention, but since I'd helped write the guest list, I was just making conversation.

"Well, I'm glad you came."

"I'll reserve judgment until I've had food," he admitted.

"I'll try and keep that in mind," I said with a wink. "I just wish Aislin were here for the fun."

He sighed and glanced in the direction of the house, maybe wishing the same thing. "Do you do a lot of things together?"

"Everything except school and sports," I said as usual. "She's not a wannabe dolphin like me."

"And you're not . . ." he prompted.

I had to think about that for a moment, because 'swan' wasn't an acceptable way to end that sentence.

"Independent," I stated. "Unlike me, she's capable of having solo adventures."

"I can see that," he said, nodding. "If you became a hermit, you'd still invite Natalie."

"I'm not that bad," I protested, even if a laugh was bubbling up in my throat, "but Aislin could see the benefits of solitary confinement."

"I didn't say it was bad." He leaned forward to rest his elbows on his knees and was comfortably quiet for a while. "I have a ten-year-old brother, but I can't tell yet if we're alike."

"You'd be surprised," I pointed out. "Every time we seem like opposites, Aislin does something patently Maeve."

"Like what?"

I turned my grin into a teasing smirk. "Getting grounded."

"Good point."

"If you can get her to tell the story, you'll have my admiration," I joked.

Ethan's smirk was just as teasing. "Deal."

White

In theory, I was still grounded. Mom wouldn't let me go out with Maeve, but as soon as I was somewhat presentable, she ordered me into the car.

"Did I forget something?" I asked immediately.

"No. I made the appointment and you're going."

I still stood my ground on principle, since teenagers were supposed to defy bossy authority figures. "Going where?"

"Out," Mom said simply.

"Then I can drive myself as soon as I have an address."

"What part of being grounded did you forget?" she challenged.

I shrugged. "You're the one who made plans for me."

She grabbed her keys and opened the door before stepping aside and giving me a pointed look. I tried to look disgruntled up to the moment that Mom tossed me the keys.

"We're going to Belmont."

I drove in my usual nervous way, avoiding the freeway like the plague so I wouldn't have to merge or deal with exits. Once I'd parallel-parked, I got out and waited for Mom to give me further instructions. The address belonged to an office building with no logos.

"You're expected on the second floor." I waited for further explanation, but she waved her hand in a shooing motion like I was a nervous kindergartener. "I'll be back for you in an hour."

The second floor was a perfectly ordinary office space that reminded me of my dentist's waiting room. I hadn't expected Mom to take me anywhere exciting, but I'd have appreciated some more clues.

I sat on a relatively comfortable couch and checked my phone for messages. Maeve had tried to convince me to sneak out two hours ago, but by now, she'd have moved on to showing off in the pool.

Whoever I was here to see kept me waiting for a few minutes, which wasn't surprising. When the side door opened, though, no one in a lab coat or scrubs came out. It was a middle-aged guy in slacks and a sweater. He walked straight over and stuck out a hand.

"Aislin Byrne?"

I shook quickly. "Guilty as charged."

For some reason, that made him grin. "So I've heard. I'm Dr. Andrew Reed."

"A pleasure to meet you."

"Come in."

He led me into another normal-looking office with more furniture and framed diplomas on the walls. I glanced at one and his psychology degree from Tufts explained why I was here. Mom had paroled me for court-mandated counseling and I immediately regretted my opening line.

"Have a seat," Dr. Reed offered. "Is this your first time in counseling?"

"No." I cleared my throat unnecessarily and stalled for time by picking out a squashy chair to inhabit. "I saw someone when I was about thirteen, and my parents thought that I could use someone to talk to who could help me with . . . stuff."

"How effective do you feel that was?"

"Not very." The problem had been that all of the ". . . stuff" couldn't be shared with strangers. "After a few months, we decided that it wasn't doing much to help me."

"Did you feel it was counterproductive?"

Honesty was going to be an issue here as well. "I didn't feel like it was needed in the first place."

"I see," he murmured. "And you're how old now?"

He probably had all of these answers, but was trying to draw me out.

"Sixteen."

He picked up a pen, but didn't uncap it or anything. "I understand that your lawyer recommended this," he commented, "but I wanted us to lay down some ground rules. All right?"

"All right," I agreed evenly. "What are your ground rules?"

"I'd like us to be honest with each other," he stated. "Someone will be taking attendance, but I promise I won't say what we discuss."

"Someone meaning a court officer," I guessed.

"Your parents too," Dr. Reed clarified.

"But there are exceptions," I responded. "If I'm a danger to myself or others, you can break that rule."

His smile thinned a little. "And that is an exception that I take very seriously," he said in practiced, reassuring tone. "I want you to remember that."

I was mostly going to avoid saying anything that would get me institutionalized. Confidentiality agreements worried me less.

"I'll try."

"I expect you to keep our appointments and show me the same respect that I afford you." He paused to allow me time to disagree, but I didn't. "Do you have anything to add?"

"I want you to take me seriously," I said after a long pause. "I don't want you thinking this is all in my head."

"In ten years of practice, I haven't once thought it was all in someone's head," he chuckled. "I don't think you're the exception."

It would be disrespectful to ask how many mythological creatures he'd treated, and he'd reevaluate that last statement. "You might be surprised."

At the end of the hour, I found Mom reading a book in the passenger seat of the car. I decided to put her out of her misery and answer obvious questions without prompting.

"Fine. It didn't come up. He's nice. Next week at the same time. Too early to tell."

She put a bookmark in her novel with a wry smile. "I *think* I can guess the questions that go with those."

"How was it? Does he know about the curse? Do I like him?

When will I see him next? Does he know what's wrong with me?"

"I wasn't going to ask that," she objected. "Other than teenage rebellion and your habit of tracking in mud, there's nothing *wrong* with you."

"I appreciate your affection," I said. "Anywhere else we need to go?"

"We're making a detour."

I stayed in the same lane until she gave me more of an explanation. "How much of a detour?"

"I've got your clothes in the back," she said. "Do you know Kerry's address or should we call Maeve?"

I didn't want to hang out with Kerry, but it would be worth it to see Maeve's face when I showed up.

"I'm not grounded anymore?" I blurted out.

"I didn't say that," Mom said, holding up her hands, "but you're out for therapy of some kind."

There were a number of reasons for why I couldn't just pull over quickly to hug her. I grinned widely in her direction instead.

"You can get a ride home with your sister before curfew," she announced.

We stopped at a gas station on Memorial Drive and I ducked into the bathroom while Mom filled the gas tank. I wouldn't be swimming, obviously, but she had brought me a blue sundress and flip-flops so I could still look like I belonged at the party. Maeve would take care of the rest.

I hugged Mom before I got in the passenger-side door. "I'll have fun," I promised. "I won't get myself arrested again, but this will be worth it."

It made me feel like a six-year-old promising to play nice, but it parroted her usual request.

"Make sure you do," she said affectionately.

Kerry had left the front door open, but the only people in the house were in search of a bathroom, so I circled around to the gate to the pool area.

I wasn't surprised to recognize Maeve as one of a dozen people playing chicken in the pool. As soon as she saw me, her concentration broke and Lydia easily unseated her, but Maeve came up coughing and grinning widely.

"You made a jailbreak," she crowed.

"Nothing that adventurous," I confided as she clambered out. "Mom snuck me out for therapy."

"This counts?" she asked.

"We came straight here after I saw my shrink."

Maeve shut up after seeing my expression and never asked for details. She finished toweling off and pulled a red version of my dress over her suit.

"I'm just glad you came and . . ."

"I thought you were grounded," Ethan interrupted.

"I bribed the warden," I joked, facing him, "so here I am."

"Good going."

"Have you eaten?" Maeve asked.

"I could use some calories."

"I'll get it," Ethan volunteered. "You get drinks and I'll meet you back here?"

I flashed my most winning smile and nodded. "You want anything to drink?"

"I'm good."

Maeve gave me an approving look as soon as he was on his way. "He's been asking about you," she informed me in a low voice. "I think he likes you."

Whenever Maeve shared a confidence, she sounded like a gossiping sixth-grader. I hadn't had much experience since then, so she was entitled to that.

"Great," I said, grabbing a soda from a cooler. "No pressure."

"You're doing great," she assured me. "Now let me look at you."

After a quick look, Maeve tugged at the dress to make it hang right and adjusted the straps. She seemed tempted to go find some makeup, but apparently decided against it. Finally, she pulled the drenched rubber band out of her own hair and pulled half of my hair back before arranging the rest of it over my shoulders.

"Much better," she announced. "I'm going to go find Nick."

Ethan showed up a couple of minutes later with the promised food and I felt immediately better. "Where do you want to sit?"

"Wherever you're parked."

His answering grin was slightly sheepish. "I've tried to stay out of people's way. That's currently over there."

He was pointing at a pair of chairs away from most of the action. It was far from the pool and I couldn't see anyone obnoxious nearby.

"Looks perfect."

I followed him over and did my best to look graceful with soda between my knees and a plate perched on my right leg so one arm was free for food.

"How long until you're sling-free?" Ethan asked.

"According to my physical therapist, a couple more weeks," I said.

I'd seen her twice and she'd been unhappy with how little rest my shoulder was getting, but I couldn't help that. She had forecast two weeks *if* I didn't do more damage to it.

"That has to be annoying."

I shrugged. "It could be worse. I don't have to do capture the flag at work."

He pointed at the plate. "I avoided anything that I'd have to dissect for you."

"Thanks for the preservation of dignity," I said solemnly. "How are you?"

"Not bad." He relaxed into the other chair and folded his hands. "I'm working at Dad's office and have no urge to follow in his footsteps."

"Filing?" I guessed.

"That's too low-tech," he countered. "I'm in charge of making sure all the computers are up-to-date."

"So, if they need something installed, you have to press the right keys?"

"Exactly." He pulled a face. "It pays pretty well and looks good on a resume, but it's boring me to death. What about you?"

I had checked out every GED prep guide at the library for daytime reading, but I stayed true to the cover story and grimaced in imaginary misery.

"Just once, I'd like a day off from keeping track of someone's inhaler or distributing craft supplies."

"I can imagine." I caught the glint of an idea in his eye about two seconds before he put it into words. "What about the 23rd?"

It was my first weekend after parole, but otherwise insignificant. "What about it?"

"What if you and I invite Maeve and a date for dinner under the stars somewhere?"

It was the first time in years that someone outside my family hadn't included me as an afterthought to a plan and I was a little bit touched. "Like a picnic?"

"Or outside dining," he amended. "Lots of places do it these days."

I did the best thing possible; I spoke without thinking about it. "I'd love to."

He'd been smart to include Maeve in the offer. No part of his invitation turned my stomach, which made this a rarity.

"Great!" He looked genuinely enthusiastic and I was able to feel the same. Maeve would be bouncing off walls when she heard. "When should we check Maeve's schedule?"

Maeve was heading our way to chaperone. "Now," I decided immediately.

Maeve took one look at my untouched food and folded her arms sternly. "What's up?"

"Don't look at me," I replied. "We've been too busy planning a double date to eat."

"A double date with you," Ethan clarified helpfully.

Her arms dropped to her sides and she bared her teeth in a slightly manic way. "I'm in," she said. "What's your idea?"

At that moment, I could have suggested algebra and she would have agreed. Ethan saved me the trouble.

"Somewhere Italian with patio dining?"

"I'm up for that," I said. "You?"

Her grin became wider. "I'm definitely in."

SCENE 2

Black

Nick was all for us going out for Italian. We'd never exactly been a *me and him*, but he'd been my go-to guy for dates since April and he usually seemed pretty comfortable with it. He'd even taken me to prom, no strings attached, and I had goofy pictures to prove it. I was the one asking the favor this time, so he was even more enthusiastic until he was told the arrangement.

"No way," he said.

"You stuttered," I observed. "Your 'I'm in' came out as 'no way.' "

"No way," Nick affirmed. "I don't double with anyone, much less nerdboy and your sister."

I folded my arms across my chest, ready to go to battle in a heartbeat. "Ethan's a nice guy . . ."

"Which is why he can't get a girlfriend," he insisted. "I'm not making small talk with him. I don't hang out with 'nice guys.' "

"Yeah," I said, "I can tell."

"Maeve . . ."

"And they're starting to rub off on you," I added.

He glowered and folded his own arms, staring down at me. "I don't want to chaperone."

"That's not what I'm asking," I protested. "Some people have awkward first date habits. Two of those people are my *friend* and my favorite sister. If I can make things a little less awkward, I will. I'd rather be there with you."

For a second, I thought I'd won. Then he gripped my upper arms and looked me in the eye. "Maeve," Nick said patiently, "do you know the meaning of the word 'codependent?' "

"I'm not codependent," I argued, whacking his shoulder for emphasis. "I'm a good sister and you're an unsympathetic friend."

"Boyfriend," he corrected.

"Not last time I checked."

We went back to the standoff, both of us trying to look impressive and unyielding. He didn't give in first, but at least his next comment wasn't something pigheaded.

"If I'm doing you this favor, the least you can do is make it official."

That was a rude thing to say, even by Nick's usually sarcastic standards. It was also the least romantic proposition that I had ever heard, even including some of the crap I heard on the subways.

"You've never wanted to . . ."

"I disagree," Nick argued. "You forget that I wanted to during finals last year."

" 'Kiss me now, for tomorrow we die' doesn't count," I reminded him, "and it was two days before you started going out with Tania Hovsepian."

"And that wasn't the best idea," he admitted. "I admit it."

"Yeah, I remember you admitting it a lot last summer," I said.

"And you've been very polite not to bring it up since then."

At his semi-repentant look, my mind circled around to how hard it always was to stay mad at him. He rarely played games, so I always knew where I stood with him. Aislin said it was a redeeming quality and that was as close as she came to approving.

"I'm not always this smart," Nick commented, "but I know when you're right and I'm wrong."

"So you'll come?"

"You'll be my girlfriend?" he rejoined.

There were reasons why we'd never been high school sweethearts. We avoided making it official because the ability to bicker was no basis for a romance, but we'd gradually learned to be affectionate instead of obstinate.

"I don't like all this hesitation," Nick pointed out. He moved closer and tapped his fingers against mine teasingly. "Do I need to give you a deadline?"

My next move was to stand on tiptoe and loop my arms around his neck. I wasn't going to seal the deal with a kiss—that was something reserved for first official dates—but I hugged the life out of him.

"We should have thought of this a while ago," I said with a grin.

He laughed and wrapped his arms around my waist, holding on for a lot longer than usual. When he finally let go, he looked like he'd grown two inches in confidence. If I had known that I could have this effect, I would have agreed to this sooner.

"I'm not going to argue that."

"Before you think about what a good bargain you got, remember this." I was on a bit of a high myself, but I had an agenda that new romance couldn't deter. "You will behave yourself, whether you're around my sister or not. My loyalty to her comes before you, my friends, or my parents."

Nick shrugged nonchalantly, but the smirk lost its luster. At least he didn't look resigned to a horrible fate. "Now that I want your family to like me," he said, "I'll treat them like it."

I could have stalled. Aislin couldn't move in my social circles, so I could have withheld my relationship status until the end of the date. Aislin deserved to know the parameters of the evening, so I decided to give her warning. The next time she came home for dinner, I was casually hanging out in the kitchen.

"Good day?" I asked.

"You'd have liked it," Aislin responded before grabbing her club sandwich. "I spent most of it swimming."

"Me too," I said. "Kerry invited some of us over for pool time and they say hi."

Technically, Sosi had asked about her and Kerry had blithely suggested that Aislin leave her cave again, but Aislin didn't need to hear specifics.

She nodded, her mouth still full, and gestured for me to continue. I waited until she'd swallowed before turning to Dad. When not on duty, he tried to sit with her for breakfast or dinner so she could keep him involved in her life. Aislin wasn't likely to dish about her social life, so I intervened.

"So, guess who has a hot date?"

"There will be no hot dates," Dad said in his best officer voice. "Who has a respectable date in a well-lit area with an honors student who has been vetted by both parents?"

Ethan fit that description, but Dad made it sound boring. I couldn't help but feel a little proud of myself for recommending a guy who wouldn't set off any warning bells.

Aislin had stopped chewing as soon as I hit the words "hot date." When she noticed me pausing for effect, she swallowed very quickly and gave me the glare that she reserved for instances of public humiliation.

"Not me," I announced.

Dad folded down a corner of the *Globe* to pay closer attention. He wisely refrained from looking shocked.

"Really," he said to Aislin. "Where did you meet him?"

"Maeve introduced us," my sister explained. "We *are* talking about Ethan, right?"

"You have *another* hot date?" I asked pointedly.

"Who's Ethan and how does Maeve know a person of whom I would approve?" Dad interrupted.

He had been discreet in his surprise with Aislin, but I wasn't shocked when he looked at me as if I'd made the whole thing up.

"Chemistry," I said.

"He's funny," Aislin added.

"And he's smart," I concluded. "I don't know his religion or credit score, but he's really interested in Aislin."

"That's a good place to start," Dad conceded.

"They hit it off at the Esplanade and he asked her out at Kerry's party."

Aislin glowered, but Dad had apparently been told about the escape, because he looked surprisingly okay with that comment. "I'm glad that your mother's clemency went to such good use," he deadpanned. "Does she know about this?"

I had chosen a night when Dad was the only parent on duty because Mom would have waxed sentimental. She would hug Aislin and before long, Brendan would know the details. Dad could at least run interference.

"I'd rather not parade this around," I said tactfully.

"I second that motion," Aislin interjected. "Does she have to know at all?"

"*Yes,*" Dad and I said in unison. Aislin sighed heavily and went back to her sandwich.

"I think it's better to give her time to get used to it," I explained. "I'll put her under a gag order."

"I'll confiscate her phone first," Dad offered. "When is this respectable date? I'll clear my schedule."

That was a worse idea than leaving Mom in the dark. "We were going to meet up in the city," I said quickly.

"*We*?" Dad looked sharply at me. "Who is your date and when will I be meeting him?"

I waved a hand dismissively. "You've already met Nick."

Dad grunted at that—he thought of Nick as an under-achiever with bad manners whose best quality was that he was hands-off.

"My boyfriend," I clarified.

Their reactions couldn't have been more in sync if they'd rehearsed first. Jaws dropped and they gave me sharp looks. Dad covered his surprise better and focused on refolding the paper. Aislin got the first word in, though.

"Since *when?*"

"Yesterday." At a look from Dad, I rolled my eyes and obediently added, "8 p.m. at Harvard Square in front of witnesses."

"That was very public of him," Dad said.

"I thought that's how you liked it."

"And I know it's not your style," he countered. "Did you approve of this public display?"

"I said yes, didn't I?"

He grunted and went back to his newspaper, apparently done with his part in the discussion.

"Wow." Aislin set down the remaining half of her sandwich so she could lean in for details. "That's been a long time coming."

"It was overdue." The distinction was important and she knew it. "But the point is, he's in."

Something about that last statement made her face cloud over. Dad didn't notice, since he had started checking the baseball scores, but I didn't miss Aislin's look of suspicion. When she stood up to put her dish in the sink, I followed.

"Did you have to *bribe him?*"

"No!" I protested. "It's not like that."

"You've been uninvolved for most of a year and now he's official," Aislin said shrewdly. "The timing is kind of convenient."

"It's not because of that." I considered for a second.

She blocked the door to the kitchen, cutting off my only escape route. "I don't want you doing this just because you need to find me a man."

I rolled my eyes at her this time. "Give me a little credit."

"Did you . . ."

"I said yes because I *wanted* to." I turned so she could see my whole expression. "We're going to have fun."

"That's what you always say," she accused.

"And when was the last time you had a completely miserable time?" I challenged.

"Your new boyfriend's Valentine's Day party."

I refrained from pointing out that she had insisted on going stag. If she had brought a date, she wouldn't have been hounded by three guys.

"That was then and this is your idea," I said confidently. "You liked Ethan enough to say yes, so you've got an edge."

"You've got a point." Her posture relaxed a little and she looked more like her usual affable self. "I'll prove my gratitude with a show of good faith."

"You'll let me pick out your clothes?" I said hopefully.

"No." Grateful or not, she wasn't going to risk anything that showed some kneecap. "I'll let you do my makeup."

It wasn't as satisfactory as having complete style control, but I appreciated the effort.

"You won't regret it."

SCENE 3

White

In a more generous mood, I would have left all the details up to Maeve, but I still wanted to look like I had a personality of my own, so I hid my sundresses and skinny jeans in the back of the closet and picked out something that could be accessorized to her heart's content.

"So?" I asked as soon as she invaded to start on hair and makeup.

"*Khakis?*"

"I'm not wearing a skirt," I declared. "This is a compromise."

"Khakis are so *preppy.*"

"And I'm going out with your lab partner," I reminded her. "What could be more appropriate?"

"I like this." She straightened the seams of my rose-colored v-neck. "Where's Grandma's locket?"

"Ready to wear," I said. "Anything else?"

Maeve tapped her finger against her lips. "Let me do your hair and we'll decide on earrings after that."

In the end, she ended up doing a Nordic braid and added heart-shaped earrings to my jewelry. She didn't overdo the eyeliner or suggest fake eyelashes, so the result was a good balance between fashionista and conservative. Dad didn't even object to it when he wished me luck.

When we got to the restaurant on Boylston, I was in for two

pleasant surprises. Ethan was already there and he actually seemed to be having a civil conversation with Nick.

"Hey," Ethan greeted once we were at arm's length. "You look great."

"Thanks. You too."

Maeve stretched up to hug Nick and I was relieved that she left the PDA at that. I didn't want to have her set the bar high on the first date I'd had in a while.

"No seats?" she asked, glancing towards the doorway.

"They're saving us a seat outside," Nick corrected. "Let's enjoy the heat before the weather gods decree a downpour."

"Good call," I complimented him. "Hope we didn't keep you waiting long."

"It's all good," Ethan said. "We got here about five minutes ago and haven't gotten bored yet."

"Yeah, well, complaining about teachers," Nick reminisced. "We could do that for years."

I guessed that Ethan would have struggled with that, but he was sincerely trying to find common ground. I could stay quiet while they commiserated over finals and bonus questions on Hawthorne, but I must have looked slightly overwhelmed because Ethan interrupted.

"Let's get the table," he suggested. "I've heard it's possible to talk and sit at the same time."

I was silently grateful that he was already on my side. Some conversations always went over my head because I hadn't gone to a normal class in almost five years.

Ethan pulled my chair out when we got to the table, which earned him a smile. The server took care of our drinks before coming back for orders. With my alfredo-based food ordered, I turned to Ethan.

"So, how was the boring day at the office?"

"Not too boring," he replied. "When I saved the day, the computer-crasher left me enough of a tip for dessert."

"Good to know." I glanced at the menu. "Any chance of making you split?"

"Not on my watch. I don't believe in sharing dessert with anyone."

"Another good thing to know," Maeve chuckled. "Is that a deal-breaker for you, Aislin?"

I wasn't going to judge something that trivial, so I shot Maeve a warning look to ask that she keep her sarcasm on a leash. She beamed in return as if I'd pledged my eternal thanks to her.

"I can live with it."

"What about you?" Ethan asked. "Still surviving summer camp?"

"I don't know why colleges will be impressed by this nonsense," I said, "but it'll all be over pretty soon."

"We should celebrate when it is," Maeve suggested.

There would, of course, be nothing to celebrate. I'd have to pick a day in August and call it my independence day. It'd probably coincide with the end of physical therapy.

"I'll check my schedule," I said vaguely.

"What, you're not counting down?" Nick teased.

"That would just depress me."

Ethan nodded and turned to Maeve. "She has a point. How did you avoid the dreaded summer job?"

"I don't need more extra-curricular activities," she responded. "I do soccer, swimming, lacrosse, freshman mentoring . . ."

"And keep up your grades," I added.

"Only because I have to compete with you," she rejoined.

I didn't like it when she downplayed her own intelligence. It was almost impossible to tell if she was doing it to look humble or dumber than her date.

"Or because you're smart."

She shrugged, but didn't argue. "Anyway, I agreed to SAT prep and a midnight curfew if I had this summer off."

"I haven't suffered enough," I explained. "Hence the camp job."

"Next year, you should try something less masochistic, like whippings," Nick said. "I just applied anywhere but offices."

"And you ended up where?" I prompted.

"Movie theater," he admitted. "I've pumped an ocean of fake butter, but it could be worse."

I lifted my glass of water in a toast. "Here's to 'it could be worse.' "

"My philosophy in life," Maeve agreed.

"So how do people tell you apart at first?" Nick interjected.

I was surprised as much by the jump in topic as his interest. "They usually think of me as Not-Maeve."

"Well, yeah," Nick said. "I can tell you're Aislin because I'm used to her, but it's gotta be harder than that."

I glanced at Maeve so she would take her cue to start talking, but she was watching me attentively. It was my turn to be the sociable one, and that was daunting.

"Maeve stands out in a crowd and I try hard to blend in," I began.

"But it can't be that simple," Ethan argued. "Maeve probably tries to lay low at times and you occasionally like the spotlight."

"Mostly when I'm in trouble," Maeve admitted.

"Say you're both strangers to me," Nick suggested. "Give me the rundown."

The ensuing conversation carried us through ordering and a shared appetizer. We covered everything from why I wasn't fond of swimming to our favorite subjects in school. We finally answered the original question when talking about the scar Maeve had sported since a diving accident in ninth grade. Nick then impressed me by knowing all of the details of the incident. I even felt a shallow stab of envy that Nick had paid attention so closely for so long. Ethan had the potential, but we'd only talked a few times, so he didn't know that my distinguishing blemish was a scar on my shoulder.

The less mundane part of the story came along when Maeve summarized by saying, "The main difference is how we deal with crowds."

"Is that why you homeschooled?" Ethan asked.

This was what Nick had been waiting for, but I shook my head. "I like working at my own pace and my parents didn't object."

"But don't you get . . ." Nick stalled to find the least offensive way to finish. "Bored?"

"Frequently," I admitted, "but I can do homework in bed, text in class, and eat non-revolting school lunches."

"Pretty good selling points," Nick conceded, "but Maeve never wanted the same?"

"Please," Maeve snorted. "Passing notes in class is an art form and I'm not leaving the playing fields."

"That wasn't a problem for me," I countered. "Soccer was fun, not my religion."

"I want *some* kind of sports scholarship," Maeve pointed out, "so being a team-playing superstar would be difficult at home."

"Then what's the one thing we'd be most shocked to hear?" Ethan interjected.

We considered that for a while. There was the obvious answer and there were about a dozen minor answers that we could honestly give instead.

"Aislin got deported once," Maeve said.

"You *what?*" Nick looked both impressed and skeptical.

"Intentionally?" Ethan added.

"What do you think?" I said, trying to look as though it were a funny story instead of a mortifying moment. Maeve was going to pay later for bringing it up. "I was visiting some friends in Montreal and lost my backpack on the way back."

"So we get this call from Aislin saying she needs a ride and proof of citizenship."

Ethan's face lit up with comprehension. "That's why you were . . ."

"Grounded for a month," I confirmed. "I told you it's a long story."

"That's pretty harsh for being scatterbrained." Nick said.

"Spontaneous road trips aren't cheap," I responded. "Since my parents drove 300 miles for my carelessness, I didn't appeal the sentence."

"Is that the worst sentence either of you has had?" Ethan asked.

"I got the same for Laurie's 16th," Maeve volunteered. "But that's just because Dad's friend issued the citations."

"If you'd told the truth, he wouldn't have been so mad," I pointed out.

"The longest sentence I've ever gotten was two weeks for getting into a fight last year," Nick admitted.

"Over what?" I asked.

"Sports," he and Maeve said in unison.

"A referee made a call in my favor at state championships last year, I got cocky about it, and my opponent threw a punch," Nick elaborated. "I didn't exactly sit there and take it."

"Did you at least win?" Ethan asked.

"What, the game or the fight?"

"Either."

"Both," he said proudly. "Have you even *gotten* grounded?"

Ethan's expression darkened slightly at the slight taunt and I guessed that Maeve would have something to say about it later. "Last time was for breaking curfew," Ethan dismissed.

"Long night at the library?"

"Coming back from Kerry's party," Ethan said. "I thought it couldn't hurt to run ten minutes late and it got me sentenced to three days."

"You were giving Jill a ride home, right?" Maeve recalled. "You couldn't have played the Good Samaritan card?"

"If I hadn't been at a party, sure," he said, "but they figured I could have left any time I wanted and I chose to break the rules."

"How did we get on this subject anyway?" Maeve interjected.

"The thing that would shock us most to hear," I supplied. "I think Maeve's would have to be something about her and . . ."

"Basements?" Maeve finished. "He already knows about that."

"Fear of the bogeyman?" Ethan suggested.

"I'm scared of what's hiding in the shadows instead of what monster's under my bed," Maeve corrected.

"I don't drive past graveyards at night," Nick said. "I had an older brother who liked me scared."

"You have a brother?"

"I have three," he corrected. "Two older, one younger. They had a lot of fun when I was an impressionable seven-year-old."

"We haven't heard Ethan's weird phobia," Maeve prodded.

"I don't really have one." He shrugged. "I don't have a fear of animals, clowns, heights . . ."

"Spiders?" Nick suggested. "Chickens? British people?"

"That's not a real one," Maeve snorted.

"Anglophobia," he insisted. "I bet it's more common than you think."

"If the world-traveling spinach-hater can admit to a weakness, you can," Nick goaded.

"Fine," Ethan said. "Agateophobia. Fear of insanity."

Maeve's blue eyes narrowed in suspicion. "I'm looking that up when I get home," she decided. "Do you think it's real?"

"I trust Ethan's obscure vocabulary skills," I said. "People think I'm holed up in my room, eating live grasshoppers, so I share that."

"At least you can laugh at it," Nick commended me.

"Not every day," I countered. "Some are tougher than others."

"You'd be surprised by the things people thought about her choice to homeschool," Maeve addressed both boys.

"Did anyone think of a convent?" Ethan asked.

"Not until today," I said with a grin.

"I think convents only take Catholics," Maeve added.

Ethan shrugged. "Technicalities."

"I think the one I liked best was that I was going to be a reality TV star."

"Which anyone who actually knows her would say is an idiotic thing to say," Maeve pointed out. "The producers would always be hounding her to do *something* scandalous.'

"It's better than the alternative," I insisted. "Given the choice, I don't think I'll ever be the reckless one in the family."

"Of course not," Maeve said. "Then I'd have to find a new hobby."

Black

Things could have been much worse. Nick took his teasing down a notch and Aislin eventually relaxed around the boys. When Ethan offered to drive Aislin home, she didn't look alarmed, which implied that we considered this a success.

The guys headed up front to pay the bills while we stopped at the restroom. It was my idea, but Aislin washed her hands while I foraged for makeup.

"Okay," I said like a coach prepping a nervous boxer. "What's your plan?"

"Walk to the car, let him hold the door, drive home, and say good night."

"No kiss?"

She gave me the withering look reserved for my efforts to make her follow my script. "I doubt it's his style."

I finally came up with a lipstick that would complement her shirt, even if it wasn't my preferred shade.

"If he tries something, will you let him?"

The withering look didn't go anywhere. "*No.*"

"But you had a good time," I said. "And you want him to ask you out again."

"I don't think he'll have a problem with taking things slow," Aislin decided.

"Good start."

"Thanks for your approval," Aislin said dryly. "Can I go now?"

I handed over the lipstick without comment and she obediently slicked it on. "Better?"

"Perfect."

Ethan had just gotten his change when we rejoined the party. "Ready?" he asked.

"Sure," Aislin said with a slightly nervous smile. "Nick, Maeve, thanks for the laughs."

"Drive safe," I exhorted Ethan. "I'll see you soon."

Nick idled at the sidewalk as Aislin and Ethan disappeared. "Why are we waiting?" I asked.

"Because we parked about a block away from them and they deserve some space."

I rolled my eyes. "I wouldn't do that. Aislin will tell me every detail later."

"Also . . ."

Before finishing the sentence, Nick stepped in and pressed his lips against mine. I drew back slightly; I hadn't seen that coming yet, and his breath smelled like Alfredo sauce, but when he kissed me again, I let him. This time, I forgot about the Alfredo sauce.

For our first kiss, it wasn't the stuff of bodice-rippers. My heartbeat definitely sped up and I forgot to think for a while, but it wasn't earth-shaking. It felt as thrilling as moving from go-to date status to official couple status.

"Hmm," Nick said once we pulled apart. "That was safe."

I stifled my laugh behind a hand. "What, you think we should try cliff-hanging kissing?"

"How many cliffs do you know within driving distance?"

"It was just a suggestion," I said. "What do you mean safe?"

"I think it means that it was pretty good for a practice."

"Thanks," I deadpanned.

"But we're going to have to practice a lot," he said.

He demonstrated, his hands cupping my face and our bodies almost flush. This time, there might have been a tremor in the ground. I participated more enthusiastically and it definitely helped.

"I think I can live with that."

Aislin's light was on when I got home, which meant Ethan had been a perfectly honorable guy or it had been a very short kiss. I still had about twenty minutes before curfew, so I didn't expect questions.

Mom was, in fact, the only one downstairs, sitting at the kitchen table with a thick stack of papers and a glass of water. As soon as I entered, she set down the top sheet of paper and looked up expectantly.

"Did you have a good time?"

"I had a great time," I assured her. "What was Aislin's opinion?"

"She seemed happy," Mom said guardedly. "You took separate cars?"

"I didn't interfere in how her date ended. He *did* walk her to the door, right?"

She nodded approvingly. "I didn't spy from the living room, though."

"We appreciate your discretion."

"Nick behaved himself?"

That question caught me off guard. "What did Ash say?"

"Nothing," Mom said, "but this was a change for him. How'd he handle it?"

My mind flashed back to a couple of times when Nick had tried to steer the conversation to awkward topics for half of the participants. "I think everyone enjoyed it," I said. "Aislin's on her own next time."

"Good." She finished her glass of water and stood up. "Thanks for the debriefing."

"Thanks for not spying," I said. "Good night."

SCENE 4

Black

In my experience, Mark McInerny was pretty laid-back around our family. Today, though, he looked downright disgruntled.

"I thought you were going to have your family here," he accused.

It was a perfect morning in July when I could have been doing anything from swimming to sleeping, but I was trying to look respectable in court. Justice didn't accommodate Aislin's schedule, so we had to go to the district where the crime occurred for a hearing. Mom had claimed that making everyone travel this far for a short conversation was unnecessary.

"Maeve couldn't make it," I said vaguely. "I thought her interview went well."

My interview had been a masterpiece of sisterly affection and according to me, God sounded irresponsible compared to Aislin.

"Her statement will be considered," Mark agreed, "but the judge might wonder why she didn't make the trip. I want your word that if we need to call witnesses next time, you'll talk her into it."

I wondered if there was a way to tilt the earth so sunset happened around eleven a.m.

"She wanted to be here," I said apologetically. "How long will this take?"

"Not long," he explained. "I'll be doing most of the work, but expect to answer questions."

Further discussion was cut off as the judge entered. I hadn't expected him to look like my ninth-grade English teacher and the resemblance relaxed me. He asked the lawyers to identify themselves and the crown attorney introduced herself as Sarah Walton.

"Your Honor, may I approach?" Mark asked.

"You may do so," the judge granted.

Both lawyers converged on the judge's bench, leaving me to try not to fidget in the interim. I tried to breathe deeply and look innocent.

After a few minutes, Mark returned. "Come with me."

We followed him to a small room, where my parents hung back and Mark extended a sheaf of papers.

"Is this where I find out what you guys said?"

"Yes," he confirmed. "Ms. Walton and I had to get the judge on board with the diversion program. He's agreed to this plea bargain, so now you sign up for it."

"That's fine," I said. "Go on."

He ran down the charges and the potential consequences. Then he read the proposed diversion program—sixty hours of community service, restitution to the store, and continuing my counseling until twelve weeks had elapsed. It was the boring formality that seemed to make up a lot of court. Once I'd read the agreement through, we returned to court to wrap up.

I was as meek as a lamb while the judge asked me about substance abuse and coercion and gave me a stern talking-to. I didn't talk back and even managed to keep my sarcasm under control until the judge set another court date to review the case. Five minutes later, we were out of court and Mark looked less likely to spontaneously combust.

"You did well," he commended me. "I just have one bit of advice."

"And that is?" I asked.

He clapped me heartily on what was supposedly my good shoulder. "Tell Maeve that the next time she lets you down, I'm keeping her graduation present."

It would have been satisfying to set the record straight then, but I just nodded. "I'll make sure she knows."

White

My physical therapist wasn't happy about my progress, but after three weeks instead of the predicted two, she grudgingly admitted that I could go back to using both arms.

The first thing I did was text Maeve to share the good news. The second was to call Ethan.

"Were you serious about celebrating when I was finally off work for the summer?" I asked after small talk.

"I was," Ethan confirmed. "How's the arm?"

"I'm allowed to use it again," I said with a self-satisfied grin. "What did you have in mind?"

"I've got just the place," he said. "What are you doing tomorrow?"

"Nothing so far," I said. "Same time, different place?"

"I'll pick you up," he said. "And wear something casual."

I left Maeve clueless this time, but I took Ethan's advice. Instead of dressing to impress, I wore shorts and a San Diego t-shirt. Maeve was already out when dusk hit, so I didn't have to sneak past her.

"Good to see you," Ethan commented as he opened the car door.

"You too," I said. He was dressed just as casually, which put me at ease. "Are you going to tell me where we're going?"

"A restaurant," he said. "I'll give you more instructions when we get there."

The restaurant was one I'd been to before, but Ethan's intentions were unclear until he opened my menu to a specific page.

"*Ribs*?"

"I've never seen them eaten one-handed," he said. "If they're not your thing, you can order steak and cut it yourself."

"It's fine," I laughed. "It's unexpected."

"Good," Ethan said. "Keeping you guessing is fun."

When we had both decided on something that was appropriately messy, he leaned over and confided, "I wasn't sure, since Maeve would have vetoed this."

"I like camping," I pointed out. "I can handle this."

"I thought so." He winced as though someone had punched him in the arm. "Sorry. I promised myself there would be less of that this time."

"Of what?" I inquired.

"Comparing you to your sister," he explained.

I was used to that, but hadn't expected him to feel remorse. That in itself was a nice touch.

"Then this is our blind date," I suggested. "Ask me any question you want."

"Any?"

"Within reason." He wasn't entitled to grooming habits or dating history, but he took an interest in me without Maeve's badgering, so I trusted him. "I do reserve the right to remain silent."

"Okay." He cracked his knuckles and sat back. "How do sick days work in homeschooling?"

The question caught me so off-guard that I snorted with laughter. "That's your most pressing question?"

"That's my most pressing unanswered question," he defended himself. "You're never snowed in and your classmates never wonder if you're contagious. What's the contract?"

"Well, for one thing, if Maeve gets a snow day, so do I," I replied.

"Fair enough."

"I have three unquestioned absences per term," I added. "I have to turn in homework, but I can bring my studying to a standstill."

It was Ethan's turn to laugh now. "So you take mental health days?"

"Officially," I confirmed.

"And here some people don't think homeschooling has its uses," he joked.

"For sick days, I can't be capable of sitting up," I continued. "When I got the flu, I traded a paper for chicken soup."

"What's the thing you miss most about regular school?"

"Having people to sit with at lunch," I said. "I have to wait for Maeve to come home before I can talk about my day."

"But you don't like classrooms?"

This was the first answer that I did have to fudge on. "If I felt like they'd be better for me, I would."

We were interrupted by the arrival of our drinks, and once Ethan swigged some soda, he sighed comfortably. Apparently, he was enjoying this as much as I.

"What's your weird human talent?"

"Bird calls," I deadpanned. "Who says I have one?"

"Everyone should have one," Ethan said.

"Then you tell me yours and I'll think about telling you mine," I challenged.

"Mental math," he admitted. "It's not much to brag about, but . . ."

"It's more than I have," I interrupted. "I can calculate tips and remember my multiplication tables, but the rest requires a notebook."

He looked flattered by my warm response. "Well, we all have something to contribute. What about you?"

"I said I'd think about telling you mine. I made no promises about actually doing it."

"That's fine," Ethan assured me, "but if you hold out on me, I'm going to have to make one up for you. Then I can refer to you as Aislin the Contortionist and enjoy the resulting rumors."

I waved my napkin in surrender, but felt both terror and amusement. "As long as my immortality's undisclosed."

"Your secret's safe with me," he promised.

On our own, we were a better match than I had originally thought, and when I stopped brainstorming other talents, I leaned in to share another confidence. "I want you to know something that Maeve did not tell me to say," I said solemnly.

He aped my posture perfectly. "Yes?"

"I think that we should do this again."

Ethan's grin was broader than ever now. "Maybe you'll change your mind after the food comes."

"Not likely," I said. "What do you think?"

"I think you're absolutely right," Ethan said.

Black

Just after freshman year, Natalie announced that two-thirds of the summer was vacation, but August was Transition Month, when we had to take ourselves seriously. We went on punishing morning runs and did laps instead of pool parties. We got our back-to-school haircuts on August 1 in case we had to grow them out.

Thanks to Coach Skandalis, I was used to running my brains out, which made Natalie's prep for varsity less stressful. Aislin and I had decided to keep our hair long.

Traditions, especially good ones, had to be upheld, though. We were upperclassmen and had to dress like it, so I saved all summer, let Nick pay for food, and came home happy from shopping. My closet wasn't going to get an overhaul, but I had new things to keep my look interesting.

"Did you have fun?" Mom asked without bothering to ask how much I spent.

"Lots," I called over my shoulder. "I'll show you . . ."

"Aislin's on a date."

I stopped halfway up the stairs and came back for clarification. "With whom?"

"Ethan," she said.

I dropped my bags and scuttled downstairs to get details. "She didn't tell me," I protested.

"She cleared it with me," Mom said. "It was your night off from social secretary duties."

Transition Month also meant adjusting to life without Aislin, but she should have . . .

I stopped that thought immediately. My sister was on a second date and I was complaining that it hadn't been my idea. Perspective changed everything.

"Great," I said. "I'm going out with Nick in twenty."

"I know," Mom said. "You know the usual lecture."

The rules were so familiar that I could say them backwards. "Yes, Mom," I assured her. "Is Dad on duty?"

"Not tonight," she said. "The Sox are playing the Yankees and someone needs company."

That 'someone' probably had a better TV and Dad would come home in a good mood. It'd be better if the Sox won, but atmosphere mattered more than score.

"If you misbehave, his colleagues have his work number," Mom added.

"No speeding or recreational drugs, check," I said.

"Have fun," she said as a parting blessing.

I changed out of my shopping uniform of jeans and a t-shirt and was finishing makeup when Nick arrived. He exchanged the obligatory pleasantries with Mom and held off on the PDA. I had him well-trained already.

"Happy Transition Month," he commented once we left the house.

"You remembered," I said drily.

"I remember that Natalie threatened to shave my head if you missed anything because of me," Nick snickered. "I'm thankful you cleared some space in your busy schedule."

"Shut up," I ordered. "She's still picking me up at six a.m. tomorrow, so . . ."

"I'll have you home by midnight," he finished. "Or, if you prefer, we can take a quick walk and let you get eight hours of sleep."

"Don't you dare."

He looked pleased that I picked him over beauty rest. I wasn't on Natalie's level, but for August, I was going to be more intense than usual and he wasn't prepared for that.

"So, I haven't seen you in two days," Nick commented. "How's your family?"

"Mom's fine, Dad's off-duty, and Aislin's out with Ethan."

I hadn't intended to make it sound like the highlight of my day, but I had to find happiness in small things where romance was concerned. Nick looked like that second date qualified as a minor miracle.

"Good for him," he commented. "Do they do this often?"

"As far as I know, not since we doubled," I said.

"Which means that she might take responsibility for her own social calendar," he considered. "You'll have to find a new hobby."

I elbowed him in the ribs. "Be nice."

"I was thinking of dragging you out for a full-day date," Nick suggested. "I'll wait until after your run so Natalie doesn't rupture an aneurysm . . ."

"I'd appreciate if you didn't kill my friends," I agreed.

"And we'll get one perfect day out of the way before you sell your soul to soccer."

"I like the idea," I said. "Did you have something specific in mind?"

His eyes glinted and I expected him to announce an excellent prank. "That's my secret," he said mischievously. "There won't be bears involved."

"I can get that in writing?"

"If you want to." He opened the car door, but I held on to the frame, waiting for more conditions. "Regrettably, sisters aren't invited."

In retribution for her dating independence, I wouldn't tell her I was escaping for a whole day. She wouldn't feel like following me anyway.

"It's my perfect day," I pointed out. "I'm fine with having you to myself."

SCENE 5

White

Tonight's post-swan scrub down was more thorough than usual. I always tried my best to smell human after a day in the woods, but I had another appointment with Dr. Reed and didn't want to smell anything like algae. I even made dinner the night before to save time. Instead of having a nice, sit-down dinner, I could scarf down my sandwich between dressing and departing.

Maeve's door was open when I passed by on my way to my

bedroom, but she didn't greet me. It was only when I was in dressed and headed for the stairs that she piped up.

"Going somewhere?"

I stopped and half-turned, staying out of her line of sight so I wouldn't be tempted to chat. I could see her feet at the end of the bed, which meant she was sprawled and reading.

"Therapy," I reminded her.

"Oh, is that tonight?"

I didn't buy her airiness—she knew my schedule before I did. Being clothed was also no basis for the theory that I had plans.

"Yes."

I heard her bed creak and she appeared in the doorway moments later. "What are you going to say to him?"

"I'm going to answer his questions without lying too often," I said.

"Fun." She leaned against the jamb and watched me interestedly. "You're not going to make an effort?"

"To do what, exactly?" I challenged.

"Use his services."

She made it sound like I was in Hawaii and boycotting the beaches, not fibbing to a shrink. "I'm going, aren't I?"

Maeve sighed and folded her arms impatiently. "Are we going to have to have this conversation every week?"

"You brought it up," I pointed out. "I still think it would do more harm than good to tell the whole truth."

"He's not going to think you're crazy . . ."

"One of the criteria for schizophrenia is bizarre delusions," I said. "Do you think that believing I molt every night counts?"

She cracked a smile very slowly; it was more fun for her to imagine the conversation than to convince me that I should have it. "You don't have to spill your secrets, just your guts," Maeve suggested. "You've got some well-earned and undeserved issues and I think he could help."

"Which is our parents' rationale," I said. "I've taken that into consideration."

"But you don't plan on listening to us?" she pressed.

"I said I was going to answer his questions," I said. "I'm just not taking initiative."

"Okay." She unfolded her arms and straightened up. "I'll walk you down."

I was mildly surprised that she was dropping it, but she probably thought she could lecture me on the way. "Come on, then," I invited her. "Maybe Mom will let you drive me."

"That's not a bad idea," Maeve said brightly. "Go get dinner. I'll work my magic."

Maeve appeared, jangling the keys in her right hand, as I was bussing my dishes. "I'm ready to go whenever you are."

"Great."

"And you're coming straight back?" Mom asked.

"I don't know," Maeve said. "I thought we might hop on the Mass Pike, see how long it takes you to panic."

"Not funny," I stage-whispered.

"Just remember: your father has a few friends in the highway patrol."

"We know," I said. "She'll drive responsibly."

"If you decide to stop somewhere afterwards, call to say where you are and when you'll be back," Mom instructed.

"We won't stay out too late," I sighed. "Let's go."

Maeve waited until we were in the car before she spoke again. "You're not grounded," she protested. "You don't *have* to give her an itinerary."

"She's still our mother," I said. "Given how much distance I covered the last time I went off the grid, I owe her an ETA."

"I suppose." She tapped the wheel restlessly as we waited at a light. "What are your weekend plans?"

"The usual," I said. "Ethan hasn't called again . . ."

"I can fix that."

"I wasn't asking you to," I said quickly. "I don't want him to feel obligated to keep me socially active."

The car lurched forward as Maeve accelerated through the intersection, but she wasn't paying attention—she had given me a dirty look the moment I mentioned "obligated."

"I wasn't planning on pressuring him," she sniffed. "It was his idea to ask you out in the first place . . ."

"And your idea to invite him to the Pops concert," I countered.

"Don't be ungrateful," Maeve chastised. "I think Ethan will be fine on his own."

"Did you want us to have plans, then?" I suggested.

"Maybe." Her impatient expression softened slightly. "I've had enough friend time that I could use a sisters' night in."

"Me, too."

"Then I say we plan to ignore everyone else on Friday," Maeve proposed. "I can still see Nick on Saturday and Ethan can make a move if he wants any other night."

"Welcome back," Dr. Reed greeted me in the main office. "You look as though you enjoyed your week."

"I did," I said. "You?"

"It had its moments," he said. "Come in."

I took the same seat as last time, but tried to look more comfortable. I wasn't apprehensive about being here this time, but I didn't know what to expect.

"What made this week good?" he asked once he'd sat.

"A lack of bad things, mostly," I said honestly.

Dr. Reed seemed to stifle a chuckle. "That's a more common answer than you might think."

"Some people in this world are happy by comparison," I replied.

"Was there nothing good that stood on its own?"

"Not really." I shrugged. "I wasn't grounded and went out on a date. I was also happy because I didn't get injured, fight with anyone in my family, or get any bad news."

He had written something down earlier, but I couldn't tell if it was an observation or today's date. I forced myself to look away from his notepad and gave him a winning smile.

"What would you like to talk about?" he asked.

"I don't know," I said. "You had the questions last time."

They'd ranged from whether I was losing interest in activities that usually brought me joy to whether I had feelings of imminent doom. He had tried several times to draw out a confession, but I had no intention of telling him my real reasons for going on my little adventure.

"Last time, I was trying to determine if you were showing signs of anxiety disorders or depression," Dr. Reed responded. "Since you answered 'no' to most of my questions, I thought we would try a different approach tonight."

"So what do you want to know?"

"What is your family like?"

"Three kids, two parents, six cousins, and no pets," I answered succinctly.

"And you're the youngest."

"By a few minutes."

He made a note at that. "You're close to your twin," he guessed. "What is your . . ."

"Brother," I supplied.

". . . brother like?" he finished.

I paused briefly to form a one-sentence opinion of Brendan. It was difficult, but easier than wasting the whole session analyzing my aversion to his teasing. "Sometimes, I don't believe I'm related to either sibling."

"Why do you say that?"

This was a complicated thing that I shouldn't have mentioned at all. Maeve would have been thrilled at my disclosure. "Maeve and Brendan are jocks, and you couldn't pay me to join a team. They *have* to go out on a Friday night and I'm fine watching TV."

"Do you identify as an introvert?"

"I don't think I've ever tried the alternative for long," I admitted. "When we were younger, Maeve and I would trade places at times, but we didn't find each other's lifestyles addictive."

"She would feel stir-crazy and you would feel overwhelmed?"

No, I wanted to answer. *She would break her neck trying to get airborne and I would drown doing the butterfly stroke.*

"Pretty much," I amended.

"You never answered my question," Dr. Reed said.

"It fits me," I said after a moment of consideration. "I'm not sure it will win me popularity, but I'm okay with that."

"How do your siblings feel?"

Here was a chance for some of the honesty that Maeve had encouraged, even if it was sparse on details. "Brendan pretty much leaves me alone now that he lives in Pennsylvania. Maeve has a very direct approach to behavioral therapy."

"Such as?" Dr. Reed prompted.

"I agreed to the date, but Maeve made the introductions, kept us in touch, and provided the other half of our double date."

This time, Dr. Reed didn't stifle the chuckle. "I see what you mean. Why do you let her get away with it?"

"Because I love her," I replied without hesitation. "She wants me to be happy, even if I'm not her."

He didn't argue with that. "How is your relationship with your parents?"

"My latest adventure wasn't their fault," I asserted.

He let a moment of silence hang between us and his smile shrank. "I'm sorry," he said quietly. "That's not what I meant."

"I was trying to make a joke," I sighed. "I love my parents and don't have problems with authority figures. They don't ask why I'm not like my siblings because Mom wants them to leave me alone and Dad expects good behavior."

"Hence your clean record."

"I'd never had so much as a speeding ticket before this," I commented. "My parents were as surprised as I was."

"Do you feel that they overreacted to the situation?"

"No. They justifiably grounded me for accidentally immigrating to Canada." I paused for breath. "Does that answer your questions about my parents?"

"I think so," Dr. Reed assured me. "Let's change the subject."

Summer vacation usually ended with Labor Day, but varsity soccer tryouts were the week before and I had to surrender Maeve. Her practices never ended at the same time and she sometimes came home after sunset, sore and full of swagger. I went to the field to watch once, but drills got old. I frequented university libraries instead and came home when those closed. Maeve was ready by then to focus on something other than soccer and I could fill her in on my day.

By Labor Day, the coach had made Maeve varsity goalie and I was a regular at BU's Mugar Memorial Library. It was reliably open later than other teenager-friendly places and I could rely on privacy while studying.

Or so I thought.

"That's looking better."

I looked up from my notebook to find a vaguely familiar man standing across from me.

"Pardon?"

At least I hadn't said "Huh?"

"Your arm," he clarified. "No more sling."

"I haven't used one in a few weeks," I said cautiously. "Do I . . ."

"Know me?" He grinned. "You had elephant ears and an anterior dislocation at the Pops concert."

I stopped myself just short of blurting out, "BU guy?" and smiled in understanding. "I just remember you're studying physical therapy."

"It was dark," he dismissed before pointing to the spare chair. "Do you mind?"

I pulled my books towards me and shook my head.

"I didn't know you went here," he commented.

"Maybe if things go well." I unearthed my GED prep book to explain. "I'm trying to graduate early."

He raised an eyebrow. "How early?"

"My parents want me to go to college instead of junior year and I agreed to it."

He let out a low whistle. "If I had known, I wouldn't have hit on you at the Esplanade."

I furrowed my brow. "That was hitting on me?"

"For a physical therapy student, yeah, that counted as flirting." He blushed. "Clearly it made an impression."

"I didn't mind," I reassured him quickly. "I just expected flirting to include comments about my gluteus maximus."

"Only if I failed to be a gentleman," he assured me, one hand over his heart.

"And I didn't expect an older guy to even notice me."

"I'm not that much older," he pointed out. "You're, what, sixteen?"

"Almost seventeen," I corrected.

"And I'm nearly nineteen." He paused. "It was still a little creepy."

"But hindsight is 20/20," I said. "No harm done."

I wasn't sure whether I should go on or resume studying. I tried to read my notes, but they were starting to blur together. A moment later, BU guy stuck out his hand.

"Hello, I'm Nate," he introduced himself.

I shook his hand politely and tried not to channel Maeve's boy-analysis techniques; she was the last person I needed to imitate right now.

"Nate, short for . . ."

"Nathaniel," he said. "Only my parents and professors call me that. My grandfather had a good, old-fashioned name, so I share it."

"I know the feeling," I assured him. "I'm Aislin and everyone born into my family has a traditional Irish name."

"I like it," Nate commented before sitting down. "I assumed you were a townie."

"What makes you say that?"

"You don't look like you're escaping your roommates. Boston?"

"Cambridge," I corrected. "You're not a townie, so I'm guessing . . . somewhere out west?"

With his dark hair and eyes, he could have easily been one of the local Greeks from around here, but he didn't dress like an East Coaster.

"Detroit."

"And you picked Boston?"

"It has baseball, blizzards, and pizza," Nate pointed out. "I'm in a top physical therapy program and the similarities make up for the distance."

Maeve's anticipated objections to my social skills kept me from my notes. He was a pleasant distraction, but I was running out of intelligent things to say and I didn't want to drive him off.

"I was born and raised around here, so I can't really compare experiences."

"It's not a bad place," Nate said with a long, slow look around the library. He eventually stared back at me across my pile of books. "What are you studying tonight?"

"I need to figure out how much math tutoring I need."

"What's the prognosis?"

"I'm okay," I said. "I was wise enough to get a really good tutor when I needed it, so I'm not panicking. What about you?"

"Bio," he answered. "There are some classes that every science-based major has and I started with the annoying ones."

I was searching for something more coherent than "Cool!" to say when he unzipped his book bag.

"Mind if I join you?"

Maeve wouldn't be thrilled with this second conversation, but she would like it if neither of us scared each other off, so I made some room for him to work.

"Be my guest."

I didn't wake Maeve up when I got home, but I left an attention-grabbing note stuck to our bathroom mirror before mapping out the next day's route.

Maeve was still breathing deeply in her room when I awoke, so romantic news could wait. A variety of breakfast options were on the kitchen table and I obediently ate cereal so I wouldn't start my trip hungry.

The house had been dark and Dad's car was gone, which meant that I had to be outside at dawn or try to turn a doorknob with my beak.

Once free of my sling, I'd worked out destinations that would keep me in easy range of home. Lake Cochituate was close but unfamiliar and I could spend most of the day there without worrying about being out of range of home. I planned to find my way to the Mass Pike, and then keep my eyes open for the signs for 95.

As soon as the skin-crawling sensations started, I peeled off my bathrobe and left it on top of my slippers. I got goose bumps immediately, but had feathers to keep me warm a moment later.

The first takeoff of the day was always the hardest, since it could tell me that I should stay home. Once, when I'd just suffered the flu, I hadn't even made it over the bushes. Today was the first the time that I was going to try getting more than a little altitude and for all I knew, it would be a few more weeks before my shoulder would let me achieve that.

Instead of waiting for more daylight, I broke into a run. Halfway across the yard, I started beating my wings and angling for takeoff. By the time I reached the two pine trees, I was airborne and catching the breeze. Today, I cleared the back fence easily. My good mood from the night before hadn't lost its touch.

SCENE 6

Black

Summer ended too early and I blamed it on the courts. I hadn't spent my whole summer running passing drills, but Mom had found a youth team for me to assistant-coach in a very hands-off way, and I gave back to the community as ordered by mid-August, but there was too little time left after that for my tastes and I celebrated my freedom with enthusiasm. Most of this year's varsity players were strangers, so I started eleventh grade with a few new friends who had liked my hustle.

On the last night of vacation, I scheduled my last bit of freedom before honors classes and after-school sports intervened.

I was ready for the new school year—I had already stuffed my slightly worn messenger bag with office supplies. This morning, I had stocked up on hand sanitizer and lip balm.

The only thing left to do was give the summer a proper send-off, and I was done with my to-dos by the time Natalie arrived. I slung my towel over my shoulder and hurried down the stairs. My hand had just touched the doorknob when my flight was interrupted.

"Where are you going?" Mom called.

I suppressed a sigh and turned back to face her, hand still on the doorknob. "Kerry's," I said. "I'll be back by curfew."

"That wasn't why I asked," she pointed out, coming to the doorway. "You don't want to oversleep on the first day of school . . ."

"I'm ready."

"With nice clothes?"

I knew Mom would approve of my khaki skirt and leaf-green sweater in the morning. "Done."

"Bag packed?"

"Done this morning," I said.

"Lunch?"

"In the fridge."

Mom looked slightly disgruntled that I had thought of everything. "All right," she granted. "Do you need a ride?"

"Natalie's waiting outside," I explained.

"Not Nick?"

"Nick isn't invited to girls' nights out," I said. "Any other objections?"

She held up a hand. "No further questions, Your Honor."

"Good." I sighed again. "I'll see you later."

"Say hi to Natalie," she responded.

Natalie was predictably impatient. "Screening your texts?"

"Escaping the warden," I corrected. "Mom still thinks I'm a third-grader."

"My parents don't give me the benefit of the doubt, either," Natalie sympathized. "They said I could go out tonight *only* if I did the dishes after dinner and cleaned my room."

I grimaced appropriately at ordinary teenager chores. "Your life is so hard."

"Yeah," she grumbled. "That's what they said."

I had to grin at a passing car to get it out of my system. "What are we doing tonight?"

"One last of everything" she announced, perking up. "Swimming, pizza . . ."

"So pizza's okay at the eleventh hour?"

"Exactly," Natalie said. "Right now, we need one last ice cream."

"This is serious," I said. "Are you sure we can do it all?"

"We have to," Natalie said with almost-religious fervor. "Starting tomorrow, we won't have a break until January."

"Which will be too cold for swimming," I guessed morosely. "Lead on."

Laurie and Sosi were already at the ice cream place, joined by some of the new soccer players. I didn't mind, even if Lupe had nearly bested me.

"We got you vanilla," Sosi announced, handing over my usual. "How's Aislin?"

"Busy," I answered. "I haven't seen her all day."

"Aislin?" Mari, one of the sophomore newbies, asked.

"Her twin sister," Sosi said.

"She decided to homeschool," I added, "so first-day-of-school pressure is different."

"Sucks to be her," Mari commented. "I would get so bored."

"That's because you care more about boys than classes," Lupe said.

"Guilty as charged," she said.

"Aislin doesn't hang out with us much," Natalie interjected. "She doesn't really like crowds."

"I wonder why," Avril muttered.

I refrained from pointing out that no one liked feeling unwelcome. Natalie knew that by now.

"But we're trying to change that," Sosi said firmly.

"Aislin can have whatever priorities that she wants," I said. "It's her business."

Mari looked slightly confused by the warring opinions, so I decided to change the subject. "How about we stop picking on anyone not here?" I suggested. "I want some ideas on how to prank Coach for the first game."

Thirty minutes later, we'd decided on shaving cream-filled cleats and Natalie was still well-behaved. Even with the last hours of summer vacation ticking down, I was able to enjoy myself.

Unfortunately, Mari shared a confidence while we were in the back seat of Natalie's car. While the front-seaters were arguing over music, Mari leaned over and got my blood boiling in two sentences.

"I have a special needs sibling too," she confided. "I think it's great that you stick up for your sister."

Natalie immediately erupted in laughter and Mari looked stricken when my jaw clenched. "I swear it wasn't me," she protested prematurely. "Honestly!"

The lady was protesting too much, but this wasn't Natalie's style. "She's right," Mari said cautiously. "I heard it from a freshman."

"Who had heard it from some upperclassman on varsity," I growled.

Natalie only snickered this time, which was as good as a confession. "You've never told us her reason for homeschooling; of course someone made one up."

"She made that decision, and just because it's not what you would have done . . ."

"Drop it," Natalie barked back with sudden sharpness.

She sounded like she'd have chewed me out if it weren't for the impressionable younglings, so I leaned forward until she was in choking range. "You and I are going to talk."

"Whatever," she said.

I grabbed Laurie by the sleeve as soon as we left the car and dragged her purposefully past the others.

"Coming?" I asked Natalie.

She followed with a dramatic sigh and we cloistered ourselves in the guest bathroom.

"You told the freshmen my sister's special needs?" I challenged.

I saw Laurie start to crack a smile, but rethought that decision when Natalie shook her head urgently and changed it to a "so what?" look.

"I didn't deny it," she said. "but I didn't start it."

"That was the first I heard of it," Natalie explained. "Sorry for laughing."

"And I'm sorry I didn't correct them," Laurie added, apparently catching on. "It won't happen again."

"No, it won't," I agreed. "And you *will* be sorry."

"We'll behave," Laurie promised.

"You'll do better than that."

Natalie's mouth pinched. "You're not going to make us *tell* Aislin, are you? We thought what she doesn't know can't hurt her."

"You're going to find a new hobby. I don't care if you never find out the real story or if I stay home with her a lot. You're going to set the record straight and then you are going to . . ." I caught Natalie's eye for emphasis. ". . . *drop it.*"

I expected them to wheedle or make excuses for their behavior, but they seemed to think they were locked up with a cranky lion and no one dared to disagree.

"All right," Natalie said. "If it means that much to you . . ."

"It does," I said.

"Then I'm sorry I didn't apologize before."

It was too much to ask that she fix her attitude, but apologizing for the behavior was good enough.

"And you?" I challenged Laurie.

"Yes," she said quickly. "I'll be on my best behavior from now on."

I took a deep breath to calm myself; as girls who could occasionally endure some disciplining, they seemed to hate me very little right now.

"Thank you," I said quietly. "Let's try to never mention this again."

Natalie cracked her first smile of the conversation. "All right."

I had just changed into street clothes after summer's final swim when someone knocked on the bathroom door.

"I'll be out in a minute," I shouted.

"Take your time," Sosi called back. "I'm your ride."

I opened the door, a hand towel still in my grip. "Is Natalie mad?"

"She isn't," Sosi assured me. "I volunteered."

It was a surprising turn of events, but I welcomed it. "Great," I responded. "Just give me a minute."

I hugged everyone on my way out and promised them we'd survive tomorrow. The moment the key was in the ignition, Sosi spoke up.

"I feel like an idiot," she announced.

"Why is that?"

"Mari told me what happened in the car."

So now everyone had heard the rumor. I'd have to bully Natalie and Laurie into acting quickly. "I feel like a cretin because I should have stopped them before now," she continued.

"I let it get this far so I wouldn't make trouble," I pointed out. "If anyone in this car is a cretin, it's me."

She sighed unhappily and focused on the turns needed to make it out of the neighborhood. I wasn't sure what to say next, but I also didn't want to change subjects until Sosi got her feelings off of her chest.

"So, here's my game plan," I said. "I'm going to hold Natalie and Laurie to their promises and make sure this rumor never hurts Aislin's feelings."

"I agree." There was another slightly uncomfortable silence. "Is that why she . . ."

"It's still her business," I interrupted. "Get her to tell you."

I doubted it would happen. Sosi wasn't pushy and Aislin wasn't crazy.

"*I* want to be a better friend to your sister without her thinking it's out of pity."

"She wouldn't think that."

"I'm going to include her more, visit *her,* call more often, et cetera," Sosi listed off. "Does that sound okay?"

As long as she didn't try to stop by after school, that could do more good than all the court-ordered counseling.

"It sounds perfect."

I overslept on the second day of school, but I had set my alarm early. That meant that I had time for a quick shower, a to-go breakfast, and a mad dash to homeroom. I grabbed Aislin's note, but I only had time to shove it into my jeans pocket.

I forgot it until I looked for an eraser during second period. My hand scraped against the edge of the folded paper and I decided to open it when Mr. Hurst had his back turned.

I got my chance a few minutes later when he bent down to get some papers. I flattened the paper casually with one hand to read.

His name is Nate.

The day had dragged until then, but it was interminable after that. Aislin only learned names if she intended to talk about them again.

After soccer, I showered in record time and got home just after dusk. Aislin was still dressing, so I laid siege outside of her bedroom door.

She looked both happy and unsurprised to see me. "You got my note."

"Who's Nate?" I asked immediately.

"BU guy," she said with unconvincing nonchalance.

"Seriously?" I squeaked.

"And for the record, he was hitting on me."

"Last night?"

"The first time we met," Aislin practically boasted, "but last night too."

It took me a second to scramble to my feet. Instead of hugging her, I planted a hand on her shoulder and propelled her back into the bedroom.

"Details, *now.*"

"You already know his name, his interest in me . . ."

"Is he from here?" I pressed on, not releasing her until we were both seated on the bed. "What did you study? When will he call you?"

"Detroit. Math and Biology. He doesn't have my number."

I gave her a reproachful look worthy of Mom. "Why not?"

"Because he didn't ask for it?"

Instead of asking when she'd ever learn, I posed a less rhetorical question: "When will you see him?"

"I'm hanging out at his library weeknights. If he's a good student, I'll run into him again."

She had a good point, but I was still right. "You should have given him your number."

"I'll offer it next time," Aislin promised, eyes crinkled in amusement. "Until then, I've got Ethan."

"Maybe," I corrected. "His first real love is his GPA, and you don't want to test that."

"So you're saying I should back off?" she guessed.

"I'm saying, don't be surprised if he forgets to call," I said gently. "I'll mention you once a month."

"Thanks." She slid off the bed and headed for the closet. "Do you have my red shirt?"

"It's in the laundry," I answered. "Do you need it tonight?"

"I thought I'd plan ahead for tomorrow. Can it be clean by then?"

I didn't like doing laundry on weeknights, but I wasn't going to let detergent stand in the way of her romance.

"I'll leave it on your bed tomorrow," I promised.

She nodded and closed the closet doors after shoving her feet into sandals. "How was school?"

"It's the second day and I haven't started hating it yet," I conceded. "That's a better record than some years."

In ninth grade, I had wanted to cry after the first hour and Aislin had intervened when I tried to play sick the next day.

"Worst teacher?"

"Grady."

Aislin frowned. "I thought you liked him."

"He lost his personality over vacation and I don't like physics as much as chemistry."

"But you get to do practical experiments," Aislin said. "Is Ethan in that class?"

"No." It would have been nice to have an ally/lab partner like him, but he was in Laurie's math class that period. "I have English and art with him, but that's it."

"That's okay," she said. "If he doesn't date me again, that could minimize the fallout."

"Listen to you," I said approvingly. "I love it when you strategize."

"Not wanting to hurt his feelings is intention, not strategy," Aislin amended.

"Either way, you're planning ahead," I insisted. "The only thing that could make me prouder . . ."

"Would be if I'd remembered the phone number," Aislin finished. "I know."

She had it in her short-term memory and that was a start. "Good girl," I applauded. "I'm going to tackle the evil physics beast. Let me know if you need any more tutorials."

White

With fall coming on, the days shortened little by little. I'd loved summer as a kid because it didn't rain much or dump a foot of snow on the city. As soon as I got used to the curse, though, I realized that fall had its advantages. I could eat dinner at a normal time because I changed back at a more reasonable hour and the long nights allowed me to see Maeve for a while before Mom ordered us back to our homework.

The exception was, of course, Wednesday nights. Dr. Reed had finally accepted that I hadn't *meant* to commit a crime and I was just a teenager who made a few bad decisions, which was the official story, even if it made me look like an idiot. With no juvenile delinquency to cure, he talked about other subjects that were making adolescence "troubled."

"How is your schoolwork?" he asked a few days into fall.

It was a question that I expected from Dad, not my shrink. Maybe he *had* run out of topics.

"It's just schoolwork."

"You don't enjoy it?"

"I enjoy finishing it," I said with a shrug. "I don't loathe it or anything."

"From what I know of you, I don't think you'd ever loathe

self-improvement," Dr. Reed commented. "What is it that you dislike about your schoolwork?"

He sounded determined to find a sore spot *somewhere*, but I drew a blank. My teacher and I didn't butt heads on homework much.

"I want to finish school in months, not years," I said at last. "That's why I'm okay with my parents' pushing for my GED."

He stopped writing mid-note. "You hadn't mentioned the GED. Tell me about it."

"Do you want to know my feelings on graduating or my parents' ambitions for me?"

"Either," he granted. "Your sister has two more years of high school."

I gave him a straight answer so he could draw his own conclusions. "I never really aspired to beat my sister," I admitted. "I always figured graduation was something else we'd do together."

"Have you talked to her about it?"

"I asked her opinion first," I said. "She's very supportive of how many boys I'll meet."

He looked amused by that argument. "Is that a concern?"

"It is for her," I said.

He made a note, probably about how I relied on Maeve's expectations. "What about you?"

If I intended to make this a long-term arrangement, I'd have admitted that I would give my right arm to obsess about something other than my love life.

"It's something I want eventually, but I wouldn't put it as my first priority," I half-lied.

"What are your priorities, then?" Dr. Reed asked.

"Getting into college someday and not flunking my exams," I said in complete honesty. "Dating can wait until after homework."

"Why?" he countered. "You said that school isn't something you particularly enjoy. What are you doing to bring yourself some joy? Do you take some time for other pursuits?"

"You mean like a hobby?"

"I mean something that you do because you want to, not because it pleases others."

Instead of asking his thoughts on a life of crime, I took some time to consider that for a while.

"I take a lot of walks," I translated my thoughts. "It clears my head without counting as gym credit."

"That's a good start," Dr. Reed commended, "but I think it would be good for you to do some pointlessly fun things for yourself once in a while."

I had to laugh at the idea. "And when do you think I should fit that in?"

"Where the rest of us do," he said. "Before we can't put it off any longer."

Black

Every teenager I've ever known has harbored some kind of grudge, usually against parents, siblings, or teachers. My grudge switched the moment my mother admitted to me that she had seen the curse coming, one hour before Aislin found out.

My anger these days was focused on Aislin's deprivation. Whenever I ran laps at practice or walked under the autumn sunlight, I'd wish she were there. I wanted her sitting at my lunch table or hanging out with a guy during a free period. When Ethan asked about her, I wished she could respond herself. With two weeks of the school year behind me, I decided to do something more than play matchmaker.

My parents were not, by their nature, the nosiest people on the planet and spent most of their suspicion on Brendan anyways. He hadn't lived here for over a year, so I figured that no one had browsed my Internet activity in a few months.

My recent searches about curse-breaking would have raised questions, even if results usually mentioned TV depictions of fortune-tellers.

When not even "Help! My sister's a swan!" turned up anything worthwhile, I tried a different direction. I knew only one person with the extra-curriculars I needed and she was a sophomore I'd known in last year's music class.

I didn't know Susanna Betancourt well, but while I liked her, the age gap wasn't the only reason we hadn't talked much since. I probably wouldn't have noticed her except her brother knew Brendan. We didn't have the same lunch period, so I simply called the number in the directory.

"Color me intrigued," she said, once I had admitted to her that

I needed her help. "Who are you trying to hex?"

"No one," I protested. "I'm not like that."

Susanna didn't debate that. "When a junior calls me, it's usually because they're getting desperate."

She wasn't far off about the desperation, but completely misinterpreted my intentions. "I'm not asking you to turn someone into a frog."

"Good," Susanna drawled. "I'm better at newts."

I relaxed for the first time since dialing; she could dish out jokes and take them in turn. "I'm hoping you can point me in the right direction on something."

She waited for an explanation, but if I pitched this wrong, she'd think I was pranking her.

"What's your schedule like tomorrow?" she asked eventually.

"I can be at school as early or late as you want," I promised. "I'm up with the birds."

"I'll be at your locker twenty minutes early," she said. "We'll go from there."

Susanna may have been the only practicing Wiccan in tenth grade, but she wore jeans and sweaters like a uniform and wore a goddess pendant like a cross necklace. She was preppy with a side of mystical.

"Morning," I greeted. "I come bearing muffins."

"Thanks," she responded. "Is this a bribe?"

"A thank you," I corrected.

"Fair enough," she granted. "How public is this conversation?"

I didn't want a crowd, so I gestured towards the doors leading to the main part of the school. "Empty classroom?"

We chose desks in my math room and Susanna didn't even grab a muffin before getting down to business. "Do you personally need help or is it someone you know?"

"I want to help my sister."

"I see. Your twin sister?"

"Yes," I said.

"I met her at the pool party," she said, opening the bag and selecting a muffin. "She hung around with my freshman mentor. She seems nice."

I felt guilty that Aislin had met her and I hadn't noticed her. "She is," I agreed. "She's also cursed."

Susanna thought about her response for two bites, so I started eating my muffin. When Susanna responded, she sounded more focused.

"What makes you think that?"

"The evidence is there," I said shortly.

Her expression was neutral, as was her question. "Does she feel cursed or do you know who cursed her?"

"It's either a curse or the world's weirdest birth defect," I said with confidence.

Susanna's expression turned wary and she even set down her food to pay closer attention.

"She was born this way?"

"It turned up at puberty, but we know it's hereditary," I elaborated.

"So there are others in your family with it?" She hunched one shoulder towards me. "Including you?"

"I wish," I said immediately. At her skeptical look, I went on. "No one living shares the curse."

"And that's why you want to help." She smiled at me for the first time since I'd brought her food. "I approve. Do you mind telling me more?"

I outlined the symptoms instead of fairytales and we both ignored the food until I was done.

"Wow," Susanna said. "If anyone knew this . . ."

"It'd probably make things worse," I finished, "but I think some people would understand."

"And have you thought about telling those people?"

"All the time," I confirmed, thinking about mutual friends and extended family. "She's against it."

"She probably wouldn't be thrilled that I know," she guessed. "This is very personal."

"My mother broke it to her gently and left out the details until later."

"Look on the bright side," Susanna commented. "Some curses are complicated, like 'find love by the third new moon of your twenty-first year.' "

Those sounded a lot more like a Disney movie than Aislin's lot in life. "He wasn't very creative, apparently."

"But the curse wins out if she doesn't find love before she . . ." Susanna coughed pointedly. ". . . makes love."

"We're responsible people," I defended. "Neither of us would have experimented with teen pregnancy, but it leaves the curse in control again."

"I don't think so," Susanna said. "Maybe that was his original intention, but we're modern women and I think your sister has more power than he intended."

I smiled and toasted her with the last of my muffin. "Good point."

I'd thought of Aislin's likely objections to Susanna's involvement already, but this was motivated by love. I was pretty sure that she would thank me in the long run.

"She's only mildly uncomfortable with my current level of interference."

"*I'm* the lesser of two evils?" Susanna laughed.

"No, you're the secret weapon."

Her smile shrunk and I wondered what mistake I'd made. "If you're serious about it, she'll have to know eventually," she said.

She didn't sound miffed or accusatory, but wounded that it sounded like a friendship I wouldn't take public.

"I don't even know what I'm asking you to do," I attempted to explain. "It's not like I've tried this in the past."

"Then why are you so hands-on in breaking the curse?" Susanna asked pointedly. "What do you get out of it?"

"My sister gets to be happy," I defended myself. "Isn't that enough?"

"I'm just wondering why now?" she commented. "Why not give her a few years to work it out on her own?"

I could just see it. Aislin would miss my mid-afternoon graduation. She'd be stuck dragging college out with years of night classes. She'd only hear about most major milestones. I could imagine getting married at midnight so she wouldn't be left out. They were things that I might have to accept, but I didn't have to *like* it.

"No one outside the family knows," I said. "Friends don't know about her condition and she can't call my aunt for sympathy on a bad day. We treat it like some shameful family secret and of all the unfair things in her life, that's what rankles me most."

"So the sooner this is over with, the better?"

I nodded. "I have a complicated and stressful life. I'd like her to be able to share in it."

She finished the muffin before responding and I followed her lead. "I'll do this if you swear to tell her eventually."

"I'll figure out a way to bring it up," I promised.

She gave me a calculating look and I half-expected her to pull out a contract. Eventually, she extracted a pen from her book bag and uncapped it.

"Breaking a curse that ancient would be tricky," she considered dourly. "It will take me some time to find a plan."

"Until then, what do we do?" I asked eagerly.

"That depends on how you want to start."

I had no idea if this would work, so I didn't aim very high. I also wasn't sure how seriously my bespoke witch took her craft.

"Is there anything you can recommend for seeking bright ideas?"

Susanna's face brightened and she flipped open a notebook. "It's more for wisdom than anything, but I think it could fit."

A half-minute later, she wasn't done and I cleared my throat. "I hope that's not the shopping list."

"The instructions," she corrected.

"You have them memorized?"

"I do this brain boost before school starts," Susanna explained.

"And it works?"

"It's worth a shot," she answered brightly. "Tomorrow, I'll bring you more homework."

She ripped the paper out and handed it over. I liked how short the list was, but I didn't know where to buy patchouli oil.

"Thank you," I said in earnest. "What can I do in return?"

Susanna contemplated that while finishing off her muffin. "I'm not expecting payment," she said, "but I'm sure you'll think of a way to show your appreciation."

Mom didn't object when I borrowed a spool of thread, but she did look curious when I used it to hang dried flowers from Aislin's ceiling.

"Do I want to know?"

It had been part of Susanna's homework. "It's just an idea I had."

"Oh yes?" Mom prompted.

"To cheer her up," I said, trying to sound convincing.

"Are fresh flowers too high-maintenance?" she asked, squinting skeptically at the sprig. "Will you do this in every room?"

"No," I responded. "There will be no random daisies in the kitchen."

She might not even notice anything else unless she went digging in our rooms. Like Aislin, she was better off being a little bit in the dark.

I finished hanging the sprig and hopped down, but Mom blocked my exit easily. "Is Aislin allowed to know?"

"That's up to her," I replied. "I'll bet she doesn't notice for a month."

"And you want it that way?" she challenged.

"It wouldn't stop me," I said with a shrug. "If she notices it, I'll explain my motives."

It was a harmless flower, but Mom regarded it like hemlock. "Are you sure you don't want to explain now?"

Explaining wouldn't get her to help me and might even hurt my cause; it wasn't like she was thinking outside the box herself. She was content to let things unfold and pass judgment on the process, and that was why I had to be the sneakily proactive one.

"I'm sure." When she still looked doubtful, I reported, "A friend of ours suggested it. It's unusual, but not sinister."

"I still want to know what secret you're keeping." Mom stepped aside with a small smile. "I'll trust your good intentions, but I'll want to know when Aislin does."

"Yes, Mother," I said meekly. "If you'll excuse me, I have some chickens to sacrifice."

She snorted but left it at that. I was just glad that she hadn't come in while I was stashing a small envelope in the lining of my sister's usual fall jacket.

INTERLUDE

White

I didn't have much experience with crisis as a twelve-year-old. Mom had spent two weeks away when Grandpa had bypass surgery, and it had been a disaster when Brendan had cheated on a math test, but I'd avoided anything more drastic than that.

It was quite alarming when my mother decided to take a leave of absence. I never knew what explanation she gave her boss, but no one argued at home. I had only been a swan-maiden for five days and I'd given everyone the silent treatment for the first two.

One morning, she came into my room, barefoot and still in pajamas, well after she should have been at work. I could have chased her from the room easily, but I settled for giving her a scathing look and ignoring her until she brought up lunch. I wasn't much better on subsequent days, but she spent every one of my swan hours with me. When I turned human again, I would usually rail at her until I ran out of original things to say, but it was unsatisfying that she didn't shout back. She would have a hot shower running for me and make something only I liked for dinner.

On the fourth day, I came downstairs after my shower to find that we had the house to ourselves. Mom sat, business-like, between a pile of maps and a stack of books. For me, she had made chicken cacciatore and even in my foul mood, I accepted the peace offering. By the time I'd finished eating, she had apologetically explained that the books were for homeschooling and I had sneered at the idea that she could fix this by letting me read about Narnia in English.

The second half of her peace offering was something that actually appealed to me. She fanned out the maps like a deck of cards and I drew a tattered guide to Rhode Island. She calculated the distance to Wallum Lake and said we'd leave two hours before dawn.

She couldn't reverse this curse, but she spent the next two weeks showing me the beauty of my new world. I familiarized myself with Todd and Walden Ponds and was floored when she brought me to Maine so I could explore Moosehead Lake.

On these trips, Mom spent some of our commuting hours brainstorming about homeschooling. She answered every question I could think of about the curse, and it was during one of these interrogations that the worst aspect of my lot in life came to light.

There had been others, Mom explained, but the curse required them to find love before they became intimate with a partner. It was a crappy way of making sure that marriage didn't necessarily break the curse, and if that happened, the girl would forfeit her human hours.

I shouted loudest of all at her for that. It wasn't her fault that she was a carrier for such a condition, but I had no one else to blame. She didn't try to stop me and I demanded that she take me home, spending the three-hour return journey in stony silence. Maeve didn't help by failing to find a single positive thing to say about that. Mom's claims that I had more freedom than those who went before fell on deaf ears.

We stayed home for two days, her respecting my locked door during the day and my stubborn silences at night. I stopped trying to forgive her because that would imply that she had wronged me personally. By the third day, I had decided that I couldn't rightfully hate her for that or any other part of the curse. It was another two years before I brought it up again.

By the end of those two weeks, I didn't like the curse any less, but it was finally something I could live with.

Black

I was often tempted to run away from home as a child. I was the more dramatic Byrne sister and that made me favor grand exits when things went wrong. When disciplined for backtalk, I stopped talking for a day. One summer, I packed clothes and food for three days into my backpack and the only thing that stopped me from disappearing was Aislin's refusal to come with me.

I grew out of this attention-seeking around ten, but the rebellious streak that caused it returned in full force when we were kicked out of summer camp.

We all tried to empathize with Aislin, but it infuriatingly accomplished nothing when we tried to say so. When she *was* in human form, she refused to discuss the matter. I was lucky that she didn't lock me out like the rest of the family. I would have picked her lock if she'd tried, anyway.

When Mom announced her leave of absence to help Aislin "settle in," I balked at the idea of Aislin getting used to this. I wanted her to fight the curse until it gave up out of sheer exhaustion. Mom had a newfound interest in New England's state parks, but it rankled on me that no one cared enough to be angry about all of this.

So while Aislin and Mom plotted the next great adventure at Lake Winnipesaukee, I planned my own escape. There was no packing involved, but when they headed out, so did I. Some days, friends would invite me over. On others, I invited myself and wore out my welcome. I even stayed at the library and read every book I could find by my favorite author in two weeks.

Mom could be counted on to arrive home a few minutes before sunset, so we knew where they'd be and when; Aislin even invited me along once. I probably hurt her feelings by declining, but Mom went ballistic when I was MIA at 11:45 that night.

I stood my ground. I pointed out that Aislin could go wherever she wanted as long as she was home at sunset. I argued against being tracked like a criminal when she could be anywhere from Connecticut to Castine. I asserted my right to run off whenever I wanted.

I still got grounded for a week, but Mom convinced me to stick around for another reason: if Aislin wasn't able to run away from this, neither was I.

SCENE 7

White

Maeve claimed that turning seventeen on October 17 called for something "uber-spectacular" and I agreed to trust her. My unofficial gift to her was not interfering and she returned the favor by forgoing a party.

Her plans in general were a complete mystery. Her texts were off-limits and her email password had been changed. Those both made me more apprehensive than the thought of some ostentatious rave.

I was encouraged when I saw that she had shown up for our rendezvous alone. Extra people would have meant that someone had to talk me into cooperating.

"Happy birthday," Maeve called boisterously.

"Happy birthday," I hissed. "Can you keep it down?"

"You wouldn't let me go all out," my older sister pointed out. "The least you can do is let me be enthusiastic."

I smiled bravely, but probably looked nervous. "Bring it on."

"You brought your ID?"

I flipped my wallet open to brandish fake and real driver's licenses. "It goes where I go."

She looked a little too pleased at that. "Perfect."

It made me anxious that she wanted me passing for 21. Few things that I could do at that age would keep me ungrounded.

"*No* tattoos."

"You promised to not interfere," Maeve pouted.

"That's sanity, not interference," I pronounced.

"We could *match*," she protested.

"We're identical," I shot back in a very low voice. "I don't want my identifying mark to be a blue butterfly."

"Why not?" my sister asked, waggling her eyebrows. "Tail feathers cover up a lot of things."

"I'm not agreeing to this," I said firmly.

"What?" Maeve teased. "Are you worried the squirrels would make fun of you?"

"No tattoos."

Maeve sighed. "You promised to not interfere and I foolishly trusted you."

"I can risk disappointment."

She abruptly grinned and waved a hand dismissively. "We're not getting tattoos," she assured me. "Don't you trust me at all?"

Before I could be brutally honest, she grabbed my hand and steered me to an unfamiliar block of Tremont Street. Our destination was an unfamiliar building, but there were no explanatory signs on the windows.

The sign on the door gave it away, though. My stomach jolted and I rounded on her, ready to fight.

"*Tarot?*"

"Come on," Maeve wheedled. "It'll be fun. I can get career advice and you can ask about your love life."

"I'm not interested in . . ."

A door opened at that moment and a very ordinary-looking woman in street clothes emerged. I clenched my jaw and shut up before entering.

"The Byrne sisters?" the woman guessed.

"That's us," Maeve confirmed. "We pay up front?"

"That *is* standard procedure."

She probably didn't want us refusing to pay if we didn't like the outcome, so Maeve passed over the credit card.

"ID?" Maeve offered hers and the woman left it on the counter. "Your real ID."

Maeve gaped. "You could tell . . ."

"I have two teenagers," the woman interrupted.

I had the urge to snicker at that insight and fought it down. The woman accepted Maeve's real license and handed it back after a moment.

"Don't try to fool me again," she admonished.

In spite of myself, I decided to like her. Maeve signed the receipt and returned everything to her wallet.

"If it's all right," the woman said, "I'll start with Aislin."

"Fine," Maeve said. "Should I come?"

It was my day too, and I didn't want Maeve eavesdropping on my destiny. "You can wait out here."

She frowned unhappily but didn't press the point. I flashed a winning smile before following the woman.

My designated psychic dressed like someone on her way to a board meeting. There were no candles, incense, or mystical runes that I could see. A small table took center stage with filing cabinets near the window.

"Happy birthday," the woman said. "I'm Marianne."

"Aislin," I answered. "Nice to meet you."

"What is the greatest question you want to have answered?" Marianne asked, crossing to the filing cabinet

"Aren't you supposed to tell me?"

She opened the top drawer and began browsing before answering. "I'm not the Psychic Hotline," she countered. "Tarot is more of a conversation between friends than a lecture."

Since this was Maeve's idea, I had expected a very different answer. I sat in the nearest chair without further comment.

"I'm not having much luck in love," I admitted.

"You're a little young for that conversation," Marianne observed, withdrawing a specific deck. "You're also absolutely in earnest."

I nodded. "It's a top priority."

"Do you want to talk about why?" she invited while shuffling.

"I thought that's what this was," I responded. "A conversation between friends."

"We can talk as much or as little as you need," she offered. "You obviously have a reason for getting a head start."

This was like being at Dr. Reed's, so I kept it equally vague. "I feel like I won't get on with the rest of my life until I see progress."

In other words, I wouldn't stop turning into a glorified chicken until I had a boyfriend. Marianne had me cut the deck in three and set the rest aside.

"Let's see what the cards say."

Black

Aislin didn't say anything when she emerged, but I had expected my notoriously private sister to hold back the reading's details. I could guess the conversation topic, but this was a new thing for me too, and her expression gave nothing away.

I had my own questions, but only one had made prompted me to drag my twin sister to a psychic. The appointment felt vaguely taboo—Mom would probably breathe fire when she saw the charge—but Aislin had focused on my happiness last year and I wanted to return the favor.

When my sister's time was up and the woman who probably knew the shoe size of my true love told me to think about what I wanted answered, scholarships or boyfriends didn't come to mind. I thought of what I'd asked since the day I found out about the curse.

"How can I help my sister?"

On Marianne's instructions, I cut the deck and handed them back to my fortune-teller. "That's a question I usually hear about a dying relative," she observed. "You're that worried about her?"

Obviously, she didn't have a twin sister, so she wouldn't understand that when Aislin hurt, I throbbed. It wasn't sympathetic pain. It was practically symbiotic. I had done my part to keep Aislin happy, but she still fought me on every curse-breaking agenda and I was pretty much flying blind.

"I'm worried I'm making things worse," I said frankly. "She has some"—'issues' was the word that came insensitively to mind—"challenges."

"We all do," Marianne replied. "What makes you think that you're responsible for them?"

"I don't think I'm *responsible* for them," I countered. "I want to make life a little easier for her and any advice would be appreciated."

"Do you know what she and I discussed?"

She didn't seem to offer details, but I guessed from her response that she knew a few. It was unsurprising and a relief to know that Aislin had possessed the guts to bring it up.

"We didn't talk about it in advance." I didn't mention that I'd sort of ambushed her. "I just know the things that bother her most."

Marianne didn't confirm that, which probably meant she respected psychic-customer confidentiality. "Fair enough."

Last year, Aislin had suffered my perception of the Sweet Sixteen. I believed that it was a rite of passage where she could have as much fun as possible. I limited most of the guest list to our mutual friends, but she was a good sport. By the end of our all-nighter, Aislin looked *happy* and claimed to appreciate the way it turned out.

This year, it was immediate family only; Mom picked the restaurant and Dad cleared his work schedule. We swung by the house beforehand and changed into something for special occasions.

The restaurant in question was out in Wayland, the place where we'd celebrated thirteenth birthdays and school achievements. Since Mom and Dad had let us do our own thing last year, we suffered it this time.

We were late by family standards, being only five minutes early for the reservation. Mom immediately hugged Aislin and then held her at arm's length to scrutinize her.

"No ink?"

"You're objecting?" I asked once Dad had side-hugged me.

"I'm confused," she admitted. "If you didn't get tattoos, where did you go?"

"You wouldn't believe it if we told you," Aislin said.

"But it didn't leave any permanent marks." Dad looked and sounded amused. "Maeve, you're losing your touch."

I stuck out my tongue like a mature seventeen-year-old and he laughed.

"If you want, we can shave our heads before dinner," Aislin offered.

"I'll pass," Mom said quickly. "Did you have fun?"

"I did," Aislin admitted convincingly. "Thanks for the late reservation."

"We couldn't resist," Dad said.

We were seated a few moments later and ordered before resuming normal conversation. Mom immediately turned her attention back to Aislin.

"How was your day?"

"I spent most of it near here, actually," she said. "The leaf-peepers didn't invade the conservation land by the college."

"And you had . . ."

"I had a pretty normal day at school," I interrupted as Mom turned to me. "I got an A on my history paper, Nick brought me flowers, and teachers gave lots of homework."

"Great work on the paper," Mom commended me.

"Thanks."

Usually, I would have been more flattered, but she didn't seem focused on our conversation. "If you're looking for our waiter, he's still in the kitchen," Aislin pointed out after Mom glanced around for the sixth time.

"I'm not . . ."

Mom trailed off and her face brightened considerably. I turned immediately and saw Brendan on an inbound path. Aislin sprang to her feet with a gasp and hugged him once he reached our table.

"No one told us you were coming," Aislin accused as I took my turn.

"Well, I was hired as a warm body, but no one brought up a birthday," Brendan commented.

"Nonsense," Dad said. "We mentioned it months ago."

"Yeah, as in, 'don't forget to send a card.'"

"We thought you'd politely hand-deliver it," Dad explained. "No family qualifies as the 'warm body.'"

Brendan bumped my shoulder on his way to his chair. "You're getting tall," he complained. "Stop that."

"No promises," I sniggered. "You'll be the shorty soon."

"Quiet, or I'll keep this."

He waved an envelope for emphasis and Aislin snatched it away. Inside was a gift certificate, but I quickly noticed one major problem.

"This restaurant's in Philadelphia."

"You catch on quick," he drawled. "You're coming to visit."

"No way," I protested. "Your dorm is a hazard zone."

"Which is why you'll be staying off-campus," Dad said. "If you're old enough for college, you can vacation unsupervised."

"As long as no one skips exams, you can go any weekend," Mom added.

"How about this?" I suggested. "We can time it to escort him back for Thanksgiving."

"You *were* planning on coming, right?" Aislin said.

"Free laundry and fresh food?" Brendan said. "I wouldn't miss it."

"I said nothing about doing your laundry," Mom protested.

He gave her a winning smile. "Don't worry. My darling sisters will do anything to keep me from saying what really happens on that trip."

SCENE 8

Black

The rest of the birthday dinner was fairly low-key. Mom got us mace in case our fake IDs got us in over our heads, and Dad bought tickets to a Celtics game. Our parents weren't exactly tuned in to our interests, but the mace couldn't hurt and I planned on using the tickets for a double date. Brendan let us interrogate him about his roommate's latest pranks and tease him about his love life on the way home. He fled to his old room once we got in the door and I followed Aislin to her bedroom.

"Am I allowed to ask what Marianne told you?"

She smirked and stepped aside so I could pass. "I'm shocked it took you this long," she commented.

"Maybe I've been waiting until you were a captive audience," I suggested.

"If you really want details, I have a print-out."

"If I really want to know, I'm not going to spend twenty minutes reading what you could summarize in five."

Aislin remained silent for over a minute, either debating the merits of telling me or reviewing what she remembered. She didn't reach for her purse, so she wasn't checking her source material.

"I asked her about my love life," she confessed.

"Me too."

Her cheeks flushed immediately. "Please tell me you're joking."

"Both of our sessions focused on how to help you," I amended.

The color didn't recede from her cheeks, but she looked both touched and dismayed. "But this was your idea," Aislin protested. "You could have asked her anything."

"Yeah," I shot back. "It was my idea, so you don't get to object to me wanting your happiness more than anything."

That seemed to make up her mind. She squared her shoulders and adopted a look of intense concentration.

"She said I shouldn't let failure set me back and need to learn from any experiences, even my mistakes," she announced. "I should be peaceful and tolerant when looking for solutions . . ."

"Come on," I prompted. "Surely she didn't spend the whole time troubleshooting your personality."

The color faded slightly from her cheeks and she didn't look too offended by that. "She said—before you had your turn—that I have more support on my side than I think."

Someone else would have had something sarcastic to say, but I rested my hand on top of hers to assert that Marianne had gotten that right.

"As for my current situation, she claims it will be resolved soon."

That made me scowl. "She didn't say *how* soon?"

"I'm more skeptical about the idea that it will be resolved," she said. "I'm not exactly on the fast track to happily ever after."

"Who cares?" I challenged.

"You," Aislin diagnosed.

"That's right," I said without remorse. "What else?"

She sighed and pulled a few papers from her bag. "While she says the problem might be resolved soon, she says I need to slow down and re-evaluate things."

"So there's no harm in taking things slow," I translated. "Maybe not as slow as Dad would like, but you don't have to rush into whatever comes next."

Aislin squinted over the top of her paper in my direction. "What makes you think I would?"

The answer was my experience of being in love with the idea of love. I wanted as much as anyone for her to find love that would last as long as it took for the curse to be overthrown.

"You want to get on with your life," I considered. "Mom and Dad think college will fix that, but I spend half my waking hours trying to figure out a permanent solution."

The squint turned amused rather than skeptical. "Only half?" she challenged.

"I have to leave *some* time for school and a social life," I explained. "Anything else you wanted to share?"

"Not for now," Aislin said.

I was disappointed, but I could always swipe her printout from her bedroom while she was out. She probably even expected me to do so.

"Me, either," I agreed. "Happy birthday, kid."

She gave me a hug that presumably meant she forgave me for my crazy ideas. "You too."

I knew the warning signs for Aislin being smitten. I had mostly seen the effects of her crushes, but I was very good at reading her moods and that told me a lot. So far, Aislin had cleared the first two hurdles: she remembered his name and initiated conversation. Once she got his number, I'd start planning the wedding.

Hurdle #3 should have been arranging a meeting with me, but instead Aislin called our first family council in years. Brendan wasn't on the phone, but the rest of us coordinated schedules and met in the kitchen.

Then she put her fake ID on the table, meaning that she wanted to Discuss Something Like Adults and the topic was not to be taken lightly. With advance warning, I would have brought my own for backup.

"All right," Dad said after a moment of contemplation. "How are things going?"

"Things are fine," Aislin responded cautiously. "I think I'll be ready for the exams by Thanksgiving."

"And the car's fine?"

The car that we got to share on the occasional weeknight was definitely fine. It didn't even have any dents.

"It needs an oil change," I contributed, "but I don't think that's why we're here."

Aislin hated small talk more than anyone else I knew, so my intervention was appreciated.

"If I'm going to be hanging around college students," she said politely, "I want to know your feelings on my dating one."

To his credit, Dad didn't immediately answer and Mom followed his lead. I prayed very hard that the words "statutory rape" wouldn't ever come up or Aislin would get scared off.

"I thought you were dating Ethan Fowler."

If Dad remembered his name, he had definitely made a good impression. Aislin took this in stride and kept calm.

"I like Ethan," she informed him, "but he hasn't made a move in weeks."

"So you're moving on?"

"No," Aislin said patiently, "I'm exploring my options."

He still looked unhappy about that, but looked to Mom for feedback.

"Did you have someone in mind?" she asked.

Aislin blushed, but I was the one who felt awkward. This wasn't going to be a comfortable topic for anyone.

"I meant in general."

Dad picked up the ID and tapped it thoughtfully on the table. "That depends," he considered. "What age do you say you are?"

"Seventeen," she said firmly.

"Good answer." He set the ID down before continuing questioning. "Why the sudden interest?"

"I occasionally notice guys on my own," Aislin stated. "How interested am I allowed to be?"

"You don't need to go into specifics," I blurted out before they could make a list.

I had asked that months ago and knew more than I ever wanted about Dad's concerns. I didn't want her subjected to that torture.

Aislin smiled to thank me for interpreting. "Are college guys off-limits?"

I could practically hear them regretting the decision to get us fake IDs. Aislin's let her circumvent curfew laws, but they'd gotten one for me out of fairness. We hadn't abused their trust yet, but that didn't rule out future irresponsibility. Aislin was picturing dinner with Nate, and Mom feared a kegger.

"Can the court recess briefly?" Mom requested.

"Go ahead," Aislin said. "We'll be here."

I waited for their footsteps to fade, and then smirked. "In general?"

"If Nate asks me out, I don't want to wait for parental permission, and I'm not sneaking around."

I snorted in disbelief. "When have you *ever* snuck around?"

She winked slyly in response. "Montreal."

I tried listening very hard to the deliberations one room over, but I couldn't eavesdrop. "Why do I have to be here in the first place?"

"Because you're like my defense attorney," my sister said.

She had a point, even if her wild side was too tame to register. "More like a character witness. What's the rest of your strategy?"

"That depends on their verdict," she said.

"And you couldn't ask forgiveness instead of permission?"

"Once in a while," Aislin responded. "I'm not a robot."

"I never said you were."

"No, but you think I can't sneeze without asking permission first," she stated.

Eager to get in a cross-examination while the jury was out, I asked, "So you're that interested in Nate?"

"I like him enough for this to be an issue," she answered.

Minutes into questioning, Aislin hadn't dodged a question yet, making me proud. "Good girl."

Our tribunal returned in under five minutes, which meant they had questions, not a decision. Instead of grilling Aislin, Dad turned to me.

"Maeve, can we have a word in private with you?"

Aislin and I exchanged the same bewildered look. "Why her?" she inquired.

"The idea was Aislin's," I answered their likely first question. "Anything else?"

"If you'll wait in the next room, Aislin, we just want to clarify some things . . ."

"No," I said firmly. "You can ask me anything in front of her."

"And I'll get the same answer in public as in private?"

"Do you want me under oath?" I deadpanned.

Instead of answering, Mom addressed her question to me. "What's Mr. Hypothetical like?"

It annoyed me when they heard truth from Aislin and refused to believe it. "I've seen college boys be gentlemen and hope Ash would pick one of those."

"How were they gentlemen?"

"They were hands-off and remembered chivalry."

Dad frowned. "I'm getting the idea that he's not hypothetical."

"Not entirely," Aislin spoke up.

I was surprised that she was confessing and Mom looked self-satisfied. "The truth at last."

"He's at the library," Aislin admitted.

"Is *that* why you chose the Mugar?" Mom demanded.

"No," Aislin answered, looking exasperated. "I go there for the resources, not the scenery."

"Okay." Dad took a deep breath that didn't sound like it was to calm himself down. "What is this student's name?"

"That's classified," Aislin protested. "He's not getting a background check unless he asks me out."

I was about to countermand that and give some details to get them off of her back, but Aislin silenced me with a razor-sharp look.

"The rule about us meeting him still stands," Dad ruled. "If he refuses an introduction, you will refuse the date."

"And curfew will not be extended to accommodate him," Mom added. "You're a minor, no matter what your ID says."

"You make every guy sound like a potential stalker," I grumbled.

Dad let that one go, but I knew that he could cite statistics. Aislin waited for my next objection, but I backed down.

"I think the terms are fair," I said.

"Glad we're agreed," Mom said. "Aislin?"

"I agree to those terms," she agreed.

"Good," Dad said. "I assume that you hope he'll ask you on a date?"

"Yes, but right now, I hope he'll enjoy studying with me."

"So if we dropped in to check your work ethic, we'd meet him?" Mom asked enthusiastically.

"Absolutely *not*," I said. "I don't want you scaring him."

"Any time you want to check up on me, you're welcome to," Aislin answered, "but I'll expect you to behave yourselves."

"I won't show up with a search warrant," Dad promised.

"And I won't bring baby pictures," Mom added.

"And you won't spy from the stacks?" Aislin responded.

Mom turned to me with a disapproving look. "What stories have you been telling her?"

"Last year, you forgot to close the door before you voted my friend Most Likely to Spread Mono," I accused, making Mom blush.

"I'll introduce you to any of my friends on campus," Aislin promised. "If and when he makes a move, I'll let you know."

"Then this court is adjourned," Dad said, rapping on the table. "May God have mercy on your soul."

White

I have always been a creature of habit and being homeschooled drilled into me the need for routine. I wasn't uptight about it, but I enjoyed following a pattern for every 'school' day. As soon as I had bathed and dined, I would check my emails and get to work with few stops in between.

Three days before Halloween, Maeve invaded without knocking and elbowed me out of the way. I caught myself on the edge of the desk to prevent falling and turned to glare at her.

"Hi to you too." I tried to drive her off, but she shifted her body to block access completely. "How was your day?"

"Jill has the flu and we won our game." She accessed my email without asking for a password I'd never disclosed. "You haven't checked your email today?"

"I barely finished dinner," I protested. "Do you mind?"

"Not at all."

She stood back, grinning triumphantly and let me see the email in question. I got as far as the subject line and shot to my feet. Maeve had stepped back to give herself a buffer zone.

"You . . ."

"You're welcome," Maeve said confidently.

"I *told you* I didn't want you . . ."

"You're *welcome,*" my sister said a little more pointedly. "You—well, we—did pretty well."

"I don't care," I snapped, closing the distance between us to corner her. "I'm not using your SAT scores."

"You are," she snapped back. "I'm not letting you go to Fill-in-the-Blank Community College on principle."

"I told you that I'm getting in on my own merits," I argued.

"Meaning you can't apply to your first-choice school because of standardized tests and I can go anywhere because I was born first? That's not fair."

"I'm used to unfairness."

"Well, I don't want you to be!"

Maeve advanced until she was nose-to-nose with me, so I instinctively felt like retreating. When she raised her hand, I thought I was in for an assault. Instead, she started ticking off things on her fingers.

"Road test, police questioning, family reunion, *court dates,* community service," she enumerated. "You haven't talked me out of helping before."

"Those weren't my choice," I insisted. "For all I know, I'd have gotten solid 500s and gone where I deserved."

Maeve didn't shake me, but she seemed to be holding back from doing just that. "Don't kid yourself," she ordered. "If anything, you would have outscored me on the essay section."

"Don't kid *your*self," I echoed.

"I did nothing wrong. Even our parents approved of how helpful I was."

She had done a wonderfully selfless thing. Finding out that her summer SAT prep had been for my sake felt like five steps too far.

"You're going to get over this very quickly," Maeve informed me. "The application deadline for winter semester at BU is in less than a week."

I blanched. "I don't even know where to . . ."

"I filled out everything except the essay part," she interrupted. "You just have to be heartwarming and send it off."

"What, like how character-building molting is?"

"If that inspires you," Maeve said stubbornly. "Just don't waste my hard work out of spite."

"I'm not . . ." I paused to adjust what I was going to say and sound less like her enemy. "I'm annoyed with the whole process, not mad."

"Me, too," she admitted. "I'm tired of having all *your* fun. If that means letting you have first pick of the college guys, so be it."

Before I could talk myself out of it, I slung an arm over her shoulders and hugged her. "Thanks," I said. "I probably won't say that again."

"You will," Maeve assured me. "Once you get in, you'll forget to be mad at me."

I could only hope that she wasn't being severely optimistic about the whole thing.

Black

Two days before Halloween, I was slaving away over math when Aislin stormed into my room, brandishing her brown jacket like a weapon.

"Come in," I greeted.

"Do you want to explain this?" she demanded.

I wasn't paying much attention yet, since I was halfway through an equation. "Explain what, exactly?"

A red envelope landed on top of my math homework.

"Oh," I said casually. "That."

"That and whatever weed you have hanging above my bed."

I could have denied everything, but I had a promise to keep to Susanna.

"Yarrow improves psychic connections between you and your love."

The arm holding her jacket dropped limply to Aislin's side. "You've got to be kidding me."

"Susanna says those envelopes are meant to improve your chances of finding love," I elaborated.

"Who on earth is Susanna?" Aislin demanded.

"Susanna Betancourt." At her nonplussed stare, I sighed. "She's the Wiccan from my music class who knows Ethan."

"Wait," Aislin interrupted furiously. "*Ethan* knows?"

"Probably not," I said. "I think Susanna can be trusted."

"Oh, *good*," she snarled. "And why did you tell Susanna about me in the first place?"

"Because she actually believes in spells," I said reasonably. "In the spirit of fighting fire with fire, I asked for help."

The look on her face now was horrified instead of angry. "You found a local witch to break the curse?"

"Yeah," I replied without a shred of guilt. "I wanted to help in any way that I could."

"You took advantage of someone else's religion," Aislin snapped. "That's like practicing Judaism because you like potato pancakes."

It was more like hanging out with Catholics and hoping for an exorcism, but that wasn't the point. I also wasn't going to tell her about the "call me spell" that Susanna had performed on her phone. I shut my math book and turned to face her properly.

"Look," I reasoned, "we're just trying to help."

"I don't want this kind of help," she snapped, grabbing the envelope and chucking it in the trash, "and I don't want you assembling some task force together to interfere."

"One person is hardly a task force," I defended myself.

"The psychic?" she pointed out.

"She was just for fun," I answered honestly. "Can you say you've never considered doing this?"

"I've considered a lot of things," she said firmly, "but I would have never gone this far."

That finally broke through my resolve to deal rationally with this discussion and I threw down my pencil. "Why not?" I demanded.

"Because it's disrespectful," she answered in like tones.

"It might work," I countered. "This could help you years before a boy finds you spectacular."

"That still exploits Susanna's beliefs," Aislin rephrased.

She couldn't stop me from interfering, but she was beating a dead horse for no reason. "Fine," I said. "I won't ask Susanna for help again until you change your mind."

"Sounds like a good idea to me," she stated. "If I find any more of these, I'm going to get our parents involved."

"If you say so," I replied mildly.

I knew her wrath wouldn't last forever, but until she settled down, I would lie low.

Our credit cards didn't have the world's highest limit, but they were for discretionary use. I usually used mine when I missed the last train home or needed food during finals week, but on both occasions, I'd paid it back with extra chores.

When Mom checked this month's activity, she came immediately to me and found me prepared with a defense. She stormed into my room while my efforts were focused on homework, waving a printout and looking thunderous.

"You spent *how much* on fortune-telling?"

Given the pitch of her voice, it was a good thing that I'd paid for the magic supplies in cash.

"You didn't say that was forbidden," I stated. "You just asked me not to do anything irresponsible for our birthday."

"This isn't irresponsible," Mom snapped. "This is ridiculous."

"Actually, I think it helped," I said. "It certainly gave Aislin something to think about."

"It won't happen again," she commanded.

"Agreed," I said, holding up my hands. "And I'll work it off, of course. That's the deal for non-emergency items."

"Non-emergency items such as thirty dollars' worth of pizza?" she challenged. "I was home that night and I don't remember anything about pizza."

Magic supplies had sold for cash, but Susanna's favorite pizza place needed payment in advance. "A sophomore did me a favor."

"She gave you a kidney, perhaps?" Mom suggested.

I shrugged, since I hadn't set the terms. "It was a big favor. That's all you need to know."

Mom crossed to my bag, which was lying unattended on my desk, and yanked my wallet out of the front pocket.

"All I need to know is that this is on lockdown until you've repaid those impulse buys."

"*What?*" I set my book down so I could give this my full attention at last. "That's not fair."

"It's just," Mom corrected.

"But what if I have an emergency?" I demanded.

"Your savings should be able to cover the small stuff," she said. "And if you know what's good for you, *everything* will be small stuff."

"But you can't guarantee that an emergency won't happen," I protested.

"I can't," she agreed. "That's why Aislin still has her card."

And Aislin would never let me abuse her discretionary credit. The only emergency she'd had was when my purse was stolen and she needed gas for my ride.

"I still don't see this as something that I did wrong," I muttered resentfully.

"It doesn't demonstrate sound judgment," Mom pointed out. "Do I need to take your fake ID?"

She hadn't done it already, which meant a very small part of her recognized my good intentions.

"No," I assured her. "Dabbling in magic is as reckless as I intend to be for now."

White

My family believed that exam prep could be put off on holidays, so I could have skipped studying tonight. I compromised by heading to the library with an arrangement to meet Maeve later.

My study session was about to wrap up when a plastic pumpkin landed atop my notebook. I was unsurprised to see Nate on the other side of the table, but the mouse nose was new.

"Nice," I said. "Budget Mickey Mouse?"

"Lab rat," he explained, gesturing to the white coat. "It's supposed to be funny."

Once it was explained, it was a dorky kind of adorable. "Sorry," I said, "no candy here."

"That's why I brought my own," he said, gesturing to the pumpkin. "Have a Twix, and tell me about your cunning disguise."

I obeyed while I considered my answer. In jeans and a grey sweater, my only concession to Halloween was my black cat pin.

"I don't have a clever lie," I confessed.

"Well, that's no good." Nate yanked the pumpkin back, looking horrified. "Give me a second."

After a few moments of rummaging, he pulled out . . . a duck nose.

"You have a disguise in case of emergencies?" I laughed.

"Preparation is my watchword," Nate said solemnly. "I think this would suit you."

"You have no idea," I said before pulling the elastic over my head and adjusting the fit. "What do you think?"

"I think it's a year-round accessory," he joked.

"And maybe someday I'll turn into a beautiful swan," I mumbled past the prosthetic. "I'll get this back to you tomorrow."

"Keep it," Nate said gallantly. "It looks better on you than my roommate."

I gave him a foul look. "Thanks."

He shouldered his bag and tossed me another candy bar. "Tell me you're not staying here all night."

"No," I assured him. "I'm keeping my promise to study every day, including . . ."

"Holidays," he finished. "How many hours have you been at it?"

I knew exactly how many, but checked my watch. Concentration had not been my friend so far and Nate's sudden appearance didn't help matters any.

"Two, but my ride will be here in ten minutes to drag me to a party."

"With your boyfriend?"

"With my more socially adept older sister," I corrected, secretly pleased that he had asked. "I must have mentioned her before."

"Not really," he said. "You just said traditional Irish names run in your family."

"Namely Brendan and Maeve," I said. "Irish for 'prince' and 'intoxicating.' Mine means 'dream.'"

"You're lucky," he said. "Mine is Hebrew for 'gift of God.'"

"Don't let it go to your head."

He grinned beneath the whiskers. "Thanks."

"Where are you off to?"

"Home," he announced. "I'm in charge of food and my roommates are trying to decide between *The Exorcist* and *The Shining*."

"And you looked for food at the Mugar?" I leaned forward to impart wisdom through my beak. "I heard the fried chicken at the Tsai Center is better."

Nate nodded sagely and mimed making a note. "I also stopped by in case workaholic friends needed some holiday cheer."

"Have fun with that."

He was about to leave when I changed my mind. "Wait up," I called. "I'll walk you out."

Maeve would sigh when she found out that I offered to walk *him*, but my intentions were good. After packing up my books, and candy, I caught up to him just before he reached circulation.

"Does this mean I get to meet your ride?" he asked casually.

"Not if I have anything to say about it," I answered immediately. "If you want to be home before Thanksgiving, she can't know that you were ever here."

That sounded more threatening than I intended, but I meant every word. He shrugged in response, apparently not offended.

"Have fun then," he said.

SCENE 9

White

I was running late today. A group of men near my hiding place had forced me to hide, shivering and nervous, behind a Dumpster for five endless minutes before I could make a mad dash for my clothes. It would have been just my luck for me to get caught streaking again.

My luck held out, though, and I didn't see anyone pass by until I left my hiding spot. I fished in my bag for my travel-size hair brush and detangled it enough for a ponytail.

Mom called on my way to the T, probably to check if I needed a ride. "Hi," I said. "I've got my books with me and I'll be on my way once I find a train."

"Do you mind coming home first?"

It would take more time to get home than to hear whatever she had to say. "I don't want to keep you waiting."

"We'll wait," Mom said, forestalling any argument. "Give us an ETA and Maeve can pick you up."

I was apparently in for a lecture or a punishment and nothing came to mind that would fit either option. That probably meant Maeve had been involved in the crime.

"Okay," I acquiesced.

Maeve met me at the station, looking exasperated instead of nervous. I welcomed the chance to get details on our way back.

"How much trouble are we in?" I asked after a minute of small talk. "She called me home from *studying*."

"Maybe she didn't want to procrastinate this discussion," my sister suggested. "It's happened before."

"*Once.*"

"Don't worry," Maeve said, grinning at the road. "Dad's not home, so it's not capital punishment."

We pulled up to the house and Mom greeted me with a plate of pork chops. "Eat," she ordered. "We'll talk after dinner."

If I was reading her right, this was mothering, not a last meal.

"Thanks," I sighed, inhaling deeply to show my appreciation. "This is much better than an on-campus sandwich."

"You had a good day?" she asked on the way into the kitchen.

"It was pretty boring," I corrected. "The tourists are flocking, so I went to a duck pond and mostly dodged stale bread."

"So you don't want toast," she guessed.

"No, thanks."

I ate quickly and as soon as I'd done dishes, Mom called Maeve down for the talk.

"If you recall, you two will be on your own this weekend."

"Have fun with Aunt Diane," I responded dutifully.

"We will," Mom answered, "but you are here to agree to the rules. This is the first time we've left you on your own and . . ."

"We know," Maeve interrupted. "No wild parties . . ."

"No parties at all," Mom corrected.

Maeve focused with unsurprising speed. It was a cardinal sin to have the house to yourself and not take advantage of it.

"Not even slumber?" my sister haggled.

"Not after what Natalie did to her parents' house last month," I guessed unhelpfully.

Maeve frowned. "Natalie had a few friends over . . ."

"I heard," Mom deadpanned. "Did she have trouble getting those stains out?"

"How do you know . . ."

"Secret raves don't belong on social media," Mom said calmly.

"Natalie's definition of a party breaks a few laws," I agreed.

Maeve's glare was sulky one. "You're not supposed to side against me."

"I've seen the pictures," I pointed out. "I'm not helping you clean up *that*."

Maeve held up her hands in surrender, still giving me an angry look. "Fine," she said. "No parties."

"What about a low-key night in?" I proposed. "We'll have one friend over each, watch a movie and show them the door during credits. I could invite Sosi . . ."

"And I could see what Laurie's doing," Maeve considered.

Mom pursed her lips, obviously debating the idea's merits. It was certainly a safe option.

"One person each," she said at last. "I *will* know if you cheat."

"How? Hidden camera?" Maeve joked.

"Worse." Mom smirked. "I'll ask Aislin."

I was a lousy liar, so that was a valid threat.

"I'll call the girls tonight," Maeve offered. "You definitely want to invite Sosi?"

"Definitely," I confirmed.

She was no longer looking like I'd canceled Christmas. "I'll make all the arrangements."

"I get to pick the movie," I countered. "What else?"

"You both have dentist appointments tomorrow at six," Mom said. "Unless you are hospitalized, you will be there so Dr. Wharton doesn't waste his last appointments of the day."

"Fine," Maeve said. "I'll need the car."

"I had planned on it. And finally . . ."

"There has to be a third thing?" I asked. "I'm sort of running late."

"The third thing is that you should be ready when Dad picks you up tonight," Mom said, ignoring my complaint.

"Got it."

Mom glanced at Maeve instead of adding another rule. "Don't you have a book to finish?"

"I'm dismissed?"

"You are liberated," Mom replied formally with a wave of her hand. "Aislin, since I interrupted your study time, I can drive you to campus."

"While I'm here, I want to grab another book," I lied. "Give me a minute."

"Go ahead."

I bolted up the stairs to Maeve's room. Her door was ajar, but I knocked first and found her staring blankly at her Norton anthology. She looked up and closed it decisively.

"Do you have that book I lent you?" I asked loudly enough for Mom.

"Yeah, just a second," Maeve responded in kind. "Sosi's in. Laurie's next."

"*Just* Sosi?" I challenged.

"I don't have time to misbehave," Maeve said, looking disgruntled. "I'll be good."

"Good." I grabbed a book at random from her shelf. "Just in case."

"Yeah, but that's not homework," Maeve snorted. A moment later, she offered the MLA handbook. "Are you seeing *him* tonight?"

"I don't know," I answered as usual.

She snatched my bag out of my hands and carried it to her vanity. She returned it with lip gloss and breath mints.

"Just in case."

I used a breath mint on my way to the car, but didn't use lip gloss until I reached campus. At the Mugar doors, I was grateful for Maeve's foresight. Nate was standing outside, talking to two guys. I smiled on my way past, but steered clear.

"Hey, wait up," he called unexpectedly.

I did an about-face and tried not to feel apprehensive, proceeding with caution around a potential date. "Hey," I responded.

"You're later than usual," Nate commented. "Everything okay?"

I felt slightly embarrassed that he was keeping tabs on my schedule. "I had business at home," I explained. "Were you waiting?"

"Sort of," Nate said. He gestured two the other guys. "These are my roommates, Noah and Foster. This is Aislin."

"Nice to meet you," Noah greeted, shaking my hand. "How's the shoulder?"

"Getting better, thanks," I responded warily. "He mentioned that?"

"He kept us waiting on the Fourth of July," Foster said, "so he told us he'd rescued a fair maiden. When he said you'd shown up here, we thought you were imaginary."

"Not a chance."

"I don't know," Noah said. "He claimed to know a pretty bookworm who needed his help. It's kind of far-fetched."

"All right," Nate interrupted. "She's real and you're annoying. Go home."

"Sure," Noah drawled. "Enjoy your privacy."

I wasn't sure why we needed privacy, but waved them away. "Good to meet you," I called.

"Save me some pizza," Nate added.

Foster gave him a thumbs-up and jogged off.

"They seem nice," I observed.

"They're good guys." He shrugged and turned back to me. "How flexible is your schedule?"

"Not very," I said apologetically. "My ride home is my cop Dad."

"Oh." He gave a grimace of his own. "If I had known that you were being held prisoner . . ."

I resisted the urge to smack him playfully on the arm for that joke, since I didn't casually strike relative strangers. "When my police escort is ready to leave, I don't argue."

"So, no midnight trips to somewhere exciting."

"Not on a school night," I said a little sheepishly. "Not while I'm a minor, anyway."

Not to mention I always felt a bit of guilt when I used my fake ID. Maeve had different scruples, but I didn't really want to use it until my ages matched up.

"Well, what about something quick?"

He was actually trying to ask me out, but the timing was rotten and I felt unprepared for the suggestion. I fumbled for an excuse or a decent answer and came up with the truth instead.

"It'll have to wait for another time," I apologized, hefting my backpack for emphasis. "What about another night?"

"I could bring you something later," he suggested. "I've already gotten my work done."

"And you waited around for me?" It seemed flattering but unlikely. "I didn't know."

"Don't worry about it," Nate insisted. "I just wanted it over with before . . ."

He trailed off again and scuffed his feet awkwardly. I couldn't tell if he or I felt more awkward at this point.

"I'd love to," I said quickly. "I wouldn't rather study, but it's just . . ."

"Bad timing," Nate finished. "I get it."

He looked relieved for a moment before he pulled a straight face. "Let me clarify. Could I take you out some other time?"

All of his mannerisms had pointed towards this, but the words made my heart flutter anyway. It was like getting a test back after I suspected that I'd aced it. I answered before I could second-guess myself.

"Absolutely," I said.

This time, the relieved grin stayed on both our faces for a while.

Black

Aislin was home before midnight with Dad as the driver. While I made detours, he rarely overshot pumpkin time.

My light was already out, but my sister opened the door anyway. "You awake?"

"I don't know," I muffled into my pillow. "Should I be up for this?"

Her answer was to turn on my desk lamp. I rolled over and noticed that she was wearing my lip gloss and a grin.

"You saw Nate," I said approvingly.

"I did," Aislin confirmed.

"With your hair like that?"

She rolled her eyes. Making her wear makeup was a major demand and asking her to try beach waves would cross the line.

"He didn't mind my hair."

If he liked her with boring hair, he would swoon on a good day. "'Atta girl."

Aislin looked grateful for my enthusiasm, even if she didn't share it yet. "He's going to call me tomorrow so we can schedule our date when . . ."

I restrained a shriek so our parents would stay asleep, but I tried to hug the life out of her. It was my go-to expression of extreme excitement.

"Glad you're happy," Aislin wheezed when I let go.

"Tell me all about it," I urged. "Was it his idea? When did it happen?"

"It was," she answered, "and he waited for me to get there tonight."

"Yes?" I prompted. She was being annoyingly circumspect. "How so?"

"Well, he thought we could go out tonight," she admitted, "but I don't circumvent rules with Dad on watch."

I nodded sympathetically. I had made that mistake once and promptly learned my lesson. "So you suggested another day?"

"I made sure he knew it could happen another time," Aislin reassured me.

"So you gave him a raincheck."

"*Yes,*" she said emphatically. "The circumstances were wrong, but my answer was yes."

Satisfied with the play-by-play, I hugged her again. She must have been just as happy about it as I was, since she didn't try to push me off.

"And then, he . . . ," I prompted.

"Carried my books to the library," she added.

I couldn't criticize her technique so far and that was a major milestone. "So he's already been chivalrous twice," I said with a nod of approval. "That's a good first step."

"No," Aislin replied, her voice very quiet now. "It's more important that he remains a gentleman."

"Whatever," I responded airily. "It's your romance."

Our smiles matched for a few more seconds before she reached for the lamp switch and I grabbed her wrist to stop her.

"When are you telling *them?*" I asked.

"Preferably before you do."

It was a low blow, but after years of meddling, I'd earned that. "Before or after the date?"

"*Before.*"

"So some time . . ."

"After they get back, yes," Aislin finished.

"Are you *crazy?*" My voice squeaked a little in horror. "You're waiting until *next* week?"

"The guy asked me out knowing my parents are involved in my life. He can wait until he's had an introduction."

"Then you can do it this weekend," I suggested.

"Not a chance," she insisted.

"You're no fun," I accused.

She shrugged and turned the lamp off. "I never pretended I was anything else," she reminded me. "Good night."

Nick and I had a standing agreement that he was allowed to drive me home three times a week. Mom and Dad didn't like weeknight dates, so this was our loophole.

Wednesday, I met him after my post-soccer shower and he kissed me in a way that wouldn't bring down the wrath of any passing teachers. Then he slung my gym bag over his free shoulder and walked me out.

"So, what are we doing this weekend?"

"Not much, I'm afraid," I said apologetically. "Nothing on Friday night . . ."

"Why not?"

"Well, for one thing, my parents are going to Florida . . ."

"Which means you bend curfew," he pointed out.

"Which means neighbors will be watching," I corrected.

"So, what are you doing on Friday?"

I liked it when he sounded jealous, even when there was no good reason for it. "Girl bonding time. You wouldn't be interested."

"Depends on the girls." He paused, considering. "If I come, can I get a facial?"

"No boys in the house without parental supervision," I mandated.

"I'm not a boy," he objected. "I'm an upstanding young man with old-fashioned boundaries."

"Yes, you are," I agreed. "Sosi and Laurie are coming over for a movie night and that's as far as it goes. Aislin's busy Saturday and Sunday, so I think we can escape then."

"If you think she might get lonely, we could double again," he offered in a weary sort of voice.

I leaned over and kissed him quickly on the cheek. Nick looked pleased by the affection, but also confused. "What was that for?"

"Caring about my sister's feelings," I said. "You're sweet."

"I try," he said modestly. "So, was that your answer to my idea?"

"Ethan hasn't made a move in weeks," I said sharply. "I'm not making him take initiative until he's ready."

"Sure," he agreed.

"And even so, Aislin has another interested party."

"*Really*?" He looked both impressed and surprised. "Since when?"

"She practically moved into the BU library," I said. "It's not what I'd do, but it works for her. I don't think rekindling things with Ethan is fair to the new guy."

"Yeah, but are you going to tell Ethan that she's moved on?"

I suspected ulterior motives, but I appreciated his concern for Ethan's feelings; if things went downhill, he knew that Aislin would come first again.

"Not unless he asks," I said firmly. "I don't want to rub it in his face."

"Then I won't bring it up," he promised.

They'd behaved on our double date, but I knew Nick and Ethan were unlikely to connect over anything but notes. He was just being the supportive boyfriend that I'd hoped he'd mature into.

"I appreciate that."

As it turned out, Nick wasn't the one to break the code of silence. When I passed Ethan's desk in English on Friday, he spoke up.

"Do you mind if I ask a question?"

He was looking resolute and good-tempered, which meant that he probably wanted to talk about the other Byrne sister.

"Sure." I dropped into Melanie's still-empty seat and gave him my undivided attention. "What's up?"

"I just aced my midterms and I thought I'd celebrate," Ethan announced.

"Was there ever any doubt?"

"I wouldn't study this hard if I didn't think there was a chance I could flunk," Ethan said seriously.

"Aislin's the same way," I chuckled. "She's convinced she's going to choke, so she studies five times harder than me. Why do you ask?"

"Well, I was hoping you could tell me Aislin's plans for the weekend," he explained.

The puppy-dog eyes were completely unnecessary, but I had the feeling that they were involuntary.

"Aislin's a free agent," I said. "You should call her and find out."

"What do you mean by free agent?" he asked quickly.

"I mean she makes her decisions," I corrected myself. "Today, she's staying in with the girls."

"What about Saturday or Sunday?"

As a previous date, he could bypass the parent-meeting requirement, but I was staying out of this decision.

"Call her, see if she's available," I urged.

Aislin was waiting for me when I got home from practice, looking unnecessarily stormy. "You ratted me out," she accused. "Ethan called."

"The most you've promised to Nate is dinner," I stated. "He brought it up."

"It would have been nice if you warned me," Aislin protested.

"So you've told him no?"

"I haven't talked to him." Her voice was plaintive, her mouth pinched. This was a bit much for a back-up plan. "I've got my first date with Nate on Tuesday."

"This means no strings are attached."

"It's still not fair to lead Ethan on."

Sometimes, we were perfectly identical and sometimes, I couldn't believe we shared any genes. "You're not leading him on."

"I'm going out with him when there's a chance that it won't happen again," she responded.

"Which is what everyone does until they get committed."

"I didn't get the impression that Ethan dates a lot of people. We take it a lot more seriously . . ."

I wasn't sure if she'd meant to admit that. "Let me hear the message," I requested.

She hesitated, but eventually handed her phone over. I put it on speaker and held it between us.

"It's, um, Ethan. I'm thinking of maybe going out for food and I thought, well, we've had fun and I didn't know your schedule . . . So, yeah. Call me back either way. Thanks. Bye."

I expected more coherence from him, but it was endearing. Leaving a message for a girl turned him from a straight-A student to a babbling idiot. I appreciated his lack of dignity and Aislin could relate to someone lacking the suave gene.

"Sounds like fun," I commented. "Why not call him back?"

"Because I . . ."

"Don't want to lead him on," I finished. "Sorry, stupid question. Do you still want him as a friend?"

"If that's possible," Aislin said quietly to her hands.

"It's not like you got a restraining order," I scoffed.

Aislin tucked her hands under her legs and hunched her shoulders uncertainly, but looked more relaxed than before. "I'm not used to this," she admitted.

"I know," I said as gently as I could. "I've been through this myself."

"So, who explained the guidelines to you?" Aislin asked.

"No one," I responded. "There are things that can be taught, like hair and makeup, but others everyone figures out the hard way. I had no idea how to ask a guy out and was a jerk to my first ex."

"In 8th grade, I had a crush and I think we exchanged twenty words total," Aislin recalled glumly. "It's not like I've had a lot of lessons."

"What, you haven't been practicing your feminine wiles on Sandeep at Dunkin' Donuts?"

Her brow furrowed at the joke. "Sandeep works the general reference desk at the Mugar, not Dunkin' Donuts. Nate's got a very rough draft of my romantic self."

"I lecture because you don't have time for trial and error," I interjected so we could get back on topic. "I don't want you making my mistakes."

Aislin's shoulders inched downwards until she looked less like a turtle and more like my sister. "I don't want that either," she conceded.

"Then you should give Ethan a chance until Nate makes more than one move."

"And you don't think he'll hate me?"

"I don't think he really needs to know."

At least for now.

SCENE 10

White

Within five minutes of the decision, I had called Ethan and enthusiastically planned dinner at 6:30 on Saturday. I went to fill Maeve in and found that she'd been joined by both of our guests.

"So?" Sosi asked immediately. "How did your pressing business go?"

I rolled my eyes in Maeve's direction. "What did you tell them?"

"That you were up there with your little black book and we shouldn't bother you," Laurie supplied. "Who's been penciled in?"

"Say it's Ethan," Sosi urged. "You guys were so cute together."

Even though Maeve claimed I was missing out on normal teenage conversation, these two were making up for it. "It's Ethan and we're going out tomorrow," I said.

"And someone else a different night?" Laurie guessed. "That's surprising."

Maeve immediately smacked her on the arm. "Be nice," she ordered.

Laurie held her hands up in surrender, but didn't look apologetic and I recognized Natalie's influence. "Sorry, I didn't think your schedule was busy."

"Not anymore," I commented, heading for the living room. "I might be in college this winter."

"Wow." Sosi looked suitably impressed by my choice to graduate early. "I didn't think you were that far ahead of us."

"Me either," I agreed, picking up the movie I'd selected. "Everyone good with this?"

"I haven't seen it," Laurie said.

"I liked it," Maeve added.

"Sounds fine," Sosi concluded, making room for me on her couch. "So, you're getting a GED and will get your PhD at twenty?"

"Not likely." It was my turn to laugh. "My parents just convinced me to benefit from professional teachers. I think they did fine, even if my usual essay topics were unconventional."

"You never know until you try," Maeve said. "I never did very well with the unconventional."

"Yeah, but you're less-skilled at satire," I said. "You take things too seriously."

"That's what I say about you," Maeve shot back.

"Honestly, if someone had me actually write a three-point thesis statement, I'd be doomed."

"You'll master the art of paper-writing," Sosi said, "but you'll get to pick a major and ignore everything else."

"And you'll have college boys," Laurie pointed out. "I'm a little jealous."

"Which brings us back to your hot date next week," Maeve concluded.

This time, I glowered at Maeve. "I plead the Fifth Amendment."

"That's not its use," Sosi said. "I can respect a gag order, though."

Which was why she was one of my friends and Laurie was someone I just sort of tolerated. "Thanks," I said. "There's little to say."

"He's cute, though," Maeve supplied when I stayed mute.

"How cute?" Laurie demanded avidly giving me her undivided attention. "Muscles?"

"He has them," I deadpanned. "He studies physical therapy, so he can probably name them."

"But you've seen him shirtless?" she challenged.

"I've seen him almost exclusively at a library," I said. "Who would be shirtless in . . ."

"Jared," Sosi and Maeve chorused before collapsing in laughter.

I had no idea who that was, but he was definitely off my list of acceptable blind dates.

"Eyes?"

I resisted the urge to avoid the question. "A very nice brown," I said to my keen audience. "Hair's the same."

"But does he have *gorgeous* eyes?" Maeve insisted. "Do you fantasize about gazing into them while he holds you in his strong arms . . ."

"Please stop."

"Does he look like he's a good kisser?" Sosi asked. "You can tell a lot about a guy by his mouth."

"Please," I repeated. "*Stop.*"

"Don't tell me you haven't thought about *any of this*," Maeve ordered.

"Do you know me at all?" I countered.

If anyone in the family could write a romance novel, it was Maeve. She used her imagination to fill in the gaps in my love life and our mutual friends weren't much better.

"Well, good for you," Laurie said at last. "Dropping the subject now."

I'd believe it when I didn't hear it, but I didn't say so. The movie distracted us all for the next couple of hours. I had chosen a non-mushy comedy and no one seemed to mind in the end.

We kicked Sosi and Laurie out a little after the agreed-upon time, reasoning that popsicles would keep Laurie from falling asleep behind the wheel.

I gave Maeve two minutes' grace during cleanup, but as soon as the house was restored to its proper order, I rounded on her. She smiled placidly in response to the severely irritated look on my face.

"I think that went well," she commented.

"Everything was great," I agreed, "except for the part where you all obsessed over my love life."

"I *wasn't . . .*" She paused and changed tactics smoothly. "So I bragged about you a little."

"And how long do you think it'll take for Laurie to tell Natalie, who will probably tell Ethan for fun?"

"Give her a little credit," Maeve said, the smile sliding off her face. "You're assuming Laurie's just like everyone else you dislike."

"I'm assuming there was more to those questions than polite interest," I corrected.

Maeve didn't seem fazed by this criticism. "I think you overestimate how much Laurie cares," Maeve criticized over her shoulder on her way upstairs. "I thought you were happy about seeing Ethan again."

"I wanted to be happy about it without an audience," I said. "Was that unreasonable?"

She didn't answer, just left me standing in the upstairs hallway with only my annoyance and apprehension to keep me company.

Black

Nick had claimed Sunday, so I staged a jailbreak on Saturday. With Aislin out, Natalie and Laurie volunteered to keep me company. All I had to do was respect curfew.

Playing it by ear usually just meant that we'd spontaneously find a new store to check out or eat at a favorite place, people-watching all the way. Natalie got two guys' phone numbers before we even boarded the T. I knew she wouldn't ever call them because she liked keeping tally more than actually dating.

"Your turn next," Laurie announced after getting one herself.

"I don't need phone numbers. I've got Nick."

"And we're very happy for you," Natalie said impatiently, "but flirting muscles can atrophy."

"Two-timing isn't my style," I retorted.

"This isn't even that," Natalie insisted. "No physical contact necessary."

"Or encouraged," Laurie added helpfully. "That's the lazy girl's way to a man's heart."

"Whoa." I held up a hand. "Now you're just fighting dirty."

"You're stalling," she shot back. "Get moving."

Nick would probably laugh at the guys I chose, but it would be fun to give it a shot and it would shut them both up.

"Nick won't find out," Natalie reconsidered. "It's just a number, not a fling."

"I'm not the type to have flings," I pointed out.

"You're not over the hill yet, and neither is green sweatshirt at six o'clock," Laurie answered. "Go for it."

Green sweatshirt guy had dark hair and a cute enough backside for me to look forward to a front view.

"Go, fight, win," Natalie added before shoving me in his direction.

He wasn't facing my way, so he didn't see me stumble like a nervous freshman. By the time I was ready to approach, I'd found my footing and was now a casual passerby. He got bonus points for not having earphones plugged in and reading a book. Since I wasn't Aislin, I couldn't use Twain as an icebreaker. That narrowed my range of pickup lines, but they were all good ones.

He turned to check the route of an incoming train and looked bewilderingly like I'd just made his weekend. "Hey," he said. "I thought you were booked today."

I suddenly forgot every clever thing I had planned to say. "I'm sorry," I blurted out. "Did I reject you before?"

"Not really," he said with a laugh. "You *do* remember our last conversation, right?"

"Honestly, no," I said. I might have seen him before, but nothing about him was familiar. "Your name starts with a D?"

"N," he corrected, his smile going a little wooden. "Well, this is humiliating."

That went for the both of us. He looked a little like one of our football players, but . . .

And then my brain caught up.

"N?" I asked quickly. "As in Nathaniel?"

"I knew we'd get there eventually," he said, looking slightly less crestfallen. "Does that mean you're not going to dinner with me?"

"Nate from Michigan, the future physical therapist . . ." It was time to let an explanation fix things. "My sister has told me *so much* about you."

Color flooded back into his face and I couldn't tell if he was blushing or just relieved that he had made a lasting impression. "Your sister," he echoed.

I dug into my purse and whipped out my real license. I held it up for comparison so he could see I wasn't bluffing, and then handed it over for closer inspection.

"I'm Maeve," I explained, "and you're Aislin's favorite person on campus."

His red face was now definitely caused by a blush. "Aislin didn't mention her sister was a dead ringer," he admitted.

"I promise I'm not crazy. We just haven't been introduced."

He passed the license back, turning the handoff into a handshake. "I'm Nate," he said. "Some crazy is good."

I wondered if he'd feel the same if he ran into my sister before she'd washed leaves and twigs from her hair.

"I'm glad you know that," I said, letting go of his perfectly nice hand. "It's nice to meet you."

"You too," he commented. "So, what were you actually doing over here?"

"Trying to get your number," I admitted with genuine embarrassment.

"Flattering," he said. "Do you still want it?"

"My gorgeous sister is the only one who needs it," I said, waving a hand vaguely.

"I thought she had plans with you," he commented.

"For about half of the weekend, but she's . . ." I couldn't think of a lie at the moment. "We had separate agendas for the evening and people-watching isn't her thing."

"Fair enough." He shoved both hands in his pockets and glanced in the direction of Natalie and Laurie. "Where are you headed?"

"Wherever the next train takes us," I said. "What about you?"

"Copley," he answered. "I have to find a budget-friendly present for my sister's birthday."

"Try somewhere less downtown," I advised. "Copley's fun, but you're not going to budget shop there."

"Thanks for the advice," Nate responded. "Any places you'd recommend instead?"

"Not off the top of my head," I said, "but come over here and we'll brainstorm."

I could have called Aislin as soon as I had cell reception, but I held off until I got home to tell her. She got back respectfully before curfew, looking satisfied with her evening instead of happy. I ambushed her in the living room as soon as soon as the coast was clear of Ethan.

"I met Nate," I announced.

She dropped her purse and turned the same shade of red that Nate had been sporting. "You *what?*"

"We were at Government Center and he thought I was you and I *met* Nate." I bent over to retrieve her purse. "You were right about him being cute."

"I didn't tell you he was cute," Aislin argued.

"No, you didn't," I agreed, "but you actually talked about his looks, which means he's special."

"Wait." She calmed down while hanging her jacket in the hall closet. When she came back, she was a normal shade of pale. "Start at the beginning."

"Well, first I made an idiot of myself trying to identify him. Then he felt embarrassed by your apparent amnesia. Then I realized who he was and we got along fine after that."

"So, who started the conversation?" she asked.

"He did," I stated. "He seemed pretty overjoyed to see you, actually."

"I wouldn't go that far," Aislin said, looking uncomfortable.

"Who's telling this story?" I challenged.

"Sorry," she replied. "I just don't think he's emotionally attached yet."

"Maybe not," I conceded, "but I practically hurt his feelings by not recognizing him."

She looked uncertain as to whether that was a good thing. "Please tell me you didn't try to flirt with him."

"No," I assured her. "I was supposed to get his number, but as he's *yours* . . ."

"He's not *mine.*"

"Give him a few dates," I said confidently.

She grimaced and turned to head for the stairs. "Maybe."

After the amount of gloating that she'd done when she got Nate's number, I expected more. Maybe tonight's side-adventure with Ethan had been a bad idea.

"Having second thoughts?" I guessed.

"Not really," she said. "Ethan didn't bring up going out again tonight."

"Oh." That might not be a bad thing, but she'd admitted to taking things seriously. "But it wasn't really a date."

"No, it wasn't," she sighed. "It was fun, and he was as nice as last time."

"But he wasn't earth-shakingly the one for you."

She gave me the familiar look that said I was being idealistic about true love. I probably looked the same way when she settled for merely liking a guy.

"And I don't know that anyone is or ever will be."

This was the problem with having a fairy-tale creature twin. She had the emotions of a seventeen-year-old and the experience of a thirteen-year-old.

"I've always expected that," I conceded.

"I know." Aislin turned and headed for the stairs, with me following. "That's why I don't get as worked up about every date as you do. I'm fine if he's always fun and nice. It feels perfectly normal."

"So you're not hoping Nate's The One?" I pressed.

"Do we have to psychoanalyze *every* date?"

"I'm just wondering," I protested.

"I'm hoping every guy's The One," she answered, turning to face me, "but if I put that much pressure on every male encounter, I'll be disappointed."

"Fair enough," I said, catching up. "Whatever it takes to make you happy, I think you should go for it."

I was sounding more like a couples' counselor than a sister again. "Thanks for your permission," Aislin muttered.

She knew that wasn't what I meant, but maybe she didn't like the idea that I'd vetted Nate on my own.

"No charge."

"And thanks for not scaring him off," she added on the top step.

She was definitely smarting about it, but it was for her own good. If Nate needed an ally in the Byrne family, he had made one tonight.

SCENE 11

Black

Third period on a Monday morning was rarely worth mentioning; the friends I had in that period were seated too far away for note-passing. Math wasn't my favorite subject, so I only raised my hand when class participation helped my average.

The most fascinating thing in math today was chewing gum on the back of Meg Larsen's skirt. I would have paid more attention to the lecture if not for that.

"Maeve."

I jerked out of my reverie and quickly checked my notes to try and guess which question was being asked. I had written down *hypotenuse* before doodling and I scrambled for the answer.

"Can you repeat the question?" I blurted out.

"You're wanted in the office," Mr. Watts said, brandishing a note. "Take your bag."

"I'll get you my notes later," Avril offered from two rows over.

I packed my bag hurriedly, but I was still lost when I finished. Maybe it was something administrative, not disciplinary.

"Thanks," I murmured to Watts on my way out.

The office wasn't far from my math classroom and I didn't take my time getting there. I theoretically had nothing to fear, so I decided to just get it over with.

"Maeve Byrne," I introduced myself.

"You've got a call," the secretary answered, pointing to the phone.

I set down my bag so I'd have my hands free, but kept out my post-its and a pencil in case I needed to take notes.

"Maeve Byrne," I answered the phone. "May I ask who's calling?"

"It's Mom," she said breathlessly. "I've signed you out for the day and Sarah Lord says she can be there in five minutes . . ."

I made it to the front steps before I realized that I had left my bag behind.

It took about ten minutes to get from Cambridge to Massachusetts General Hospital on a good day. The traffic wasn't bad this early in the day, but ten felt like thirty in a crisis. Mrs. Lord, our neighbor, had the decency to not make small talk or give advice. She kept the music off so I could only hear my quick breathing and the engine humming. The turn signal clicked occasionally, but I barely noticed.

I wrenched the door open before we came to a stop at the hospital and she uttered her third sentence since picking me up. "Call me if you need a ride home."

"Thank you."

"You're in our . . ."

I slammed the door before she could finish that sentence and grimaced apologetically before turning to go. Right now, I didn't care much about manners.

I got quick directions at the information desk and broke into a run. I missed the turn the first time and twice stopped for staff or patients, but I finally found Mom in a waiting room. I caught her looking vulnerable, her fist pressed against her mouth and her eyes squeezed shut against the glare of the overhead lights. She looked very close to vomiting.

After a few seconds, Mom opened her eyes and half of the tension left her. She unfurled herself from the chair and hugged me tighter than usual. Our ragged breathing matched, which made sense.

"Dad's still in surgery," she reported.

"For what?" I challenged. "You just said he was hurt."

Her sudden pallor made me feel guilty. "He broke up a knife fight," she said. "They didn't tell me many details."

"Where's his partner?"

"Doing his job," Mom explained. "He said he'd be by later, but he had to stay behind . . ."

She swayed for a moment and I adjusted my stance so I could hold her up if it got worse. "Let's sit down," I said. "Did you drive here?"

"Yes," she said as she found her way back to the chair. "I couldn't wait for a ride."

"Have you told Brendan?" I pressed.

She nodded and replaced her elbows on her knees, hands clasped behind her neck. "He's driving up now. I didn't want him to panic, but there was a chance . . ."

"We want to be here," I lied.

I didn't want to be here, but I disliked being in the dark more. I wanted to rewind the day to my boring math class, but she had done me a favor by calling.

For lack of anything better to do, I wrapped an arm around her shoulders and held on until our synchronized breathing stopped sounding like we'd just run a 5K.

"It's bad," Mom murmured some time later.

She was answering the question that I had been afraid to ask. It didn't help when she read my mind. It made me worried that she would answer the questions that I was trying to secret away.

"Did you get to talk to him beforehand?" I asked patiently.

"I got to see him," she responded. "I told him . . ."

Her voice broke and I didn't want to hear how brave and comforting she'd been, since I was neither. "What time do you think Brendan will be here?" I asked. "It should take about five hours, but I bet he'll be here in four."

She nodded absently and let her hands unclasp and fall to her sides. "Brendan's checking in every hour and I'll tell him if there's news."

"I can take care of that," I offered. "Is there anyone else waiting by the phone?"

"I hadn't gotten any further than immediate family," she said.

"That's okay—it can wait. Once we have more news, we can let everyone know how well he's doing."

She went through a kind of full-body shudder and rocked forward into a standing position. "They'll want to know before then."

I couldn't try to keep my grandparents from panicking when they were a thousand miles away. Mass emails would only lead to dozens of phone calls. If I told Laurie, I could be sure that everyone this side of the Mississippi would know what happened, but that wouldn't help.

Mom checked her watch and her mouth tightened. "Where does Aislin land today?"

I had thought that she was counting the length of the surgery and hadn't thought once about how long it was until the sun set on this terror.

"By the skate park," I said without having to think about it. "I can pick her up once Brendan's here."

This was usually when TV characters suggested eating, but panic kept my throat tight. I couldn't stop thinking about the tremor in Mom's voice and wanted to get as far away from here as possible, but I couldn't leave without news. I wanted to stay until her fear eased, but I wanted to be at the skate park before sunset and swan-nap Aislin.

Aislin would transform exhausted and grubby and not care that she hadn't showered yet. We would probably have answers to her million questions by then and she'd deal with fresh hell when the rest of us were veterans of it.

I didn't know whether or not to envy her.

White

I touched down just before sunset to find Maeve holding my clothes by the idling car. "Come on," she said without preamble.

I didn't wait for night to fall, just scrambled into the front seat so she could get going immediately. I ducked down just before the transformation and spent a very uncomfortable minute pulling on clothes between the seat and glove compartment.

"Brendan's with Mom," Maeve said simply once I was upright in my seat.

I suddenly forgot how to buckle a seatbelt. If Brendan was here, this was a significant crisis.

"Where are we going?"

"MGH," she said. "It's Dad."

My gorge rose immediately and I had to swallow several times before I could croak out one word: "Gun?"

"No," she said sharply.

"But something happened," I insisted. "He wouldn't be there if it weren't serious."

"It wasn't a gun," Maeve said in her reasonable voice. "It was a knife."

The world spun suddenly and I barked, "Pull over!"

She obeyed in time for me to free myself of the car and vomit all over the side of the road. I dry-heaved for another minute, but by the time that stopped, I was sobbing. I heard Maeve turn on the hazard lights and park the car, but it took a minute for her to circle the car and pull me into a hug.

"I know," was all she said.

That was a lie. She was the shoulder to cry on and Brendan had known long enough to drive from Philadelphia to Boston. I couldn't tell if I was more furious or traumatized.

"They pulled me out of school, but when I left, he was out of surgery and they think . . ."

"Someone with a knife put him in *surgery*," I keened. "Someone *intentionally* . . ."

I couldn't get another word out. With Dad, I couldn't stomach the thought of him being close to such danger. This was the guy who tutored Brendan in French and wore mouse ears for our entire trip to Disneyland. The mental image of someone knifing him made me pull away and dry-heave again.

"I know," Maeve echoed herself.

"When?"

"This morning," she supplied. "The surgery was to repair damage to his liver."

My palms covered my face, but I kept seeing a knife being thrust purposefully into my father's stomach, a spray of blood . . .

"He's out of surgery," I rasped.

"Yes, and it went fine," Maeve insisted. "He'll probably be in the hospital for a week."

The nausea and vertigo passed in another minute, but the tremors that stayed felt like hypothermia instead of horror. No embrace could stop them yet.

"He won't be lucid tonight," she commented. "Do you want to go home?"

"No," I said, pulling away. "Drive."

After a long moment in which I didn't pretend to be fine, she nodded. "Strap in," she ordered. "I'm going to break the land speed record."

I did as ordered and she returned to the driver's side, only stopping to grab me a water bottle from the trunk. My shaking hands failed to open it, so she twisted the top off.

At the moment when Maeve finally found an opening in the traffic, her phone rang. "You answer it," she suggested.

"Hi, Mom," I greeted on speakerphone.

"Maeve found you," she breathed.

I could have asked Maeve how many swans she'd kidnapped before me, but it wasn't time to lighten the mood. I'd feel slightly less guilty for being absent for most of the crisis if I took all of this seriously.

"Yes," I said. "We're on our way."

"Dad woke up," she said. "He wasn't very alert, but it's a start."

"Good," I muttered stupidly.

"Did he say anything?" Maeve prompted.

"He asked why Brendan was here."

At least he hadn't been awake long enough to notice our absence. "If he wakes up again . . ."

"I'll let him know you're on your way," Mom promised, "but I don't think that will happen."

"So we shouldn't worry about being stuck in traffic," Maeve called out.

"Call Brendan when you're getting close," Mom instructed. "He'll show you up. And drive safe."

"Yes, ma'am," Maeve responded. "We'll see you soon."

Mom hung up and I held the phone in my hand just in case it

started ringing again. "Are you okay?" I asked belatedly.

"I'm not great," Maeve admitted. "It was a long day in the waiting room."

"You were probably just what Mom needed," I said in an attempt to be consoling.

She glanced sideways at me, her expression neutral. "She knows you would have been there if you could have."

"I'm not blaming anyone," I lied. "I'm just glad she wasn't alone."

Her expression didn't change, but she let out a very quiet sigh. "Me too."

After hugging me hard enough to bruise, Mom offered the chair closest to the bed. "We've all had our turn," she said.

I fit my hand around Dad's, but he didn't stir at all. He looked better than I had imagined in those first few minutes of panic, but seemed somehow worried and uncomfortable. I immediately moved the chair closer and rested our hands on the bed.

"Did the doctors say anything?" I asked. "Maeve's answers don't cover a lot."

Maeve shot me a dirty look. "I told you what I knew," she said defensively. "You wanted lab results."

"We don't know much," Mom interjected, "but he's out of immediate danger and we'll know more later."

"But there was liver damage . . ."

"They were able to repair that for now," she assured me. "He's under excellent care."

The door opened and I looked up to see Brendan enter. "Glad you could join us," he commented.

"You too," I rejoined.

"Be nice," Mom and Maeve said in unison.

"I didn't say anything," Brendan protested. "I found the cafeteria if you need it."

"Good idea," I said. "I'll stay here . . ."

Mom shook her head. "Have you eaten anything since breakfast?"

"Have you?" I countered. "I haven't been worrying all day."

"I'll keep you company," Brendan offered. "The others deserve a dinner break."

I nodded. "And there are probably some guidelines as to how many visitors he's allowed to have."

"They recommend two," Mom said after a moment of hesitation. "Maeve and I won't be gone long."

"Me?" my sister protested. "Why do I have to go?"

"Because you need more than four glasses of water and half a granola bar," Mom responded. "Come on."

Maeve followed grudgingly and Brendan took the corner seat, dropping a bag on the floor.

"Some home comforts," he answered my inquiring look. "I ran back to the house for the phone charger and the legal thriller from his nightstand."

I grunted in approval. "You know the one bright side of this?"

"Getting to spend quality time with me?" he suggested.

"Think of all the sports he'll have time to watch," I corrected.

Brendan rolled his eyes, but couldn't deny that I had a valid point. "Too bad he missed the World Series," he reflected. "I'll check the listings."

"It would be unpatriotic not to have NESN," I said confidently.

Brendan's grin widened a bit. "I've missed you," he admitted.

"I've wished you were here occasionally," I responded.

"Aw, shucks." He stretched his legs out so he could tease comfortably. "So, no wild adventures while I've been gone?"

I screwed up my face as if in concentration. "I eloped to Mexico."

"Isn't that a little far, even for you?"

"Not if you stow away in the cargo hold," I pointed out. "I spent some time in Cabo, got a decent tan, and hitched a ride back on a flight going my way."

"And no one noticed?"

"No one," I teased. "I just made sure I didn't answer my phone anywhere with a mariachi band."

"Seriously," he chided. "Please tell me you've been keeping out of trouble."

"I've been a saint," I reassured him, feigning indignation. "I haven't had to use my fake ID in weeks and the most exciting thing I bought was a textbook."

He shook his head, letting the grin fall completely off of his face. "Youth is wasted on the wrong people."

"I don't want to get a record after all of Maeve's hard work."

"I'm sure the parents are thrilled."

I shrugged indifferently. "Not as much as Maeve."

Dad's fingers stirred in my palm, but when I looked in his direction, he was still unconscious. It didn't keep me from tightening my grip in case some part of him was trying to reach out to me and my mind shifted back to the matter that Brendan was trying to distract me from.

"Next topic," I requested.

"What?" Brendan asked. "Not in the mood for a fraternal lecture?"

"I don't like ordinary teasing in an extraordinary crisis," I said bluntly.

"I know," Brendan responded after a moment. "I was hoping I could take your mind off of this."

"It *has* been off of it," I shot back.

"That's not your fault." I looked up and found him staring at me with uncomfortable intensity. "Nothing could have gotten you in here sooner."

There was nothing untrue about his statement, but it was only underlining one thing: I was useless in a crisis. I dropped Dad's hand and shot to my feet.

"I need some air," I lied.

"No," Brendan said, moving to block my exit.

"I'm going to be sick," I threatened.

"Best place for it, a hospital," he deadpanned, "but you're not allowed to go wallow somewhere."

"I'm not going to *wallow . . . ,*" I began hotly.

"You're running away from me so you can blame yourself," Brendan pointed out. "I don't think you're in your right mind."

"Would you be?" I challenged, trying to sidestep him.

He held up a hand as if to hold me at bay. "I'm not," he said in a low voice. "I just think you should trust me."

"I don't want to . . ."

"I'll get Maeve to back me up," Brendan threatened. "Besides, as soon as she's back, we're all going home."

"No, I'm not," I protested.

"They don't accommodate overnight visitors," he said.

"But if he wakes up again . . ."

"They also don't allow therapy swans," Brendan interrupted me again. "I checked."

"So, what?" I demanded. "You want me to go home, drink some tea, and study before bed?"

"Those aren't bad ideas," he commented. "You could also keep an eye on Maeve and listen if Mom needs to talk. I might even need a shoulder to cry on."

I didn't like his attitude, but he was showing an unexpected amount of level-headedness. I backed away a few steps, folding my arms over my chest.

"What if he asks for us?"

"He has a phone and we have horseless carriages that get us here in minutes," Brendan asserted.

I returned to the chair and stubbornly wove my fingers through Dad's. There was no response this time.

"You don't think he needs us now?"

"I think we need to be with him more than vice versa right now," he said.

My breathing steadied after a few more moments. "If majority vote is for it, I'll go home," I granted.

Brendan's mouth twitched a bit and I suspected he was anticipating dragging me by the hair to the car. "We'll see."

Black

Dinner wasn't much more fun than waiting all day had been. We ate quickly and Mom invented an excuse to check on my siblings after only a few bites. I didn't eat much more, so I didn't hypocritically try to force-feed her.

When we returned, Aislin looked somehow more upset than before and Brendan looked like an undersized bouncer.

"Anything new to report?" Mom asked Aislin.

"He's acting restless," she said immediately. "I think he might wake up again."

Brendan shifted uncomfortably in his chair and I guessed that he disagreed. I shot him a warning look, but he didn't speak up.

"I'm sure what he needs is rest," Mom said. "We were thinking of heading home."

Aislin glowered at Brendan, meaning that the tension had been caused by a similar conversation. "I want to stay."

"It's been a long day," Mom reasoned. "We could all use some rest."

"Then I'll take over for now," Aislin offered. "You can sleep, field calls from concerned friends and family . . ."

"I'll stay," I offered.

Aislin's eyebrows arched. "You've been here longer than I have," she protested.

"I don't care," I said honestly. "Brendan can take Mom home and we'll be home by curfew . . ." I waited until Mom nodded. "We can stay here in case he *does* wake up."

Mom had apparently felt as uncomfortable with the emotional tension as I had. "I think that'll be best for everyone," she agreed. "School's not an option tomorrow, so you can sleep in."

That was good, since I had planned on skipping.

"Brendan," she said in a more commanding voice, "go find Aislin dinner."

He stood up and saluted somewhat grudgingly. Once he was out of the room, Mom turned to Aislin.

"I'll talk Nurse Arirang into ignoring visiting hours," she assured her. "If you break curfew, I'll still punish you."

"We'll be home by then," Aislin promised. "Thank you."

Mom bent to kiss her forehead. "Try not to make him laugh too hard when he wakes up," she advised. "Just be content that he'll be happy to see you."

"We weren't planning on juggling," I scoffed.

"Good."

Brendan returned a minute or so later with pretzels and a candy bar.

"These should tide you over," he guessed. "Ready to go?"

"Yes," Mom answered. "We'll see you at home."

Once Brendan had left, I pulled a chair over and took Aislin's free hand. She didn't fight back.

"Thank you," she murmured.

"I knew they'd try to rush us out of here," I commented. "I wanted you to deal with this on your own terms."

"Brendan wanted me home to take care of the rest of you," she said.

"I doubt that," I said.

"But he said . . ."

"He was probably trying to be sympathetic," I translated. "Not that he'd admit that."

"So I get to be miserable here instead of home."

"You asked for it," I reminded her. "I'm just being supportive."

When she didn't respond to that, I shifted in my seat so I could rest my head on her shoulder. "Dad's going to be okay," I promised.

"Eventually," she added.

"True, but think of the board games we can make him play on bed rest."

"We could watch every Jane Austen adaptation ever made."

"Maybe when he's feeling better," I suggested. "We don't want him to suffer."

White

We returned home just before Maeve's alarm signaled curfew. She reset it without looking and opened the front door.

"What time are you going there tomorrow?" I asked.

"Whenever Mom goes," she said.

"So as soon as they have visiting hours," I muttered.

"Do you want me to stay with you?" Maeve asked after a moment of peering at me.

"No," I admitted. "I want there to be a way for me to be there."

She nodded without a change of expression. "Me too," she said. "If you want, I can sit next to you with my phone on in case there's an update."

"What's the point of that?" I challenged. "All it would accomplish is . . ."

"You wouldn't be the only one excluded," Maeve interrupted. "I'll do it if you just say the word."

In that case, we would be equally helpless. It was a punishment for something she hadn't done.

"I want you to call with any news," I said. "If you pick me up at sunset again, I won't hold the rest of the day against you."

Maeve spent another moment trying to read my mind, but finally broke eye contact. "I'll take care of it myself."

"Any updates?" Mom asked from Dad's armchair as I entered the living room.

"He's getting a good night's rest," I said. "I'm sure he'll be ready for human contact tomorrow."

Mom frowned sympathetically at the turn of phrase. "I'll wake you if we get a call during the night," she promised.

I doubted if she would, given her efforts to bring me home; interrupting sleep for any conversation with Dad was unlikely.

"Okay."

I crossed the room and bent to hug her, since I had nothing helpful to say. She stood and pulled me into a firmer embrace.

"He'll be fine," she murmured. "He'll say so tomorrow."

"I know," I reassured her. "It doesn't make today easier."

I pulled away first and sighed. "I'm going to bed," I announced. "Call me if you need me."

I wanted to get horizontal without even undressing, but I first took a few minutes to let a scalding shower wash away my tension. I was just tying my bathrobe when I remembered the other thing scheduled for tomorrow.

I texted Nate immediately and asked him to call me in the morning. Ten seconds later, my phone started ringing and I picked it up.

"I hope I didn't wake you," I said quietly.

"I'm just finishing up," he assured me. "Hello."

I found the words stuck in my throat, since I hardly wanted to cry to my date. I was momentarily at a complete loss for words.

"Raincheck," I finally said.

His pitch rose a few notes. "Are you all right?"

I was relieved that he worried instead of objecting; I should have expected that from a guy who'd befriended me because of a dislocated shoulder.

"There was an emergency today," I blurted out. "I don't know when I'll be able to . . ." I broke off, breathing hard, but he didn't interrupt. "I'm sorry. My family needs me right now."

"I understand," Nate said quickly. "You're not hurt?"

I hesitated for a moment before deciding that he was owed a little detail on a second raincheck. "My father's been hospitalized."

He let out a long breath and when he spoke again, his voice had dropped back to its usual range. "I'm sorry to hear that," he said in what seemed to be a sincere tone. "Take as much time as you need."

The fist clenched around my stomach loosened its grip a little. He wasn't asking for any commitments or details and that was exactly what I needed.

"Thank you."

"I probably won't see you at the library for a few days."

Right now, I didn't know when I'd next feel comfortable leaving the house. "Not for a while," I agreed.

"Then that's all I need to know for now," he said.

Black

I found as many messages on my phone that night as I usually got in four days. Most of them would be from friends wanting to check on me and once I was in less of a shell-shocked state, I'd appreciate most of what people said.

There was one person I could count on to care about my absence without prying too much. I dialed Natalie's number and she predictably picked up after the first ring.

"Hey," she said cautiously.

"Hey."

After waiting a minute for me to explain myself, she took charge. "I didn't see you today."

Subtlety wasn't her strongest suit, but we'd known each other long enough to fine-tune our approaches. It was why I had called her first.

"I got a call at the office," I explained, "and couldn't come back."

"About Aislin?" she guessed.

"About Dad," I corrected.

She inhaled sharply. The stakes were considerably higher for a cop than a hermit.

"Is he going to be okay?"

"Yes." I took a moment to summarize so she could inform mutual friends. "He got hurt at work and needed surgery, so I'm probably going to be out for the rest of the week."

We hadn't officially decided that or even discussed it, but this terrible new world would take some adjustment. Right now, the only thing keeping me from staying in bed all week was the promise of visiting hours.

"Ethan will take care of getting your notes and they'll be legible and filed by subject."

I almost heard that as an insult, but she was assigning it to the guy who wouldn't complain or expect compensation. He also would care about Aislin's well-being.

"Who ratted me out?"

"Avril's sister saw you on the sign-out sheet," she explained. "Genevieve asked Sosi, who said you'd left in third period . . ."

"And the rumors started."

"Not really," she said. "It's bad taste to speculate, so your three hundred texts won't be rude."

"I hope so."

"If anyone gives you crap, take names and I'll set them straight by Monday," Natalie swore.

I doubted that she would go that far, but I appreciated the offer. "I appreciate that," I said.

"How's Aislin doing with all this?"

Even if she cared, I wasn't going to tell every detail. No one needed to know about her vomiting on the side of the road or crying for ten minutes about an hour ago. I had my moments of vulnerability to hide and I figured that Aislin had equal rights to her humanity.

"We're all stressed," I said before she could draw any conclusions.

"Well, yeah," Natalie sighed. "No one should be okay with their father getting hurt."

"Exactly. Brendan's even here and you know how thick his skin is."

"Almost as thick as his skull," Natalie recited the old joke.

I had nothing more to say on that subject that felt appropriate to the conversation, so I elaborated on an earlier conversation.

"They said Dad should be home by the end of the week. He won't be out on patrol for a while, but he can take desk duty."

"That's good," she said, sounding glad for a change of subject. "When I had my appendix out, I went so stir-crazy that I actually *wanted* to go to class."

"I think Dad is three days from yelling at us to stop hovering," I predicted.

"You think it'll be soon?"

I tried to reconcile that mental image with my memory of the grey, exhausted man in the hospital and then tried to push it from my mind.

"Once he's home, he'll get sick of everyone mothering him," I guessed.

"Good luck with that," Natalie snorted. "I can just see Aislin trying to serve him a tenth cup of tea and doing her homework nearby in case he needs anything."

I could picture that with relative ease. "She's not his dog, but other than playing fetch, that's pretty accurate. She'll follow doctors' instructions to the letter and make the rest of us feel like slackers."

It was a quirk that Aislin filled a lot of her human time trying to make a contribution. It was like she felt she had to cram the productivity of our days into the night hours.

"So, how can I help?" Natalie asked.

"If Ethan's willing to hound my teachers, sic him on them," I requested. "Tell Coach Skandalis what happened, update friends who ask and pick up the phone if I call."

"Yes, ma'am," Natalie said cheerfully. "Do you want me to check in at a set time?"

I didn't like the idea of putting anything on a schedule right now, even if her offer was tempting.

"Can you just be on call?"

"Anytime, anywhere," Natalie promised. "Especially during gym and English."

"Yes, ma'am."

"And let me know if you need company or a ride," she ordered.

"Got it."

"Good."

"Then I'll let you get to bed," I said. "Thanks for being on call."

"Any time."

Even with my exhaustion, I didn't sleep well. I slept at midnight, but woke up at 3:43. After trying in vain to get my brain to shut off again, I surrendered and got up.

It was no surprise to find Aislin sitting at the top of the stairs. At my approach, she moved over to make room for me without comment.

"Have you slept at all?" I asked. Aislin shook her head, making me sigh and sling an arm over her shoulders. "I can't sleep either."

She didn't shrug me off and after a minute, she wrapped her arm around my waist. I didn't mind that it took her a while to speak.

"I can sleep after dawn," she reasoned, "and so can you."

"I don't think it's going to be that easy," I admitted. "I got some sleep, but . . ."

"I can't," Aislin blurted out.

I momentarily couldn't tell if she was mounting a defense or asking for help. Either way, I didn't budge.

"Do you want something to eat?" I offered. My mind flashed back to Natalie's comment about the tenth cup of tea, but I could live with fussing. "You haven't had real food since yesterday morning and I'm a champion omelet-maker."

"I'm not in the mood," she muttered.

"Then what do you feel like?"

I knew what was probably bothering her and she felt she hadn't put herself through enough hell yesterday.

"I don't know."

"All right," I conceded. "I'm going to go down in a minute. If it's your thing to eat cold cereal in the dark, I'll join you. But you're going to keep me company."

Aislin shrugged, but didn't argue with that. "I think Mom finally fell asleep," she observed.

"What makes you think that?"

"She talked to Aunt Diane for a while," Aislin explained, "but she stopped tossing and turning a while ago."

"You're too awake and the walls are too thin in this house," I commented. "I don't want four zombies visiting Dad, so we need sleep."

When she didn't answer, I pulled her to her feet. She didn't resist, but I had to be the one to steer her downstairs.

In the kitchen, I set out two bowls and poured over-sugared cereal into a few ounces of milk in my bowl before offering her the same. I wasn't hungry, but she wouldn't eat unless I took charge. I stuck a large spoonful in my mouth and Aislin picked listlessly at one of the marshmallows.

"Come on," I chided. "You can do better than that."

By the time I finished the bowl, she'd eaten four pieces and rummaged through the rest without any real interest.

"Take your time," I encouraged her.

She rewarded my kindness by picking up her spoon and eating one spoonful. It was hard-won progress.

"I can't sleep," she said quietly, "because every time I close my eyes, I see it happening again."

I immediately felt terrible for trying to talk her into sleeping. I just couldn't put those feelings into words.

"It's the nightmare I've always had," she rushed on. "Not this specifically, but every time there's a school shooting or some bombing, I worry that you'll be at the next one. I worry about Mom getting in five-car pileups and riots happening on Dad's watch. I even worry about Brendan getting mugged."

Her spoon clattered on the table and she buried her face in her hands. Her shoulders hunched and I thought for a moment that she was going to be sick all over again, and after that recitation, I didn't blame her.

"I spend a lot of time worrying that I'll never be able to protect anyone," she admitted.

"That's not necessarily true," I insisted.

"Oh, no? Where was I yesterday morning?" After another moment, she clenched her fists and lowered them to rest on the tabletop. "Can you call Susanna later?" she requested. "If anything she can do can cut this short, I'm game."

It was a Pyrrhic victory to get her cooperation after a trauma, but I nodded reassuringly.

"As soon as it's a decent hour," I promised.

White

I stayed in the house for the rest of that day and slept a little. I checked my phone for updates when awake and Maeve, understanding my worries, sent texts when Dad next woke up. He even texted a short, drowsy message.

At sunset, I took the world's most efficient shower, dressed and was ready to go within ten minutes. Maeve showed up fifteen minutes after the sun disappeared.

"He's looking forward to seeing you," she reported. "I think he's getting tired of the rest of us."

"Not possible," I asserted. "I think he dislikes being the center of attention."

"That's true," Maeve admitted. "So the plan is to enter the room and completely ignore him?"

"If it helps," I agreed. "I'm planning on playing it by ear."

I hugged Dad as carefully as I could for the first minute. He didn't complain and gestured to the empty chair at his bedside once I'd pulled away.

"I've saved this for you," he said.

I took it without protest, giving him the once-over that I hadn't managed earlier. He wasn't as chipper as Maeve had implied, but he was conscious and that was reassuring.

"Good day?"

"I didn't do much," I said dismissively.

"Well, that's disappointing," he murmured. "Try to have some fun tomorrow for me."

I couldn't speak for a moment, since my throat had tightened, but I nodded. "Sure," I muttered. "I'll get Maeve to give me ideas."

"Maeve can stay with you," he suggested.

"What?" she objected. "Trying to get rid of us already?"

His mouth curved up on one side. "I want all of you to take turns being distracted," he corrected her. "Why do you think Brendan's gone?"

"Because he has a paper?" I guessed. "He complained about it last week."

"Because he can study while Nurse Arirang watches over me," Dad said. "Your mission is to entertain Aislin."

"All right," Maeve grumbled. "Does that mean we can stay late tonight?"

"If you like," he granted.

"Okay," I interrupted. "Witty banter aside, how are you doing?"

His smile shrank, but didn't disappear. "Your mother has notes from the doctor, but they're going to watch for signs of complication or infection. I'll probably be out by Thanksgiving."

"You may not be here for Veteran's Day," Mom asserted. "Stop frightening them."

He winked at her, smile still in place. "If I don't make terrible jokes once in a while, they'll think I'm an imposter."

"But the doctors think you're doing all right?" I asked.

"I'm healing as well as expected," he said gravely. "I'm not going to try to push myself before I'm ready just to look macho."

"If anyone can be macho in a hospital gown, it's you," Maeve called. "You just don't have to prove it."

"Good," Dad said. "Any other questions?"

"Do you need anything?" I asked.

He mulled that over for a minute. "Sudoku or crossword puzzles. If you can find a picture that doesn't make us look robotic, I'd like to have something to show off to staff."

I knew the perfect one. It was from Brendan's birthday party last year and someone had caught us all laughing at some joke. We all looked fantastically relaxed.

"Done."

Dad had probably intended for us to watch a movie or shop on our day off, but I came downstairs after sunset and found Maeve and a guest in the living room.

"Susanna?" I guessed.

"Yes," she confirmed. "How are you?"

"I'm okay," I answered before turning to Maeve. "I didn't know you were doing this tonight."

"You didn't say you had other plans," she rejoined.

I shrugged in acknowledgment that I had nothing set in stone. "What news from the hospital?"

"He's improving," Maeve recited. "There's no infection and they'll run tests later. Have a seat."

I didn't appreciate my concerns being dismissed, but the house rules put guests first. I pulled out the chair opposite Susanna and sat obediently.

"How much do you know?" I asked.

"As far as I can tell, Maeve has told me everything that your family definitely knows about the curse," she explained.

"So, everything from the daily schedule to the fine print?"

"Yes," she said. "Including the complication."

I supposed that this sort of detail was necessary—a doctor couldn't treat a condition without knowing the symptoms—but I didn't like anyone knowing about the intimacy issue. We hadn't even told Brendan about that, figuring that he'd either find it hilarious or horrifying.

"Personally, I find it very medieval," Susanna commented.

"Glad we're on the same page," I muttered.

She waited for a few moments for me to pick up the conversation, but finally glanced at Maeve for permission to continue.

"You asked Maeve to call me," she said. "Why was that?"

"I couldn't be there when disaster struck," I blurted out. "I want this to be over and I don't know if anything you've done has worked . . ."

"It may not be something that you can measure for a while," Susanna responded. "We've been doing things that don't require your participation, but that was Maeve's choice."

"All right." I clasped my hands in my lap and leaned forward. "I don't want to take advantage of what you do."

"I'm happy to help," she said, sounding genuine. "Would you like to take a more active part in all of this?"

"This isn't my thing and I don't know where to start," I said. "Otherwise, the answer's yes."

"Right," she said with another glance in Maeve's direction. "I want you to be comfortable with this. You're not tying me down and making me chant. I'm willing to kick things up a few notches, so don't worry about that for now."

"And what can I do?"

"There are a couple of things you should know about curses," Susanna responded. "First, they're empowered by your belief in them."

Something in my stomach twinged and my jaw clenched. "I don't think so," I said.

"It's true," she rejoined. "The spell-caster can do his part, but the curse is only as effective as you make it."

"I'm *sorry?*" I asked, my voice rising a few notes on the scale. "You're saying I chose this?"

She seemed to wisely realize that she had misspoken and even Maeve looked wary.

"I really think that logic's crap," Maeve said authoritatively. "It's as medieval as the curse itself."

I thought that was going a bit far, but I was grateful for her support. I had wondered for the last few days whose side she was on.

"I'm sorry," Susanna back-pedaled. "Let me put it a different way."

"Please do," I encouraged her a little less sharply.

"You know the curse's power," she said, "but I want you to believe in your ability to overcome it."

That made more sense than what she'd said earlier and Maeve relaxed a little. "Positive thinking's better," Maeve commented. "What else?"

Susanna reached into the pocket of the jacket that she had draped over the back of her chair and pulled out a folded piece of paper. I opened it to find a list of four websites.

"I'd like you to do your own browsing," she suggested. "You might find an approach you'd like us to take."

"And you will . . ."

"Keep up what I've done since September," she said. "Once you've come back with an answer, I'll see what changes need to be made."

Black

With hospital visits in our daily routine, I tried to turn on the shower minutes before sunset so Aislin could get started and take care of the details once hair replaced feathers. When she woke me up the morning after our consultation with Susanna, I promised to have dinner on the table when she finished dressing so we could visit Dad soon afterwards.

I was running late that day, but with friends and family contributing lasagnas, soups, and even a pizza sent by Brendan's roommate, dinner would be easy. I had decided on Mrs. Kerrigan's chicken a la king by the time I parked the car, but I didn't notice the person on the front steps until I reached the walk. I recognized him from our one previous encounter, but that didn't explain his presence.

"When did you get our address?"

"Hello, Maeve," Nate answered, standing up and stretching languidly.

"How do you know I'm not Aislin?" I challenged.

He dropped his arms to his sides and grinned. "I hope you're well."

"You too," I said. "How did you find the place?"

I wasn't trying to be rude, per se. I was wondering if his decision to track us down was a red flag. He'd probably found the Byrne residences on the internet and tried each one in alphabetical order.

"Well, Aislin would remember that she gave me the address where I could pick her up," Nate explained.

"Oh . . ." I closed my eyes for a moment to process the disaster I'd stumbled upon. Maybe Aislin was hiding. "For that dinner you mentioned last weekend."

"Actually, we agreed on a raincheck," he assured me. "I don't mind waiting."

"She probably didn't mean for you to wait on the porch," I pointed out.

He waved a gloved hand dismissively. "It's not that bad."

He was wearing a coat, so Detroit-boy was cold enough to mind.

"Besides," he continued, "I haven't been waiting long."

"You haven't said why you're here," I reminded.

"You haven't asked," Nate responded. "Is Aislin here?"

I pulled my phone out of my pocket to check and found one new message: STALL.

"She came home for a while earlier and I'm her ride back to the hospital," I improvised.

By the glow of the porch light, I could see his cheeks turn slightly redder. "I was going to offer her a ride."

"Anything else?" I asked.

"I don't know if she's eaten yet," he said, bending down to retrieve a fast-food bag.

"I know she hasn't had dinner," I said brightly. "That makes you a lifesaver."

"It's only a hamburger," he protested modestly.

"We're living off of neighbors' casseroles," I expounded. "She won't have to wait for it to defrost either."

"Well, when you put it that way . . ."

At that moment, the front door open and Aislin stepped out. "Nate," she said breathlessly. "I wasn't expecting you."

"I wasn't sure you'd be here," he said. "How's your father?"

She shot me a look that radiated gratitude for my intervention and backed up so the threshold was clear. "Come in and I'll tell you about it while you warm up."

"I can do that," he agreed.

I followed him inside and shucked my coat immediately to signal that she should take her time. Nate followed suit as soon as he'd handed off the bag of food.

"I wasn't sure what you'd like," he admitted, "but this seemed pretty safe."

"Thank you so much."

Her cheeks were just as red as if she'd been standing out in the cold with us, but I doubted it was because of exposure to the elements.

"They say he'll be out in a few more days, provided everything goes well," Aislin added.

"That's good," he said. "Are you going over tonight?"

"After dinner," I replied. "Let me know when you're ready to go."

I went to the kitchen, heated up the chicken, and took my place at the kitchen table where I could eat *and* eavesdrop.

"You didn't have to come all the way out here," Aislin commented.

"It's not the sacrifice you're expecting," Nate replied. "I avoided the traffic by leaving early and the longest delay was at the drive-thru."

I heard her try out an uneasy laugh. None of us had cracked many smiles since Monday morning and we'd forgotten how to act casual.

"I appreciate you checking in on me," she amended, "even if you won't admit it."

"I promised I'd buy you dinner this week," he replied. "This is a down payment."

"It's very sweet," she clarified.

After a slightly awkward silence, Nate spoke up again. "Well, I'd better let you get going."

"Thank you again," Aislin said. "I'll let you know how everything goes."

"I'll call you tomorrow?" he suggested.

Aislin hesitated for a moment, but didn't sound nervous when she replied. "I'd like that."

White

Nate had offered to pick me up after dinner the night before Dad was supposed to get out, but Maeve invited him to eat with us and then invented unfinished homework. I was left to eat leftover stroganoff with Nate, which was a poor substitute for a date.

"I'm sorry about this," I commented. "I'm sure you have better things to do than help me empty the freezer."

"I wouldn't have offered if it bothered me," he said.

"But this isn't what you pictured when you asked me out," I rejoined.

"And I'm sure you didn't accept hoping that I'd spring for fries," Nate teased. "Neither counts as that dinner."

"So I still owe you."

"No," he said after a moment's pause. "You just owe me for a raincheck."

"You're too kind." He modestly shrugged in response to the compliment. "I stood you up and you were *nice* about it."

Nate set down his fork and I prepared for a minor speech. "You didn't stand me up. If a family emergency were a deal-breaker, I wouldn't be worth knowing. You should also know that as long as we know each other, I'll want to be a friend to you. If I can find a way to make your life easier, I will."

That was both the sweetest and most honest thing I'd heard in days. "And I hope to return the favor someday," I responded earnestly. "I just feel like I'm taking advantage of your patience."

"You're accepting help," he answered firmly. "You shouldn't feel guilty about that."

"All right," I surrendered.

"You promise to rethink your issues with this setup?" Nate challenged.

I tilted my head to the side and shrugged. "I promise to give it some thought. It's all I feel comfortable with right now."

"I know." Nate sighed. "Can you just try to stop worrying about if I think of you as an inconvenience?"

"That's tactful," I scoffed.

"It's honest," Nate retorted. "Promise you'll try?"

"I promise to not let it worry me as much as it has in the past," I negotiated.

"That's not what I asked for," he objected.

"But it's the best I can agree to for now," I said. "Can you live with that?"

"I can certainly try," he promised.

SCENE 12

White

Dad came home in the middle of an afternoon. Mom and Brendan helped him upstairs, which made him look as exhausted as he had on Monday. As his therapy swan, I curled up next to him like a needy housecat, which made him laugh. When he drifted off a few minutes later, I followed suit.

Mom woke me up about five minutes before sunset when she came to check on him. "I'm making dinner," she said quietly. "Are you in the mood for anything specific?"

I shook my head and slid as gracefully as I could from the bed. I could hear her murmuring something and Dad responding, but I was sprawled on my bed within reach of a towel when the sun set.

When I returned to the master bedroom later, Dad was awake. "Your mother said you'd been here all afternoon," he observed. "It must be nice to not have visiting hours."

"I hope you didn't mind," I responded warily. "If it was too crowded, I can clear out."

"It's no problem," Dad reassured me.

I settled on the end of the bed to give him some of the space I'd stolen during the afternoon. "I bet you're happy to be home," I commented.

"I miss the needles, and no one's woken me up to see if I need a sleeping pill," Dad said with a slight smile.

"If you miss it, I can talk Maeve into poking you several times a day," I offered. "Brendan can be in charge of bland food."

"You treat me so well," he joked.

His eyelids drooped and I stood up, anticipating that he'd be too unconscious to notice in a minute. At my movement, though, he cracked one eye open.

"If you want to help, you can call the young man Maeve described and schedule your dinner for tomorrow."

"Maeve snitched," I grumbled.

"Your mother approves. I wish you'd followed orders and found a distraction."

"I'm not very good company these days," I said.

"I disagree," Dad replied sympathetically, "but I'll feel better if you do everyday things nonetheless."

I did *not* believe that his healing process was tied to awkward first dates, but I acquiesced this time.

"All right," I said. "I have a phone call to make."

Without meaning to, Nate and I had somehow gotten through most of the awkward first-date moments long before now. I blamed that both on study sessions and his kindness towards me during the crisis.

I knew already about the after-school work at a doctor's office that led him to physical therapy. We'd covered family names and his parents' professions. He was afraid of heights and dogs.

In turn, he knew how long I'd homeschooled and that I wished I could study abroad in college. One night, Maeve had confided to him that I sang in the shower and hated turkey. I had no idea why she thought this was relevant, but I hadn't been there to stop her.

By our first date, we had advanced as far as third date conversations. That stripped the situation of some tension, but that meant he was close to finding a deal-breaker and that made me more nervous than ever. Nate instructed me to be casual, but I didn't know if that meant preppy or laid-back for my first collegiate date.

I eventually let Maeve pick everything and she kept my look pretty casual with jeans, a black tank top and a dark green shirt. I wore no jewelry except a watch. As for makeup, she didn't go much further than lip gloss because she knew he liked it.

Nate had offered to pick me up without my prepared warning about gentlemanly behavior and showed up exactly on time. He correctly assumed that he would have to pass a first interview.

I was under orders to stay upstairs until then, but the bedroom door was open and Dad was within earshot downstairs. I was ready to spring into action the moment it got out of hand. Dad went easier on him than he did on Maeve's usual choices, but he still managed to sound authoritative from his semi-recumbent position on the couch.

"I'm Officer David Byrne."

"Nathaniel Baron. A pleasure to meet you."

"You're a student?"

"I'm studying physical therapy at Boston University, sir."

"You're from Michigan?"

"Yes, sir."

"You don't have to call me sir."

"Yes, Officer."

I liked that he was so nervous that he wound up being deferential.

"What are your intentions?"

"To take your daughter to dinner in a well-lit place and a family-friendly movie, sir."

This was starting to sound like something out of boot camp. Dad had that effect on some people, even though he wasn't a tyrant. Unlike most tyrants, he actually tended to smile. It was the police questioning that caused the breakdowns.

"What time will you have her home?"

"What time is her curfew?"

"Midnight."

"11:55."

"Good answer."

That was my cue. Maeve gave me a quick hug for luck, and then shoved me out the door. I wasn't the type to glide down the stairs, but I was also wearing boots.

Nate's face brightened when I came into view and he looked happy instead of relieved. He was also wearing jeans, which eased my mind.

"I'll see you by midnight," Dad said. "Do you need any money?"

"I've got everything covered," Nate said.

I had a twenty in my pocket in case of emergencies. I leaned over to kiss Dad's cheek.

"Don't wait up."

Nate didn't talk until we reached the car, probably remembering that anything he said could be used against him. I caught Maeve watching from the upstairs window and waved while Nate's back was turned.

"You have any music preferences?" he asked once the car was on.

"Whatever you usually play," I said automatically.

Maeve had instructed that I should let him pick the music and look impressed. He put on something I had at home and buckled up.

"So," he said once we were under way, "how do you feel about Chinese food?"

I let out a short sigh of relief. "Maeve was convinced you'd take me out for sushi."

"You want sushi?"

"Anything but," I countered. "I don't like most fish."

I could see his smile in profile. "So Legal Seafoods is out?"

Legal Seafoods was also too pricy for a first date, but I didn't want to point this out to him. "If that's all right with you."

"That's fine." He glanced over. "So, Chinese food?"

"I like it," I said simply.

"Good. There's a great place near campus."

He didn't seem to have the same kind of nervous need to please me that Ethan had shown. Maybe it was the age, but he seemed confident without arrogance.

"How were classes?" I asked.

"They were okay," he said. "We need a vacation between midterms and finals."

"I know the feeling," I commiserated.

He held the door open for me at the restaurant and pulled my chair out once we got to the table. I took mental notes for Maeve, even if I felt guilty for keeping tally.

"So, I knew that you had a sister," he said conversationally. "You didn't once mention the family resemblance."

My face burned with embarrassment and I covered it with both hands. "I didn't want you to meet her *that* way."

"People probably mix you up all the time."

"No," I corrected, letting my hands drop after a moment, "they're always mistaking me for Maeve."

"Sorry," he said.

"It was a nice change," I only half-lied. "Don't worry about it."

"I'll try," Nate sighed, "but the official story on meeting your family refers to tonight."

"You won't take credit for coming to my rescue earlier?" I asked. "You were fantastic while Dad was in the hospital."

"I suppose so," he granted modestly. "If my flirtation with Maeve comes up, I'll admit my guilt."

"And I'll admit that I didn't prepare you at all," I said. "I'm sorry."

"We're allowed a few mistakes at first," Nate answered. "Let's split the blame and say this is strike .5 for both of us."

That didn't make sense metaphorically, but I let it slide. "Does that mean that after three strikes I'm out?"

"No," he assured me. "After three strikes, we both figure out what we can do to boost our IQ."

As far as I could tell, neither of us did anything to earn a strike that night. Sure, I dropped sweet and sour chicken on my shirt and he called Maeve Mabel once, but it was the kind of date that she would have approved of.

My only regret was how quiet we were during the movie. We weren't comfortable enough to hold hands, much less make out in the back row. I caught him glancing my way more than once, probably to see if our senses of humor meshed. We didn't always laugh at the same things, but we didn't have to.

Ten minutes before curfew, we reached the front steps and another crossroads.

"I'd like to do this again," Nate said.

"I completely agree," I said. "But only if . . ."

"We do something more interactive than a movie?" he suggested.

"Exactly," I said. "I liked the conversation best."

"I'm glad you find me more entertaining than Hollywood," he said. "Give me some time to get creative."

"We can take turns," I offered. "I'll come up with the brilliant plan next."

"I think you were pretty brilliant tonight," he said.

It was then that I noticed Nick's car approaching and a cold knot formed under my ribcage. I wasn't ready for an audience, but he miraculously decided to pass by.

"So," Nate said.

"So you said to give you some time to be brilliant," I continued. "How much time?"

"Until this weekend?"

"Sounds good."

"We'll work out the details at the library," he suggested. "You are going to be there tomorrow, right?"

I nodded with a tight smile. "Same time, same place until further notice."

"Okay." He shoved his hands into his pockets and met my gaze before giving me a tentative grin. "I had a lot of fun."

"Me too," I replied. "Thanks for that."

Maybe I gave off the dreaded don't-touch-me vibe or he was respectful, but he left a kiss on my cheek. I failed to not blush at any rate.

"Thank you for a great night," he said. "I'll see you tomorrow."

"Bye," I blurted out.

His grin broadened. "Good night."

I slunk in the door and only saw Dad asleep on the couch. Maeve was still out, so I had time to regroup.

It hadn't been a romantic-comedic, life-changing experience, but this had felt like a natural next step after friendship and I was happy to see where this would go next.

For now, I turned to one of the suggestions from Susanna's websites. I lit the green candle on my desk and whispered a hope to myself.

"All of the luck that I might own
Running with marrow in my bones
I borrow its energy that I may use
Only in good fortune, not to abuse . . ."

Black

I didn't plan my bad timing, but Nate and Aislin hit the awkward front porch moment as soon as Nick started pulling up to my curb. He swerved back and accelerated, making me laugh.

"You read my mind," I said.

"I did," he agreed, "but if you'd have brought binoculars, we could have stayed."

"I would not," I protested.

"This is new territory for her," Nick pointed out. "You don't want to see how it goes?"

"I do," I admitted, "but I want the play-by-play from Aislin, not spying."

He shook his head, laughing quietly. "He must be something special if you're showing this kind of restraint."

"Give me a little credit."

"I'll do better than that."

He found a parking spot two blocks away and leaned over for a goodnight kiss. With no one to interrupt us, he didn't bother keeping it short and sweet. He even gave Aislin a few minutes of extra privacy.

"If this is the tradeoff, my spying days are over," I commented once he turned the car back on.

"No, they aren't," he said, "but this way, we don't have to wait in line for the doorstep."

It was a very selfish rationale, but I didn't mind it very much at all.

"I think we're safe to go now," I said.

Aislin was more likely to give a friendly handshake than a goodnight kiss. She wasn't prudish, just careful. Nick gave me a quick peck at the door and retreated. I opened the door as the clock struck twelve.

"Good timing," Dad commented from the couch. "Did you enjoy yourself?"

"I always do," I said, flashing a smile. "What about Aislin?"

He jerked his head towards the kitchen. "Ask her yourself."

She wasn't looking flushed enough for a first kiss, but she looked happy enough to have come close.

"Cheek kiss?" I guessed.

"Yes," she confirmed. "He's going to talk to me tomorrow about a second date."

"And you're going to tell me first-date details tonight," I practically commanded.

"The Chinese food was good and we're going out again," she recited. "The rest is my business."

"I'd like to disagree."

"You always do," Aislin said, "but all you need to know is that I'm happy. You'll get more details if that changes."

Her summary was what she would have reported to our parents, so I probably wasn't getting much more out of her.

"Okay," I said. "But if you need to go into details . . ."

"I know where to find you," she concluded. "Thank Nick for the space."

So she *had* noticed our discretion. "Any time."

SCENE 13

White

By the time we had a few dates behind us, Nate and I established a routine. He would call the next day after classes or, when he was feeling eager, during breakfast. When he called just after dinner this time, I was only surprised when he named the venue.

"We're spending the night in *another* library?"

"Don't worry," he said casually. "We're just meeting there."

"Dress code?"

"You should wear clothing," he said unhelpfully. "Jeans are fine."

It was a typical weeknight date. He'd taken me somewhere nice over the weekend, but dinner and a walk counted as a date on Wednesdays. I didn't mind his efforts.

"I'll be there at 7:30."

On weeknights, Maeve also had no say in my appearance. She balked at that, but I agreed to dress up on weekends. Since we had variety and excitement in our relationship, she surrendered.

I met Nate in front of the Boston Public Library at 7:30 as planned, wearing jeans, and a blue sweater layered over a t-shirt in case the weather was warm.

"Hi," Nate said, giving me a quick hug. "You look great."

"I look comfortable," I corrected.

He was just as casual, but had a leather jacket in place of a sweater. I had the dress code down, all right.

"You look great."

"I can't take the credit," Nate said modestly. "The coat's Noah's."

"Accidentally lose it in your closet," I encouraged.

"What are you in the mood for?"

"Something to-go," I suggested. "You have a test in two days."

"You've got a good memory." He looked flattered and relieved by my attention to detail. "Indian food acceptable?"

"Perfectly acceptable."

We hadn't reached hand-holding status, but he kept a hand on my elbow. It was protective instead of intimate. We settled in the chairs at the front of the restaurant after placing our orders and, to my surprise, Nate pulled out a sheaf of papers.

"Did I miss something on the syllabus?" I teased. "No one mentioned a quiz."

"Not everything's about school," Nate chided. "But in this case, I found a list of things every couple should know about each other to kill time."

I scrunched up my face. "That's still a quiz," I pointed out.

"Aren't you a little curious about . . ." He rifled through and chuckled. "My shopping habits and pet peeves?"

"Not as much as you are about my work ambitions," I said, reading upside-down. "I think I need to update my résumé."

"That won't tell me enough about you," Nate protested. "Are you game or do you have something else to say?"

"I would hope I have a lot to say," I countered. "As long as we both have to answer, I'll consider this a fair trade."

Nate paused after "favorite vacation" to pay for dinner, but the list was more addicting than I'd originally thought. I found out about his best friend Niko during dinner and he drew out a few confessions about living in Maeve's shadow. By the time we got back to campus, we'd run through half the list, but had to actually study after that.

That didn't stop him from being mischievous. I had just finished a set of practice equations when he glanced up with a glint in his eye.

"Pet peeves?"

"Guys who won't let me study," I answered flatly.

"Girls who don't know when to have fun," he responded.

"Good thing you're not dating one of them," I stated, turning a page in my notebook.

"Good thing," Nate echoed solemnly, highlighting a paragraph.

A moment later, though, I reached across the table and pulled the top paper towards me. "Religion?"

"Jewish," he said immediately. "I don't go to temple as often as I should, but I had a bar mitzvah, I celebrate the holidays, and I try to eat kosher."

"So I won't schedule things on Fridays and I shouldn't save you a pork chop from dinner?"

"Right," he said. "You?"

"Gentile," I said.

"Yes, I gathered that," he said with a smile. "Anything else?"

"I'm not very religiously active." Mostly because services didn't accommodate my schedule. "I celebrate the holidays and try not to do anything too scandalous."

He arched an eyebrow and closed his book to pay closer attention. "Define scandalous."

"I'd rather not," I said. "I don't want you knowing the limit just yet."

"But then how will I . . ."

"You'll know if you're about to cross a line," I assured him. "Don't you have some reading to do?"

He executed a mock salute and started looking for his place again. A few minutes later, though, I gave in to the temptation to continue the conversation.

"What do you like best about living in modern times?"

"Indoor plumbing," Nate confided, "but I have studying to do."

"Yes, sir." I grinned at the next page of the book. "I'd pick women's suffrage."

He just grunted in response, so I closed the math book and reached for my notes from the previous night.

"On the other hand," he considered a few minutes later, "go back a couple of hundred years and there are other disadvantages."

"Like our families living on different sides of Europe and the chances of us meeting being slim to none?"

"Mind reader," he labeled me, with a grin of his own. "We'll pretend the plumbing answer never happened, right?"

"Your secret's safe with me," I vowed.

He went back to reading, but his left hand snaked across the table and clasped mine. I didn't mind if he noticed my sudden pulse acceleration—I wanted him to realize the effect he had on me. I just held on for dear life and enjoyed it.

Tonight, when he aimed a kiss for my lips instead of my cheek, I was taken aback, but didn't have much time to think about it. He kissed like a kid testing the temperature of a pool and I couldn't concentrate on how to kiss back. I enjoyed it too much to overthink it, and when he pulled back, his expression suggested I'd done quite enough.

"I'll call you tomorrow," he repeated his usual promise.

"I'll be waiting," I answered, resisting the urge to touch my lips.

"I was thinking we could double," Nate suggested a few days later.

He mentioned this in passing while tapping his pencil rhythmically on his Lit textbook and, for a few moments, I thought I had hallucinated the sound.

"Double as in double date," I clarified.

"You, me, your sister, and the date of her choice. Dinner and a movie."

"Bad idea," I said without hesitation.

He stopped tapping and looked up with a surprised expression. "You don't want me befriending your social secretary?"

"It's not that I don't want to show you off . . ."

"I *hope* you want to show me off," he interjected. "For all I know, you're living a double life."

"That's not my style," I argued. "And if I were, I'd still prefer the one with you in it."

"But?" he prompted.

"But it's a bad idea," I reiterated. "You haven't met Maeve's current boyfriend and I'd like to keep it that way."

"So you're afraid that I'll be a jerk and word will get around?"

"You're not the one I think would act like a jerk," I countered.

"But you want me under wraps," he summarized.

I had the impression of being cross-examined, even though I could see his mile-wide mischievous streak.

"I think that if Nick is even slightly impressed by you, he'll rub it in the face of the last guy who looked my way. That's the last thing I want to do to him."

"Okay." He nodded, his expression not changing. "It's a bad idea."

"Thank you."

I didn't have to analyze the intention behind his agreement, just enjoy the fact that he did agree. He went back to tapping his pencil and I went back to review questions.

"But . . ."

I didn't expect to be the one to break the silence. Nate glanced up again, surprised that the conversation was only half-over.

"You have a closing statement?" he asked.

"An alternate idea," I amended. "I only said double-dating with my sister was a bad idea. What about your roommates?"

His brow furrowed in confusion or pain. "I'm confused. Have you not hit your pain quota this week?"

"No, but I don't know them well," I said. "Do you think one would slum it with a nearly graduated teenager?"

"We're all teenagers and some of us act like it," Nate considered. "The real problem is finding them dates."

"And neither of us wants to see the results?" I guessed.

"Bingo," he agreed.

"Okay." I considered for a few minutes, mind more on the idea than my homework. "What if we give them a while to find a date and try not to be revolting for now?"

"When were you thinking?"

"Just before Thanksgiving week," I suggested.

"Bad idea."

I didn't laugh at his echo of my objection, but I couldn't keep myself from smirking. "Why?"

"Because you're not canceling my plans that week, even for roommate-humiliation."

"Am I entitled to details?"

Nate shrugged. "I'm not sure you'll be involved but I'll let you know."

If I felt more secure in our relationship, I'd have pressed for details. I wasn't used to being in a committed relationship and didn't know how far I could go without being overbearing.

"I'll be waiting."

SCENE 14

Black

"Are you feeling all right?"

Nick asked this between dinner and the goodnight kiss on one of our study dates. I had been scouring a book for a quote to support my paper's thesis and didn't hear the question properly. When he asked it again, I looked up.

"Fine," I said. "Why?"

"Because it's been more than a week since you lectured me about Aislin," he observed. "I'd call that unusual."

"Huh." I never tracked such things, but it *had* been a while since he'd said something worth a chastisement. "My sister can take care of herself."

"I've never said otherwise," he said, "but that's a new policy. When did she declare independence?"

He was being flippant, but his turn of phrase was amusing. "Last week."

"Really?" he asked skeptically.

I wasn't ready to declare victory, but . . . "She's commendably self-sufficient these days."

She'd worried me several times, but Nate inexplicably found her habits endearing. She was just what I wanted these days—a love-sick teenager.

"Well, good."

After another few equations, Nick closed his book and stowed his homework away. I took this as my cue to devote my attention to him, not my notes. Study dates gave us unusual privacy. Instead of exploiting the circumstances, he clasped my hands tightly and looked very serious.

"You're giving your sister some breathing room?"

"Maybe," I said cautiously, taken aback by the subject. "Why?"

"Because that means you can concentrate on other things."

I had a theory about what those other things were, but I was obligated to torture him. "You're right," I said. "The SATs . . ."

"Which you already took."

"For practice," I fibbed. "I'm not settling for my first score."

"I meant . . ."

"Are you asking to skip studying one of these nights?"

"Have you been reading my notes?" he growled.

"No, just your mind. You're a little bit transparent."

He looked ready to disagree, but decided to keep his mouth shut at the last minute. I reached past him to retrieve the soccer schedule.

"I can't promise to be there for every one . . ."

"I wouldn't expect you to," Nick interrupted. "Your team would object."

"The second one next week is an away game, so I can ride up with one of the girls and then we can take a detour on the way back."

"And the last game of the season is a home game," he recalled, "so I'll drive you back the long way."

"For food?" I suggested.

"And maybe even music," Nick said very seriously. "Should I put it in my calendar?"

"Don't make fun," I chided. "This was your idea."

He looked momentarily hurt that I wasn't looking forward to this, but then he either covered it up or got over it. "Okay," he said. "It's a date."

After the first few days of panic and constant vigilance, our family's approach to Dad's recovery was fairly hands-off. We took care of the heavy lifting and spent a few more nights at home letting him pick the movie. By the time Aislin had to sit her exams, I was back to my normal routine.

The problem was that by all reports, Aislin hadn't strayed more than twenty yards from home during daylight hours since that first day. She had let Nate take her out, but that was during the hours when she could pick up a phone or show up at a hospital if needed. I suspected she'd stay home more if Dad had been tolerant of her standing guard.

When I brought this up discreetly and while she was out, Dad nodded gravely. "I've been thinking about that," he admitted. "I've talked to the department and they aren't trying to drag me back, but they're willing to put me on desk duty as soon as I feel up to it."

"When do you think that will be?" I asked.

He grimaced. "Sometimes, I feel like it could be any day now, but I also feel like I won't feel normal for months." Seeing my expression, he held up a hand. "It's going well," he promised, "but I'm fine with taking it slow."

"So you'll be going back soon?"

"I was thinking the day you guys leave for Philadelphia," Dad suggested.

So we would be on the train while Aislin worried about whether some nut job was going to storm the precinct. I had those same fears, but dealt with them differently.

"Do we have to tell her?" I asked.

"Yes," he said, "but I'm going to order her onto that train as tactfully as I can. This can't bring life to a standstill anymore."

"We just wanted to be there," I protested quietly.

"And you were a great help, but I'm getting on with life and I'd like to see all of you do the same."

Aislin probably wouldn't take it gracefully, but I knew it was my duty to talk her into that.

"I'll see what I can do to help," I promised.

White

I tried my best to find out what Nate's mysterious pre-Thanksgiving plans were, but he was being secretive and his roommates claimed to be oblivious. All I knew for certain was that we hadn't made plans by the time the GED exams came around.

Dad picked me up from the last test, but didn't grill me for information. He respected my need to stop thinking now that I was done with homework.

I had worried that Maeve would turn tonight into a graduation party, but there were no extra cars in the driveway when we pulled up to the house.

"Are you hungry?" Dad asked on the way in.

"I had dinner before the test," I mumbled. "I can wait a while for breakfast."

"Okay," he said. "I like seconds."

From that comment, I was anticipating some kind of buffet, but I found *pastel de tres leches,* my go-to celebration cake, on the counter. Mom smothered me in a hug as soon as I got within arm's reach and I returned the affection readily.

"Diane sent a card," Maeve announced as soon as I was able to breathe again. "Brendan called to hope you didn't flunk. Grandma wants to know what color quilt you want for your dorm."

"I haven't ruled dorm life out, but Brendan might be on to something," I said. "What about . . ."

"Nate?" she interrupted. "I think he's giving you some space."

Great. The person I wanted on interrogation duty was giving me radio silence. I accepted the first enormous slice from Mom and tried to not look dour at my own party.

"So, you think it went well?" Mom prodded.

I probably would have burst into tears the moment I got in the car if it hadn't gone well.

"I think I survived," I said modestly.

"I think you aced it," Maeve corrected me with a wink. "You had all those . . . *study sessions* under your belt."

"Subtle," I said. "I think we managed not to ruin each other for academics."

"Whatever your results, we're proud of you," Mom said.

"And you'll be the youngest Byrne to graduate by three months," Dad pointed out. "We have a new family wunderkind."

"Have *you* called Nate?" Maeve asked. "He'll want to know how everything went."

"Not yet," I admitted. "Where's my phone?"

"Charging upstairs," Mom said. "Go share the good news."

I waited until I'd finished my cake and then hurried upstairs. I could see the glow of my phone's screen on the desk, but when I flicked on my light, I saw that my bed was partially hidden.

"*Maeve*!" I bellowed.

She was there in few enough seconds that I knew she'd been lying in wait. "You called?" she asked drolly.

"You let him into my *room?*"

"I did not," she said, admiring the spread. "He left everything downstairs and I set it up."

That explained why it had style and symmetry—Nate wasn't this artistic. There were white roses, a Dr. Seuss book, and lots of candy, among other things.

"Call him," Maeve ordered.

"You said you hadn't heard from him," I protested.

"I said he hadn't called," she reminded me.

"I applaud your sneakiness," I said solemnly.

"Thank you," she responded with a mock bow. "*Call* him."

I moved the champagne-scented bubble bath and roses so I could sit down and grabbed my phone. It started ringing seconds later.

"Hi," I said cheerfully. "Did Maeve signal you?"

"No, I'm just psychic," Nate answered. "How are you feeling?"

"Very relieved and spoiled," I said frankly. "Thank you for all of this."

"Don't thank me yet," he said. "We haven't discussed my mysterious agenda for the week."

"I don't mind." I had forgiven him for that long before he left me half a Valentine's Day commercial. "What is there to discuss?"

"My sister in California wants to meet you," he stated. "I told her there was no chance until after exams."

I dropped a candy bar, suddenly suspicious of a bribe. "What's your point?"

"She arrives tomorrow night," he announced. I could tell he was grinning too much to sound serious. "I was hoping we could all get dinner."

"Oh."

It was a lousy comeback, but it gave me time to reason it out. I could eat at a decent hour due to it being November and if she came in late enough, I could probably shower first, but that wasn't my concern.

"Is she a trial run?" I asked bluntly. "If I'm not embarrassing, your parents are next?"

"You're not going to embarrass me," Nate chuckled, "but sure, we'll call this the trial run."

"And is 'no' an acceptable answer?"

His next laugh was confident. "I doubt that's your answer."

"Why?" I challenged. "Maybe this is moving too fast."

"Maybe," Nate echoed, "but I think you want to."

"I want to spend dinner worrying if my pizza toppings are making the wrong impression?"

"Yes."

"*Why?*"

"You want to know if my insanity is hereditary."

After a moment of contemplation, I sighed. "That's true."

"I know."

"What time does she get here?"

"Six thirty," he said. "We can pick you up on the way home from the airport."

"Not a chance," I decided. "I don't want to be stuck making small talk in a car."

"Good point," he conceded.

"I can go to that place on Thatcher and hold our table . . ."

Nate snickered. "You're a mind reader."

"I know it's the only one that lives up to your standards," I pointed out. "She'll probably feel the same way."

"Go on," he encouraged. "We'll be there around seven thirty and try to show her a good time."

"Emphasis on try," I concluded. "What are the chances?"

"Better than you'd expect," Nate insisted.

I was feeling less sanguine about the whole thing. "It'll only be better than expected if none of us spontaneously combusts."

Black

It was no surprise that Aislin came to me for advice after tonight's surprise. Where dating rituals were concerned, she was like a novice ballroom dancer who liked to count out loud to make sure she wasn't off-beat. She looked happy, but she also looked like she was trying to find the hitch in her plans.

"How was your day?" she asked. "I want details."

"My day was entertaining," I sighed. It was a weird time to want a thorough account, but she wouldn't give up in this mood. "When Nick carried my books to class, he mixed them up. I had his French binder and he tried to turn in my English paper in history. Dewitt let him take a quick break to swap. Aaron was a jerk to Avril at lunch, so I won't be talking to him until she does. I tripped over the ball and have a bruise to prove it. Then Nate dropped off a portable gift shop." I stopped for breath and gave her a pointed look. "Is that detailed enough?"

"What was Aaron a jerk about?" Aislin asked, frowning.

"Does it matter?"

"I like Avril and you mentioned it," she pointed out, "Is she okay?"

Avril hadn't cried in the girls' room for the last two periods, but she hadn't been happy after lunch. I walked her home and let her talk about basketball tryouts instead of annoying boys. The whole thing would probably blow over soon.

"She'll be fine." I folded my arms, closing the subject to debate. "What did Nate say?"

"That his sister is coming into town and we're going to dinner tomorrow."

"Whoa." This announcement didn't need exaggerated excitement of any kind. "I don't think Brendan's ever reached that milestone."

"Brendan doesn't usually get this serious," Aislin reminded.

"And how are you feeling about it?" I asked, switching naturally into therapist mode. "Feel like fleeing the country again?"

She didn't laugh at that last joke. "Not just yet."

I was tempted to check her temperature. "Are you sure you're still conscious?"

"I'm pretty sure that I can handle his sister," Aislin defended herself. "I'm in charge of wardrobe, though."

I grunted in displeasure. Nate liked her in any outfit, but it didn't mean that his sister was the same way.

"So, why are you telling me?" I queried.

Aislin smiled with minimal teeth exposure. "Well, gloating, obviously."

"Obviously," I echoed. "And to ask for an impersonation?"

"I wanted you to understand why I'll be nervous until her flight leaves on Sunday."

That sounded more like her. She didn't spend much time in normal human interaction, so she sometimes felt the need to explain herself. It also gave the information needed to brief our parents.

"I'll keep that in mind," I promised.

White

Boston was home to enough pizza places that I still hadn't gotten to all of them, but Nate was most fond of Pizzeria Regina. I didn't have to wait long for a table, so I chose the chair facing the door and ordered water for everyone.

I recognized Janet before she saw me. I'd never seen a picture, but she resembled Nate and headed in my direction as soon as she saw me. I immediately stood up and tried to smile in a friendly way. To my surprise, her smile matched mine.

"So he wasn't exaggerating."

I had expected her greeting to include the word "hello," so my anxiety ratcheted up a level. I tried not to look petrified.

"I thought he'd call any girlfriend gorgeous on principle," Janet explained. "You must be Aislin."

"Guilty as charged," I answered. "Thanks."

"My parents say hello and Mom says he improves with age. I can testify to that."

Their mom sounded a little bit like Brendan, which meant that she was probably an acquired taste. I tried not to look dismayed at that prospect.

"So do I," I commented. "Where's Nate?"

"Trying to find parking," she said with a roll of her eyes. "It's worse than I thought."

I smirked and took my seat as soon as she had. "The stories about Boston drivers and record-breaking snowfalls are true."

"We're from Michigan," Janet said dismissively. "We can deal with being snowed in."

I let her get seated, minus her coat, before resuming small talk. "Are you here for business or pleasure?"

"A little of both," Janet replied. "One of my friends got me an interview with his law firm in Wellesley, but it was too last-minute for Isaac to come along."

"And I'm your unofficial reason?" I said, only half-joking.

"This is your preliminary hearing," she quipped back, "but our time is short, so the psychiatric evaluation and credit check will have to wait."

"I'm seventeen," I protested. "I haven't had time to get a credit score."

"Then we'll check you off as financially responsible," she decided. "And here's your public defender."

Nate's hand landed on my shoulder a moment later and I turned to give him a baleful look. "You left me alone with the *lawyer?*"

"She's our family's goodwill ambassador," he countered. "You just have to excuse her legalese. Dad would bring up your English grades."

"He's not that bad," Janet protested.

"Dad didn't approve of Isaac until after their first Dostoevsky discussion," Nate stated.

"Mom at least can leave work at the office," she sighed.

"So if I meet them, I should study harder for that than I did for any of my exams?"

"*No,*" Janet protested.

"Absolutely not," Nate agreed. "Isaac had to be worthy of Janet. It's a given that I should be worthy of *you.*"

"My dad certainly thinks so," I teased.

"And your dad is . . ."

"A cop," I supplied. "So far, he approves."

"And Nate seems to return the favor," she commented. "I think this is a good sign."

"I'd like to think so."

Nate coughed pointedly as the waiter approached. "How much do you trust my judgment?"

"Who are you asking?" Janet retorted.

"I know Ash will let me order whatever I want, but you're new here."

"If no broccoli is included, that's fine," Janet assured him.

With the order placed, she turned back to me. "So," she said seriously, "how free is your schedule?"

"With such short notice, I only have evenings free," I replied.

"You're not spending every waking moment at the library anymore," Nate pointed out. "I thought you could relax now."

"I'm relaxed," I promised, "but I still have college to prepare for, even if the campus is a mystery."

"You're going to BU," Nate asserted. "The other applications are a formality."

"That's the hope," I agreed.

"So I can drag Nate to Plymouth," Janet suggested, "and you're on call after dark?"

"I can't wait."

"That's because you haven't seen us in action." Nate said.

"There's a reason why we belong on opposite coasts," Janet confided.

"This much wit is a controlled substance?" I suggested.

Janet grinned and raised her glass. "I like you already."

SCENE 15

Black

Two days after Janet Long introduced herself to Aislin Byrne, extenuating circumstances happened. Aislin had bribed me to babysit her phone in case of changes in plans. If Nate wanted to reschedule, I was to use my judgment and relay results to our back-porch loiterer.

This text was low-key, but it was something Aislin would want to know about immediately.

"I'm heading out," I announced once I had her attention. "Janet's schedule changed and today might be your last chance to see her before she reports back."

Aislin's head came up as if I'd just presented her to a hungry wolf. I could practically hear her opposing argument running through my head, so I talked my captive audience into it.

"I know Janet thinks you're wonderful, but I'm not going to pass this up because of scheduling conflicts."

Before she could try to intervene, I turned on my heel and headed upstairs to re-dress. We were going to be outdoors mostly, so I grabbed jeans and a down-to-earth red plaid shirt. She would have disapproved of my makeup, but once I put my hair in a ponytail, you could barely tell the difference. Aislin hadn't moved from her spot when I returned and I crouched so she could hear me.

"My phone's on your desk," I informed her. "Call me when you're back."

She snapped at my wrist to feebly protest the idea, but didn't chase me when I turned to go. I headed for the front door and found Mom returning from the store.

"Going somewhere?" She frowned thoughtfully at the clothing choices. "As Aislin?"

"Doing her a favor," I corrected. "She knows."

"And she approves?" she asked skeptically.

"She only tried to stop me once," I reasoned.

Mom looked uncertain about the logic, so I handed over the phone and let the message speak for itself.

"So this impersonation is benevolent?" she guessed.

I bristled at the implication that I would maliciously impersonate her. I was at least giving everyone warning this time.

"I can't really screw things up on the Freedom Trail," I asserted. "I just have to behave myself between historical sites."

Mom handed back the phone, but still stood in my way. "How worthy is your cause?"

"Very worthy," I insisted. "If we argue any longer, I'm going to keep them waiting. I'll be back before you know it."

Janet's rental car pulled up to the curb five minutes later. I opened the back door and found an unfamiliar person across the seat.

"Hey," I said.

"You remember Noah," Nate assumed.

"Nate found out that I couldn't find Old North Church on a map and ordered me along," Noah explained.

It probably had more to do with uneven numbers than Noah's lack of historical education. Janet was no longer the third wheel and that suited her well.

"Cool," I said, sliding in. "Hey, Barons."

"Sorry for the short notice," Janet said from the driver's seat. "I didn't expect to visit New Hampshire, but I couldn't pass the chance up."

"I don't mind," I assured her.

"Our native guide is in charge of not getting us lost," Nate called over his shoulder.

I hadn't walked the Freedom Trail in years, but it was almost impossible to get lost when following a red brick road through the city. I could also navigate by T stops.

The real problem would be keeping the PDA platonic without seeming distant or uninterested in Nate. That wouldn't be too hard with Aislin's reserved style, but she would overreact if I even held his hand.

"For twenty bucks per person, I'll get all of you back to the car in one piece. For thirty, I'll make sure the car is in one piece too."

In hindsight, it was a very Maeve thing to say, but Nate smiled at me in the rearview mirror. I'd just have to watch myself.

"I've got five bucks and a water bottle," Nate volunteered. "What will that get me?"

"I'll show you how to find the Trail and take the T to the end with the five bucks," I negotiated. "You can keep the water bottle."

"For ten, you'll tell us about the history?" Noah guessed.

"Yes," I said. "I can show you where Paul Revere signed the Magna Carta on Bunker Hill."

"And you expect us to believe that?" Janet asked.

"I'm the native guide," I reminded her.

When she looked in the mirror, her grin matched Nate's and I knew I was on the right track.

We managed to follow the Trail to its conclusion without any mishaps and Janet offered to buy celebratory dinner. Aislin could make it to Harvard Square quickly, so I picked a restaurant near there and everyone agreed. Once seated, I stepped outside for a phone call.

I called Aislin immediately and I heard the ringtone a few yards away as she approached. Aislin was in my jeans and a red sweater, which wasn't really my style, but fit me better than today's lumberjack look.

"Biggest mishap was losing Noah's sunglasses by Faneuil Hall and we didn't get lost once," I assured her.

"How witty have I been?" Aislin asked in resignation.

"No more than usual," I answered. "You've also been very hands-off."

"How hands-off?" she challenged.

"I think he'd do anything for a goodnight kiss," I sighed. "The poor guy has been deprived."

She didn't look suspicious about my answer, so she was giving me the benefit of the doubt. I appreciated that after the miles I'd put on this personality.

"Thanks," she said.

We found a public restroom with available adjoining stalls and started swapping clothes over the wall.

"You know, I think you'd make a bigger impression if you wore pants in my style," I called as I lobbed the shirt over the stall wall.

"Yes, but that's not what I'm trying to achieve," she said. "Anything new with Janet?"

"She seemed to like us as much as you claimed," I reported, "and you're coming along to see her off on Sunday."

"Oh." She draped the sweater over the wall. "Who decided that?"

"Janet," I said.

She let out a sigh, but it sounded less disgruntled this time. "Thanks."

"Any time," I said. "You should have trusted me."

The creak of her door didn't drown out a sigh. "You know it wasn't about . . ."

"It's about me deciding what's best for you," I interrupted. I was in familiar territory. "Today wasn't the end of the world and you should remember that."

"I will," Aislin said, rolling her sleeves up. "Want to come to dinner?"

"Are you sure?"

"I know Noah's already there," she pointed out. "There are worse things than letting Janet meet both of us."

White

Sometime between the appetizers and entrée, I squeezed Nate's hand. He responded enthusiastically, probably since I'd been so hands-off all day. We took breaks to eat, of course, but as soon as he paid for our part of the bill, he went back to clutching my hand for dear life.

"How are you getting home?" Nate asked Maeve, assuming that she knew where we were parked.

"I borrowed the car to make things easier," she said. "I thought I would save you a trip."

Nate's grip tightened and there was more tension than usual in the gesture. "Sure," he said. "Thanks for thinking of that."

This meant that we had to end this adventure with an audience for our PDA. I expected him to ask for some privacy, but he kissed me before I could negotiate. It was a "we'll finish this *later*" gesture instead of a "until we meet again," but I didn't mind. Noah and Maeve cleared their throats in near-unison a few moments later and Nate pulled away.

"You can put up with us or wait in the car," Nate pointed out.

"But we're your chaperones," Maeve alleged.

"I think I should get her home before she gets any crankier," I suggested.

"Good call," Nate approved with a final kiss to my cheek. "Drive safe."

We made it back to the car before Maeve decided to talk again. "Well, that was fun."

"They like this composite me," I agreed. "Don't ever do it again."

"No deal," Maeve stated. "Until you go from being in passionate like to inevitable love, I'll have to help out once in a while."

She didn't know how close that "inevitable love" was right now, but it was impossible to tell how committed Nate was.

"And that kiss," Maeve continued, fanning herself. "Is he always like that?"

I shrugged, but didn't bother to quash my grin. "When making impressions."

Maeve sniggered. "Tell him I was definitely impressed," she commanded.

It was unexpectedly satisfying to have her approval.

ACT III

"If we could decide who we loved, it would be much simpler, but much less magical."
Trey Parker and Matt Stone

SCENE 1

White

In any relationship, there were secrets to be kept. I figured that Nate withheld his roommates' opinions of me and wouldn't disclose past indiscretions. I likewise kept mum on Canadian adventures and when I'd taken my driving test. I had no compulsion to disclose the reason they'd happened.

I hadn't lied about my post-exam itinerary, but I'd fibbed about the schedule. Mom wanted to shop for back-to-school clothes and re-equip me for classes, but we always raided the mall after her work day. Until that happened, my days were my own.

I was unofficially in charge of keeping Dad company like a devoted pet these days. He couldn't take me to doctor's appointments or meetings with his boss, but he let me sit next to him on the couch when he watched TV.

Today, I knew he would be out of the house for the morning, so I awoke for the transformation, but went back to bed after leaving the bedroom door open.

The front door slammed two hours later and I glanced at the clock to find that it was just after 8:00. A car started in the driveway, which meant that Dad was driving Mom to work so he could have reliable transportation to his appointments. Maeve was long gone.

I heaved a sigh and got my feet under me to hop from the bed and stretched my wings out to their full span. It was then that I noticed that I had no wings and my human knees buckled in surprise.

A few moments later, when I'd regained my senses, I grabbed my usual robe and wrapped it around myself for warmth. Then I hastened to the bathroom mirror to stare at myself in proper daylight.

According to the reflection, I was myself, down to the scar on my shoulder. When I pinched myself, it hurt, and surely dreams wouldn't be this cold.

I didn't scream in joy, but I couldn't stop myself from dancing back to my room, where I headed straight for the phone. I had just finished dialing Maeve's number when sense caught up and I abandoned that plan to with the tumble of emotions and theories that were running around my head.

Maeve deserved to be the first one to know, but if I called her at school, she'd unwisely skip the rest of the day. If I called Mom, she would take time out of her day to check that this wasn't a hoax. Most likely, Dad was going to overreact when he found me like this after his doctor's visit.

The person I really wanted to tell would be at his dorm until 9:30 today, so I did the only sensible thing. After a shower and dressing for sunlight, I headed to campus.

Nate answered his door with a toothbrush in hand and an amused expression in place.

"You played hooky," he blurted out, sounding impressed.

"My wardens have other things to do this morning," I responded, "so I thought I could walk you to class in my spare time."

"Great idea," he said. "Come in."

He beat a hasty retreat to one of the bedrooms and I heard him warning his roommates that there was a *lady* in the area. This led to Foster poking his head out to confirm his story and waving cheerfully.

"All right," Nate said after ridding himself of the toothbrush. "No one's going to traumatize you now."

"I don't think we'll be here long enough for that," I pointed out.

"I'm almost ready," he replied. "If I save pleasantries for later, I can even buy you breakfast on the way."

I was more interested in the idea of holding hands with him on the way to the student union, but I would take a bagel where I could.

"Go for it."

He returned a few minutes later with his backpack over one shoulder and smelling of mouthwash.

"If I didn't mention it before, this is a great surprise," Nate commented.

"I should do it more often, then?" I suggested.

"I wouldn't say no to a repeat performance," he agreed. "Good thing you'll be here next semester."

I didn't want him to jinx anything school-related, but today, I was feeling a lot more optimistic about the future than usual.

"Good thing," I echoed. "Shall we be going?"

He laced his fingers through mine. "Have you picked where you want to eat?"

"It's your turn for the surprise," I replied. "I trust your judgment."

The weather seemed to be in a good mood as well. It was cold enough that he pulled our hands into his coat pocket for the walk, but the sun cut through the late-autumn chill to make me not mind it at all.

"I assume you have great plans for your liberty," Nate prompted.

I wanted to talk him into skipping Bio and sharing a real adventure, but I had other ideas. I wanted to reacquaint myself with the city without taking a single subway, for one thing. "Whatever I want."

He laughed at that and tightened his grip on my hand. "Now I'm jealous," he said. "What made you start off this wild ride with a visit to me?"

I came to a halt and he turned to face me, which had been the point. I had three words that I wasn't brave enough to speak, so I paraphrased.

"I wanted you to know I think you're fantastic," I admitted.

This time, he didn't laugh. He just pulled me closer and kissed me as if there were no witnesses. This only served to back up my claim, so I wrapped one arm around his neck and returned the gesture.

When we pulled apart, I was grinning like an idiot, but his expression was perfectly neutral.

"The feeling's mutual," he said unnecessarily.

I wasn't the type to raid the refrigerator, since milk jugs and bowls of pasta were hard to grab with a beak and dinner was always waiting for me at sunset. I wanted to use my new freedom to do a hundred things, but the first thing that came to mind when I got home was a grilled cheese sandwich.

Dad had still been out when I returned from campus, but he walked into the kitchen after eleven to find me flipping my sandwich and stopped dead in his tracks. "Don't you have a class to get to?" he asked a bit warily.

"Not today," I said. "Sit down and I'll make you one."

He obeyed, but followed up with, "Did I forget a half-day?"

"Not as far as I know." I kept my back to him so he wouldn't see my grin. "White or wheat bread?"

"White," Dad answered. "Is there a perfectly good explanation for why you're taking your lunch period at home?"

"Am I not welcome here?" I challenged.

He ignored that question. "Can I hear your perfectly good explanation?" he requested.

I turned and leaned against the nearest counter, trying valiantly to keep a straight face. "I haven't had opposable thumbs at this time of day in five years," I said. "Forgive me for living a little."

I turned back to the stove and flipped the sandwich while waiting for that to sink in. Five seconds later, his hand landed on my shoulder and I turned to grin at him. He didn't say anything, just hugged me as if I'd been away for five years. I wrapped my arms around his waist and we both held on until something started to burn.

"Let me take care of that," Dad said in an oddly choked-up voice.

"Don't you dare," I ordered, pulling away and reaching for the spatula. "I'm enjoying this."

Instead of nudging me out of the way, he took my recently vacated spot against the counter and made our smiles match. "Is this the first time it's happened?"

"I'm as surprised as you," I confirmed.

"And your mother doesn't know," he prodded.

"By the time I woke up without a beak, no one was home."

Dad laughed, running a hand through his hair at the mental image. "Good thing. Maeve would have never left your room and the same goes for your mother. Teachers and bosses would wonder why."

"So I'm perfectly happy to have you witness this phenomenon first," I assured him. "You can also help me figure out how to break the news to everybody else."

He reached for his phone and dialed a number before I could say anything else.

"Hey, Sarah," he said casually. I quickly shut my mouth and fought the mad urge to laugh. "I'm done for the morning and home alone. Can I bring you lunch?"

In the middle of frying chicken, however, I felt the dull nausea that often preceded transformation. I backed away from the stove abruptly in case it happened immediately and Dad rested a steadying hand on my shoulder.

"Need a break?"

"The curse thinks so," I responded breathlessly.

"Okay," he said quietly. "I'll handle this and you take it easy. There's no rush."

I wanted there to be a rush. I wanted to show up mid-afternoon and laugh myself silly at Mom's reaction to my miracle.

"We'll tell her tonight," I decided.

Ten minutes later, I was back to my swan form. It immediately felt like a defeat, like I could have held it off if I had been stronger-willed. I had to console myself that if it happened today, chances were very good that it could happen again.

Black

As a year-round athlete, I rarely had dibs on the car. Mom had to have it for some errands, but promised to respond in cases of emergency. That also meant that if she arranged to pick me up, I didn't waste her time.

Soccer season had ended the week before Thanksgiving, so I didn't have anything to look forward to until winter sports, when I could trade in a mouth guard for swimming goggles. I could have taken the T home, but on Monday, I found Mom's car sitting at the curb fifteen minutes after last bell. Avril was keeping her company and laughing at some joke. I quickened my pace so I wouldn't keep them waiting.

Only it wasn't Mom driving.

"Hey," Aislin said casually. "I thought I'd give you a ride."

I wasn't on hallucinogenics, so I had no explanation for Aislin being behind the wheel in broad daylight.

"Hi?"

"Surprised?"

I still was too stunned to remember how to get into the car. "Hi?" Eventually I'd remember two-syllable words. "You're here."

Avril laughed at my complete lack of coherence and straightened up. "Aislin bet you'd keel over in shock. I'm disappointed."

"Give me a second and I might," I assured her. The illusion didn't fade when I blinked. "I had a dream like this once, you know."

"Come on," Avril teased. "When was the last time . . ."

"Never," we chorused.

Avril looked a little taken aback. Aislin had sounded entertained by the question and I was used to it.

"House rules," Aislin lied easily. "I'm not allowed to borrow the car until all my homework's done and that's usually long after dinner."

"But now that you're between schools . . ."

"I hadn't heard about that," Avril interrupted.

"Yeah," I said. "Brainiac here is off to college soon."

"We don't know that," Aislin corrected modestly. "I'm still not accepted."

On principle, she'd picked two colleges that didn't require standardized tests, but Avril didn't have to know that and it would require more explanation than it was worth.

"BU is where her boyfriend goes," I confided in Avril.

"Wow." I was relieved that she didn't look shocked, since Aislin wouldn't have responded well, no matter the reason why. "Good for you."

"Yeah," my sister drawled contentedly. "He is good for me."

"What are you doing Black Friday?" I asked. "We should do something that afternoon."

I glanced at Aislin, but she didn't object or correct the schedule.

"Good idea," Avril said a little more enthusiastically. "I'll call you."

She stepped away, raising a hand. "Happy Thanksgiving."

Her part of the conversation was over, but I was going to make Aislin drive until heard the salient details. After a few more moments of my stunned silence, Aislin sighed and turned the key.

"Get in. You look ridiculous just standing there."

I lobbed my bag into the back seat and got in so we could continue the conversation.

"You're here and the . . . sun's still . . . you know . . . shining." My wording was awful, but it made its point. "That's not common."

"It's a first for me too," Aislin stated.

"When did this . . ."

"Um." In private, her air of self-confidence diminished a little. "I don't know."

"You must have *some* idea," I said, more impatient than curious now. "How long has this lasted?"

She rolled her shoulders in a shrug and put the car into drive. "My transformation times have been off for three days, but today I was human until noon and swan until 2. It was really confusing."

The look on her face wasn't confusion; it was enjoyment of my befuddlement.

"So the curse isn't . . ."

"I don't know," Aislin interrupted. "It's not gone, but it's been tweaked and I don't know how."

"This is unprecedented."

She nodded. "Crushes and casual dating have never had an effect." She glanced over as we came to a stop sign. "You're going to dry out your mouth like that."

I quickly closed my mouth, but that didn't last long. "We're going to celebrate," I announced.

Her self-satisfied look came back, and she checked for traffic before pulling out of the parking spot. "Where are we going?"

"The T," Aislin decided. "I want some gelato . . ."

"It's forty degrees out."

She considered that for a second. "Okay, not gelato, but we're eating outside."

"It's *forty degrees*," I repeated. "You really haven't been out since . . ."

"I was twelve years old," she finished, her smile fading a little.

I felt like a complete creep for making a joke and I still had no idea what was going on. "This isn't how the curse worked in the ballet," I observed when we'd parked the car.

"We don't *know* how it works," Aislin contended. "It's family hearsay that happened to be true. Apparently, being head over heels gives me a little leeway."

She was sounding testy, so I gave her space until we found a café downtown. She stubbornly insisted on taking our drinks outside, but as soon as we were settled outside with our cupcakes and cocoa, I tried to reason it out again.

"So you love him?"

She didn't answer immediately, probably not wanting answer that impulsively. I took a sip of my own drink and waited very patiently.

"I think I've loved him for a week," Aislin answered.

"Since *when*?" I prompted eagerly.

"Since . . ." She tried to hide her blush behind her cup. "We've only been going out, what, a month?"

"I'm not keeping track," I lied.

"Having his sister meet me is significant. I thought it would be too much, but Saturday aside, I don't think it could have gone better. He proved that he takes our relationship very seriously, which . . ."

"You're not used to," I finished. "You've never dated anyone quite like him."

"Something between Nate and I flipped the switch," Aislin concluded. "I've loved him in one way or another since before then."

"Since Dad was in the hospital?" I guessed. "You weren't even dating and he went above and beyond."

"Yes," Aislin agreed.

"So you know when *you* fell in love," I said slowly. "Want to hear my theory about today?"

"I probably know the answer, but go on," she invited.

I wanted a fanfare for the next sentence, but it spoke for itself. "I think he's starting to love you back."

Aislin closed her eyes against the sunlight and grinned a little wider. "That's what I think too."

After the café, I made sure we covered as much ground as possible. It wasn't sunset yet and Aislin was still looking like a kid on Christmas morning.

"Think of all the things we can do with this," I commented. "Disneyland, tans . . ."

"Ski trips," Aislin commented. "Cross-country flights."

"The Boston Marathon."

"Whoa," Aislin protested. "You're getting ahead of me. The marathon was never in the plans."

"That's not the point," I said firmly. "We could go to the same high school."

"No way." The smile vanished and she looked suddenly intense. "Since someone went behind my back and got me the SAT scores I needed . . ."

"You're welcome," I answered modestly.

"I'm going to register for classes at any hour I want. I'm not going to take a single night class and I'm going to *enjoy* it."

I sighed and saluted her. "Here's to the nerds," I said. "You could even take a class with Nate."

"Best idea I've heard all year," she said.

"I'd save that for my next one," I advised. "Sunset's when . . . 4:30?"

"Something like that." Aislin answered. "What are you thinking?"

"Mom doesn't know, right?"

"Not yet," she agreed. "I tried to surprise her and turned into a swan instead."

It was a throwaway comment, but I could hear a tinge of annoyance in there. She would talk about that if she wanted, so I let it slide.

"So, I figure we break it to her gently," I proposed.

If Mom found it odd that Aislin's phone sent her an invitation to get off early, she didn't mention it. She texted back that she had loose ends to tie up before the holiday.

We flagged a random pedestrian down and asked him to take a retaliatory picture of us in the late-autumn sunshine. Within two minutes, Mom bolted from the building, looking pale, but not horrified. We waved innocently in return.

It was a good half hour before the sun was expected to set, but

Mom checked her watch at any rate. "What are you *doing* here?"

"I think that's obvious," Aislin commented. "We're your ride home."

"I mean . . ."

"I know what you mean," I interrupted. "I had the same reaction after last bell."

"Dad's known longer," Aislin contributed. "He wanted me to bring you lunch, but this isn't an all-day reprieve."

Mom, momentarily at a loss for words, just stared at the pair of us. It reminded me of the year that Aunt Diane had given us gerbils for our eighth birthdays; Mom understood the thing in front of her, but had no idea what to feel about it. After a long moment, some color returned to her face.

"All right," she said with a slightly nervous laugh. "I'll clock out now if you explain yourself on the way home."

I had been to the office twice during the daytime, but Aislin spent the minutes that it took Mom to wrap up business staring out her office window. She could only see other buildings and whatever was on the street and sidewalks below, but I think she enjoyed something other than a bird's-eye view more than anything else.

"So, where are we parked?" Mom asked.

"Within walking distance," Aislin replied.

"Meaning somewhere between here and Vermont?" she joked.

"Meaning a half mile away," I clarified.

"After all," Aislin concluded, "the weather's nice. Let's enjoy the sunshine while we can."

Mom snorted in amusement while pulling on her coat. "You make it sound as though we're under cloud cover for ten months of the year."

"Sorry for the slight exaggeration," she amended. "I just think I'll be walking everywhere until the snow's thigh-deep."

"I think you should," Mom said, pulling her into a side hug for the trip out of the office. "You've earned it."

White

I'd originally been thrilled about our planned trip to Philadelphia, but Dad's injury had changed things. When he announced his proposed work schedule, the urge to stay home grew stronger.

Dad eventually threatened to pack my bag himself, and after

setting some guidelines, I consented to leave him unattended.

The earliest Amtrak from South Station got us to Philadelphia before noon, so we checked into the hotel and went to all of the historical sites that Brendan would have refused to stomach. After a mere hour of swan time at the hotel—absence made the heart grow fonder, apparently—I headed back to the city to keep Maeve's 3:00 rendezvous. She probably channel-surfed while I waited on Market Street for Brendan to arrive.

"Hey," Brendan greeted from the driver's seat. "Good trip?"

As far as he knew, we'd arrived early this morning so Aislin could find a nice park. He could hear the details once he caught on to the real schedule.

"You know over-nighters," I said casually. "We played card games until we passed out."

"Good." He was silent until we were on the road again. "Have you had a cheesesteak?"

"Every single time we've visited you," I laughed.

"Good, then traditions must be upheld," Brendan decided. "We'll get one before we leave."

He didn't say much else during the drive, but once we neared the hotel, he raised the issue I'd been waiting for.

"So, who's this college guy I've heard so little about?"

"His name is Nate, he's at BU and yes, he loves her."

He grunted at that. "He loves her and she . . ."

"Loved him first," I said.

He grunted again—he had nothing intelligent or polite to say about that. A minute later, he spoke up again.

"Is he worth it?"

"By whose criteria?" I countered.

"Mom and Dad have a weird checklist of worthiness, but you don't just hand out approval."

"I don't," I agreed. "I definitely approve and take partial credit."

"Of course you do," Brendan snorted. "What did you do, lend her a sweater for the first date?"

"No, but she met him at the Pops concert on the Fourth," I pointed out.

"Where you were busy introducing her to someone else," he recalled.

"Nate wasn't with us," I corrected. "He just happened to be nearby."

"So I haven't met him."

"No, but he's coming to Thanksgiving . . ."

"Good," Brendan said. "I've always wanted my own reign of terror."

"You're going to be on your best behavior," I finished sharply. "You know he's important to her."

"I know that if this only happens once, I'm not allowed to ruin it," he sighed.

"With any luck, this will only have to happen once."

"No matter how deep first love is supposed to be, it's usually temporary," Brendan philosophized.

The brotherly concern in his voice was the only thing that kept me from starting a fight. He was convinced that this was going to end badly and was preparing for the fallout. I could live with that ignorant expectation of failure.

"There are a lot of people who marry their high school sweethearts and make it work."

"I know." He glanced over to gauge my hostility levels, something he rarely did when he thought I was Aislin. Our conversations usually made me feel like he saw me as a kindergartener, which made me wonder why Maeve got special treatment. "I promise to be on my best behavior."

"And no sending him on quests to prove himself," I commanded.

"No King Arthur stuff," he agreed and I recognized the familiar teasing in his tone. "Anything else I should know?"

"That you should have asked Aislin," I told him.

"She'll think I'm questioning her judgment," Brendan ruminated. "She doesn't deserve me running Nate out on a rail."

"I think she can handle it," I said.

"Then I'll talk to her about this sometime," Brendan promised as we parked.

"You haven't asked me what happened to my lip," I observed halfway up the sidewalk.

"I know what happened," he countered as we left the car. "Four stitches in ninth grade."

I pulled my hair back and turned to face him. "Where?"

He frowned after a moment of concentration. "Elective surgery?"

"No," I said. "Maeve has the scar on her lip and Aislin has ones on her shoulders."

Two steps later, it clicked and he dropped his keys.

"Knew we'd get there eventually," I gloated.

"You're . . ."

"This is why Maeve believes things are serious with Nate," I explained.

"You didn't think to tell me?" Brendan spluttered.

"I just did," I sighed. "Yours isn't the funniest reaction, though."

"Thanks," he muttered.

I turned around to find him grinning in the way that meant he was enjoying the thought of others' discomfort more than his own. "Congratulations?"

"Thanks," I said, walking backwards to enjoy the show. "Now do you believe me?"

"I'm converted," Brendan admitted. "Are we having Thanksgiving dinner at a decent time?"

Of course that was his first concern. "You mean in the middle of the afternoon when no one else needs feeding?"

"Just ask Nate. College boys need food every three hours."

"I thought it was every hour," I countered.

"That's in high school," he corrected. "We're less needy in college."

"Today, I only spent about an hour with feathers," I changed the subject. "A normal dinner time is almost guaranteed."

He slung an arm over my shoulders to show his appreciation and I turned to match his stride. "I'm happy for you," he said. "I don't think I said that yet."

"It was kind of vague," I admitted. "But thanks."

When Maeve answered the door with a hopeful expression, Brendan detached himself from my side and rested a hand on her shoulder. "Turn around," he ordered.

She obeyed and he pulled her collar aside for inspection. "Just checking," he said. "Hello, Maeve."

Her face contorted melodramatically with disappointment. "You told him," she accused.

"I didn't," I protested. "I just dropped a hint."

"But that wasn't our plan," she groused.

"We didn't have a plan." I threw my hands up in exasperation. "Can we at least argue inside?"

"Sure."

She stepped aside and I found my things on the window side of the double bed. Maeve had hogged the entire mattress for her nap, but we'd work it out.

"He was getting weird," I explained. "Do you guys always obsess over my love life?"

"When we're bored," Brendan said apologetically.

"What do you mean?" she asked.

"Brendan just had an opinion on my relationship longevity and how realistic my infatuation was . . ."

"Wow, that came out wrong," Brendan interjected. "I turned off the filters on my older brother instincts."

"So you don't filter with Maeve?" I challenged. "That's not fair."

"On most things, you're even," he said. "Maeve doesn't take my jokes as personally, though."

I understood *that* because Maeve and Brendan approached things from similar angles. "I don't know why you never asked me those questions."

He sat on the edge of the bed, his arms folded. "I already told you I was caring without making life more of a living hell," he reasoned.

"I'm not scared of skepticism," I protested.

"And now I know that," he said calmly, "but I still don't want to talk about it. God willing, I don't have to."

With his sudden lack of guile, I lost most of my will to argue the point. Instead of picking a fight, I gave him what I hoped was a forgiving smile.

"Let's not dwell on it," I suggested. "When are we using our birthday gift?"

"Tonight at six," Brendan answered, "and after your life-changing spanakopita, I thought we'd catch a movie without parental supervision."

"And tomorrow, you're all ours?" I asked hopefully.

"As soon as I hand in a paper," he said.

"And then you'll show us around?" Maeve said.

"I don't know," he said with a grin. "I was hoping to lose you on the subways."

We threw our pillows at him in perfect sync. He just ducked.

I wondered when he'd stop being touchy-feely, and it happened on the drive to dinner.

"So, all the guys in the world and the love of your life and you picked the burger boy?"

"He's not a *boy,*" I defended.

"He's younger than me. If he were your age, I'd call him the Ketchup Kid."

I shot Maeve a warning look at her stifled snigger. "You're supposed to be on Nate's side."

"I'm on your side," she giggled. "I just think Brendan achieved humor for once."

"Thanks, wise one," Brendan said. "Aislin chose the . . ."

"No more nicknames or I'm taking our spending money home with me tonight," I threatened.

"Fine," Brendan snapped. "The curse is losing its effectiveness because of *that guy*?"

"*That guy* is a university student who doesn't treat me like an annoying chew toy," I shot back. "Mom and Dad approve of him in ways that they'll never approve of you."

He looked indignant, meaning I'd hit below the belt on something. "That's low," he informed me.

"So is calling him everything short of Hamburger Helper," I retorted. "I'm not asking for your approval because that's not your place. You're not morally obligated to hate him."

"I'm entitled to have high standards for my sisters," Brendan stated.

"And you'll check him against those standards," Maeve said. "But the seal of approval isn't yours to give."

"It's not our parents', either," I added.

Maeve didn't argue with that, but nodded for me to answer that challenge.

"It's my business if he's worthy of me," I pronounced. "The rest of you are just there for commentary."

"Hear, hear," Maeve agreed from the backseat. "Your body, your choice."

"How about my life, my destiny?" I counter-proposed.

"That's better," she conceded.

"Tell that to the guy who cursed you in the first place," Brendan suggested. "He seemed to think he had a say in all of this."

"He did, but I'm here in daylight because the curse recognizes that Nate's met some of the conditions of breaking it."

"He's a smart guy; I'll give him that," Brendan said. "What else should I know about him?"

We drove back on Wednesday night with new inside jokes and matching sunburns. Mom would lecture us on skin cancer, but it was the first time in five years that I'd been at risk for that, so I'd forgotten sunblock.

The kitchen fridge was overflowing with enough food for a whole dorm, but Mom hadn't limited her shopping to that. She left a red paisley skirt and sweater that had probably been meant for Christmas on my doorknob.

My body still thought I should wake at dawn, so I helped stuff the turkey. As soon as it was roasting, I went back to bed and set my alarm for noon.

I got my wings tangled in the sheets upon waking. Maeve checked in on me, her expression dour, about ten minutes later. Instead of going outside, I pecked at my keyboard and listened to music until the phase passed.

At 2:05 by my clock's reckoning, I felt the lethargy that meant I was minutes away from human hours. At 2:10, Maeve cleared out of the bathroom so I could hog the shower.

Even on a home-bound day, my hair disliked the transformation process.

At 3:30, I was letting Maeve finish my makeup when the doorbell rang. She immediately grabbed a tissue to fix the lip-liner.

"Sorry," she said. "I'll stall him. You get shoes."

I hurried back to my room for my black flats. From the sound of two male voices, I guessed that Brendan had answered the door. I headed downstairs before damage could be done.

"You made it," I greeted Nate.

"I heard there was going to be pie," he replied, "and it beats the cafeteria. Plus, you invited me."

"My mother invited you," I corrected. "You should be flattered by *that*."

"Good point," Nate said. His posture straightened and his smile became a little more genuine. "How are you?"

I shrugged casually and reached for his hand. He latched on with casual ease and I pulled him to available chairs in the living room.

"It's been a pretty boring day," I admitted. "I helped cook and slept the rest of the time."

"That's more than I did," he said, laughing. "I didn't get up until noon, when Mom called to make sure I had somewhere to go."

"And you told her . . ."

He shrugged. "That I might not survive meeting your brother."

"Nice." I shifted in my seat so we were both facing the only entrance to the living room and prepared for battle. "How bad was it?"

"Brendan wouldn't let me in the house until he saw some ID."

"Don't buy the drug test requirement," I advised him. "He just likes having more power than the guy under the spotlight."

Nate grimaced. "Then I should probably get the sample back."

"You're not serious," I said quickly. "He's never tried that before."

"No, I'm just playing along to amuse you," Nate drawled. "Is it working?"

"One step at a time," I said. "We don't joke about criminal careers in this house."

His mouth twitched, but he kept an otherwise straight face. "Maeve vouched for me since your Dad's on a butter run and your mother . . ."

"Here we go," I muttered.

Mom had just swept into the room, still wearing an apron and beaming as though posing for pictures. "Sorry to keep you waiting," she said genially. "Good to see you again, Nate."

"Thanks for having me, Sarah," Nate responded

"Has anyone gotten your drink order?" Mom asked. "Aislin can bring you both something."

"I'll get it," he suggested.

That had been a test and he'd aced it without a second thought When he returned with apple cider, Maeve accompanied him.

"I found her in the kitchen, trying to give us some space," he said lightly.

"That's not fair," I said, shaking my head. "I can't be expected to babysit him the whole time."

"That's what football's for," Brendan called from the doorway. "You're not a Princeton fan, are you?"

"No?"

I rolled my eyes. "Two years ago, he couldn't tell you the Princeton mascot, but he's taken his rivalries seriously ever since freshman orientation."

"I get it," Nate said, nodding. "My dad went to University of Michigan and wouldn't have forgiven me if I looked at Notre Dame. He's lucky to have married a neutral UC San Diego alumna."

"So BU is neutral territory?" Maeve asked.

"Neutral enough," he reasoned, squeezing my hand for no apparent reason. "I think it's been worth it."

"I still haven't heard from them," I said helpfully, "but they claim I'll hear by mid-December."

"Which means I need to bribe my friend in the admissions office for a sneak peek."

"Don't you dare," I insisted. "I want to *enjoy* opening that mail. You're invited, of course."

"I've got a better idea."

"Name it," I invited.

"As you get the letter, I'll bring pizza and drinks and we'll visit your new campus afterwards."

"Can I borrow your confidence?" I joked.

"I'm happy to believe in you when you can't manage it yourself," he said solemnly.

That was the sort of statement that made me wish we could share a couch instead of parallel seats. "I'd like that," I said. "Could I sit in on a class sometime?"

"I'll set it up," he said.

"You guys don't date like normal people," Brendan added.

I had completely forgotten that he was still there. He took that opportunity to occupy Dad's usual armchair.

"What will you do if you need a safety school?" he asked.

"Just in case, I've picked four alternatives."

Brendan suddenly perked up. "Please tell me at least one of them is out of state."

"So she can help you conquer Philly?" Maeve guessed.

"To see what mischief she could manage without supervision," Brendan replied. "I think she's got a wild side and Montreal's just the tip of the iceberg."

"What happened in Montreal?" Nate asked.

"Absolutely nothing," I said firmly.

"It doesn't sound like nothing," Nate considered. "Should I ask Brendan?"

If it took an actual threat, I would make sure it never came to light. It turned out to be slightly unnecessary.

"I wasn't there," Brendan complained. "The hearsay's great, though."

"It's not important," Maeve claimed.

"One of the colleges is even out of the country, just in case no one wants me here," I answered the original question.

"You're twice the student you think you are," Maeve complained. "I should go dress uncomfortably for dinner. Can you knock off the humility when I get back?"

"Nerves, not humility," Nate corrected. "It happens to me too."

"You're all very funny," Mom commented drily. "Does anyone need a refill?"

"No, thanks," Nate said.

"I'm good," I added.

"Why don't you come help me?" Mom suggested to Brendan before he could answer.

"I just got here," he protested.

"Yes, but you're antagonizing everyone," she said. "And it's time you learned how to make gravy."

"We'll come," Nate said.

"Don't you dare," Mom said. "House rules say that guests aren't allowed near the stove. We can manage on our own and you can have some privacy."

I was saved from Maeve's inevitable protest by Nate's impulse to be useful.

"We have that all the time," he said, "and I've learned the fine art of mashing potatoes from my mother."

"All right," Mom sighed, beckoning him forward. "Aislin, go fetch your sister, will you?"

I found her pulling on a pair of nylons. "How's it going?" she asked. "Has he run screaming yet?"

"Nate is the helpful son Mom never had," I reported. "I'm not sure if Mom approves or wants to banish him from the kitchen."

"Well, Dad hasn't requested a protective order against him and that's a good sign," she pointed out.

"It's never happened to one of yours," I argued. "What makes you think he'd go that far?"

"For a cop, Dad's pretty low-key," Maeve informed me. "When he disapproves, he names one or two flaws and trusts me to find the others. If Dad hasn't told you to watch your step with Nate, he's practically part of the family."

I considered for a while before agreeing. "I think Dad recognizes this relationship as being the best thing that's ever happened to me."

"First love," Maeve sighed. "It's always the best thing that's ever happened to someone."

I didn't think my feelings would have been different if he were my thirtieth relationship, but I didn't want to ignore Nate while we philosophized.

Nate had taken over the gravy by the time we got back and was chatting amiably about classes. Mom probably didn't find this enthralling, but she supportively paid enough attention to commit things to memory.

I knew things were going well, though, when we were allowed to sit together. Dad could have kept Nate next to him several seats away. We took advantage of that to hold hands surreptitiously while dishes were passed.

To my relief, no one balked when Nate passed on the football game. Brendan was emotionally invested, but didn't expect our newcomer to share his zeal.

"We can do dishes," Nate suggested with a glance at me.

"Leave it for Dad," I said. "The cooks don't clean on holidays."

"But all I did was make gravy," he pointed out.

"It counts."

"You can relax anywhere you like downstairs," Mom directed. "Has he seen the photos in the office?"

"No," Maeve and I responded sharply.

"No baby pictures ever," I reasoned.

"He's not seeing our school pictures," Maeve added. "We *were* going to build a fire later. Get kindling if you're bored."

"That sounds like a plan," Nate said approvingly. "Coming?"

The weather was pretty mild today, so we didn't need outerwear. Nate wrapped his hand around mine immediately, though.

"You looked like you needed a hand warmer," he said with a sly grin.

My hands were fine, but I accepted the affection gladly. "So," I said casually, "have they scared you off yet?"

"Your dad hasn't changed at all."

I nodded. "He hasn't in seventeen years, so why should he change now?"

"Your mom is very . . ."

"Enthusiastic?" I supplied.

"Supportive," he corrected. "I think she knows my classes better than I do."

"You've gotten in her good graces," I assured him. "Brendan . . . can't be helped. He and Maeve treat every stranger like that."

"Like what?"

"Reserving judgment."

He let out a quiet snicker and his grip tightened on my hand. "Thanks for the interpretation," he said. "And the invitation."

It had been a collaborative effort, but I didn't want to make light of the situation or exaggerate its significance. I settled for smiling back.

"My pleasure."

The woodpile was within sight of any self-appointed chaperones, but it was a good place to talk out of earshot of anyone in the house.

"So," Nate said as we surveyed the various stacks, "did you really feel like raiding the woodpile?"

"We could burn it out here," I granted, "but the others probably wouldn't enjoy that as much."

Plus concrete was not the most comfortable place to cuddle.

"I mean . . ." His fingers flexed for emphasis. "I thought we could . . . take our time."

I instinctively pulled back so he couldn't make a move; out of earshot or not, I knew Maeve would spy on us, either for my good or on Brendan's orders.

"I'm *not* making out with you next to the kindling," I said indignantly.

Nate grinned wickedly. "So you'd be willing to make out next to the tinder?"

We were serious enough that I didn't mind the suggestion, but I was still awkward teenager, so I grimaced. "You're missing the point."

"No, just getting some entertainment," he corrected.

I waited for my embarrassment to fade, and then arched an eyebrow. "If you're that desperate, I can tap dance."

"Really," he said, surprised.

"Badly," I admitted.

His grin converted into a smirk. "I'll keep that in mind," he threatened.

"You're missing the point."

"Which is, I'm guessing, something about privacy?"

"We've got privacy." Nate waved towards the house, and I turned to see Maeve keeping watch. "We'd have more of it on a walk."

"I can get behind that," I said. "We should tell . . ."

"Maeve can do that," he quipped. "In the meantime . . ."

He released my hand and bent me backwards in a posture worthy of *Gone With the Wind* for an equally dramatic kiss. The long, almost lazy kiss took all the time it needed without needing embellishments. It went on so long that my bosom should have heaved, but it was hard to heave in a twinset. He finally got around to coming up for air and I made a show of readjusting my hair.

"We'll be back in half an hour," I called to Maeve. She flashed a thumbs-up through the window before retreating from view.

"That was fun," Nate announced. "Can we take that on the road?"

"Only if we visit everyone who's called me a hermit," I retorted.

"Are they in walking distance or should I get my keys?" he asked with a perfectly straight face.

"I was *kidding*," I said hastily.

"I wasn't."

"I like to show you off, but that's not necessary," I promised. "Let's get going before anyone stops us."

Nate marched me around the house and to the sidewalk. I stifled a laugh and quickened my pace to keep up. Once we were invisible to anyone in the house, he stopped for breath.

"How many people would have been on this tour?" he wheezed.

"Five started the rumors," I said. "They're still not worth the detour."

"I'll trust you on that," he said. "I wouldn't have minded."

"They usually don't care if I exist," I pointed out. "I don't want this to be what changes their minds."

He looked actually offended by that and that was more flattering than the display he'd put on for Maeve. "Just give me one address," he demanded.

I squeezed his hand in gratitude, but I turned left on Lake Street to avoid Natalie's neighborhood. We got about two blocks before I decided to try conversation again.

"So, my family's that bad?"

Nate's brow furrowed. "What are you talking about? I said nothing like that."

"Yeah," I conceded, "but you had to escape after dinner."

"I had to escape with *you,*" he pointed out. "Your family's great."

He was being the perfect guy by lying through his teeth about loved ones. "They're weird," I admitted.

"Mine too. That's why you and I work."

That didn't sound like a lie, but I had to dig for details anyway. "How weird?"

He considered his answer for a while. "You know Janet's competitive about . . ."

"Everything?" I supplied politely. "So you claim."

"Yes, she was on her best behavior so she wouldn't scare you off," he said.

"What's your point?" I prompted.

"She doesn't like anyone following her lead. Not her bratty younger brother and not our parents."

Now my interest was piqued. "Did she get it from them?"

"Not as far as I can tell," Nate said. "Dad would have been

proud if I imitated him, but I'm not cut out for teaching. Mom just wants me to be happy."

I liked his parents already. "Which makes me wonder how that's working out for you."

He glanced in my direction, his expression guarded. "You don't know?"

"It's important to me," I admitted. I held up a hand in warning. "Try to answer without channeling Rhett Butler."

He couldn't quash his grin at that. "You know I am."

It was reassuring to hear it confirmed. "Have any plans for next Thanksgiving?"

I wasn't supposed to scare him off with long-term plans and I immediately wanted to smack myself. Maeve would be appalled.

Nate relieved me by not looking horrified. "There's something you should know before I answer that and it's waited too long."

If he turned out to be a werewolf, I was swearing off men. He pulled me to a stop under the next tree and turned me to face him with one hand cupping my chin.

"I love you," he said very quietly.

It was a secret shared that I had known since I reclaimed some daylight hours, but I was thrilled that he had divulged it in private. The intimacy of the moment made it feel more authentic.

"I love you too," I answered.

"I'm really glad to hear that," Nate said. "I've been trying to say that for a week and it's harder than you'd think."

I kissed him the same way that he had kissed me at first, only caring if he felt safe. I preferred it to bosom-heaving any day.

"It was worth the wait," I assured him.

Hours later, after Mom had foisted leftovers on Nate and I walked him to the curb, I visited Maeve in her room.

"Can you do me a favor?"

She looked up from her phone with a mischievous grin. "From what I saw today, I've done you enough of those."

"*Pro bono*," I suggested. "Can you let Susanna know her services are no longer needed?"

That made her abandon whatever she was doing on the phone entirely. "You're that confident you don't need it?"

"I'm optimistic that we can pick up the slack on our own," I said. "Tell her I say 'thank you.' "

"I will," Maeve promised. "Two months of her work paid off."

"Or it had no ill effect," I countered. "Don't tell her that."

"Then what do I tell her to explain this decision?" she asked.

"After two months of her hard work, life is good," I stated. "I'm grateful for that, but I'd like her to get back to her own priorities now."

Maeve nodded. "I'll tell her as soon as I can figure out how to make that sound better," she agreed.

I wasn't sure what she expected to improve, but she could change the words if the meaning was the same.

"Thanks," I responded.

She smiled and retrieved her phone to resume whatever she had been doing. "Any time," she said. "But for the record . . ."

"You think it's a bad idea?"

Maeve's smile spread into a smirk. "The opposite," she said. "For the record, I think you'll do just fine on your own."

It was the most confidence she'd ever expressed in my methods, but this was the first time I'd been in love. I was willing to take her at her word.

"Thanks for the vote of confidence."

SCENE 2

White

I felt stuck as soon as Thanksgiving passed, since college plans were still unconfirmed. Everything that fall had led up to the exams and it felt as though I had nothing to focus on until letters started arriving. Nate offered twice to break into the admissions office, but it wasn't a temptation.

The envelope finally arrived a little over a week after the holiday, stuck between bills and a holiday card from cousins.

"I have an answer from BU," I texted the interested parties immediately. "I'm opening it at five no matter what."

Dad could only participate by speakerphone, but Mom, Maeve,

and Nate were all there and Brendan promised to call once his test was over. Nate had brought the promised pizza, but everyone was too apprehensive to eat.

"Are we all ready?" I shouted at the speakerphone.

"This is a business call," Dad said almost inaudibly. "Don't worry if I start talking about a break-in on Boylston."

"Can I have the envelope, please?" I requested, trying to feign bravado.

Maeve handed it over with a flourish and everyone present leaned a little closer as if they could read the answer through the envelope.

"I'm in," I blurted out a few seconds later.

I hugged the lunatic who had taken my SATs first. Mom opted for a group hug, but Nate hung back until I freed myself and wrapped my arms around him.

"Officer Byrne," he called in the direction of the phone, "I'd like to take your youngest to her new campus. Is that all right?"

"Enjoy it," Dad allowed before hanging up.

Maeve cleared her throat and offered a glass of soda. "Do you mind?" she asked. "You're holding up a celebratory toast."

I took it, but didn't let go of Nate's hand as Mom raised her glass. "To Aislin, her college career, and many more great things to come."

I wasn't sure what she meant by that last bit, but I didn't mind the sentiment. I clinked glasses with everyone and drank up.

"I'm calling Brendan," Maeve said. "Do you want to tell him or . . ."

"Text him something cryptic," I ordered. "I'll tell him after the tour."

She did as instructed while we dished out slices of pepperoni. Nate hadn't stopped grinning since the toast and our expressions matched.

"Are you as happy as you look?" he asked in a low voice.

"Everything's feeling surreal," I admitted. "But I couldn't be happier about it."

"Good," he said. "You should be."

I wanted to thank him properly for getting me through this, but not with witnesses. I set down my pizza and put that gratitude into another hug. Under the circumstances, I was at a loss for words.

Black

I escaped to my room as soon as Nate and Aislin headed for campus. The time for being demonstratively happy was past and I knew from seventeen years of experience that Aislin's instinct was to worry about the unknown. Nate could get her through that, since her default setting around him was happiness. I didn't like being outgrown, but I couldn't really resent the pay-off.

Instead of moping, I called Nick. When Aislin's text had gone out, I'd canceled our plans and promised to make it up to him. I had just decided to call tomorrow when he picked up, yawning groggily.

"Is it good news?"

"It's very good news," I said.

He sighed into the phone and I patiently waited for the news to register. "That's awesome," Nick said finally. "Tell your sister I'm happy for her."

"I will," I promised. "Will I see you tomorrow?"

"Ask me then." He'd apparently gone to bed early, so I wouldn't call his bluff if he started snoring. "'Night."

Apparently, he'd taken my silence to be consent. I hung up and went back to the kitchen to do dishes.

"Don't look now," I commented, "but I think things are finally looking up for my kid sister."

Mom turned with an amused expression on her face. "I was just thinking that," she said.

Since she was taking care of the dishes, I cleared the table before commenting again. "I don't want to jinx it . . ."

"Or be skeptical," she added.

"I don't want to be waiting for the other shoe to drop."

Mom shrugged at the dishes that she was rearranging. "I don't think any of us want that," she said, "but this is the best year she's had since . . ."

"Forever?"

Mom's shoulders dropped back into their normal position. "Since I can remember."

"And all winning streaks have to end."

She turned to face me and there was weariness behind the smile. "Just don't tell her I said so."

Somewhere down the line, things would go wrong again and all I could hope for was a long wait. It was a traditional and inherited sense of pessimism.

"I won't tell if you won't."

White

I didn't often get the chance to answer the door these days, but it was a standing rule that if I was human and home alone, I had to see who it was. This year, I'd met two deliverymen and a pair of missionaries.

When I opened the door tonight, Natalie looked frankly ill. "You're home! Can I come in?"

Natalie was rarely happy to see me, so I suspected she mistook my identity. She looked devastated, though, so I decided to get her out of the cold.

"She's not here," I said immediately to forestall a misunderstanding.

Natalie gave a diffident shrug. "She has to get out sometime," she replied.

Now I was certain that she thought I was Maeve and wasn't paying attention.

"Do you want to . . ."

I never finished the thought; without warning, the walking superiority complex who treated me like the village idiot started sobbing. I had no preparation for this scenario, but I knew that it was my responsibility to let her stay until Maeve got back.

I went immediately into Mom mode, taking her bag and steering her to a chair. I wasn't making her a soothing cup of tea, but I got her a glass of water. It took her a while to drink it, but after the second glass of water, her sobbing had become the sort of crying that I associated with the ending of a really good movie.

"Okay," I said cautiously, "do you need some privacy?"

She nodded miserably and accepted the third glass of water, but only drank half of it before heaving a great sigh.

"I don't want this out in the open," she admitted.

"Okay," I agreed. "Upstairs it is."

I left her purse sitting on the counter where Maeve would find it.

My immediate plan was to find out whatever was bothering Natalie and sympathize long enough for Maeve to return.

"Does anyone know you're here?" I asked before we left the kitchen.

"I'm *not* talking to my parents," she snapped.

That narrowed down the reasons for her distress and gave us common ground. I had a lot of experience with being at odds with family.

"Go on up," I offered. "I'm going to cover our bases."

Natalie's brow furrowed and she halted immediately. "I don't *want* to talk to my parents."

"I'm not going to call them," I promised. "I'm just not interrupting therapy because you're dehydrated."

It was an accurate impression of Maeve, striking the balance between practicality and impatience in a crisis.

"All right," Natalie muttered. "I'll be upstairs."

I got enough ice water to last us for a couple of hours and didn't look up a way to check in with her parents. I *did* text Maeve that there was a "Natalie 911 @ home."

Said emergency was sitting on Maeve's bed and looking no less miserable than she had been a few minutes ago.

"Family trouble?" I prompted.

"My stupid brother decided that being busted for possession once a semester just wasn't thrilling enough."

I clenched my jaw so I wouldn't say something stupid or insensitive. I knew that Natalie had an older brother, but knew less about him than she knew about me.

"This time, he's being charged with intent to distribute," she continued. "I doubt he's smart enough for that, but those are the charges."

"And he's not a first offender, so the rules are different," I recalled Dad's occasional lectures on law enforcement.

"Dad's trying to find a lawyer who can get the charge reduced so it won't be as bad, but that's up to the judge."

"And you want that?" I asked blankly.

Natalie's look was suddenly venomous. "He's an idiot, but he's my brother," she defended.

"I just . . ." I couldn't figure out where the person who had no sympathy for my introversion ended and the staunchly supportive sister began. "Are they talking about some kind of outpatient rehab program?"

"That's what they want," she said, reaching for the water pitcher. "That's better than him being stuck in some facility where he's treated like a murderer. I want him to get the help that brings the old him back."

"I get that," I said honestly.

I wondered if Maeve felt the same way about my circumstances. It would certainly explain how persistently she meddled.

"Don't they usually get family input on this sort of thing?" I asked.

"He's eighteen now," she pointed out. "I'm not sure they're going to be as sympathetic as the last time."

"You can still find out," I suggested. "Even if they don't want input, he'd like knowing you haven't given up on him."

"Of course I haven't given up on him," Natalie bit out. "I wouldn't be this mad if I had."

"Have you told him that?"

"Not in that many words, no," she conceded, "but I can't hammer it into his thick skull."

"I would," I informed her. "You're on his side when he probably thinks no one is. It couldn't hurt to state the obvious."

Maeve had taught me the most about loyalty, so I didn't feel guilty about imparting her wisdom to her best friend.

"Can I call your parents?" I requested.

"Why?" Natalie sniffed sullenly.

"They should know you're staying over," I said firmly. "You don't need their permission, but they'll appreciate you showing respect."

Natalie's glower faded into an exhausted expression. "Okay," she agreed, "but I'll call them. Where's my purse?"

I hadn't expected her to give in at all, much less that easily. "I'll get it," I excused myself. "Pajamas are in the bottom drawer."

I retrieved her purse and a spare toothbrush. When I got back, Natalie was wearing Maeve's grey flannel pajamas and a guarded expression.

"Here you go," I announced. "Come find me when you're done."

I grabbed the water pitcher and beat a hasty retreat to the

kitchen. The pitcher was half-full when Dad came in.

"Natalie's staying over," I announced. "This is non-negotiable."

He stopped dead in his tracks, looking just as confused as our guest. "Those are very strange words to be coming out of your mouth."

"They are," I agreed. "I feel strongly about the matter."

His mouth curved up on one side. "Do her parents know?"

"Yes," I said. "Maeve doesn't."

"So this was your idea?" Dad finished skeptically.

"Yes."

"All right."

If I'd met Mom first, I'd still be working out the details. Dad was good enough to follow my lead.

"I'll let your mother know I approve," he promised. "What does Natalie like for breakfast?"

I successfully kept a straight face. "How should I know?" I deadpanned. "She's Maeve's friend."

Black

Aislin's text didn't reach me until after the movie, but it was followed soon after by instructions to knock on my own door. She'd called it an emergency, so I followed orders.

Aislin opened up immediately and slipped out, closing the door behind her. "Hey," she said. "Did you have a good night?"

"I had a great night," I said cautiously. "Why are you in there?"

"It's a one-time thing," Aislin explained, "but I don't want you tripping over Natalie."

"What are you doing with *Natalie*?" I blurted out.

"Plotting world domination."

"In *my* pajamas," I responded.

Aislin shrugged. "You've borrowed my wardrobe often enough."

"So you were impersonating me with my best friend," I summarized. "Mind explaining?"

"Come with me," she ordered. "I'll get you up to speed while you change."

Three minutes later, we'd swapped pajamas and I was somewhat flabbergasted by her account.

"It's as much as you would have done," Aislin summarized. "You'd have done it with finesse and understanding, but . . ."

"I can believe that you'd help her, but I never thought you'd have that put to the test."

"Nor I," Aislin admitted. "But I owe you, so it was the least I could do."

Be that as it may, I spontaneously hugged her and she returned it after a brief hesitation. She didn't look thrilled with the situation, but seemed relieved that I hadn't bitten her head off.

"Don't mention it," she said. "Dad wants breakfast suggestions."

"Pancakes," I decided. "It'll make us all feel better."

I figured that a last-minute request was better than interrupting Dad's sleep, so I headed back to my room and cracked the door open just wide enough for me to squeeze through.

The bedside lamp clicked on and Natalie blinked at me. "You're back."

"Yeah." I climbed into the makeshift bedroll on the floor and propped myself on my elbow. "I just had to run to the bathroom."

"That's not what I meant." She was now awake enough to look sheepish. "Your sister is a lot nicer than I've ever given her credit for."

I was sure Aislin would have mentioned Natalie recognizing her, but it was possible that she hadn't caught on to Natalie's realization.

"Yes, she is," I replied. "I've been saying it for years."

"I know," Natalie admitted, "but I was too stupid to believe you."

"You weren't stupid."

"Not tonight," she agreed, "but in general."

It would have been tactless to remind her of a similar statement in an earlier lecture, so I shrugged it off.

"What gave her away?" I asked.

"After five glasses of water and three pep talks, I noticed she didn't have your scar."

"I told you her Florence Nightingale tendencies were strong," I joked with a grin.

Natalie didn't smile back. "I felt like a jerk."

She was willing to admit to at least one mistake, so I had mercy on her. "You shouldn't," I advised. "Feel lucky that I don't exaggerate my sister's qualities."

She considered that for a moment, and then rolled onto her back with a sigh. "Should I tell her?"

"No," I decided immediately. "She'll enjoy this most if it's an unknown act of kindness."

"If you say so," Natalie said.

"But I think this will make it easier to behave yourself," I added. "Any time you feel like taking a crack . . ."

"I said I was sorry," she interrupted.

She'd technically only admitted to feeling like a jerk, but that was close enough.

"Okay," I said. "I suspect she feels like a jerk, too."

Natalie turned to stare in disbelief. "Why? She spent her whole evening babysitting someone who hasn't been very fair to her."

"She spent her whole evening learning why I'm friends with you," I pointed out. "You underestimated each other and that stops now."

She was quiet for so long that I thought she was drifting off. It was a minute before she turned off the light. "Yes, it does," she promised.

SCENE 3

Black

There were certain traditions that had been stopped by the curse, but most of the time, we found workarounds. We didn't take normal vacations, but we spent New Year's Eve together. We rarely flew, but road trips were on every year's schedule.

Winter holidays were no exception. We were probably the only teenagers who still woke our parents up in the middle of the night to open presents. The first Saturday of December was Christmas tree night. We all enjoyed that most festivities didn't require daylight.

This year, I dragged Aislin out for a *day* of shopping and she agreed to go to three malls as long we also tried stores that were more her style. She helped me pick out jewelry and I suggested a book that Mom had expressed interest in. We combined our funds when I found Brendan a movie collection that was out of our individual price ranges. For Dad, she got a gelato gift card and I got a book on the Red Sox.

I didn't want to bring up Nate's present before she was ready, but figured that quest would take the longest. I already had a Syracuse sweatshirt for Nick to provide inspiration for his last semester.

When everyone else was taken care of, I finally spoke up. "It's your first major holiday as a couple," I prompted. "What's your plan?"

"I've already checked," Aislin informed me. "He doesn't expect gifts for all eight nights of Hanukkah."

There was a way to work with Hanukkah, but he would have to settle for eight smaller gifts.

"Any caveats?"

"He's leaving before Hanukkah starts," Aislin said. "We're exchanging gifts on the 17th."

"That's okay," I said.

"Not really," she said. "I still have *no* idea what to get him."

"Mistletoe?" I suggested with a sly smile.

"Not on your life," Aislin answered firmly. "We don't need help."

I smirked at her until she turned away, still capable of embarrassment. "You know what I mean," she said.

"You're not allowed to give him a book."

"He's read half the science library this semester," Aislin pointed out. "That never crossed my mind."

"Good girl." I considered. "Redecorate his dorm room?"

"I'd have to clean up after his roommates to find the floor, so no."

"Make him dinner?"

"I need something memorable," Aislin considered, ignoring me.

"Given the right amount of tabasco sauce, food can be memorable," I pointed out.

She tried to look stern, but her sudden laugh ruined the effect. "Come on," she begged. "I'm being serious."

"Okay," I muttered. "Define memorable."

"Maybe clothes?"

I shook my head. "He'll get that from his mom."

"But it's all I can think of," she said. "And that's what you're giving Nick."

"Yeah, but he's my boyfriend, not my happily ever after."

Her next look was slightly pitying. "Why are you with him if he's not your happily ever after?"

"Because regular teenagers don't have that kind of pressure," I stated. "I can afford to have a bit of innocent fun. Yours is serious."

"So clothes are a no?" Aislin asked despondently.

I decided to take pity on her since she was starting to look frazzled. "It depends on the clothes." I checked my watch. "Why don't we hit the Garment District and see what we can scrounge up there?"

That store was never the same twice, but it had unhealthy amounts of reasonably priced clothes in one building. On some days, I could go in there and find the perfect top for myself. On others, I struck out. If Aislin was determined to find clothes for Nate, a famous thrift store might work for her.

"Let's split up," I suggested. "I'll pull some options and we'll meet back here in twenty minutes."

I didn't know Nate's style or tastes, so I looked for something that would make any guy look good. My collection included a few shirts, a belt, and even a vest that he might just be able to pull off.

When I met Aislin at our spot twenty minutes later, she was folding a receipt into her wallet and looking smug. Had my hands not been full of clothes, I would have rubbed my temples.

"I think you missed the point," I said.

"No, I just found something irrefutably perfect for him," she informed me.

"Let me see," I ordered.

"Not until we get home."

"Why not?"

She smirked. "Because you'll try to talk me out of it."

I immediately lunged for the bag, but Aislin gently elbowed me out of the way. "We never agreed to let you choose the gift," she insisted. "You just get to admire my good taste."

"Fine," I huffed. "I'll admire it now so we don't have to come back later."

"Wow," Aislin sighed. "You really are as arrogant as I thought."

From anyone else, that would be an insult. I just smirked back and held out my hand for the bag. Instead of yielding, she turned and left. Once I'd put everything back, I dashed out of the Garment District and chased her down.

"Do you need anything else?" she asked.

"I've got everyone covered," I bit out, momentarily annoyed by her escape tactics. "Are you sure you wouldn't rather . . ."

"I'm sure." She hefted the bag and grinned. "We're good to go."

She handed me the mystery bag the moment we parked at home. I pulled out the item and frowned.

"It's good, isn't it?"

"It is," I agreed, "but this isn't his style."

"Which is why *I* got to pick it out," Aislin said decisively. "You're just here to tell me if it's unsightly."

"I think he'll look great in it," I replied cautiously, "but why?"

"One of our longest-standing jokes," she confirmed. "I'll tell you the story someday."

"Okay."

"And no asking him about it," she added quickly. "It would be a dead giveaway."

I had no intentions of dropping hints into casual conversation, but she had no faith in my ability to be sneaky.

"I'm guessing you don't have a lot of inside jokes," I commented.

"We have enough."

She slid the present back into its bag and opened the door. I gathered my own bags, opened the door, and followed her indoors without another word.

I didn't recognize the number on my caller ID, but I definitely recognized the area code.

"Nate?"

The first thing that came over the line was his laugh. "How did you know?"

"How many guys with a Michigan area code do I know?"

"Not enough," he said.

"This isn't a social call," I guessed.

"It might be," Nate protested. "How was your day?"

"Full of boring tests and conjugations," I said. "Yours?"

"Full of memorization and exam panic," he admitted. "I hope your tests went well."

He wasn't very good at small talk, so I decided to cut it short. "You're exchanging gifts with my sister soon. Do you want an opinion or a wish list?"

"The latter," Nate admitted. "Would you be willing to tag along? I've never done this before."

"Don't worry," I confided. "Neither has she."

"I got that impression," he answered. "Still, I'd rather have an expert weigh in on what I find. Please?"

I didn't want to spend my weekend in another bookstore, but there was a certain appeal to practically picking out the gift.

I sighed to give him the impression that it was a burden. "Because you asked nicely, what's your schedule like?"

"I have study days from the 13th to the 15th and no free time after that," Nate said. "Can we meet up on the 14th?"

Vacation didn't start until just before his exams ended, but I could take a night off for such a good cause.

"As far as I know, yes," I said cautiously. "Can I call you back?"

"Sure," he said. "Just make it before exams."

"I'll make sure you're taken care of," I promised. "This is your first holiday as a couple and pressure is built-in. After this, Valentine's Day will be easy."

Due to the horrified silence that followed, I was about to change my tactics when he spoke up again. "*Thank you.*"

"Glad I could help," I said cheerfully.

I could only hope that he wasn't as picky as my sister.

INTERLUDE

White

One of the most terrifying conversations of my life took place when I was fourteen. I knew from that the curse could take over permanently under certain circumstances, but I didn't feel like I was under much threat from that condition at twelve.

At fourteen, I finally asked about the generations past who had passed it on. She got very quiet at that, but spoke up with some persuasion.

The sorcerer's cruelty meant that love had to be found before a relationship was consummated. In his time, that meant that a girl could be condemned by an arranged marriage for alliances' sake. Two generations later, a second daughter died without falling in love. A few generations after *that,* a woman had fallen in what turned out to be unrequited love and acted on it.

Mom's voice had cracked when she told the final story of my great-great-aunt. Great-great-grandmother's older sister had been violated when she was fifteen. Four days later, she had not regained her human form and she chose to die from exposure instead of living the rest of her life like that. It was because of that violation that it had been passed to me.

It was a grim fact of life, but one that convinced me of my purpose. No matter what it took, I wouldn't be the one to condemn another generation to the curse.

Black

I think it's inevitable that every high school student read Kafka's *The Metamorphosis.* Gregor Samsa, a traveling salesman, wakes up one day as a giant cockroach. He tries to live a normal life, even when everything's changed. He can't work or go out. He can't find joy in things that used to make him happy. He overhears conversations about what a burden he is to the rest of his family. Eventually, he allows himself to die to put an end to that.

In all of Aislin's years of homeschooling, I only asked to change the curriculum once. When Mom mentally replaced Gregor with Aislin, she removed it from the planned reading list without further argument.

It may be just a story, but I've seen some of the guilt Aislin feels for the circumstances she didn't ask for. If anyone in this world knew what it was to wake up one day with a different life, it would be her.

Aislin has always said that I try to compensate for her lack of a life with my own activities. She scoffs at my attempts to keep her life normal, but I would rather risk her scorn than let her believe that she has nothing to contribute to our lives.

As far as I know, Aislin has never read that novella, but I'm sure that she knows the story too well.

SCENE 4

White

Nate was being cryptic again. He'd stopped dictating a dress code after the first dates, but this time, he told me to wear something nice.

His exams started on Friday and ended on Tuesday, but we planned to go out on the weekend so we could exchange gifts with time to spare. I didn't want to shove his package into his duffel bag as he was trying to get a ride to Logan Airport on Tuesday afternoon.

I recycled my outfit from Thanksgiving, adding tights instead of nylons to ward off the freezing weather, and borrowed Maeve's more formal black coat.

"My favorite," Nate commented as soon as I opened the door.

I suspected that he would have only said something different if he hadn't seen it before. He was wearing a black suit with a scarlet tie under a heavy overcoat.

"Thanks," I said. "You're looking pretty sharp yourself."

I leaned across the threshold to kiss him. His warm lips were a nice touch in the frigid air.

"If you insist on doing that, there's handy mistletoe in the living room," Mom offered nearby.

Nate pulled away, grinning. "Nice to see you too, Sarah," he called. "I have a cab waiting."

"Go," she called. "Have fun."

I scooped up my purse and his gift bag and he offered an arm for the walk to the cab. "Why not bring your own car?" I asked.

"This way we skip parking and can open presents," he explained.

We climbed into the back seat and he called "The Wang Center" to the driver, which immediately explained the dress code. I turned to stare.

"You're taking me to *The Nutcracker?*"

He grinned. "You said you hated *Swan Lake,* but you never said anything about the rest of ballet."

"I love it," I assured him quickly. "But it's a Christmas story and you . . ."

"Only for the first half," Nate interrupted. "Here."

The wrapping had definitely been done by someone with

professional skills, since it actually fit the white cardboard box inside. I opened it to find a thick scarf in various shades of red, woven through with ribbons. A pair of black, lined gloves was tucked into the fold of the scarf.

"Wow," I said, pulling it out to admire it. "This is gor . . ."

He looked nervous at the break in the sentence and my sudden look of comprehension. "Did you use Maeve as your personal shopper?"

Nate had the decency to look slightly abashed. "You recognize her handiwork?"

"I recognize her style," I corrected. "This is gorgeous."

"I picked it out," he admitted. "Maeve just pointed me in the right direction."

"Well, Maeve was probably eager to help because I wouldn't let her see this," I pointed out. "Happy Hanukkah."

He removed the ribbon tying the handles together and lay the bag flat to extract the item. His grin broadened as soon as he pulled the paper away.

"You got me a jacket," he said.

"So you don't have to forget to return your roommate's," I pointed out.

The black motorcycle jacket was cut along the lines of what he'd worn on that early date. As I'd anticipated, he enjoyed the humor behind it.

"Perfect," he said before leaning over to continue the PDA that I'd started at the threshold. Closer to the Wang Center, he decided to try conversation again, but I didn't mind letting him direct the flow of commentary. "So you like it?"

"It's fantastic," I said, reaching into the box to lift the scarf out. "I think I'll break it in . . ."

"No." Nate reached over and shoved the lid of the box back into place. "This is for New Year's Eve."

"Really." I arched an eyebrow. "What's happening then?"

"Well, I convinced my travel agents . . ."

"Namely your parents . . ."

"That I needed to be back earlier than the start of the semester," he said. "I want you to meet me at First Night wearing the fanciest thing you own and that scarf."

I was homeschooled. My current outfit *was* the fanciest thing I owned, but Maeve would be thrilled to help under special circumstances.

"Fancy, huh?" I prompted, hoping for another clue.

"Yes." He lifted my hand to kiss my knuckles. "Something fancy meant for dancing."

"Oh, no," I protested. "I haven't danced with a guy since the sixth grade."

"It's okay," he insisted. "Wear something long and no one will notice."

He had a point. "As long as you wear this," I requested, gesturing to the suit.

"I was planning on it," he assured me.

In typical Massachusetts fashion, it was snowing again when we got out of the ballet. Nate took it as an excuse to draw me under his arm and I didn't need persuasion to stay there. I was feeling pretty giddy right now.

"I take it you enjoyed the show?" he asked with a grin.

"I loved it," I said, my arm wrapped around his waist. "Thank you."

"I'll have to remember that," he laughed. "We can talk about it someplace warmer."

"Like a cab?" I asked hopefully.

"Like the T," Nate said. "Cabs will be hard to find and I'm not making you walk all the way to my dorm."

"How chivalrous," I complimented him. "After you."

Nate took my hand and pulled our hands into his pocket for warmth. Boylston Station wasn't far, but he didn't speak again until we were out of the elements. Then he freed our hands from his pocket but didn't let go as we stood waiting for the B train.

"So," he said conversationally, "it's not ballet that you object to."

"I never said I had a problem with it," I corrected. "I just haven't been in a while."

Nate raised an eyebrow. "I asked you your thoughts on ballet and you said that you hated all that *Sleeping Beauty* nonsense."

That comment had been in mid-November and I had worried that he'd blow grocery money on impressive, elaborate dates.

There were other reasons that I objected to that particular story, though.

"*Sleeping Beauty* is nonsense," I defended myself.

"How so?"

"The girl knows the conditions of her curse for sixteen years and still lets a complete stranger trick her. When the curse is broken, she marries the first guy she's presumably ever kissed and lives happily ever after."

His eyebrow lowered and he let out a vague "Hmm."

"You disagree?" I challenged.

"No, I'm just confused," Nate admitted. "You balk at *Sleeping Beauty,* but have no problems with a child being abducted one night by a grown military officer . . ."

"Her boy toy," I corrected.

He grimaced at the term, but plowed on. "A child is abducted by a man who takes her to the magical Land of Every Diabetic's Nightmare."

"Of course I have no problems with it," I said earnestly. "It's sweet and the bad guy's a giant mousie who can be thwarted by ballistic pointe shoes."

Nate let out a bark of laughter at that. "That has to be the world's least likely weapon of mass destruction," he said. "I'm not sure I even want to know your opinions on *Swan Lake* now."

"Probably not," I admitted. "What are yours?"

"I think I hate it."

"Is that because it's also nonsense?" I challenged.

"Because it turns out all right for nobody in the end," he said. "The sorcerer is defeated, the lovers commit suicide, and no one at court knows what happened between the prince and that Odile chick . . ."

"No pun intended," I teased. "I didn't think you were all that familiar with it."

"Janet made me see it," he explained. "I think the story is pretty crummy to all of its characters."

Not for the first time, I had the impression that he would understand the curse better than I expected. I was determined to put it off as long as possible, but he didn't make it easy.

"Good call," I said after those moments of reflection.

Nate kissed my hand again, triggering my blush. "I'm glad you approve, milady."

The B train showed up at that point and we were lucky enough to find adjoining seats against the windows where we could give each other undivided attention.

"I also think the prince is a moron," he announced.

"How so?"

This time, he took both of my hands and my blush got more severe. "When you love someone, you aren't fooled by a pale imitation."

"You thought Maeve was me in November," I said bluntly. "You didn't treat her like a pale imitation of the real thing."

"Be fair," Nate protested in mock indignation. "I didn't love you before the first date."

I paused for a moment just to pretend that I was letting him sweat, but he was on the verge of giving me a hangdog expression just to gain some sympathy. "Okay, you're forgiven," I said mercifully.

"Nowadays," he said without responding to my clemency, "I know you're nothing like your sister."

"I wouldn't go that far," the identical twin in me objected.

"Well, you *are* different," Nate reconsidered. "I think you're prettier."

"Now you're just lying," I asserted.

"And kinder."

"I'd like to think so, but you're probably still wrong."

He leaned across the few inches between us and let some things go without saying for a while. Someone nearby suggested we get a room, but I didn't try to pull away first or take the lead. I just enjoyed the attention.

He withdrew by about an inch so that we were still in danger of bumping noses if the train rocked too hard. "You're definitely the better kisser."

That ruined the moment, since my first instinct was to laugh. I turned my hands so the palms faced towards him and gently shoved. "You've done a first-hand comparison?"

His face had turned red as soon as I started laughing, since he had apparently caught on to his mistake. "Okay, I admit I made that one up," he said.

He leaned in for another kiss, but I turned to put both my feet on the ground and it landed on my cheek. "This is going to make some very interesting girl talk," I mused aloud.

His face stayed red; so did his mortified expression. "Don't you dare."

"You brought it up," I reminded him. "You will have to suffer the consequences. But I can be persuaded to be wise and lenient."

"I have no doubt," Nate said. "How do I persuade you?"

I turned and smiled benevolently. "We've got the whole ride home to discuss it," I reminded him. "Let's hear your ideas first."

My dancing into the house caused raised eyebrows from Maeve. She was waiting up in the kitchen and was clearly amused by my pirouette entrance.

"Where *did* he take you?"

"He didn't tell you?"

"He just told me the scarf was for New Year's," she stated.

"He brought me to *The Nutcracker,"* I explained before dropping the gift box on the table. "And he loved the jacket."

"Does that mean you'll tell me the story behind it, then?" Maeve asked.

"Not yet." I finished one final arm reverence and sank into a chair, grinning. "So, he told you about First Night?"

"Vaguely," she countered. "Did he say where you're going?"

"No." I leaned in to stage-whisper the next part. "He said to wear something fancy meant for dancing."

Maeve's sudden burst of laughter was not unexpected, but it was unflattering. "Really? You let him know that you're not the ballroom dancing type?"

"I told him," I assured her. "He wouldn't change his mind."

"Well, more power to him," Maeve said gravely. "What are you going to wear?"

"Not. A. Clue."

Her expression, already giddy at the vicarious romance, turned radiant. "You need my help again."

"Consider it an early Christmas present," I said.

"Oh, I will."

Maeve stood and almost skipped out of the room, heading for

the stairs. The low murmur of voices probably meant that she was checking in with the chaperones. I took the steps at a much more relaxed pace and joined her in the doorway of the master bedroom.

"Come in," Dad invited.

"Sorry Nate couldn't say hello," I said. "He has a final at nine and we were late getting back."

"Did you have a good time?"

"Yes, Dad," I said truthfully.

"Maeve was just explaining the dress code for First Night," Mom added, "and she proposed an interesting idea."

"Since you started homeschooling, we've have had to pay for Maeve's sports equipment, school clothes, dresses for homecoming and prom, tutors, library fines and field trips. You've gotten through high school on a much smaller budget."

"Which made me think," Maeve interrupted. "You *could* borrow something of mine, but since you've never begged them for a prom dress, you're owed at least one splurge."

"Which means," Dad concluded, "that we will be giving you a budget for your New Year's Eve dress. Maeve will take charge of the trip, but you will absolutely have the final say in the dress."

As soon as my brain caught up to this logic, I blurted out, "Thank you."

"If you go too far, I reserve the right to charge you for indecent exposure," Dad added as an afterthought. "Again."

"Yes, sir," I said obediently. "Thank you both."

Maeve wanted to go straight to work, but I convinced her to hold off until tomorrow against her better judgment. She protested, but since I had final veto power, she shut up quickly.

She did, however, come home from school with a stack of papers. Each one showcased a different dress, ranging from ball-gown to tea-length. Most were sleeveless and some were strapless, which I quickly forbade, but I let her walk me through the pros and cons of each one.

I dismissed one with "Mom can wear that in twenty years." Another was vetoed because "I'm an introvert, not a Puritan." We agreed not to make me wear anything that might cause a wardrobe malfunction. I flatly refused to wear anything with slits on both sides due to the tripping risk.

I vetoed sequins and spangles, but agreed to consider something with applique or brocade. Maeve pointed out that as my makeup artist, she'd make me wear something shimmery, so I agreed to anything short of looking like I fell into a vat of body glitter.

After an hour of haggling and arguing about the practicality of wearing a very short dress under a long coat, we had a short list and a better idea of where we both stood. We parted ways amicably with websites to check and an appointment to hit *one* mall on the 23rd. It wasn't prudent to try and buy something two days before Christmas, but at least it was a place to start.

Two days later, Maeve found a short red dress speckled in black with a corseted top and just enough taffeta to make it poof. I vetoed it immediately because I wanted to leave things to the imagination, but I was oddly charmed by the polka dots. Closer to Christmas, we found a polka-dotted dress with a sweetheart neckline that made me look less like a 1950s vampire. The hem hit the middle of my calf, which meant I wouldn't worry about hypothermia.

Once we had the dress, Maeve was off on a tear. She loaned me her bow earrings and silver ribbons to weave into my hair. My contribution was a shiny red vinyl purse that I didn't expect to like, but it somehow completed the look. The heels on my red shoes were higher than I'd wanted, but I stashed a pair of travel flats in my purse for outdoor use and probably the dancing part of the evening.

Christmas was a bit of an anti-climax with the excitement geared towards some kind of New Year's Eve extravaganza. Maeve made sure that I had enough makeup to keep me in lipstick until grad school, but my small array of lotions and body sprays for her were just as whimsical. Brendan, home for the holidays, teasingly gave us turtlenecks that left everything to the imagination. Mom and Dad gave us all winter coats that could withstand most New England weather, but rather than buying a handful of smaller gifts, they gave their daughters what we called "investment gifts." I'd expected this, since Brendan had gotten one his last Christmas before college, but was still surprised that they had splurged on a nicer-than-average laptop. Maeve wasn't off to university yet, but they kept things fair. She opened the smallest of her present to find keys to a used, but perfectly functional, car. Needless to say, we both refrained from being obnoxious teenagers for a few days after that.

On New Year's Eve, Maeve devoted the afternoon to getting me ready. I let her subject me to hair, skin, and makeup products that I had never heard of, but I came out of the process looking ready for a red carpet and I could live with that. She then instructed me to keep my coat buttoned and cinched until our first stop. Nate would know that the dress matched the scarf and gloves that he'd given me, but he wouldn't get the big picture for a while. I was, Maeve said, to take his breath away at the latest possible moment. I was personally fine with keeping my coat on until the actual dancing.

The only problem was that Nate called from Chicago to say his flight was delayed and we'd have to meet downtown. Dad grumbled all the way to the train station, but wished me a good time when I got out of the car. I kissed his cheek as a thank-you for caring and told him I'd see him next year.

There was no point in trying to drive into the city, so I had instructed Nate to meet me at Copley. I had the buttons that were required to get him into all of the First Night events with me. Nate had bought them in mid-December and entrusted them to me, so I kept my hand wrapped around them in the pocket of my coat.

Several trains came and went, but he still didn't materialize out of the crowd. I was starting to get paranoid when a D train coming outbound pulled into the station and Nate practically forced his way out of the first car. I met him halfway and made sure he set his duffel bag down before he caught me up in a tight hug. The next order of business was giving me a kiss that almost made up for all of his time in Michigan.

When we finally came up for air, he grabbed my right hand and lifted our arms so he could get a better look at my outfit.

"Nice outerwear," he commented, flicking the end of my scarf. "When do I get to see the rest?"

"Not until absolutely necessary," I said. "Where are you going to change?"

"In the first public bathroom I can find," he said. "I could swear I've got a suit in here somewhere."

His bag looked stuffed to the seams, but I didn't comment on that. I just let him pull me along to the stairs so we could make our way out of the underground.

"You have the buttons, right?"

"How could I forget?"

"You carried them in your pocket wherever you went?" he asked hopefully.

"I wouldn't go that far." I still had an hour or so per day when I had no use for clothing. "I made sure they were locked away someplace safe until they were needed."

Once we were up the stairs and breathing tandem white puffs of air into the night, I handed over his button and pinned my own to my lapel. "How was your vacation?"

"I spent half of it being told that I should have brought you along," he informed me.

I mentally took a step back, since I had been prepared to hear that my name hadn't come up once. I hadn't wanted to assume that the rest of his family took me seriously.

"Who was doing the reprimanding?"

"They took turns," he informed me. "Janet wouldn't shut up about you."

"And I'll send her a receipt for the bribe later this week," I joked. "Was she there?"

"No," he said, taking my hand in his. "Isaac dragged her off to Miami to visit her in-laws."

"Did she send presents to apologize?" I asked.

"She got me a restaurant gift card for every night of the holiday," Nate chuckled. "Apparently she wants to encourage me to spend money on you."

"To spend her money on me," I corrected.

"It's mine by adoption," he reconsidered. "Do you mind?"

"I hope you don't feel as if you have to spend money on me," I said after only a moment of hesitation.

"I don't feel like I *have* to, but I like to."

That was as good a summary as any and I wasn't going to insult his romantic side by telling him to knock it off. Whatever his views on the subject, I could learn to adapt.

"But your vacation was good otherwise?" I pressed for more details when he didn't continue that thought. "Did you see Jared and Niko?"

"Every chance I got," he admitted. "My parents didn't make me spend all of my quality time with them."

"And they're doing . . ."

Nate came to an abrupt halt and turned to face me. "I appreciate the interest, Aislin," he said formally, "but I spent thirteen hours traveling to talk about you, not Niko's GPA."

"Sorry," I said meekly. "I'll try to be more selfish."

"Good." He spotted a convenience store on the next corner and immediately started heading for the door. "If you'll browse fervently for something for us to drink, I'll be back in five minutes, tops."

He came back wearing the sharp-looking black suit that I had previously suspected was his one dapper outfit, saved from either a cousin's wedding or his high school graduation.

"Find anything?"

"Hot chocolate," I suggested. "It'll keep us warm while we decide where to go first."

"Oh, I know where we're going first," Nate said emphatically with a tug on his lapels. "I told you to dress for dancing, didn't I?"

"Against my will," I conceded. "Is that far from here?"

"Not at all," he said. "You'd be more cheerful about a death sentence, so we're going to start there and stay until you agree that it was a good idea."

"Great," I said with little enthusiasm.

"You won't know until you've tried," Nate argued.

I decided to not whine that I didn't want to try, lest he decide that he should have picked someone a little less high-maintenance to love.

"And after that?"

Nate grinned confidently. "I'm getting you to dance," he said firmly. "If we never get around to the rest of the festivities, I can live with that."

"But realistically . . ."

"Realistically, we'll take turns," he assured me. "You get to pick the last stop of the year, but we'll get around to that conversation when we feel like it."

Our first stop was a hotel where the ballroom was fairly full of people with the bright idea of breaking a sweat before going out in the freezing cold. We found a table after a few minutes of threading our way through the crowd and Nate dropped his duffel at the foot of his chair before pausing to listen to the music. I unwound my scarf and gloves, feeling slightly apprehensive. After making me suffer for about a minute, Nate turned back to me with a very serious expression and I prepared to fight.

"So, tell me about your skills," he requested. "Are you a waltz or cha-cha kind of person?"

"I haven't danced with a boy since the 6th grade," I reminded as a deterrent. "I'm very good at side-to-side and sometimes turning on the spot."

"So you're practically a blank slate," he said approvingly. "That's good."

"What about you?" I challenged.

"One of my friends is on the BU ballroom dance team and after months of practice, I only fall once in a while."

If he fell and took me down with him, my dress would rip and Maeve would kill me, even if it made for a funny story. I had promised to use this dress for dancing, though.

"If you fall, do it with panache and I won't know it was an accident," I confided.

"As long as you promise me panache," he said. "I'll try to catch you before that happens, though."

"And then we'll both hit the floor," I predicted. "It'll be adorable."

"I think so."

He leaned over to kiss me, his hands firmly attached to the lapels of my coat. It wasn't a Hollywood kiss—all fire and show—but was meant to last for a few searing seconds. It was the kind of kiss that was just meant for the two of us and was all about unchangeable love.

"You make it very hard to resist loving you," Nate said quietly at last.

It was, without question, the most romantic thing he had ever said, but I had to repress a giggle because it belonged in a romantic comedy.

"Likewise," I said. Noting that he was still holding me by the lapels, I cleared my throat. "If you can take my coat, I'll let you start the dance class."

He grinned and released the coat so I could turn my back to him. I unbuttoned and let it slide off my shoulders.

It was a few moments before Nate remembered to help me out of the coat. I made a mental note to thank Maeve for all her hard work when I got home. The red was receding from his face when I turned around, but it felt unusual to enjoy seeing him affected.

"Nice dress," he said quickly.

"I thought you might like it," I said.

He managed to stop blushing by the time he hung my coat on the back of the chair, but it took some obvious effort for him to find words again.

"For the record, I still love you for your mind," he said. "Give my thanks to Maeve."

I adjusted the strap, feeling a little like blushing myself. "I will," I said. "Any other thoughts?"

He was now giving the entire ensemble a thorough looking over. "I think," Nate said, "we'll try you first on cha-cha."

Black

Nick was pretty adamant about our New Year's Eve plans. As soon as we'd gotten back to school after Thanksgiving, he had announced that he wanted to keep it low-key. I thought that meant limiting the guest list to ten people and watching a movie before the ball dropped on TV. He decided that it meant going to a normal party. I compromised that he could drag me to Sang's party if he promised not to disappear on me.

"So I'm not allowed to be out of your line of sight until midnight?" he teased as we headed up Sang's walk.

"I'll let you have some privacy if you need the facilities," I assured him.

"But otherwise, not being around you is considered disappearing?"

"Last year, you came with me to Sosi's party and stayed long enough to get me a drink. Then I had to hunt you down for a ride after the countdown."

"Yeah," Nick said without a hint of remorse, "but this year I'm your significant other."

"And I want you to stay that way."

I pushed the doorbell before we could delve any further into the subject and Natalie opened the door almost immediately.

"*Hi,*" she said enthusiastically. "I was wondering when you guys would show up."

The number of people there probably broke a few fire codes, but she had been waiting for us, or at least me. I let her pull me inside, but kept my hand latched on to Nick's.

"Do you mind if I steal her for a . . ."

"Yes," Nick and I said in unison.

Natalie arched an eyebrow. "Feeling clingy?" she guessed.

"Feeling like having a good time with my boyfriend," I corrected. "Is it an emergency?"

"It can wait," she said after a brief silence. "Come find me when he gets distracted."

"I won't," Nick said under his breath, just loud enough for me to hear him over the music.

Nick stayed with me through my perusal of the entire snacks selection and let me opt for the movie about to get started in the basement. He even ignored the game being played very loudly in the living room. He let me pick the couch against the wall, where we could have both privacy and a fairly good view of the screen. The view wouldn't matter until they started the next movie, but he let me curl up next to him and pick at the food on his plate.

"I can find you something else if you don't like it," Nick offered drily. "There's plenty of food out there for the both of us."

"I'm fine with what I have," I said, eating a peanut from my own plate for emphasis. "You?"

He extended his plate to me and I exchanged a few items for variety's sake. "One of my New Year's Resolutions is to be more tolerant when you do weird stuff."

"This isn't weird stuff," I protested. "It's couples stuff."

"Same thing," Nick asserted.

I complacently ignored that comment and went back to eating my own food. When Jill and Andrew started arguing over the choice of movies, Nick turned to me with an almost bored expression.

"Maybe it would be more peaceful upstairs," he suggested.

"I'm comfortable here," I replied. "And this never lasts long."

Sure enough, Jill caved a minute later and Andrew went to circulate the news that we were starting something new.

"What about you?" Nick asked.

I had been focusing on a green olive that I wanted to steal from his plate and therefore missed the original question. "What about me?" I asked evasively.

"New Year's Resolutions," he clarified. "Let's hear them."

Resolutions were something that parents loved and I ignored. Nick seemed serious, though, so I gave him the first answer that I could think of.

"I want to make sure you finish high school on a high note."

"I'd settle for getting into college," he murmured back.

"And you're going to," I said confidently. If Aislin could get into a college with my SATs and her extra-curricular activities, Nick could find a place that would want him. "Until then, I'm going to be a ridiculously supportive girlfriend."

"I'm not surprised," he said.

Andrew came stomping back, having made the appropriate announcements. I was still processing our conversation.

"What would have surprised you?" I challenged.

"I figured that with Aislin taken care of, you'd find a new hobby," he reasoned. "I don't mind being your new project."

In the spirit of being the best girlfriend known to mankind, I nodded. I didn't need to argue about that perception right now.

"I should take your advice more often," I said sagely. "What else is on your resolutions list?"

"Spend less time arguing with you and more time making you hope I'll come back for a visit."

That didn't fit with his usual confidence, but I respected the painful honesty to the confession. I moved my plate and reached over to take his hand. I hadn't much liked his first resolution, but the second was something we could both work on.

"I don't think you'll have a problem with that."

White

Around 11:30, when we had worn ourselves out and seen as many things as the laws of time and space would permit, Nate got around to asking for the final directions of the night.

"Lady's choice," he reminded me. "What's your pleasure?"

"Well," I considered, "Do you want to get hypothermia or a view of the fireworks?"

"It's your choice," he reiterated, "but I wouldn't mind being able to feel my lips at midnight."

"I have just the place, then," I said.

We arrived at our destination a few minutes later and he smirked. "I know you so well," Nate announced.

"You do," I agreed. "Stop rubbing it in."

The music was still going and it looked as though we weren't the only ones who had thought to stay out of the elements. Nate took my coat immediately this time, not really noticing the dress at this point, and found a chair where we could leave things and still be close to the dance floor.

"We stayed here until I agreed that you were right," I informed him. "I think it was fantastic."

Nate pulled my right glove off so he could kiss my knuckles. "May I have the next dance, then?"

I hadn't taken to the cha-cha very well—I kept losing track of direction and stepping on toes—but he'd taught me the basics of a waltz. He also hadn't gotten around to showing me the moves that lessened body contact. He occasionally insisted on letting me do a still-clumsy turn, but I spent most of the time being swept along to a count of three. He didn't let me fall once.

The next dance reminded us that we were in the 21st century, so we went back to the old standby of side-to-side. I caught my breath without having to disentangle myself and clasped my hands behind his neck while he repositioned his arms to go around my waist.

"This isn't as exciting," I apologized, "but I think we can make this work."

"I'm following your lead," Nate joked. "So, we're dancing our feet off until the countdown?"

"I never said that," I said.

"What's the plan, then?"

"There are a couple of places across the city setting off fireworks," I said. "I plan on finding a nice street corner where we can watch."

"So, as soon as we finish this song, you'll want to leave?"

"Yes. So enjoy it while you can."

He laughed and pulled me just a little bit closer. "I am," he promised.

Locating a place to watch the fireworks wasn't a problem since they were easily visible in many places. Finding a place for two people to fit into the crowd was difficult, though. I was about to suggest that we go inside when Nate wedged himself into a spot. After waiting patiently for two girls to move, I nearly got pinned against an older man when the crowd moved to fill their spot, but Nate tugged me to him and pinned me. I couldn't turn to see him, but I was at least within arm's reach.

"See?" he asked smugly. "There's room for both of us."

"Please tell me you know where your duffel bag is."

"Between my shoes," he said. "I think we're just in time."

It was about a minute later that that the crowd joined in the countdown and his grip on me slackened. With great difficulty, I twisted my way around so that we were facing each other by the time that they hit "Three . . . two . . . one . . ."

We didn't bother shouting "Happy New Year" with the rest of the crowd. The fireworks were probably great, but we didn't even watch them until the chorus of "Auld Lang Syne." Nate belatedly handed over a noisemaker and I blew it in his face.

"Thanks," he teased. "That alone made thirteen hours of travel worth it."

"No, you traveled thirteen hours for the dress," I said, stowing the noisemaker in my pocket. "I know *that* was worth it."

"You know that isn't true."

"You got me to dance," I mentioned. "Was that worth it?"

"You're missing the point," Nate said more loudly. "I didn't come here just to force you to look gorgeous on a dance floor."

"Though that was hopefully a highlight," I shot back.

Nate ignored my comment and cupped my chin in his hand so that I was meeting his gaze. "I traveled thirteen hours because I couldn't imagine spending this moment with anyone else."

I had to go precariously on tiptoe to kiss him for that, but I sacrificed dignity to communicate that I felt the same way.

SCENE 5

White

The first advantage I noticed to college was that classes didn't start until midway through January. That meant that Maeve was complaining about her first oral presentation while I was still killing time.

Nate took my freshman orientation upon himself, making sure I got my student ID and helping me find all my textbooks. These were things I had looked forward to doing on my own, but I didn't protest his helpful urges. As long as he didn't hover, I could put up with his tour guide side.

What I didn't expect was to find him sitting at the kitchen table on the morning of the first day of classes. "Hi," I said warily.

"Good morning, incoming freshman," he said cheerfully once he'd stolen a kiss behind Dad's back. "I heard you have a nine o'clock class that's within walking distance of *my* nine o'clock . . ."

"And you thought you'd walk me there," I finished the sentence. "You could have just met me at the T."

"Don't worry about it," Nate said dismissively. "It's your first day of school and I'm here with pep talks on several topics."

"And I appreciate that," I reassured him. "You just caught me off-guard."

I ignored Nate completely for a few moments, just in case Dad thought I hadn't noticed him. He returned my hug and handed over a plain bagel with strawberry cream cheese. The amount of supplies on the counter suggested he had been hoping to give me a proper breakfast, but Nate had spoiled the surprise.

"This looks great," I said, surveying the options. "Can we reschedule for tomorrow?"

"Sure," Dad said amiably. "If you can stay up until ten tonight, I'll want to hear everything about college."

He didn't pack the food away immediately, just began frying bacon so *someone* could enjoy their breakfast. I kissed him on the cheek and headed back to the kitchen table.

"You ready to go?" Nate asked.

"Ready as ever," I said with false cheer.

"Very convincing," my boyfriend sniggered. "Come on, before you lose your nerve."

"I'll see you tonight," I called to Dad.

"Have fun," he ordered.

"I'll just be happy when the first day is over," I admitted once we were in the car.

"You'll make it," he insisted. "I won't hover, but if you get completely lost, you can call me . . ."

"I'll be *fine*," I said. "I appreciate the ride, though."

He glanced over, but returned his attention to the road. "If you want to make it a regular habit . . ."

It was time for a compromise. "I think I can find my own way to campus," I responded. "I won't say no to someone sitting with me at lunch, though."

"You'll be just fine," he reasoned, "but we should synchronize our watches and pick a place to eat. Anything else?"

"I'll be fine once I stop having curriculum-related panic attacks."

"You didn't say anything about a panic attack," he said, his voice rising a little bit in pitch. "How long has this been going on?"

It was a relief to know that my fear had not been as obvious as I thought. "Ever since you started treating my enrollment like some kind of terminal illness," I informed him.

"All right," he said. "I'll admit that I've hovered a little if you admit that I was helpful."

"No worries there," I said. "I don't know who would have kept me entertained in the bookstore line, but it'll be days before I'm used to seeing this place in daylight. I'm lucky to have you to help keep it all straight."

Once more assured that I did need him, he let the subject drop.

Black

I've never been a calendar person, but Mom insisted on giving me something to mark the passage of time every year and this Christmas was no exception. My desk calendar came with motivational quotes that sounded like fortune cookies and served to remind me of things I would forget otherwise.

I had circled today's date as soon as I checked the appropriate schedule. A quick call to Nate convinced him that he should have "car trouble" after classes. Naturally, Aislin was suspicious.

"I'm supposed to meet Nate," she said as a greeting. "If you have him bound and gagged somewhere, I'm not speaking to you."

"I ran into him and he's on his way to a mechanic," I said sympathetically. "He was supposed to leave you a message."

She pulled out her phone and was apparently satisfied to find a voicemail. "So you're here as a stand-in?" she guessed.

"No, I'm here to see if this was worth the SAT scores," I said loftily. "It doesn't look too bad."

Currently, I was admiring a long hallway with about as much personality as a storage unit, but I was trying to be polite.

"I like it," Aislin replied before I could pose a first question. "I think I'll stay."

"Even if you don't have a single class with Nate?" I challenged.

She hadn't jumped at the chance to find one of those, since she *was* here to focus on other things. She gave me another annoyingly neutral shrug that didn't answer anything.

"I can live with that."

I didn't like her vague answers and she didn't want me dragging the details out, so I went on the offensive.

"You know," I suggested, "now that we're on the same schedule, we could switch places once in a while."

She smirked as if borrowing from my repertoire. "Meaning you could sneak into my classes and I'd go see if no one notices that I can't swim? Not a chance."

And with that, I believed she was actually as Zen with the whole thing as Mom had suspected when we discussed the matter last night. It wasn't just optimism.

"Come on," Aislin said, correctly interpreting my expression as one of amused shock. "I'll buy you a drink and give you straight answers."

"You're just humoring me," I accused.

"Yeah," she admitted, "but you used to do that all the time. It's my turn."

We found a table in the food court that was pleasantly out of the way in case we wanted to have a private conversation.

"How was your day anyway?" my collegiate sister asked. "You never told me if Ethan's playing basketball again."

"He's playing and he says hi," I answered. "He's still on JV and most of his friends moved on. I don't think he'll ever get to varsity, but that's not why he's playing."

"Good for him," she commented. "What about Nick?"

"Nick is starting forward," I said proudly. "He would have liked to be captain, but the job went to Danny Keene."

It wasn't like Aislin cared about any of this, but she took interest in the small things the same way that I did.

"So, back to this whole college thing," I added before she could ask another question.

"This whole college thing just started today," Aislin pointed out. "I didn't faint at the sight of the workload and I think I'll be fine."

We had gone over the general requirements a few days after the acceptance letter arrived and Aislin had signed up for as many of them as possible. While she had been sleeping, I had revised that schedule for more fun. The result was that while she was taking Readings in American Literature, she was also signed up for Intensive Beginning Spanish, which she could ace with relative ease. We allowed her a two-hour break after her morning classes to accommodate any midday swan hours that she had.

"And do you ever run into Nate?" I prompted.

"By arrangement," she responded. "On a campus this size, it has to be."

"And you still won't try and find a class in common?"

"I have no idea what I want to do yet and he has program requirements." Aislin shook her head. "There'll be time for that later."

Her whole attitude was still annoying me, which justified all these questions. "And you're really all right with all of this?"

"No."

I suspected that I was about to witness a moment of weakness. I took no pleasure in it, but I liked it when Aislin confided in me and that seemed inevitable right now.

"It's really too early to make a judgment call," Aislin insisted. "Do you have any questions that don't mean you think I'm on the verge of a nervous breakdown?"

"None that you'll answer."

She saluted me with her cup and nodded. "Glad we cleared that up."

"I just want to make sure you're enjoying yourself," I rushed on. "I want this to work out for you."

"Ah, she confesses," Aislin mused.

Her tone slightly irritated me; according to her, I only resembled myself when I was over-bearing. "I never denied that I want you to be happy, but I had other reasons for picking you up."

"Really?" Aislin countered. "You asked me about my classes and I predict that this is a one-time thing."

"You never wanted to gripe about classes and teachers before," I protested in annoyance. "Don't be prejudiced."

"Sorry." She looked away, apparently just needing something else to focus on. "I wish everyone would shut up about how hard it was to get this far."

"Oh." I set down my cup so she would recognize that she had my undivided attention. "Just to be clear, are we putting too much pressure on you or is it a different issue?"

Aislin hesitated before speaking, but decided that I wasn't making fun of her. "Too much pressure," she said quietly. "I want to get on with life."

She was making it sound like she was in remission from cancer and waiting for bad test results. "Okay, then," I said cheerfully. "The next person who badgers you gets smacked, even if it's me."

"Be serious," Aislin requested.

"I'm absolutely serious," I said. "Tell me what you think your favorite class will be."

After a few moments of skepticism, Aislin sighed and smiled a little unconvincingly. "Introduction to Movement for Theater," she replied. "I can get grades for stretching and being creative. I won't ever need it . . ."

"You never know," I countered.

"But I think I'll enjoy it," she concluded.

"And you don't have to sit at a desk for the whole time."

"Exactly," Aislin said. "It's P.E. of a kind I haven't gotten in years."

"Do you miss it?"

She arched an eyebrow. "What do you mean by that?"

I hunched my shoulders and leaned closer. "You had almost five years on your own schedule," I reminded her. "Is there anything about it that you miss?"

That gave her pause, but the speed at which she came to the conclusion meant it wasn't the first time she'd thought about it. Most likely, she hadn't considered it today.

"I haven't had a good flight in weeks," she confided. "I have swan time on most days, but it's not the kind where I can go exploring or see what the aftermath of this week's ice storm looks like from a hundred feet up."

"I'd miss that too," I admitted. "How are you handling swan time here?"

Aislin grinned sheepishly. "I locked myself in a bathroom stall until it passed," she explained. "Luckily, no one tried to kick me out."

That would have been something that I would pay to see. "It might be worth moving into the dorms so you can have a place to crash closer to classes."

"I know," she sighed, "but I don't think Mom and Dad are ready for me to grow up *that* much."

I was about to make a crack about that when I spotted a slightly unwelcome figure. "Uh-oh."

Aislin stayed stock-still, looking suddenly apprehensive. "What?"

"Don't look," I said quickly. "The ropes weren't tight enough."

Aislin waited until Nate was inches away before drawling, "I have eyes in the back of my head, you know."

"No, you have a sister keeping watch," Nate said. "Good evening, ladies."

"I stand by my statement," Aislin said even more placidly. "I always liked that shirt on you."

He immediately glanced down and I smirked to let Aislin know that she had produced the desired effect. She smiled back and turned to face him.

"How's the car?"

Nate bent down to kiss her quickly in greeting. "It'll live," he assured her. "I thought you'd be long gone by now."

"I couldn't resist letting my sister hang out with a real college student for a while," she said. "It's not often that the younger twin gets to act superior."

"Bull," I snorted. "You get to be superior all the time. You just don't flaunt it."

"Which is one of the things I like about her," Nate said. "Can I walk you to your car?"

He was probably trying to sound chivalrous, but it came off as a dismissal. "Why?" I challenged. "Is there something you don't want us to see?"

"Yeah," he said, "a bunch of ravenously hungry college boys who have forgotten their manners."

"We were about to leave anyway," Aislin said pointedly. "We'd love an escort."

Nate picked up her messenger bag and slung it over his shoulder before offering his arm. Aislin accepted it and we headed to the car with Aislin now enthralled by Nate's description of his classes and me enjoying the view.

SCENE 6

Black

There were a hundred things to do today, including a paper and a project proposal to write after I was done with flashcards and math problems. That would have been bad enough, but I also had a swim meet.

Mom and Dad were usually pretty intense about grades, since they wanted their girls to get into good colleges. Now that Aislin was living the dream, I was the only one with applications to fear. I'd never been a slacker, but I had renewed my efforts to get better-than-decent grades for the last semester of junior year.

I hid in a corner of the locker room with my books from last bell until the rest of the team started to trickle in, and then tucked my handwritten half-draft of my paper into my English folder and joined the others.

I had a lot of things on my mind today, like the feeling that my paper's thesis was completely useless, but those weren't things I could think about mid-race. I pictured a good launch and kicking off the far wall seconds ahead of the next person. Thoughts of drag vs. propulsion were for practice, where I could worry about my stroke rate. There was no reason to pile up calculations. I just needed to get in the water and get moving.

By the time I left the locker room, I didn't need any pep talks. I heard the cheers from the sidelines, but I didn't need to look for familiar faces. This wasn't a big meet against our chief rivals, so there wouldn't be that many people here to watch anyway.

I didn't even look at the crowd until they called my race. The small crowd made up for numbers in enthusiasm. Three of the guys were there for girlfriends, and two parents had turned up.

One was Aislin.

The only thing that kept me from staring longer was that everyone but me was taking their marks. I raised a hand to acknowledge that I saw her and Aislin waved cheerfully back from her seat next to Avril.

The next minutes were swallowed up with all the things I had been visualizing. My start wasn't as smooth as I had hoped, but I made up for it with a good, strong burst of energy. My arms scooped the water away, not effortlessly, but at least effectively, and when it came time for the tumble turn, I kicked off the far wall sooner than I expected. I put that spare energy to good use and shut off the worrying part of my brain until my hand touched the wall.

It was impossible to know the immediate results, since I didn't turn around to check who was struggling to catch up, but our fans were treating this like the Olympics. I clambered out of the pool once I'd caught my breath.

"Good, good," Coach Keller murmured, clapping me on the shoulder. "Good start."

He could have given me some encouragement, but he was already talking to Melissa Chambers about the next race. I grabbed a towel and swiped at my eyes so I could see the spectators more clearly.

The illusion hadn't faded. Aislin and Avril were still sitting on the second row, but they headed to the front row as soon as I approached.

"Surprised?" Aislin asked blithely.

"Thrilled," I corrected. "Where's Nate?"

"At lab and then allowed to have personal time for homework," Aislin answered. "I knew you'd ask that."

"She claims you have his schedule memorized," Avril explained.

"Do not. I thought his lab was on Thursdays. Do not." They just grinned back at me and I shrugged indifferently. "I pay attention to what they say about their schedules like any friend. Of course I know what he's doing."

"Please tell me you're not more obsessed with him than your sister is," Avril said.

"I don't think that's possible," I shot back.

"I agree," Aislin said. "I think you're just very happy that I'm happy."

"As I should be," I said. "As a good sister, I'm always happy for you. Can we continue this conversation another time? I sort of need to . . ."

I gestured vaguely in the direction of the rest of the swim team. I wasn't here to catch up on gossip, just show my appreciation for support.

"Sure," Aislin said.

"Abandon us," Avril added. "We'll survive."

"I'll make it up to you if you stick around," I promised.

"You'll buy us food?" Aislin suggested.

"If you behave yourselves," I agreed.

"We'll sit down and shut up then," Avril decided. "You won't even know we're here."

"I wouldn't go that far." I smirked. "You have permission to cheer if it looks like I'm winning."

"Yes, Your Highness," Aislin quipped. "Your coach awaits."

Coach Keller was giving me the kind of look usually reserved for someone texting during practice. I hustled over and he had the grace to not say anything about it just yet. When he had his back turned to me, I snuck a clandestine wave at my cheering section.

Avril was treating this like any other day and I didn't think Aislin would ever tell her why this sort of thing was a treat. I could hope that Aislin would make it enough of a habit that it would stop being a thrill.

Team habit was to grab pizza after a victory, but I wasn't in the mood to make Aislin sit through a play-by-play of what she'd already watched. I snuck out of the locker room while everyone was debating where to go and found the girls waiting.

"Pizza as usual?" Avril guessed.

"Not tonight," I said. "Where do *you* want to go?"

"I don't know." Avril elbowed Aislin in the ribs with an innocent expression. "I hear Aislin's had a hot date at every restaurant in the state."

"You exaggerate," Aislin protested. "I've only been on hot dates to a quarter of them."

"I stand corrected," she said. "I'm going to let my parents know I'll be home late . . ."

"We'll finish deciding," I responded.

I dropped that subject once she was gone. "This was a great surprise," I commented. "When was the last time . . ."

"I hid under the bleachers for a couple of your soccer games," Aislin admitted, "but this is the first time I've been here in the flesh."

It irked me a little that she had never confessed to being a spectator before, but I let that slide. "That's what I thought. And Nate is . . ."

"Doing homework," she said. "I plan on imitating him after dinner."

"I'll drop you off," I offered immediately. "Are you interested in making this a regular thing?"

"You mean, will I be at every swim meet, soccer game, et cetera? Probably not."

I didn't blame her. Sometimes, *I* didn't want to show up.

"If you're asking what I intend to do with my new schedule, the answer is, 'what are you doing on Saturday?'"

"I promised to spend some quality time with Laurie in the morning and Nick in the evening. What were you thinking?"

"I have a list . . ."

"I'm not tanning until it's at least 32 degrees," I interrupted.

"No, but we could go to a movie after a late breakfast," she proposed.

"You actually have a list of things you've missed during daylight hours?" I asked incredulously. "I thought that was a joke."

"It's not a formal one," she said, "but you get the idea."

It was as good a coping method as whatever I would have come up with. I linked my arm through hers and sighed wearily.

"I think we need to shop for your first pair of sunglasses in five years this weekend," I suggested. "After that, we can just improvise."

White

While Nate was unusual in a lot of ways, he had obviously decided to test the theory that college students could survive on ramen and caffeine. It was probably why he tried to include a dinner in every one of our dates.

I reserved our kitchen for my lightest day of classes of the week and Maeve promised to make herself scarce. With Dad at work and Mom out on errands, we were guaranteed to have the place to ourselves myself.

With the shopping done the previous weekend, I was ready by 5:30 p.m. when the doorbell rang.

"Hi, gorgeous," Nate greeted me, stepping across the threshold for a quick kiss in case we were being watched.

I wasn't wearing anything special, but I needed fewer layers indoors. If he thought that was gorgeous, I wasn't going to argue.

"You're not so bad yourself," I teased. "Everyone's out."

"Oh."

He shrugged in a sort of "in that case" way and closed the door behind him before kissing me into a wall. I squeaked, more out of surprise than pain and Nate immediately pulled away.

"Sorry," he said hastily. "I don't usually get you all to myself."

"Well, except for the hard surface, I don't mind a little enthusiasm."

He arched an eyebrow. "What's this enthusiasm thing you mention?"

I pulled him closer by the lapel of his jacket and gave him a demonstration. "Got it?" I asked breathlessly a little while later.

"I think so," Nate smirked. "What smells so good?"

My focus shifted to why I'd invited him over in the first place. "Come and see."

I thought trying candlelight for ambience would have been ridiculous—but I had used table linens and background music. The enthusiasm wasn't for the table settings, though. It was for what I had set out about two minutes before he showed up.

"Salmon," he said. "I thought you didn't like seafood."

"I said I wasn't the biggest fan of fish, but the lady at the kosher . . ."

"Wait, wait, wait," Nate interrupted. "You went to a kosher deli to make me food you might not like?"

"She said that I didn't know what I was missing," I said, "and she wanted to help me be supportive. Impressed?"

"Very," he commented. "Only one significant other has ever made me food before now."

"And I'm guessing it wasn't kosher."

"It was pork," he answered. "It was like taking a Hindu to a steakhouse."

I clapped a hand to my mouth to stifle my laugh. "I see why you're so easily impressed."

"Well, that's just one of the things that make you worth writing home about."

I blushed at the comment, but it inspired skepticism as well as embarrassment. "You write home about me?"

"My parents insist," he explained. "You get more mention than my GPA."

"Just as long as I'm not ruining it."

"I spent more time at that library than my dorm so I could talk to you," he pointed out.

Now he was actually trying to make my cheeks stay flushed. "I don't believe it."

Nate shrugged indifferently this time. "Believe what you want, but you can dance and cook and they will definitely approve."

That hadn't been my top-secret goal in life, but it was nice to hear that I had a seal of approval. "Hold off on your accolades until we find out how it tastes," I instructed.

At that, Nate stepped away and pulled my chair out for me with a flourishing bow. "Then let us take our seats and let the test begin."

Mom and Maeve made it back in time to find me nursing a glass of water at the table and Nate up to his elbows in dish soap. Maeve apologized for my slave-driving nature, but Nate shrugged and got back to scrubbing a pot.

"If they weren't constantly checking up on us, you'd be someone to write home about," I commented once Nate had finished up.

He paused in the middle of drying his hands and checked his watch. "Should I make this a regular thing? I can probably do dishes on Saturdays too."

"That won't be necessary," I responded. "But speaking of committing to a date . . ."

"Such as February 14?" he asked.

"I suppose so," I said.

"Neither of us has a test that day, so I was hoping you might take a sick day with me."

It was a very good thing that Mom and Maeve weren't eavesdropping, since Mom would have lectured the both of us about academic responsibility.

"Define sick day," I requested.

"Dawn to dusk adventure of my design," he suggested. "You agree to the time and date and I'll take care of the rest."

It was a bold idea, but I couldn't guarantee that I'd be human the whole time and this was not how I wanted him to find out. "Afternoon to night?" I negotiated. "I really shouldn't miss my morning classes that day."

"I was hoping to make you breakfast," he sighed.

"And I can come to your dorm for that," I promised, "but I'm committed to my studies first and you later."

"That is so freshman of you," he chuckled.

"It sounds great, but we'll have other Valentine's Days. We can be irresponsible then."

Nate's expression was momentarily difficult to read. I got a vibe of disappointment or something else that I couldn't describe accurately.

"So we will," he said. "So you can finish by noon?"

Now he was sounding like a debt collector, but at least he was teasing me now.

"I'll make sure of it," I promised.

ACT IV

"Life has taught us that love does not consist of gazing at each other, but in looking together in the same direction."
Antoine de Saint-Exupery

SCENE 1

Black

I was in a bad mood and there was no other way to describe it. Aislin had agreed that I needed to consult on Valentine's Day gifts, since I'd actually had more than one boyfriend. She needed a gift that expressed all of the mushy stuff that she had been waiting her whole adolescent experience to share.

And then she ditched me. I waited for two hours at our rendezvous point and headed home after leaving her a very annoyed message.

An hour after I got home, she called. "I'm *so* sorry," Aislin blurted out. "It was one of those days."

"Tell me about it," I ordered. "In detail."

If she noticed the warning tone, she didn't comment on it. "I was trying to take the B line out to BU and we broke down just before Kenmore. By the time I got there, Nate had already left for work and was mad that I stood him up . . ."

Okay, I had asked for details and was now pretty sure she wasn't fibbing. If she put in too many details, I'd cry pretense, but I'd been stuck in similar straits myself.

"Why didn't Nate call me?" I asked.

"Probably didn't want to bother you," she guessed. "What are you doing tonight?"

"Seeing Nick," I replied shortly.

Her voice got quiet then, and I knew that she wasn't faking her remorse. "I didn't mean to stand you up," she said.

Now that I felt a stab of guilt at her cowed tone, I felt less angry. "I know," I said. "What are you doing tomorrow?"

"Homework," she answered. "What about in the morning?"

If we both got this over with in the morning, maybe we could finish homework together in the afternoon . . .

"I'm seeing Nate after lunch," she continued, "but if you had time before then, we could hit the stores together."

I wasn't one to upstage a date with the guy who loved her, so I agreed. "Sure," I said. "Are you coming home soon?"

"On my way now," Aislin responded.

She showed up twenty minutes later and immediately claimed the shower, which reminded me of the days of hosing off lake water. I took that time to look for evidence. There was nothing immediately suspicious and I felt a little guilty for even questioning her story. The shower might have just been a response to being stuck on the subway for too long.

I slipped out the door as soon as the water turned off and returned to my unfinished homework. Halfway through the chapter on refraction, Aislin tapped on the door.

"Come in," I called, swiveling in my chair.

Aislin padded in, hair still damp. "Sorry again," she said immediately.

"You haven't taken an evening shower in a while," I commented.

"You would, too, after a day like this," she pointed out. "Where are you going with Nick?"

"Out for a movie," I said with a shrug. "I promised him an action/adventure if he promised to put up with couples stuff on Valentine's Day."

"Isn't Valentine's Day always supposed to be about couples stuff?" Aislin asked.

"When done right," I responded. "Has Nate given you any hints on what to expect?"

"Not even a dress code," she said solemnly. "I spent enough money on First Night that I won't need something new until graduation."

"And you won't wear something slinky," I lamented.

"New Year's was slinky," she reminded me. "I'd like to just look ordinarily pretty."

I shook my head in bemusement. "You know that's a contradiction in terms," I pointed out.

"I want to be Aislin pretty instead of Maeve stunning," she amended.

"I can help with that," I offered.

"I'd rather have your shopping suggestions." Without waiting for an invitation, she sat on the end of my bed and curled in on herself, arms wrapped around her knees. "I need a more typical guy present to show I care."

"Gift card," I suggested. "A movie you both liked. A watch."

"Well, that's vague," Aislin said disapprovingly.

"No matter what the commercials say, there isn't a typical guy present," I pointed. "Nate and Nick are pretty normal guys, but Nate wouldn't like Bruins tickets and Nick wouldn't go dancing for fun."

"So you're basically saying you can't help me with the present?" she sighed.

"You know him better," I corrected, my voice gentle. I didn't want to make her day any worse. "Just get him something less emotionally significant than your Hanukkah present and more special than an impulse buy. You'll know it when you see it."

"That's what I'm hoping," Aislin admitted.

There was something very off about her voice right now. The stress combined with her posture also made her look exhausted.

"Was your day really that bad?" I sympathized.

"You have no idea," she commented.

Before I could grill her for previously undisclosed details, she unfurled herself and stood up. "I've got homework to do," she announced. "Try to have a stroke of genius."

I couldn't believe that she had been stuck on the T and hadn't used the time to do her homework. Since she probably needed a wireless connection to finish some of it, I would let that slide. If she looked this miserable tomorrow, I wasn't going to put up with it, even if I had to go to Nate.

White

The day had started out all right. I made it to my nine o'clock class on time, turned in my paper and contributed intelligently to the discussion. In Lit, we got the guidelines for student presentations and I started brainstorming.

Halfway to the Mugar to return books, I blacked out. I came to with feathers, a beak, and a full-blown anxiety attack. I managed to stash my clothes and backpack without being chased off by any students.

I hadn't spent more than an hour as a swan in weeks and the transformation left me feeling like I had run a marathon without stretching. I returned before sunset and sacrificed dignity to dress in record speed in some bushes.

Nate didn't call me once that day.

Black

I wouldn't have known something was wrong if it weren't for Aislin's blue floral shirt. I'd forgotten to plan my outfit for my history presentation and it wasn't until after my shower that I realized I didn't want to be in jeans when my grade depended on good impressions. I even knew that she had washed it the other day, so it wouldn't have stains on it.

I forgot about that when I opened the door well after dawn to find a swan under Aislin's quilt. I checked my watch in case I was wrong about the time, but she should have been featherless and getting ready for class by now. I closed the door quietly and decided to address the crisis instead of my wardrobe problems.

Mom answered after three quiet taps on the door, fully dressed and frowning at my bathrobe. "Shouldn't you be getting ready?"

"I need an emergency orthodontist note," I announced.

She immediately looked towards Aislin's door, wondering what role my sister was playing in this request. "Any particular reason?" she asked delicately.

"It's important," I assured her.

"But you have your presentation second period," she stated.

"Which is why I'm asking to leave after that," I responded. "I promise it's important."

"Can I ask why?"

I could have brought her to Aislin to explain, but I kept my expression neutral and nodded. "Aislin needs my help and I don't know how long it will take."

Mom folded her arms and leaned back to rest against the door. "Aislin didn't mention anything about it."

I mirrored her pose. "Emergencies don't give much warning."

"I think, then, that I'd like to hear about it from her," she said.

I blocked the path with an arm immediately. "Can you not? It will just make things worse for her."

Mom stepped to the other side and met the same resistance, which made her look stormy. "What do you mean 'worse'?" she challenged.

"I mean that there's a problem today," I shot back. "I'll get you details by the end of the day."

"If you don't know the details, how do you know there's a problem?" Mom demanded.

"I have my reasons."

"And you're being very vague about what they are." She gestured over her shoulder towards her bedroom door. "Would you like me to call the cop? He could probably talk you around."

"I'd like you to trust me about this—I wouldn't ask for a little faith without a good reason." I hastened to explain, "I'm not breaking any laws or doing something unethical."

Mom unfolded her arms after another half-minute of standoff. "Third period?" she asked.

"Leaving third period for the day," I said.

"All right," she said. "You get ready and I'll write the note for you to get your non-existent braces checked."

Once she was gone, I ventured back into Aislin's room. She was too asleep to protest when I borrowed her button-down and a black skirt. I brushed my hair and braided it so I could look formal and limited my makeup to lip gloss. That left me plenty of time to print off both my notes and Aislin's schedule and find shoes. I cleared out most of my school books and made a quick trip to Aislin's room to stock up on what I would need for her day.

Mom had a sealed envelope next to my plate of eggs and toast and I immediately stashed it next to my notes. "Thank you."

Mom nodded from behind a cup of tea and sighed once she had swallowed. "You'll tell me if there is anything that your father and I should know about Aislin," she stated.

The main reason for my silence was that I was as confused by the situation as them. I wasn't letting Aislin get away without an explanation tonight.

"I'm hoping this won't happen again," I responded before eating most of my eggs.

"Then I hope your presentation goes well and that your good intentions pay off," she said seriously.

I checked my watch and found that I would have to finish my last piece of toast on my way to school. I wrapped it in the napkin that had been under my fork and carried my plate to the sink.

"Will you be telling Dad about my truancy?" I asked.

"Not yet," she promised. "He'll be there for the explanation later, though."

"Yes, mother," I agreed, stepping away from the sink to give her a quick hug. "I'll see you tonight."

The first part of the day went without a hitch. I did well enough on my presentation that my teacher actually smiled at a few points and after ditching, I found parking quickly enough to get to class ten minutes early. I didn't participate, just took notes on everything and kept my head down.

I thought that the simple approach to the first class was a good sign, but that feeling of ease didn't last long in Lit class. The person in front of me passed a stack of papers back and I grabbed an exam. Instead of swearing loudly, I felt like vomiting my toast all over question #1 about "Young Goodman Brown."

My first option was to have a nervous breakdown and hope the professor was merciful. I could claim there'd been a death in the family, but that would be tricky to corroborate. I decided to do the best that I could with what I remembered from Honors American Lit and hope that it applied to Readings in American Literature.

I was relieved to find that there were a lot of multiple-choice questions and the short-answer questions didn't start with "Compare and contrast with at least three examples . . ." The essay question was like that, but I could worry about that later. I pulled out a pencil and tackled the first multiple-choice questions.

At the end of the period, I had probably done an average job. I had never heard of some of the material, but had I elaborated to my heart's content on the rest. I had tried to make up for my lack of familiarity with the second work on the essay question by being heavy-handed on my analysis of the first. I didn't know the professor's grading policies, but I hoped for partial credit.

I spent the hour between the second and third classes feverishly looking through Aislin's emails for any red flags about the next two classes. I found that if I had thought to do this earlier, I would have seen the study guide for the exam. There were a couple unread emails from Nate, but I was leaving those where they were.

I was heading to the third class of the day when I heard someone calling my surname. I turned to find the Lit professor strolling towards me, a slightly bemused expression on his face.

"Ms. Byrne," he greeted me. "I just checked my emails. I'm glad to see you're feeling better."

I froze and resisted the urge to close my eyes until he went away. Of course Aislin would have found a way to call in sick, even if it required the hunt-and-peck method of typing.

"False alarm," I croaked. I didn't know if Aislin had claimed food poisoning or a life-threatening injury, but I figured I could get by with flu-like symptoms. "I'm not great, but I could stay upright, so I decided to come anyway."

The professor chuckled at the lame joke. "The exam could have waited in extenuating circumstances," he assured me. "I appreciate you thinking ahead."

"I'll bear that in mind."

He nodded sympathetically. "This being your first semester, you're wise to play it safe, but if your sinus infection keeps you from attending the other classes this week, I'm sure someone will lend you their notes."

Aislin had picked something that wasn't drastic but debilitating. It was reassuring that she didn't expect to take a few weeks off.

"Thank you, sir," I responded. "I hope to see you on Wednesday."

He hurried away, probably off to a class of his own, and I turned to find Nate walking away. By the time I thought to call out his name, he was gone.

White

I wasn't surprised to wake up with feathers, but I wasn't prepared. I hadn't felt anything the night before, so I couldn't work out why I had woken up feeling like a bewildered twelve-year-old.

It didn't help that I had overslept my alarm and woke up with sunlight in my eyes. Maeve was at school and my parents had headed off to their respective jobs, but there was no indication of whether any of them had noticed my change in plans.

The next things I thought of had to do with notes on Puritan theology. I couldn't call Dr. Andress before the exam, though. Wings were useless for typing and I couldn't exactly poke keys with my webbed foot. I tried to peck at the keys, but kept hitting several keys at once. I eventually found a pencil to use as a stylus and painstakingly punched in each letter. In the end, he had a badly punctuated explanation of my miserable health. I'd heard on day one that he would work with us in the event of one illness or major emergency per semester and that meant I could get away with something a little more serious than a cold. I sent a copy to Nate so he wouldn't wonder where I was at lunch, trusting that he'd accept an explanation later in the day.

With that accomplished, I curled up on my bed with my head turned towards the clock. I didn't know when I'd revert, but I wanted to know the exact moment. I heard my phone buzzing in the distance, but didn't feel like getting out of bed to not answer the phone. I used my beak to pull my quilt up to my neck and settled in to wait.

The doorbell woke me next and my eyes snapped open to find that it was just after three. I rolled onto my back, feeling my wing scrape the underside of my top sheet, and knew there was no chance of someone answering the door for a while.

The bell sounded again, followed immediately by my ringtone. I found Nate's name on the caller ID, so craned my neck far enough to tap it with my beak and send the call to voicemail. That only made the person knock firmly on the door and that meant Nate was trying to badger me out of bed. If this went on much longer, he'd start looking for a spare key, but the key box had a passcode.

My bedroom didn't have a front-facing window, so I hurried to Brendan's old room and peered out the window. I couldn't see anyone on the front porch, but Nate's usual mode of transportation was parked at the curb. If I had been capable of human speech, I might have said something consisting of four letters that my mother would have disapproved of.

After ten minutes of cycling between leaning on the bell, pounding on the door and calling my phone, he hit the front walk looking like a vengeful god off to smite someone. It was then that something flipped and I found myself with opposable thumbs once more. I scrambled off the bed and grabbed my bathrobe on my way back to my room. By the time I got to the front door, he was back at the car and I had to chase him in fluffy slippers.

"Nate," I called breathlessly. "Wait up."

He turned and my impression of a vengeful god wasn't changed. He looked both furious and disappointed.

"Nice of you to turn up," he deadpanned. "Sorry if I kept you waiting."

I could have responded that he was stealing my lines, but this wasn't the moment for a playful joke. "I haven't been out of bed since I got back from the doctor's," I invented.

"Oh?"

"Yeah. I have orders to stay there for a few days, so I hope you don't mind if we have to put a hold on some . . ."

"Don't give me that," Nate snapped unexpectedly. "There's more to that story and right now, I don't know if I want to hear it."

I was as confused by his claim as his hostility; I had called in sick to life today and he was treating me as though he'd walked in on me shooting a puppy. It was out of line and after the stress of this morning, I wasn't inclined to be submissive about it.

"I'm not letting you inspect my phlegm," I asserted. "I don't know what you mean by . . ."

"I know your sister was covering for you today," he interrupted. "I saw you on campus when you claimed to be in bed."

I was going to have to strangle Maeve. If she had been on campus, there was a chance she had benevolently gone to my classes and flunked my lit exam with the best of intentions. I had been stupid not to check my messages or emails before charging after Nate, but I had also been desperate.

"That wasn't what I intended," I blurted out.

"So she did that on her own initiative?" Nate challenged. "Does she get impostor privileges on date nights?"

That, more than any of his aggression, brought an angry flush to my cheeks. "Don't be petty," I ordered. "When has she ever given you reason to mistrust her?"

"That's what I'd like to know," he said. "I don't like having to second-guess you."

"I don't *want* you second-guessing me," I protested. "I want you to believe that it wasn't my idea and that I . . ."

I couldn't bring myself to tell him that I'd never deceive him. I also couldn't deny that this was the second time in three months that Maeve had crossed the line.

"Why are you angry at me?" I asked at last. "This was her doing."

"I'm furious that you couldn't be bothered to talk to me for the last ten minutes," Nate explained through gritted teeth. "Did you think it was funny?"

"I came as I soon as I could," I answered in complete honesty. "I'm not going to apologize for you trying to break down my door because of some paranoia."

"I saw someone in the upstairs window," he pointed out. "You were enjoying the view for at least part of it and the least you could have done was answer the door."

"Which I've done now."

This was the time that I could have reached out a conciliatory hand, but I was feeling too defensive to bother with that.

"This is an asinine argument," I asserted. "The only thing I'm guilty of is not being awake enough to stop Maeve and being too asleep to answer the door for a while. I don't know why you're having some kind of nuclear meltdown over those two things."

"I don't like that you're not taking this seriously," he answered. "I don't want you thinking that it's okay for it to happen again."

"It *won't* happen again."

"That's all I ask."

"No," I shot back. "You want me to stop being dishonest with you, which means you don't trust me in the first place."

"I'm trying," he argued.

"And you think I'm not?" I challenged.

"I think you're doing a lot of yelling for someone too sick to go to campus."

At this rate, I was going to wind up with pneumonia. I stepped away. "Call me tonight when you feel like being less of an idiot," I requested. "I'm going back to bed."

I returned to the house without letting him say anything else, anger pulsing in my veins. I heard his car door slam before I reached the stairs and didn't even bother to care.

The voicemails weren't much better than the fight. He started out with sympathy and suggesting we take things indoors until I was feeling better, but by the time we got to the door-pounding, he was getting intolerable. I deleted all of the messages and didn't bother to read any of the texts.

I had another half hour before Maeve would get out of my last class and when she did, there would be no mistaking my feelings on today's events.

Black

My phone rang as soon as I left the classroom, which was not a surprise. It was, however, a relief to see Aislin's name on caller ID.

"Hello," I said as cheerfully as possible. "Feeling better?"

"What did you do?"

"Took lots of notes, correctly answered a question about Plato and . . ."

"Took my exam on colonial literature?" she demanded.

A few hours after the fact, the exam seemed a lot funnier than it had been. "I think it went fine."

"It did *not*," Aislin snapped.

"He couldn't have graded it already," I defended.

"I had this covered," she squawked. "I could reschedule it and at worst, take a few points off of my score. Now, if I flunk, I'll have to claim that I was too delirious to remember the difference between Puritans and Protestants."

I stepped out of the flow of traffic and leaned against a wall. "I don't think I was *that* bad," I protested.

"Don't you have your own school to go to?"

"I went until third period," I reported. "Then I went to your rescue. Can't you be grateful?"

"Not today."

I read into the momentary break in her voice that the stupid exam was the least of her problems and remembered that she had been too feathery to have a life today. Just like old times.

"I'm going to pick up Mom from work," I informed her. "When I get home, you and I are going to talk."

Aislin hung up in response.

I called ahead so Mom was waiting outside of her building when I pulled over. She ducked into the car and skipped the pleasantries.

"Is your sister all right?"

"Aislin is fine," I said. "She hit a snag, but it turned out all right in the end."

She inhaled deeply as if she'd suffocated all day and let it out slowly. "I trust it won't happen often."

"We went over that this morning," I reminded her.

"I know, but it's like when I nag you about homework or your room," Mom explained. "I'm saving up for when I don't have time to remind you."

"And I sometimes deserve the nagging," I admitted. "I don't want this to happen again."

She glanced my way to invite details. "That bad?" she prompted.

"That unexpected," I corrected. When Mom didn't respond for a few minutes, I broke the silence instead.

"This is Aislin's story to tell. Do you mind letting her decide when?"

She glanced at me with a slightly amused expression. "Is this client-attorney or doctor-patient privilege?" she teased.

"Twin prerogative," I countered. "We didn't do anything illegal or dangerous, but she'd appreciate some space."

"That's what I thought," Mom said grimly. "That's why I trusted you today."

"So you'll hold off on the interrogations?" I prompted.

"I won't bring it up with her," Mom promised, "but your father deserves to know that there was a snag. I'll leave it at that."

It wasn't the compromise that I had hoped for, but until I consulted with Aislin, I wasn't promising anything else.

"I can agree to that."

I was tempted to avoid my sister when I returned, but she had sounded on the verge of an apocalypse when I spoke to her after class. That meant stalling would be adding insult to injury and would definitely make things worse.

I knocked on her bedroom door and entered without waiting for an invitation. "I have your notes and books, plus three handouts from today and a flyer for the ornithology club," I announced. "I thought you might find that amusing."

She wasn't exactly glaring at me when I stopped speaking, but she was carved from ice and giving off as much heat as your average Nor'easter. I set her things on the desk for easy access and backed away, hands up in surrender.

"I said I'm sorry."

"Actually," Aislin bit out, "you never did. You tried to talk me into agreeing that it was a good idea. You told me I should be grateful. Never once did you say you're sorry."

All right, so that had been a bad choice of words and a worse attempt at reconciliation. It still rankled me that she wasn't giving me a shred of credit for the hard work that I had put into this day.

"Do I get to know what I should be sorry for?" I asked pointedly. "Other than the exam, I was practically inconspicuous . . ."

"I disagree," she snapped. "Nate saw you . . ."

"I know," I protested, "but I didn't talk to him."

"Things might have turned out better if you had," my sister responded. "Unlike my classmates and professors, Nate can tell us apart and had a lot to say on the subject when he came over here looking for me."

"While you were human?"

"While I wasn't," she shot back. "That fixed itself after a while, but he felt like I was being deceitful by letting my sister try to pass herself off as me. I called him petty and you can imagine how well that went over. So *tell me again* why I should be grateful."

My knees didn't exactly buckle in horror, but I sat in her desk chair as soon as I remembered how to move my legs. "Well, this could have been coordinated better," I confessed.

"You don't say," Aislin said flatly.

The time for apologies was past. While they might be socially acceptable, they wouldn't make a dent if Nate had made her angry enough to fight him. I could only try to make something right and wasn't exactly sure how to do that right now. It was especially difficult to make amends when she was likely to kick me in the shins at any moment now.

"Do you mind me asking what happened?" I asked carefully.

She shook her head firmly. "I would mind even if I knew," my sister snapped. "I had a lousy day and that should have been the end of the story."

I had wondered all the way home who she was blaming and why. Now that I had recognized this as equal parts self-flagellation and sibling-resentment, I didn't feel better. I stood abruptly and left the room without another word. A few minutes later, I returned in my own clothes and knocked on the door. She invited me in this time, sounding a little less murderous.

"Hey," I greeted. "I'm sorry I crossed a number of lines. Do you want to talk about your day?"

Aislin had her knees drawn up to her chest and looked more defeated than anything. "I want to talk to Nate," she admitted.

"Then call him."

She shook her head. "I think I need to give him time to stop hating me."

It took every ounce of self-control that I had not to sigh in exasperation and Aislin looked up from her toenails.

"What?" she demanded. "I can practically hear you keeping your big mouth shut."

"I'm going to have to cite experience here," I said. "May I approach?"

She gestured to the desk chair, accepting that I came in peace. I hung up the shirt and skirt, then sat in the offered chair.

"He doesn't hate you," I asserted. "I don't doubt that he's angry and hurt, which you can relate to very well right now."

She didn't dispute that.

"He doesn't like finding reasons to feel that way," I explained. "Do you take that as true or false?"

"True," Aislin responded after only a few seconds of hesitation.

"I didn't mean to do anything wrong," I asserted. "Do you take that as . . ."

"True."

We were at least getting somewhere in our own conflict. "Nate thinks you hate him too."

Aislin tilted her head to the side and contemplated that idea with her cheek against her knee. "I don't know," she admitted.

"Then find out," I urged her. "Maybe not tonight, but as soon as you think you can express that without hurting feelings. Do you accept the assignment?"

She nodded still curled in on herself. "I'm sorry for blaming you," she added after a few more moments of more amicable silence.

"I don't hold it against you," I replied.

Her shoulders slumped slightly and she let her knees lower to their normal position. "How much do our parents know?"

"I've gotten them to back down," I responded confidently. "You can't plead the fifth for long, but Mom knows there was a snag."

"A snag," she echoed. "That could mean practically anything."

"She no longer thinks there was a nuclear meltdown–style disaster," I admitted. "I had to talk her down, though."

"And she didn't tell Dad?" Aislin asked with obvious incredulity.

"She is telling Dad as much as she knows and I said that this is your story to tell," I said diplomatically. "I trust her to honor that."

Aislin breathed deeply for a few moments and when she spoke again, she sounded like herself. She had moved past being angry with me and she could probably admit that I hadn't ruined her day.

"I'm sorry for ripping your head off," she commented unnecessarily.

"Apology accepted," I replied. "I'm sorry I ever set foot in your English class."

Aislin sniggered at that, which meant she could forgive me. "I'm sure I'll survive."

She didn't make me promise not to interfere again, but she let me give her a conciliatory hug before we parted ways. It was acceptable progress.

I woke up early on the next day and stopped by Aislin's room to spy on her. There wasn't much light coming through the window, but I could see her fingers curled around her pillow and her hair tangled around her face.

Reassured that the crisis had passed for now, I closed the door and moved on with my day.

White

When the next day dawned, I was still in my natural state, but I didn't take any chances. I claimed to still be miserably sick and in the aftermath of yesterday's fiasco, the miserable part wasn't a challenge.

I awoke human and stayed that way, which I took as a sign that we were both feeling appropriate amounts of regret. When I heard someone crunching across the snow on the front walk around three, I hurried downstairs and peered through a window to find Nate approaching with a plastic grocery bag.

I opened the door before he could knock and he came to a halt at the top of the stairs, looking both uncertain and apprehensive.

"I didn't want to wake you," Nate greeted, "but I wanted to apologize."

"I don't think you can fit roses into a bag that small," I observed.

"No," Nate agreed, "but chicken-flavored Ramen is the perfect size."

I couldn't restrain a smile at that. "I don't think I've ever had a boy bring me chicken noodle soup."

"Well . . ." He looked somewhat abashedly at his shoes for a moment. "I probably made things worse yesterday."

He was clearly not referring to the cough that I would have to fake for a while longer, but I appreciated the circumspect way in which he was bringing up a touchy subject.

"I didn't help," I said in the same vein. "Come in."

"Are you sure?"

"Don't question my motives."

He met my eyes and grinned back. "If you say so."

He kissed my cheek on the way in, which was probably as good as I could expect in my alleged condition.

He invited himself into the kitchen and remembered enough from Thanksgiving to know where the pots and pans were. A few minutes later, the water was on its way to boiling and we'd progressed to hand-holding at the kitchen table.

"Do we want to take turns being sorry or should I just say it all in one go?" Nate asked.

"I'll start," I offered. "I'm sorry for calling you petty."

"I'm sorry I earned it," he countered. "I was being irrational . . ."

"And we both overreacted . . ."

"Aislin-impersonator or not, your sister didn't deserve what I said," he stated. "Does she know?"

I never had gotten around to telling Maeve *why* I'd called him petty. I wasn't sure how easily she'd forgive him, since it had taken the better part of the night for the anger to fade from my mind. Waking up human had helped a lot.

"She knows we upset each other," I replied candidly.

"Which she'll translate to something I said," he guessed.

"Which she'll translate as both our faults," I corrected. "She's a loyal sister, but knows me too well to blame you for everything."

Nate chuckled at that, a reassuringly quiet sound after all the arguing we'd done yesterday. "Tell her I appreciate having an ally."

"I won't." At his arched eyebrow, I pulled a straight face so he would know that I was in earnest. "If anyone in this house is your ally, I demand that it be me."

That earned me a kiss that went on long enough for the water to boil over. At the sound of water hissing on the burner, we broke apart with a mutual laugh and Nate turned his attention back to other ways of making me feel better.

Half an hour after he left, I was back in swan form. I felt it coming on this time and hung out my Do Not Disturb sign. Two hours later, Mom checked on me, but I was human-shaped by then.

Since the curse kicked in, travel had always been an adventure. I had stopped booking flights and gotten into the habit of taking overnighter trains. On the occasional road trips, I had the option to sit in the back seat like some kind of family pet or stretch my wings for a while.

In theory, falling in love with Nate should have made things less complicated, but based on the last few days, I couldn't rely on any kind of set schedule. I knew that I could rely on my humanity between dusk and dawn, though, so I spent a few hours at the library and headed for South Station instead of making my way home. No one had noticed this morning that I was packing more than my textbooks and binders into my bag and Mom wouldn't get the credit card bill until long after I returned. With any luck, this would be worth it.

I should have told someone that I'd be on an Amtrak instead of the Red Line around 9:30, but I wasn't going to let anyone talk me out of this. I hadn't exactly lied to Mom when she called at five to ask if I needed a ride home from campus. When Maeve texted to see if I was on my way home yet, I just responded that I wasn't there yet. No one asked where "there" was, so it wasn't until around eleven that the questions about my whereabouts got a little more pointed. I stopped answering calls and texted two words that would have to do for now: *Trust me.*

I couldn't exactly wake Brendan up to ask for a 4 a.m. lift from the 30th Street Station, so I decided to hang out there until a more decent hour after group-texting every relative in Cambridge to say I was still alive and well and hadn't crossed any international borders.

Three minutes before dawn, I found a restroom and waited for the inevitable change to happen, but nothing happened. It was the first good sign I'd had in days.

My next signal was a mixed one; I left the station to find Brendan waiting in the dawn chill for me. Without saying a word, he handed over his phone.

"Needless to say, you're grounded again," Dad announced. "Brendan will see you back on the train."

Without further commentary, he hung up. I mutely handed the phone back to Brendan, who looked surprisingly cheerful for this time of day.

"I assume you have a return ticket?" he asked.

"For tomorrow morning," I confirmed.

"Good." He reached out and pulled my bag off my shoulder before I could offer any kind of proper greeting. "Have you eaten yet?"

No matter the obligatory conflicts that I had with Brendan, I was grateful that his first priority wasn't seeing how fast he could get rid of me. We headed for the nearby Dunkin' Donuts so I could at least explain myself on a full stomach.

One breakfast sandwich, five minutes in the car and a flight of stairs later, Brendan directed me to the couch and sat within arm's reach, my bag perched on his knees.

"So, everyone has their theory on why you're here," he announced.

"Including you?" I prompted.

"I'm guessing that if you wanted to run away from home, you'd pick somewhere warmer than Pennsylvania and tell Maeve first," Brendan considered. "That means that you're not running away. You're just out of your mind."

"Because I'm here at four in the morning?"

"Because you came to *me,*" he clarified. "Back home, you have two parents who want the best for you, a sister who would take a bullet for you and a therapist who would see you as soon as his schedule permitted. I don't get why you're *here.*"

"All of them would encourage me to be rational about my current situation," I stated. "You're more likely to try the alternative."

He steepled his fingers together at that, looking contemplative instead of scheming. "I thought you objected to that."

"I don't always appreciate it, but it's what I need," I corrected. "What do you say?"

"I say you came a long way for a short conversation."

I didn't believe that. On the rare occasion when I'd actually asked his advice, Brendan hadn't dismissed the problem in a few minutes. If I'd stayed at home and called in my crisis, he would have broken this up into half a dozen phone calls.

"Are you going to hear me out or not?"

"You've got, what, twenty-four hours until your train?"

"Twenty-six," I amended.

"And you don't know when you'll be human?" At a stern look from me, he shrugged. "If you're here about a crisis, I'm guessing it's not about where you should spend spring break."

"You're right," I admitted. "I'll have some warning, but I'm pretty sure I'll lose some daylight hours."

Brendan nodded and tossed my bag to me. "That's what I thought," he said. "Hose down. I'll find you a place to stay for the night, tell Dad when to pick you up tomorrow, and talk to my boss."

I obeyed and emerged, dressed in clean clothes and smelling a little less travel-worn, ten minutes later. He held up a hand to forestall any conversation and, from the sound of things, finished arranging housing for the night.

"All right," he said upon hanging up. "It's too short notice for on-campus guest accommodations, but Dad was willing to spring for a hotel once he heard that this might take a while."

"You didn't really say that, did you?" I asked.

"I told him you'd already gotten a return ticket for tomorrow and I wanted to do this right," he replied.

"And he was fine with that?"

"He put me under oath to try to be helpful," Brendan said drily. "It's like he doesn't know me at all."

I didn't confirm or deny that, just pulled my damp hair back in a ponytail holder. "What has Mom said?"

"That she hopes you find whatever you're looking for," he replied. "Maeve had to be talked out of taking the next train south."

That was what I had expected, including my sentence. I had considered the punishment worth whatever happened down here.

"Does Nate know?" he asked pointedly while I took my seat and pulled my hair out of my face.

I grimaced, but gave an honest answer. "Nate might wonder where I am today or he might not even notice."

"Ah." He paused to stretch languidly and made himself comfortable before continuing. "Who knows?"

"As far as I know, only Maeve, but that might have changed since I last talked to her."

"Probably," he agreed. "The first thing Dad asked was if any of us saw this coming."

That didn't necessarily mean that Maeve had spilled her guts about her recent college visit. If she acted in-character, she would have told them to ask me for an explanation.

"But you haven't dumped him?" Brendan prompted, "Or vice versa?"

"I haven't done anything stupid," I defended.

"I didn't say you had, but that doesn't answer my question."

"We're still together," I replied.

"And you approve of that?"

I cocked my head to give him a skeptical look. "Why shouldn't I?"

"Don't ask me," Brendan said. "You're the one who took an overnighter to talk to me about your feelings."

I still wasn't completely sure that it was a brilliant idea, but it had felt like the right thing to do. I'd probably understand afterwards.

"I want to be with him," I answered. "I think he still wants to be with me."

"But that's where it gets too complicated to talk to Maeve about?" he guessed.

"Sort of," I confirmed.

Brendan didn't exactly look excited by that, but looked for all the world like he was about to defend my honor in a duel.

"All right," he said. "Talk me through it."

So I did. I didn't give him hours and minutes, but he knew how long I'd been having problems and the nature of those problems. He knew what I'd told Maeve and what I had yet to disclose to our parents. While Maeve would have interrupted with a thousand questions, he let me finish my recital before opening his mouth again.

"It's not the disaster you think."

"Come on," I protested. "You, of all people, should be willing to tell me it's a disaster."

"Who says I'm not willing?" he shot back. "I took a solemn vow when I got younger sisters that I would teach them the brutal and unpleasant ways of the world. I don't think anyone can say I've slacked off in that department."

"Which is why I came to you," I confirmed.

He bowed his head in acknowledgment of that compliment. "I'd rather die than break that vow," he explained.

"So, why isn't it a disaster?" I challenged.

He held up his hands. "You're getting ahead of me."

That was a product of up-all-night nerves, the orange juice I'd gotten at Dunkin', and my waning conviction that he was in the process of lying to me. I dropped my eyes to my lap for a moment and nodded meekly. "Sorry."

"I'd rather die than break the solemn vows that got me into the Order of Older Brothers," he reiterated, "so I'm not allowed to lie when you ask me if something makes you look fat or if you screwed up with the parents or if you're in way over your head. It's a disaster, but it's not the disaster you think."

The second use of that phrase caught my attention and I lifted my eyes so I could stare him down. "Explain."

"Gladly." He held out both hands as if weighing two options. "Tell me what you think a disaster is. Not anecdotes, just a definition."

"It's a sudden accident or catastrophe that causes a lot of damage."

"Yes," he agreed, "but not what I'm looking for. A disaster doesn't have to be sudden. It can be years in the making. Your definition of disaster explains why you had a few feathery days and felt the urge to run away from home."

I wasn't running away from home, but I had fled my problems before I could make them any worse.

"The meaning I'm looking for is something that has unfortunate consequences," he continued. "When you hit puberty and the curse flipped the switch, it was a disaster by both definitions. When you discovered how far you could fly without stopping for a map check, it was the sudden catastrophe kind."

"And Nate falling out of love with me is the kind that can take years to fester?"

For the first time since we returned to his dorm, his wise-old-mentor image cracked. It was just a moment where I could see his exasperation, but it was reassuring that I wasn't the only one struggling to make sense of this conversation.

"Do you really think he's fallen out of love with you?" he asked simply.

Yesterday, my immediate answer would have been yes. Today, I was an hour into the day and showing no sign of swanhood.

"I don't think it's that cut-and-dry," I admitted.

"Good," Brendan grunted. "I didn't feel like talking you out of thinking that, so that'll make things easier. I don't think he's stupid enough that he's stopped loving you, but that's where it gets complicated. You didn't leave any gruesome fights out of your story, right?

"Then there are any number of reasons for this to go south," he speculated at my nod. "You both have responsibilities outside of the relationship and that can cause stress. You don't have as much free time as you used to for the mushy stuff, so you're both feeling that distance. And you're out of the honeymoon period, so you've settled down into a more normal relationship than the stuff of fairytales."

"But apparently, normal relationships aren't enough for the curse," I pointed out.

His back straightened suddenly as if we were trying to navigate a half-remembered course and he'd finally recognized a landmark. "Okay."

"I don't think of it as 'okay.' "

Brendan waved the comment off. "Here's the deal," he said with utter conviction and confidence. "You could break things off now and find someone who will get you back to the honeymoon period of wild, impulsive, passionate love again."

I saw any kind of love as something slightly miraculous and that would be tempting fate. "You're sweet to think I have a chance."

"Do you want to?" he asked.

"*No,*" I protested. "No one should think that's an option."

"I'm glad you think so. Second question," he continued is, "do you still want to break up because things are waning?"

That was a messier question and one that I didn't have a ready answer for. "I don't think so," I said cautiously.

"Why?"

"Because I love him and I want him to still love me."

"And based on my intimate knowledge of the male brain, I still say he does."

Which was why he didn't claim this was the disaster of my imagining, but that still didn't solve the problem that had brought me to Philadelphia. "So, what now?" I challenged.

"So the springboard question of the day is this: Do you want to stay in love with someone who might not always have a positive influence on the curse?"

If we had been speaking in rhetoric, I would have seen that as a no-win situation. I would have asserted my right to absolute happiness and moved on to the next question.

"I want to stay in love with Nate," I answered. "I'm having trouble accepting that it'll mean days where the curse is in charge."

Brendan reached over and took my hand, which was a much more concrete sign of his affection than a hug. "None of us has ever thought less of you for having a problem with that."

I doubted that, but I hadn't gotten him up at the crack of dawn to start a fight. "I still need to know what I do now," I reminded him.

"My advice from the start of this conversation was going to be pretty simple," he said. "You have to either stop in your tracks or keep moving forward. You know you're not stopping, so how do you move forward?"

"Exactly."

"You tell him."

The next sensation was one of someone grabbing a neck muscle and wringing it. A dull ache followed. It was not the psychological or physical response I had hoped for.

"I can't," I argued, abandoning my meekness.

"You have to," he said. "The best way to move forward is to be completely honest with him."

"I can't."

"Why not?" he challenged. "Because he might feel some kind of obligation to you?"

I pulled my hand back, irritated. "Well, yeah. If I'd wanted to hear that . . ."

"You'd have stayed in Cambridge," he finished. "Yeah, it's not what you wanted to hear, but you've now heard it from two people who are honor-bound to tell you the truth."

I could have protested a third time, but he had a point. "I promise to think about it," I said.

He scrubbed one hand over his face and the exasperated look returned. "Try thinking aloud," he requested. "I can do this all day."

When he walked me to the platform the next morning, I still hadn't committed to that leap of faith, but I had other plans of action in mind. I put one more question to him before boarding.

"How did you become the expert on this stuff?"

Brendan patted my shoulder in a commiserating and slightly patronizing way, as any older brother would. "You're too young to hear that story, kid," he said.

Black

After that first panicked day, things seemed to be better. I checked on Aislin the next two mornings until she greeted my concern with a heartfelt "I'm trying to *sleep* here." If she was human enough to be that cranky, I counted the day as some kind of success.

The problem was that even on good days, she didn't look like herself. I got the impression that life was causing her a constant headache and that didn't add up to head-over-heels love by any definition. She would look thrilled any time Nate picked her up and what I heard of their phone conversations didn't sound problematic, but I couldn't balance her exhaustion with her relationship.

If I had any sense of self-preservation, I wouldn't have planned to go to Aislin's campus at all. It was her turf and to say my last visit hadn't gone well was like saying that the *Titanic* hit a patch of black ice.

On the other hand, I was honor-bound as a loving sister to fix things. I wasn't sure that was possible, but Aislin was, so I had to at least *try*.

Then she pulled a vanishing act of the kind that had gotten her arrested last year and I decided that drastic measures were no longer optional. I was polite enough to call first, though, and Nate accepted my invitation.

I would have preferred to track him down between classes so he would be less inclined to yell at me in public, but this was a Saturday and I wasn't about to visit his dorm. We met on the fairly neutral ground of a pizza place in Kenmore Square.

Nate didn't say it was nice to see me or thank me for coming. He left the pleasantries at "hello" and led me to a table in back. Once we had decided to share a pepperoni pizza, he folded his hands on the table and looked my way with the attitude of a diplomat heading into difficult negotiations.

"I would have thought that, if Ash told you about the fight, she'd have told you about the makeup."

"Not in so many words," I corrected, "but she stopped moping and I noticed the ramen. Thank you."

"Thank her," Nate suggested. "I came to my senses, but she had to forgive me and I'm not completely sure that I deserved it."

I didn't like that the uncertainty of his love had driven Aislin to go to *Brendan* for advice, but I liked his attitude today.

"Relax," I requested. "I'm not here to lecture you about my sister."

The waiter arrived with our drinks then and he swigged half of his soda before responding. In the wake of this latest statement, he looked wary instead of defensive. I tried to slouch slightly so he'd feel more ease.

"I have the feeling you're still here to lecture me," Nate observed.

"Yes," I admitted. "To lecture you about *me*."

That wasn't very comforting, apparently. Nate looked as on-guard as he had half a glass of soda ago. I wanted him to take this conversation seriously, though, so that was a good thing.

"Before you think she's turned against you, you should know that she hasn't quoted anyone but herself in that argument," I said before coming around to my main point. "I can tell, though, when she's censoring herself and I know that the whole mess started because you noticed me taking her place the other day."

"Pretty much," Nate confirmed. "I didn't like what you did."

"If it makes you feel any better, neither did she."

He smiled quickly before taking another drink. "And that's one of the reasons why I stopped being mad at her."

"But that's also why you shouldn't have blamed her in the first place," I argued.

"I already admitted that it was a bad idea," Nate objected.

"But you don't get something fundamental about this whole situation," I insisted, leaning forward to share a confidence. "You tell her you love her, but trusting her isn't a reflex. I don't get how that works."

"Is it for you?" he pointed out, adopting a similar posture. "I'm pretty sure that you're here because you don't give me the benefit of the doubt. You think that I dealt her a pretty hard blow and I'm poised for another one. That doesn't sound like you trust me."

He was right for the most part. "It's not my job to trust you," I said, "but I can try very hard to do that."

"And I promise to trust your sister."

"That's not why I'm here." On some points, he was grasping my meaning immediately, but that wasn't my goal in coming here. "You can trust Ash because she's practically allergic to making you unhappy. You can trust me because I have the same reaction to making her life more difficult."

Nate retreated and folded his arms across his chest, his wary expression gone now. "Then how do you explain that you went behind her back?"

"Because I honestly didn't know that it would have that effect," I asserted. "I thought that I could get to campus, get her notes, and get home without bothering anyone, and the only price she'd have to pay would be reading my handwriting. Now that I know how bad an idea it was, I'm less inclined to do that again."

"Then I can also promise to try very hard to trust you," Nate offered. "Does that seem fair?"

Having anticipated that he would be reasonable, I was ready for an answer and a handshake. "Agreed."

White

Brendan saw me onto the train Sunday morning with a hug and another reassurance that things weren't as bad as I thought. When Maeve met me on the platform at South Station, she pulled me into another hug.

"You're going to be fine," she asserted confidently.

I nearly laughed at the parallel messages, but pulled away with a quizzical smile. "What makes you say that?"

"Dad is only grounding you for a week and that's only because of the price of tickets," Maeve said.

"As long as I'm still allowed on campus, I can understand that," I replied.

Maeve shrugged and reached for my bag. "You'll have to take that up with the warden, but there's a second thing you should know before life gets back to normal."

I slid the straps off my shoulder and handed the bag over. "And that is?"

"I talked Nate into accepting my apology," she announced.

"*When?*"

"Lunch yesterday," Maeve responded calmly. "I bribed him with pizza and we talked rationally about why he shouldn't blame you for what I did."

I was dumbstruck for a few moments. She had gone behind my back, again with good intentions. The basic facts were the same as the disastrous day, but it felt like less of a betrayal than before. Maybe that was a side effect of listening to Brendan for hours.

"I don't think you're mad at me," she prompted. "Tell me I'm right."

"You are," I said. "But *why?*"

"Because you ran off to Philadelphia and I had the time to have an honest dialogue with him," my sister stated. "I figured there were worse ways to spend a Saturday."

"Do I get to find out what you said?" I asked.

"Not unless you tell me what he said during your fight," Maeve countered.

It was forgiven, if not forgotten, so I was going to keep it there no matter how tempting the offer was. "No deal," I said.

Maeve grinned and tightened the straps on my backpack. "Then let's get you home so the others can stop worrying."

SCENE 2

Black

I didn't know what Aislin's day had been like on Monday, but she wasn't home when I got back from school and I chose to optimistically think of that as a good sign. It was even better when I texted her before sunset and got an immediate response.

She came to my bedroom looking exhausted, but her mood seemed to fall between the good mood of yesterday and the misery of a few days ago.

"Hey," she said, failing to sound casual. "Any messages for me?"

"Nate called twice," I pointed out. "Do you guys have something going on tonight?"

"Sort of." She dropped her purse on the bed and dropped down next to it. "We're meeting up on campus in about an hour."

The weariness in her voice was so noticeable that I decided to give up on subtlety. "Are you sure that's a good idea?"

I expected her to lie about her feelings, but she sighed heavily. "No, but whatever he has to say, I have to hear it."

"He hasn't said anything yet?"

"No," Aislin responded, "but I think I know some of it. It hasn't been easy."

I believed that more completely than she might think. "I've noticed more than you realized," I reminded her.

"I know."

"If this goes on much longer, I may have to spill your secrets to the offending party."

She must have been miserable, since she didn't even fight back on that. After a minute, I pulled her into a hug and didn't let go until she did.

"Do you need to talk it out?"

"Yes," she answered dully. "With him."

"Then I'll drive you to campus," I decided.

Aislin nodded in agreement. "I'm going to lie down until it's time to go."

I wanted answers, but I wanted her peace of mind more, so I let her go.

When we left a little over half an hour later, she was looking either rested or resolute. I let her out after a short hug and she walked away without acknowledging my "Good luck." I just hoped that I wouldn't have to beat Nate up after tonight's conversation ended.

White

Nate met me, as requested, at our usual table. I figured it was the place that we had been the most honest with each other and that was a good place to start. When he leaned across the table for a kiss, I turned and let his lips land on my cheek. He drew back, looking wary, and took a seat. I extended a hand to clarify that I wasn't completely shutting him out and he took it, but his expression didn't change. We were both on guard here.

"You look nice," he commented.

"You too," I responded. "Thanks for coming."

I had called him after classes and asked him to clear his schedule immediately for some us time. I just hadn't specified anything but the meeting place and time.

"Do you want to get something to . . ."

I cut him off, shaking my head firmly. "I need to talk to you," I said.

The comment came out as a desperate rasp, not the way I intended. I had imagined confronting him and stridently demanding answers. Instead, I felt as I had in third grade when trying to make sense of an act of bullying. The thought that I was responding to this situation the same way was harder to deal with than the change itself.

"Something's off," Nate observed. "What is it?"

I took some time to breathe deeply and after a minute, the tightness in my throat eased a little. This was the person I had trusted enough to love and he was not here on the offensive.

"That's my line," I stated.

He didn't deny it, but his grip tightened on my hand. I focused my gaze on the point where our fingers laced together and took another minute to rewrite my questions.

"We're pulling away from each other," I confessed. "I need to know why."

I had been brave enough to admit my part in this and I hoped he would do the same. After a pause of his own, Nate sighed.

"I don't want you to feel like that," he commented. "I've had some issues and I hoped you wouldn't notice until I worked them out on my own."

I felt the absurd urge to laugh, but he wouldn't understand that impulse unless he knew the secrets that I had kept from him.

"I feel like we were heading in a very good direction . . ."

"And I don't think that's changed," Nate said.

"Really?" I tried to take deep breaths, but the tension in my throat had now moved to somewhere in my ribcage. "You weren't willing to talk about whatever issues you have with me."

"Let's be clear then," Nate requested, sounding ready for cross-examination. "What exactly are we doing here?"

"Being honest with each other, I hope."

"I'm willing if you are," he assured me. "What makes you think I'm not?"

I had spent four daylight hours as a swan today, which was fairly damning evidence.

"It's nothing concrete," I stated. "It's not like I've been grilling your roommates or reading your diary . . ."

"It's none of their business and I only journal when there's a grade riding on it," he said with a slight smile. "So, it's just the impression that you're getting?"

"Is it off-base?" I challenged. "While we're being honest, what were the issues?"

He looked momentarily as if his fight-or-flight instinct was kicking in; when he stood, I prepared myself for him to storm off. Instead, he rounded the table and took the chair next to me.

"I don't want you to think that I'm blaming you," he murmured in my ear. "This is just an impression that *I'm* getting."

"Then what is it?" I asked.

"I feel like I'm in love with someone waiting for the next big disaster," he said. "I remember what it's like to feel like a relationship is all or nothing, so I don't blame you."

He wasn't off-base, but I didn't enjoy that he'd noticed. I had hoped that it wouldn't be as glaringly obvious to him as it was to me. I suddenly found it a little more difficult to look at him, so I averted my eyes.

"You think I'm just being naïve?"

"I think you're seventeen and I'm nineteen and neither of us knows how love works yet," he explained.

"You didn't have a problem with my age before," I rejoined quietly.

"It's not about age," he asserted. "It's perspective. Love isn't supposed to be black and white."

"I know that," I reasoned. "But can you tell me what I can do to understand this better?"

"Understand that it's not the end of the world if this whole relationship is a bit of a roller coaster," he requested.

There was a slight edge to his voice and he paused for a long moment. I expected him to elaborate, but it was apparently my turn. I unlaced my fingers and turned my attention back to him for the serious questions.

"Is it someone else?"

"*No.*" He scrubbed his free hand over his face. "I said I didn't want you blaming yourself."

"You said that I haven't figured out how love works," I pointed out. "I'm not supposed to take this personally?"

"You're supposed to trust me."

"I want to," I answered honestly. "What other issues?"

"Let's be fair," Nate suggested. "What issues do you have where we're concerned?"

"Other than thinking of love as black and white?" I asked in clipped tones.

"That wasn't an attack," Nate protested.

"I don't want you to hold it against me," I retorted. "I want you to have patience with the fact that I'm new to this."

"And you think I won't?" he asked.

That question didn't sound like a challenge or attack. It rang with genuine concern and that did more to calm my nerves than any other sentence that he'd uttered since sitting down. The tightness still remained in my chest, though.

"Maybe this is a long-term thing," I mused, "or maybe this is practice for both of us."

"Maybe I'm your happily ever after and maybe I'm just your first love," he replied.

"I don't think we're anywhere near knowing which it is."

"I agree," Nate said quietly, "but I don't want us to treat that uncertainty as a deal-breaker."

"Me either," I admitted.

"Then I want us to be free to talk about things like this," he insisted. "What can I do to help you?"

I wanted to selfishly demand that he love me as he had in the past. What came to mind next was a different form of the same request.

"Don't give up on us," I requested in a near-whisper.

This time, when he tried to kiss me, I accepted it. It had little of the previous fire to it, but it was a comfort and a promise wrapped into a moment of honesty. Instead of feeling like we were pulling on opposite ends of a fraying rope, it felt like we were weaving a new one from the remains of the old one. He pulled away after a few moments, but kept his lips close enough to my ear to share one last confidence.

"The last thing I want is to give up on a good thing."

Maeve had put me under oath to call her if I needed a ride home. I suspected that she took a scenic drive along Commonwealth Avenue, hung a right by the Academy and circled around courtesy of Storrow Drive just in case I needed a quick getaway. I sent her a text with two letters—O and K—at the first opportunity and let Nate bring me home.

She was back on my bed, her knees drawn up to her chest and her expression defiant. She was spoiling for a fight with *someone* if I just said so and I couldn't grin at her, but I waved a hand.

"Stand down," I requested. "It's not the end of the world."

Maeve didn't budge, but a wary glint came into her eye. "Are you sure?" she challenged. "You've had a rough week and I'm very willing to bet I can beat him up."

"I wouldn't have let you, even if we broke up," I said, crossing to the bed and sitting next to her. "This week wasn't entirely his fault."

"You're my sister," Maeve growled. "If someone makes you unhappy, of course it's his fault."

That was exactly why I hadn't wanted to bring my issues up. Maeve felt honor-bound to be on my side and, while I appreciated that more often than not, I wanted that honor reined in.

"For me, can you not hate him?"

Maeve turned her head sharply, eyes narrowed in suspicion. "I thought you said you didn't break up."

"We didn't," I protested. "After tonight, I don't think that's happening any time soon . . ."

"But there's a reason to hate him?" she asked.

"You think there is," I explained. "But I'm choosing to stick this out, no matter the temporary consequences."

"Like losing your human hours?"

I wasn't about to give her a transcript of the conversation, but I could give her some assurances to keep in mind. "I don't know if that will happen as much after tonight."

Maeve's legs relaxed and she shifted to mirror my position. "You know there's one way to fix that."

"I know what you think will fix that," I retorted.

"Then you know that I'm *this* close to telling him myself," she threatened.

"So you said."

"And that doesn't make a difference?"

I finally smiled, but the expression felt rigid with anxiety. "It doesn't," I said, "because I am telling him very soon. Threatening me won't change that."

Maeve breathed in so deeply that she might have just been released from a noose. "Really?" she asked skeptically.

"Within the week," I promised. "Can I trust you to keep silent until then?"

She looked ready to squeeze the life out of me, but settled for nodding enthusiastically. "You have my word."

CODA

"If you are not willing to risk the unusual, you will have to settle for the ordinary." ~Jim Rohn

White

Valentine's Day dawned cold and snowy, but with no transformation. That made five days in a row that I had awoken human and, while my days were not entirely human yet, this was progress. It was also, by design, the first day that I was free from my latest punishment; I figured my parents had seen the harm that could be done by sequestering me on the most romantic day of the year.

I had promised Nate the latter half of my day and he agreed, with the provision that I get to pick the meeting place. I had endured half an hour with feathers, but managed to be only slightly late to my 11:00 class and explained it away as a transportation problem.

I hopped the B line at BU Central and got off at Copley not much later. I expected Nate to intercept me somewhere along the way, but our paths didn't cross until I reached the rendezvous point.

Nate was waiting at the Prudential Arcade, one hand clutching tickets and the other shoved into his coat pocket. "You found the place all right?" he teased.

"I don't know," I commented. "These places are a dime-a-dozen."

"Then I'll ask for a refund," he suggested. "We can always find somewhere more unique to hang out."

I had a difficult conversation ahead of me, so I should have been feeling too nervous to joke. The almost transformation-free morning had given me unusual confidence, though, and I greeted him with a properly affectionate kiss once I had snatched my ticket from his hand.

"I hope you didn't peek," I said.

"At the destination?"

"At the view," I corrected. "For all I know, you went up there and practiced looking awestruck."

"I promise I waited for you," Nate assured me.

He asked me about classes and told me about a job he was thinking of applying for over the summer, but once we got to the elevators, we didn't say much. He kept a comfortable grip on my hand and didn't avoid eye contact once. By the time we got to the Skywalk, my nerves were humming instead of jangling. I hoped they would stay that way for a little while longer.

All conversation cut off when we passed through the entrance. Nate caught his breath and stared for a long moment. He let a sigh out and shook his head.

"I'm glad I waited," he commented.

This was the best place to get a view of the city; there weren't many obstructed views from fifty floors up. I didn't answer, just tugged him along until we reached the windows.

"Since you told me to skip the audio guide, you're in charge of telling me what to look for," Nate informed me.

I could have pointed out anything from the Hancock Tower to Fenway Park, but that wasn't why I'd brought him here. "I have a good reason for skipping the tour," I admitted.

"You didn't want to be listening to a lecture on history when I wanted some PDA?" he suggested, kissing my hand.

"I wanted to talk."

His face fell comically. "You brought me all the way up here to ignore the view?"

"Not quite." I turned my back on the cityscape so he would know I was serious and he immediately met my gaze. "I wanted to take you here so you could see the world as I do."

"Go on," Nate invited.

The nerves returned then, but they weren't out in full force. They were just nudging me to remind me that I had thought of this conversation as an extremely bad idea for nearly five years. To steady myself, I took his other hand.

"This is how I'm used to the city," I said. "I sometimes get lost on the streets, but everything's familiar from a bird's-eye view."

He frowned slightly. "Is this a clever metaphor . . ."

"Be patient," I requested. "I'm getting there."

He tightened his grip on my hands. "Sorry. You were saying?"

"There is something you should have known a while ago," I blurted out. "I don't know if you were entitled to it on the Esplanade, but you earned it in November."

"Sounds complicated," Nate said.

"It's very straight-forward if you know the basics," I countered.

"The basics being . . ."

"*Swan Lake*," I stated.

His brow furrowed for just a moment before he grinned uncertainly and cocked his head as if trying to figure out where he was missing the joke.

"I don't follow."

"Girl under a curse must fall in love . . ."

"I remember that part," he interjected. "What does that mean for you and me?"

"Until 'you and me' happened, I hadn't spent a daylight hour as a human since middle school."

The smile disappeared, replaced by puzzlement. "You wouldn't joke about this."

"My family can back me up on it," I said a little defensively. "I promise I wouldn't lie about this."

His eyes focused on something over my shoulder, but I knew he wasn't admiring the Back Bay. After a few moments, he turned and released my hand so he could lean against the window as well.

"That doesn't make any sense," he said to no one in particular.

"I know." I was relieved that he didn't laugh at me or call me crazy, but I suspected that those reactions weren't far off. "It's a curse handed down from one generation to the next because no one has broken it yet."

"So there have been swans in your family before?"

"A few," I confirmed. "Maeve isn't one of them, so when I have to make an unavoidable human appearance, she steps in. The most recent example was . . ."

"On the day you were too sick for class," Nate provided. "And that's why you had her sense of humor on the Freedom Trail?"

I was profoundly grateful that these circumstances had been few and far between. Her impersonation seemed to bother him more than the need for it in the first place.

"Most of the time, it's not an issue," I said. "Neither of those times was my idea."

Nate exhaled very slowly, but didn't pull away. "That's why you burned the midnight oil at the library," he deduced.

"We've found a lot of ways to work around daylight," I confirmed.

He blinked and turned back to face me. His expression was more neutral, but there was nothing pleasant about it.

"So, if you've been working around daylight for five years, how are we here?"

The next word took more courage to utter than anything else: "You."

I wasn't sure what reaction to expect to that, but his tentative smile was an unexpected relief. "Are you sure?"

"You believe me?"

He raised an eyebrow. "We've agreed that you wouldn't make something like this up," he said. "Why shouldn't I believe you?"

"The fact that it makes no sense," I pointed out.

"That's not the point," he said firmly, latching on to my other hand. "I can take what you say as truth. I just need . . ."

"Details?" I suggested. "Proof?"

He considered that for nearly a minute and took that time to focus on my face again. He seemed surprised to find me unchanged.

"I don't have to see it to believe it," he assured me.

That was a relief; love or not, he wasn't seeing me naked. Spending a few hours with me in swan form might also prove to be too weird for him.

"As soon as we started thinking of what we had as love, I started becoming more human," I explained.

"That's fantastic," he said. "Is that also why you could tell when I was having doubts?"

"Exactly."

He whistled quietly. "And that wasn't fantastic."

I smiled wanly. "It wasn't my best week," I confirmed.

His expression became guarded and if I could have browsed his thoughts, I suspected that I would have found guilt sparring with skepticism. "What happened to the other swans?" Nate asked after a long moment. "Why did you inherit the curse?"

"I don't know all of the details."

I had hesitated over that phrase and he caught it. "What details make you uncomfortable?" he prodded.

"That they all failed to break the family curse," I hedged.

"What else?" he pressed. "You're still holding something back and . . ."

"It's not something you need to know about," I interrupted.

"Why don't you let me know?" Nate rejoined.

"Because it's not the sort of thing I want to bring up in public," I admitted in a near-whisper.

For the first time since I broached the subject, he looked on the verge of amusement. "Now I *have* to know. It's not a state secret."

"No, but it's a personal matter."

"Then I can wait for a little more privacy," he decided.

His hand found mine and I joined him in city-watching until the other visitors had moved on. I took that time to consider how deep he was allowed to dig before I refused to explain things. I could only hope that he agreed with my boundaries.

"I'll tell you the unpleasant details, but I don't like to talk about some of it," I explained when we were once more alone. "Can you live with not getting to pry?"

"I promise to stop when you ask me to," he promised.

I squeezed his hand briefly, then turned my back to the city. "There's a deadline."

He didn't look disgusted, just intrigued. "What age?"

"An event," I corrected.

"You have to be in love and loved in return by the time you get married or it passes on to the next generation?"

I had the urge to look away, since this was my least favorite part of the story to tell, but I didn't want him doubting any part of this. "Some people don't wait for marriage," I said.

Now he looked a little mortified.

"And the others didn't wait?" he guessed. "Or were married for reasons other than love?"

"Basically," I said. "That's all you need to know on that subject."

"Not quite."

"It's all I'm willing to tell," I amended.

Nate tightened his grip on my fingers. "I'm not asking for those details," he said. "This is on the same subject, though."

He trusted me enough to leave the stories untold, so I decided to believe his intentions to be honorable.

"What makes you think that we'd get that far without being in love?" Nate asked.

"After so many generations of the curse, I have the right to be a little paranoid," I said after a moment of consideration. "I don't think you'd pressure me into anything and I'm not even sure if we'll ever get that far, but until the curse is broken, there's a chance it will win in this generation."

He nodded, eyes clouded and expression back to its neutral expression. "And until the curse breaks, there will be days when you can't be human."

"It may be in days, months, or years," I confirmed.

"Then I'm sorry for every human hour I've cost you," he responded quietly.

His regret was appreciated, but it was also myopic. "What makes you think it was entirely your fault?" I challenged.

"I had some part in it," he countered. "The point is, no matter what you did, I didn't mean to hurt you."

On an impulse, I wrapped one arm around his waist so that we were no longer at arm's length. "Thank you," I murmured.

We stayed like that for an unknown time, not capable of conversation until that settled in. He pulled away first, but kept his arm around my shoulders.

"So, what now?" he asked. "You had some problems earlier, so I didn't break this curse just by falling in love with you. Does it ever go away?"

"When things become more permanent," I confessed, "and that's exactly why it took me seven months to tell you."

I could see Nate's frown in profile now. "Because you don't know if I'll want to make this permanent?"

"Because I don't know if this will be permanent," I corrected. "Remember, it takes two people to fall in love."

"Either way, that's a lot of responsibility for one guy," he said.

"I know."

"I'm not sure I'm ready for that," he replied.

The words felt like a punch to the gut, but he was still there. Whatever his doubts about himself, he wasn't running yet. It was the most I could ask of him right now.

"I don't want that to be all you think about. I don't want you waking up every day wondering if you've ruined my life. You haven't," I continued hastily. "But any time I have to skip class or see you after sunset, you might blame yourself and that's not why I told you."

His arm relaxed slightly and I turned to see him watching me once more. "Why, then?"

"Because I trust you with my heart," I said. "I trust you with whatever comes while we're together. That's why I can love the roller coaster."

The kiss that came next was unexpected and felt as if a vow were passing between us. It tethered me to him and promised that the bond would remain strong.

"If you can promise to let me love the roller coaster too, I'll promise to make the hills as gradual as possible," he swore. "Deal?"

I couldn't be sure when the next slope would come, but I had a reason to believe that it would be for our good.

"Deal," I vowed.

Black

Aislin had promised to tell Nate on Valentine's Day and I agreed not to divulge the secret before then. The conditions that she outlined on February 13 were less simple than that. There weren't many of them, but they started with me swearing to not interrogate him and ending with "Don't hate him for my swan days."

"There shouldn't *be* days," I protested. "He knows what's at stake, so he should know better."

"And I should know better, but I'll probably have my part in causing the transformation," Aislin argued. "I don't want you holding it against either of us."

"Then I don't want you holding it against me when I have hard feelings about it," I said.

That was a violation of her request, but she contemplated the issue for a moment before nodding. "I recognize your right to have them," she conceded, "but I have another stipulation."

"I don't like anything about this," I reminded her.

Aislin ignored that in favor of a different request. "I don't want you to hold my choice against me," she reiterated, "and that means I want you to stop interfering."

"You want me to give up?" I squawked in honest dismay.

She looked close to tears, but she shook her head. "I want you to leave this to me," she said. "I want you to be able to love your sister even if she molts at night."

It was my turn for the waterworks, but it wasn't out of frustration. It was because she thought there was any reason that I would stop loving her, swan or not.

"I'll always love you," I promised. "That's why I'll trust you to take care of this on your own unless you say otherwise."

On February 14, when she returned, she was aglow with the kind of contentment that I'd first seen in November.

"We've come to an understanding," was all she would say.

I shouldn't have kept track, but I was now the one waiting for something to go wrong. It was nine days before something happened, but I awoke on the 23rd to hear Aislin being conspicuously quiet on the stairs. That could only mean that she wanted no questions asked.

She wasn't that lucky. I opened the back door about twenty minutes before dawn to find her sitting in her usual tattered bathrobe.

"I brought breakfast," I offered lamely.

She didn't look my way, but accepted the orange that I handed over. "I think it'll be one of those days," she said.

"Any idea why?"

She shook her head, but made no move to unpeel the orange. If a transformation was coming soon, I knew she would be feeling nauseated at this point.

"Any idea how long . . ."

"I don't have any ideas," she said. "Can we leave it at that?"

For all her conditions, I had the feeling that she was holding today's dawn against herself. Since she wouldn't explain that, I could only be a witness to the event. I reached over and unpeeled the orange for her, in case she didn't feel up to it.

"I thought it would be easier this time," she admitted.

"You're blaming yourself," I observed. "You shouldn't."

"The alternative is blaming him," she responded. "And I promised myself I wouldn't, but I don't want to hear 'I told you so.'"

That hadn't occurred to me today. I just wanted to say something that would make her feel as all right with the whole mess as she had claimed to be nine days ago. That was too much to ask, though, so I went back to being her audience/waitress.

"It never crossed my mind," I said.

With that truth as the last word, we sat together and watched the sun drag its way inevitably over the horizon. By the time dawn crept over the horizon, the orange was gone and I helped her out of the bathrobe. She transformed a moment later and nipped my ankle as a sign of gratitude.

She took flight today with desperate energy today, charging across the yard without a backward glance. It looked less like a bid for the freedom of the skies and more like an attempt to escape the life she'd enjoyed too temporarily.

It was then that I made another promise: Whatever it took, I would someday make sure she found a way back to her humanity.

ACKNOWLEDGMENTS

My first thanks are to this book's first fans. Kate Reynolds was its first audience and has supported it through two apartments, three years, four countries, and ten drafts. She came up with the prologue, voraciously edited the third draft, and has yet to turn me down for a fairytale philosophy session. Elaine Sangiolo talked me into pitching an unfinished manuscript to an editor, and though I never signed with them, her encouragement got those first two drafts done. Emma Parker took a book with potential and helped me wrangle it into something worth printing. I'll trust her forever, even if we may never completely agree on the ending.

I will publicly embarrass only a percentage of my other contributors lest the acknowledgments outstrip the length of the book. Marianna Roberg was Aislin's fashionista and my web designer. Becky Greenwood, my secret agent and friend, turned up as my cover artist as well. When I needed radical feminists, I counted wisely on Hillary Stirling and Sarah Doherty. Jonathan Ellis kept me supplied with peanut butter sandwiches and motivational fluffy toys, while Laren Dowling lent me her actual pet as a therapy dog. Clem, Mandy, Tangie, Chino, and Radar preserved what little sanity I have left.

To the Badgers and the Botosphere (including Andrew and Del), you know who you are and how much you helped. You vetted major plot points, checked my anxiety levels at midnight, treated me like a rock star, and even let me plug my laptop into your camper when I had an editing deadline to meet.

In the penultimate spot are the librarians in Weston, Massachusetts; in years of shelving books for them, I discovered that I wanted to see my own work in the YA section someday. My final thanks go to my family, who always said I should put down my fanfic and write my own books.

ABOUT THE AUTHOR

Kaki Olsen is always on the brink of another adventure. If she couldn't be a writer, she'd be a full-time musician or travel guide, and she would take her lunch breaks at Fenway Park. Until that happens, she speaks both Spanish and English at her everyday office job, but she has vacationed enthusiastically in such places as Istanbul and Ireland. She has lived in five states, but will always refer to Boston as home. She regularly contributes academic papers on zombies or wizards to Life, the Universe and Everything, a sci-fi/fantasy symposium originated at her alma mater, Brigham Young University. Her published works have appeared in such magazines as *Voices* and *AuthorsPublish*. She is a doting aunt and the librarian of two bulging bookshelves.